THE GIRL WHO CLONED LIGHTNING

A NOVEL

CLIFF RATZA

THE GIRL WHO CLONED LIGHTNING

A NOVEL

CLIFF RATZA

The Girl Who Cloned Lightning

Copyright ©2025 by Clifford Ratza

ISBN: 978-1-967375-76-9 (Paperback)
ISBN: 978-1-967375-77-6 (E-book)

Library of Congress Control Number: 2025918585

Printed in the United States of America

Published by:

info@thequippyquill.com
(302) 295-2278

About the Book

This book, the fourth in the Lightning Brain Series, is the sequel to The Girl Who Commanded Lightning, and it traces an action-packed trail of technological and political intrigue running through Electra Kittner's professional and personal lives. Electra – now an Electra-Alisha split personality infected with an STD-like T-Plague mutation – must cure herself first before battling a new set of enemies in Cyber as well as 3-D Space. She must also contend with a relentlessly harsh government as well as random acts of terrorism masterminded by a rogue paramilitary force allied with China and Russia.

The theme for all books in the series is this: extraordinary people are sometimes victims of a primitive world that can't handle the truth, but no matter how exceptional they are, they must still deal with the complexities of being "merely human," best handled with an optimistic and pragmatic philosophy.
There are three storyline threads:

1. The adventures of Electra and her closest friends.
2. The adventures of Electra as she reaches out to her allies.
3. The battles against "S-Cubed" super soldiers and other adversaries.

Readers should enjoy the book on whatever level they wish:
- Gripping action-packed thriller
- Glimpse into a plausible near-term future
- Insight into dealing with the "human condition"
- Illustrative, optimistic, and pragmatic worldview philosophy
- Fast-paced, suspense-filled, emotive narrative and imagery
- Introduction to topics every reader wants to know
- Interesting talking points going beyond sound-bytes

There is a glossary and appendix at the back for readers who wish to know more about terms or topics referenced.

At least two more books are being developed for the Lightning Brain Series, which means readers will have more enjoyment in store. Electra's exciting odyssey continues.

Main Characters

The Electra-Alisha Duo
Su-Lin Song Chou
Kameyo Kato
Indira (Indy) Jaswinder Ramanujan
Hudson (Hud) Haller
Sam Ryder
Blake (Woolly) Wolker
Robin Setdarova
Zoe and Matt Fortier
Jennifer and Russell Conklin
Carter Quavah
Professor Ravenhill
Angus McTear
Jared Gardner
Kathi Lauret
Tyger Riddley
Vincent Valdez
Winona Kota
Carley Kota
Tim Godfrey
Kwame Chyril
Darla Tinibu
Maksim Popovitch
Ziarmal Thaqaf
Sergei Zeitsev
Chen Xu
Brandon Marshall
Cassandra Marshall
Lisa Perugino
Vito Buono

Book Series Dedication

Of course, I wish to thank my parents, Clyde and Betty Ratza, for their loving patience and generosity that gave me the freedom to explore the limits of my world, and my sister, Claudia, for introducing me to poetry and literature. Thanks also to Robert Williams and the Quippy Quill production team, who have made our Lightning Brain Series resonate with readers. And a special thanks to Martin Caylor for his careful draft reviews and suggestions.

My entire series is dedicated to those readers who wish to follow the adventures of Electra and her friends. And just like Electra, we must always remember to engage life not tomorrow but today, an admonition often given in verse. Whether you prefer Elinor Wylie's "welcoming madness and the most" or Indira's "blowing a kiss to the future," the sentiment is much the same.

Nonsense Rhyme	The Mystical Memory Garden
Whatever's good or bad or both There's grace in either love or loathe Sunlight, or freckles on the sun. The worst and best are both inclined To snap like vixens at the truth But, O beware the middle mind Beware the smooth, ambiguous smile That never pulls the lips apart Salt of pure and pepper of vile Must season the extremer heart A pinch of fair, a pinch of foul And bad and good make best of all That climbs no fractional inch to fall. Reason's a rabbit in a hutch, And ectasy's a were-wolf ghost But, O beware the nothing much And welcome madness and the most! Elinor Wylie, 1920	Tomorrow's memories made today, Just go about your merry way, They are a future mystery. No crystal ball for what will lead, What fruit your current effort bring. Just tend the present plant the seed, Tomorrow's harvest rests with you, It's bounty whether short or long. Remember today in all you do, Blow a kiss to the future keep singing your song.

CONTENTS

Chapter 1
March 2126

"On the Beach"
(Thread 1 Chapter 1)

The ocean, it's said, never gives up its dead when storms of a season come roaring. But that somber sentiment might prove false as seething waves cast a lifeless body face down onto a stone-strewn beach well past midnight, fingers of lightning strobing the blackness while a howling wind and rumbling thunder whip squalls ashore midway between Fukushima and Tokyo. But perhaps events now unfolding will prove the rhyme true; the lightning brain is about to summon Electra Kittner back from limbo.

Why am I tossing in an angry sea? Where have I been? What's happened to me?

These and other foot-soldier questions – the who, what, why, where, when – flash into Electra's brain as she bobs back to consciousness, raising herself onto hands and knees. Suddenly, the lightning brain shifts to a higher gear.

Get with it, soldier! This is no drill. Check for injuries, get your bearings, and get going.

Though disoriented from a forty-foot precipice plunge, the ice-cold water has kept contusions and lacerations from worsening.

Nothing broken or bleeding. Clothes in shreds, and I'm missing a shoe. Where to go? What to do?

Flashlight beams crisscrossing uncertainly far down the shore point the way.

That must be my extraction team. The van explosion shot me over the edge, but at least I kept Su and Kameyo safe from the blow. Now I must get to the searchers before they give up and go.

But now the rains came, whipping horizontally and obliterating everything except Electra's personal space. She could do nothing until the squall blew through, so she curled into a shivering ball, back to the wind. A few minutes later, the squall left as abruptly as it came, but so did the flashlight beacons, replaced by ascending points of light.

My team is roping up to the ledge. I'm SOL if they leave without me.

Electra stumbled towards her rescuers, but darkness and rocks got in the way. She yelled out as the lights disappeared but was too far away for anyone to hear. Then she saw what could only be a fading glow from a vehicle; by the time she reached where the team had ascended, there were only sibilant sounds of wind and waves, and a dim outline of an abandoned rope extending upwards into blackness. There was only one thing to do: climb for survival and that she did. The exertion helped keep hypothermia at bay and reorient her to the situation. When she reached the ledge, she recognized the burned-out remains of her overturned van. Now she climbed the remaining slope to the road, coming to the car that had rammed the van. She rummaged for anything of use; nothing salvageable from the body slumped over the steering wheel except wrong-sized shoes and a windbreaker. Once again, there was only one thing to do: jog as best as possible on the coastal road towards the Tokyo staging area, many miles away.

There's nothing here, but something will come along when the sun comes up. I've gotta keep moving until then.

As her jogging rhythm adjusted to conditions, so did the lightning brain.

I'm a survivor; I can deal with what I've been dealt. I've done it all my life, pretty much all alone.

But then she remembered she's never alone. Her inner voice, Indira – her practically perfect mother – is with her, as is Alisha, her alter ego.

I'll ask them for help when needed, but for now, the lightning brain has put Electra in charge. That's who I am.

Chapter 2
March 2126

"The Race for Survival"
(Thread 1 Chapter 2)

As the sun cleared the horizon, promising to chase away the early morning mist shrouding the shoreline, Daisuke knew it would bring him what he had desired ever since graduating from high school four years ago: membership in a local yakuza family headquartered in Sendai. Yakuza, the Japanese equivalent of Italy's mafia, traces its samurai roots that originated centuries ago, and its 75 thousand members worldwide still adhere to a rigid tradition that includes elaborate tattooing, membership qualifying exams, and demonstrating family loyalty.

Wedged between family leader Hiroto and his second-in-command Kage, Daisuke was charging south towards Tokyo on a desolate stretch of the coastal road, their all-black appearance crowned with black-visor helmets matching the ominous bellow of their black Honda CBR superbikes. But only deserted shacks and occasional trees witnessed the procession.

Daisuke had not a doubt that he would pass the exam being administered today by the regional chapter located in the coastal city of Chosi, 60 miles east of Tokyo. He had studied diligently, and even though a vocational training dropout, he was smarter than what his stocky build and pugnacious face projected. He knew that his yakuza family handled two of the top three criminal markets: drugs and sex. Sex trafficking – slaves, sado-masochism, and prostitution – was his favorite, and he knew how to strike deals using the Deep-Dark Web. Daisuke knew the numbers too: 25 million women and children sex slaves worldwide, over a million recruited annually, valued at $10 billion. And if he concocted another useful demonstration of his fealty, Hiroto would allow him another tattoo, signifying Daisuke's yakuza membership.

Daisuke was too busy thinking about his initiation party to notice the surroundings until the group slowed as it approached a woman limping along the side of the road. She wore only a windbreaker, but Daisuke's mind went to work as he noticed a striking pair of legs. As the three bikers surrounded the woman, Daisuke took the rear position and checked his equipment while Hiroto barked out guttural Japanese phrases.

Though Electra had tried valiantly to jog, after 90 minutes the pain of blisters caused by ill-fitting shoes forced her to walk, but she maintained a pace that kept the damp chill at bay. And as the sky cleared while the sun rose, so did her mood.

Though I'm on a road less traveled, I know there'll be traffic because I encountered some when driving here a couple of days ago. Alisha decided to join the conversation.

"Very good. A Road Less Traveled is a book, poem, or metaphor for our current predicament, as well as what we've been on since the lightning bolt at birth." Alisha had more to say, but the hum of approaching motorcycles pushed her into the background as Electra turned to face an uncertain encounter. She waited for at least one of the three bikers surrounding her to remove a helmet and talk. None came off, and only unrecognizable words came out of the designated speaker.

"I'm sorry, but I don't understand Japanese. Do you speak English?"

"What here you doing?"

"I'm heading towards Tokyo to connect with friends. If I could borrow a cell phone, I could call them."

"Accident we pass 10 miles back. In it you?" Electra's warning system elevated.

"Why yes, but I have to aagh —" Daisuke whipped several turns of chain around Electra's legs and drove off, dragging her behind his angry-sounding motorcycle as his two escorts stared at the spectacle.

Daisuke raced through a rock-strewn meadow that bounced him just enough for a joy ride but his victim more than enough for cuts and bruises. He slowed enough to trace loops while checking his passenger for damages because he wanted to terrorize, not spoil the merchandise. Five minutes later he crashed through the side door of a deserted building, stopping when his now unconscious victim was completely inside. He removed his helmet and dismounted, then exited through the front door to greet his escorts as they roared to the entrance. Both removed their helmets as they faced a grinning Daisuke, who waited for Hiroto to speak. Small and wiry, the leader's muddled words matched his confused expression.

"What intentions got you? What thinking you?" Because he was younger, Daisuke spoke better English.

"No sense raping and pillaging until we know what we've got. We have plenty of time before my exam, so why don't you wait here while I prepare my hitchhiker for an interrogation. Then you can decide how to use her. She might fetch a tidy sum."

Hiroto blinked once before looking at Kage, who remained mute. Then he blinked again before issuing a verdict.

"Woman good looking. Could drug and sell for sex or slave. Go preparations make. Call ready when." Then he pulled a roll of toilet paper from his travel bag in preparation for hiking to a clump of bushes about a hundred yards away. Kage did likewise.

Daisuke bowed before saying, "As you wish," then reentered the building while joking to himself that although Japan's number one fishing port is Chosi, he had hauled in a most valuable catch while on dry land.

Electra had bounced back to consciousness while Daisuke was talking to his partners. And luckily, she heard everything through the open door so she knew what would be coming her way.

Daisuke closed the door before removing his boots, leather jacket, and pants, then decided how best to sample the goods once it could talk. He would chain the woman to a chair afterwards, but first he propped her to a sitting position and started kissing different parts of the anatomy. Sleeping Beauty had come awake from a prince's kiss; Daisuke expected the same. But as his lips sucked hungrily on those of the unconscious woman, he did not get a repeat performance.

Electra's eyes flashed open just before she nailed a lightning-quick punch into Daisuke's prominent Adam's apple, muffling any words as he gasped for air. As he collapsed backward, Electra grabbed hanks of his hair with both hands and fell atop this mass of inert flesh, then rose to her knees and smashed his head two, three, four times onto the barren concrete floor.

Get with it, soldier. Get dressed, get your gear, and get out.

Electra followed orders. Though a head taller and a hundred

pounds lighter, she made do with Daisuke's clothes and would do even better with his equipment. The phone showed five-bar signal strength, and the SIG Sauer magazine held 15 rounds. She retrieved from memory the phone number of her support team, but before calling, glanced warily out a window.

No one in sight.

Electra punched in the number and two ring tones later recognized the calm voice of a female support team member.

"This is Gemini Kittner calling for any Team Gemini. Do you copy? Over."

"This is Gemini H-2. I copy. What are your intentions? Over."

"In two minutes, I will be in flight mode on black Honda motorcycle, heading south on coastal road. Possible pursuit motorcycles. I have one SIG Sauer and 15 rounds. Requesting extraction. Can you see location of cell phone? Over."

"Affirmative. You are 80 miles north of staging area. Gemini T-1 and T-2 will drive van. Estimated interception in 40 minutes. We are good to go. Ganbatte kudasai. Over."

"Good luck to all of us. Gemini Kittner, Over."

Electra disconnected the call, then crept on hands and knees towards the bigger motorcycles parked out front, intent on rifling through their saddle bags for keys or weapons. She found none, so she emptied them and toppled one bike on top of the other, hoping to slow the pursuit of her adversaries, who were squatting in the opposite direction. Then she ran into the building, strapped on the helmet and blasted out the side door.

Caught with their pants down, Hiroto and Kage were interrupted by the buzz of a motorcycle. Both stood and stared at what appeared to be Daisuke rocketing towards the coastal road and then racing south. They stumbled back to the building, pulling up pants while trying to run.

Hiroto bellowed, "Get you up!" after tripping over a disoriented Daisuke. Four minutes later, after telling him to guard the scattered gear, Hiroto and Kage roared off in pursuit of the escapee.

Electra's altered brain state reveled in the thrill of this race for survival. She was an expert bike handler, thanks to having spent time in the saddle touring Texas towns, and the roar of the exhaust combined with the lurching motion of the bike gave her a now-here focus. Both bike and lightning brain were in high gear.

Their bikes are bigger, so my head start won't be enough to get me to safety. It's time for a contingency plan. When I find the right place, I'll set up an ambush.

Electra zoomed through two curves because they weren't sharp enough, but the next – a double switchback – rewarded her patience. After hiding the bike, she concealed herself at the entrance to the second hairpin before checking the cell phone.

I've been on the road for twenty minutes. I should hear the bikes in about five more, which might be only minutes ahead of my extraction team. This could turn into a three-way Mexican standoff.

Electra shifted to another gear that synchronized all three personas: the physical, emotional, and cognitive. She was armed and dangerous and totally focused on survival.

Faint buzzing built into a penetrating crescendo until her pursuers braked while downshifting to handle the first hairpin. Lying prone with arms outstretched for a two-handed grip, Electra exhaled before firing two quick shots that brought down the lead bike. The second couldn't avoid the road kill; it somersaulted over the first and came to rest pinning the rider underneath. Electra rose and approached for the second kill. She could feel the Monster from the Id stirring and it thrilled her, but just then the commotion of a screeching van broke her concentration. Two hazmat uniforms leaped out, one pointing a weapon at Electra, and the other at the downed riders. Electra dropped to her knees, put down the gun, and interlaced fingers behind her head before yelling.

"I am Gemini Kittner." A muffled voice from the nearer uniform spoke.

"We are Gemini T-1 and T-2. Remain where you are. We will interrogate others."

The Ts dragged the bikes and riders into the grass, and though she couldn't decipher the words, Electra knew they were harsh. Two gunshots terminated the discussion before the Ts ran to her.

"Gemini Kittner, Gemini Su told us of T-Plague virus contamination. Please come to van and don hazmat uniform. Then we drive to staging area."

Electra limped to the van where she stripped off all clothes before putting on the uniform. She was about to fasten the helmet when one of the Ts spoke.

"Gemini Kittner, are you hungry or thirsty? We have refreshments." Electra smiled for the first time in twenty-four hours as her brain shifted to a lower gear. She bowed before saying one word only. "Doumo."

"Gemini Kittner, welcome. We serve you in van; then we must make haste."

Chapter 3
March 2126

"Homeward Bound"
(Thread 2 Chapter 1)

Electra guzzled a bottle of water, then devoured several packets of Oreo Double Stuf cookies that she washed down with Coke before locking on her hazmat helmet. The sugar-caffeine combination helped restore some energy and sense of humor.

Su must have told the Ts what my favorite snacks are. I hope my manners didn't offend them. A glycogen-depleted 29-year-old can gobble as fast as a teenager. Now I can sit back and enjoy the ride.

The 45-minute trip gave her time enough to prepare for a reunion with Su and Kameyo before negotiating with the Ts. After the van pulled inside the staging area building, the Ts escorted her into the same conference room used before. Sitting at the table were her hazmat-clad research partners and one of the handlers, who motioned her to sit.

"Greetings, Gemini Kittner. I am Gemini H-2. Please do not remove your helmet. Your partners told me about your misfortune and the Ts told me about cuts and bruises. May I recommend your partners help you refresh and medicate for your comfort? Then we will meet here to arrange your journey home."

"I would like that. Thank you for your hospitality." The female T led the trio to a shower room. Su and Kamayo removed their helmets before removing everything from Electra and seating her for an inspection led by Su. Electra spoke first.

"Did the new vaccines work? Are both of you symptom-free and no longer contagious?"

"A weary-looking Su said, "Yes to both questions, but H-2 insists we wear the suits. But how about you?"

I have a new secret to keep, so I have to stretch the truth.

"I feel fine, but I don't know if I'm contagious. All of us should wear our hazmat suits. Put your helmets on." Su and Kamayo followed orders, then Su talked while examining Electra.

"You have grass burns as well as cuts and bruises all over your body. Two cuts look like they might leave a scar. They form an inverted cross high in the middle of your chest. We'll dry and patch when you come out of the shower. Will you need help?"

"No. I can shower myself. Give me ten minutes." While Electra did that, Kameyo talked to Su.

"Electra has a practically perfect physique, like that of an athlete-turned-model. Do you know how she acquired it?"

"It's another of her enigmas. And though I know her better than anyone does, she often puzzles me. But I do know she heals quickly. And when she does, she'll tell us how to rebuild the lab and what to get for her cloning project." Electra's exit from the shower ended the conversation. Su and Kameyo carefully dried and patched their leader before encasing her in the hazmat suit and returning to the conference room.

H-2 and a traditional Japanese breakfast awaited: natto rice, pickled vegetables, and tea. Everyone ate quickly and quietly, keeping a safe distance from Electra before H-2 started the discussion.

"We are most pleased you arrive safely, but your adventure has produced expediencies. Alas, your van was destroyed and you brought back two people. This will complicate your homeward journey." H-2 smiled briefly, waiting for Electra.

The Japanese are world's best negotiators. I might need H-2's help in the future, so I shall offer a win-win proposition.

"We are indebted to you for saving our lives, so please allow me to pay in advance for whatever you must arrange to deliver us to Austin." Smiling again, H-2 continued.

"We did lend assistance, but the two Ts said you were in command of the situation when they arrived. But let me not digress. Back to travel plans. Timing is everything. We know of a FedEx flight late tonight carrying hazardous materials to America, so your hazmat uniforms provide a natural cover. And as a demonstration of our best wishes for future business, we give you discount on van and laser bazooka that went missing on your adventure."

"You are generous. If you would please logon for a wire transfer, I will send money to your account right now."

"As you wish."

The trio lounged in the conference room after H-2 completed the exchange and left to make travel preparations. Su spoke after she and Kameyo removed helmets.

"I was getting claustrophobic. Keep yours on if you wish, but Kameyo and I think the new vaccine will keep us protected, even if you're contagious."

"I'll play it safe and keep mine on, but let's discuss plans. We have to rebuild the lab, and since we already have the Fukushima manufacturing site, I recommend we rebuild nearby. And because Kameyo will be leading our cloning project at this lab, let's hear from her."

"Yes, I agree, but when we get back to Austin, will you please explain to Hud what happened?"

"I'll put it at the top of my list. And when we get back, I'll tell both of you what cloning we'll do. But we've been through enough. Let's ask H-2 for laptops so we can surf for whatever we want until we depart."

While Kameyo and Su rested on the 15-hour Memphis flight, Electra planned a solution for the most pressing issue facing her and her alter-ego. After four hours, she was ready to explain but let Alisha speak first.

"I thought you might enjoy a traveling verse from Henry Van Dyke's poem America for Me. Born in 1852, he was a prominent American poet and professor of literature at Princeton.
'Oh, it's home again, and home again, America for me!
Our hearts are turning home again and there we long to be, In our beautiful big country beyond the ocean bars,
Where the air is full of sunlight and the flag is full of stars.'

And let's always remember what the great philosophers say about the arts. We should read poetry, listen to music, and look at paintings for creative inspiration that comes only when we break away from the quotidian."

"That's good advice, and I particularly like that last word. You know how clever I am when playing word games, but you're better artistically and emotionally. Did you like our escape?"

"I was simultaneously frightened and thrilled, especially by our 'Monster from the Id.' It's difficult to control until it's had its way. It would've killed the bikers if the Ts hadn't arrived."

"Perhaps, but we tell no one. And we tell no one that we are T-Plague carriers. We'll add that complication to our list of don't show don't tell items."

"I trust you have a solution."

"In fact, I do. Let me walk you through what I'll do. Please review the white paper I prepared." Alisha said more ten minutes later.

"You – or should I say we – are sui generis. Only you could develop this solution path so quickly. I agree you should modify the vaccine instead of our immune system. And you already know the techniques and have the tools at our Austin lab for inserting our genetic marker into the vaccine structure so our T-cells won't consider it an antigen. Our immune system will then let the vaccine put the virus into remission, making us no longer contagious. I can't think of any additional contingency paths if what you're proposing doesn't work. But knowing you, I'm sure you do. And please make remission top priority so we can proceed with all our activities."

"I'll lock myself in the lab after briefing Hud and won't come out until I have it. Then you can handle our Hollywood adventure and social schedule while I concentrate on cloning, bio-drugs, and artificial intelligence software. And both of us handle our political career. We should be back in Austin late Thursday evening. Su and Kameyo will stay at the lab until we brief Hud first thing Friday morning. And you and I should be clean by Monday."

"Wonderful. I'd say that's a wrap. Now let's rest while the lightning brain shift gears and keeps working."

Hud Haller, president of the privately held H&H business empire, wore an expression that matched his Texas-sized dimensions and personality. It was clear to all sitting across from him in the conference room that he was pleased to have three of his people back, but judging from their uniforms, they might have returned from the Moon rather than Japan. Electra and Kameyo fit into theirs, but Su's petite proportions left plenty of room. Her eyes looked like they were peering up from the bottom of a goldfish bowl. Hud spoke after Electra delivered an edited version of what had occurred.

"Too bad the lab blew up, but what counts is your safety. Glad to have y'all back in one piece. But when can you take off the hazmat suits? Electra pointed to Kameyo for the answer.

"Su and I will do so after confirming we are no longer contagious.

We will test ourselves once more today. And if we test negative, then we know our modified vaccines work. Su, please tell Hud more."

"Kameyo and I will come back Monday to make preparations for our plants here and in Japan to begin making the modified vaccines. We should also make plans to depart for Japan soon. And you and Electra must make plans to rebuild the lab. Electra should describe what she has in mind, but only after she confirms she is not contagious."

"Su's right. I intend to stay in my lab all weekend until I'm certain I'm clean. And then first thing Monday I need to meet with you to outline next steps. Hud looked relieved as he ended the meeting. "Well then, let's have all of you carry on so you're out of those space suits and back in the saddle on Monday."

Electra accomplished everything needed during her isolation. Early Monday morning she summarized to herself all the results.

My assorted bruises and blisters are healing nicely, and the cuts on my chest look like a tattoo. When Robin sees it, she'll say it looks sexy.

And my specially modified vaccine works, but I have to take it every day to keep the virus in remission. So now I have a chronic condition. If I don't do so, the dormant virus grows enough to make me contagious, even though to me it's harmless.

Lots of people take medication for chronic conditions, like diabetes or high blood pressure. And I'm lucky, I can make my own pills. But I must keep my condition a secret, even from my friends. And the Government must never find out. It will treat me badly if it does.

Electra met briefly with Su and Kameyo, relieved to hear they were good to go. Then she parked herself in a chair on the other side of Hud's desk after closing the door, waiting for him to talk. A smiling Hud got right to the point.

"Well your Highness, I guess you're not contagious because you're not wearing that space suit. So tell me, where do you want to rebuild the lab? Any chance picking a closer continent? Or putting it in the U.S.?"

"Remember why we chose Japan? It's pro-biotech and plays by international rules of law. Russia and China don't, and Europe is afraid of biotech. The Middle East and Africa lack biotech infrastructure, and you know from dealing with our Government that

they could nationalize your biotech business. The accident was a one-time fluke, so let's have Kameyo and Su coordinate a rebuild close to our plant. I'll tell them what additional equipment to get."
"OK, you sold me. So, what else is on your list?"

"This isn't new, but I have additional A.I. and Neuro-Knitter projects for Tim and Kwame that we'll run through our Neuro-Device Lab here in Austin. I'll keep you posted on progress."
"Anything else?"

"They're Texas-related. The first affects your West Texas oil and gas business. Reserves and demand continue to decline. What business do you want to build to replace it?"

"Uh, I haven't thought about it. Oil's gonna be around awhile longer."

"Don't bet on it lasting as long as you think. Look at what happened to Saudi Arabia. And besides, you're a great entrepreneur. You need to keep busy. I'll give you three choices that use land, technology, and people in the Permian Basin. Solar panel farms, Martian farming, and water reclamation and transportation. Why don't you discuss these ideas at your next Permian Basin Roundtable meeting?"
"Fair enough. But what got you to thinking about this?"

"Do you recall that I'm going to run for Congress, representing Congressional District 11, which is in the heart of the West Texas Permian Basin? Well, if I'm going to represent those folks, I should look for opportunities to replace oil patch job losses. Woolly Walker has put in place my campaign organization, and I need you to help him make it work. You have lots of contacts. Would you please arrange for us to meet with him as soon as possible?"

"Now that's something I can do. And I'll include Sam Ryder too. He owes you a lot for how you helped his Austin T-Breds win the Co-NFL championship last year. But aren't you spreading yourself pretty thin? You've already got biotech and artificial intelligence projects at two universities as well as a budding Hollywood career. And now you want to piggyback on the work you're doing in Washington for our Governor. Don't burn yourself out." Electra smiled as she rose to leave.

"I have help on the way, thanks to you. See you soon." Electra shared the news with Alisha as soon as she could.

"Now that we're no longer contagious, we have a clean bill of health to charge ahead. And we have a lot to do. Good thing we share the load. Are you ready?"

"Of course I am. You've divvied it up using one of your favorite economics principles, the law of comparative advantage. Since you're the smart one, you do all the heavy lifting while I handle the lighter stuff. I'm going to focus on Hollywood this week while you handle the rest. And I think you should call Robin. Depending on her mood, she sometimes needs the Electra touch."

Robin picked the pancake house near Walnut Creek Park when Electra called yesterday, partly to remember Holy (Hud's father and Robin's first caregiver patient) as well as to celebrate Sunshine's anniversary (the abused puppy she found two years). All this and more flitted like a butterfly through her thoughts as she waited for Electra while talking to Sunshine, who was sitting attentively next to her at the booth often occupied by herself and Holy until he died nearly a year ago.

"Electra and you are my best friends, but I've known her since grade school days when she and Christi and I were known as the Three Queens. That was long before Electra decided to sometimes call herself Alisha. Christi's dead now, and I'd be too if it weren't for Electra. She brought me back from the edge when I tried to kill myself, but with Holy's help she made me what I am today. Electra says she has a surprise. Well, we have one for her too."

Robin had always been emotionally brittle.Ambivalence toward males, a failed music career, and an aborted college program had fueled her mental breakdown, but though still borderline psychotic, she had developed enough mental stability and an eldercare business to keep centered. While training Sunshine for a therapy-dog role, she discovered that her empathy for the elderly carried over to animals. Those traits, along with Hud and Electra's help, had launched Sunshine Eldercare soon after Holy's death.

Blue-eyed and ashe-blonde, Robin's high cheekbones and Russian heritage accentuated a European profile, though the stress of recent years had matured her physically and emotionally. She had lost the bloom of youth and now looked her age, the same as Electra's. But Electra was taller and thinner, looked several years older, and had an emotional hardness that she constantly worked to soften. She had become more empathetic, and her Alisha alter-ego had become a tony dresser who fussed with her raven-black hair and makeup that highlighted hazel eyes and a darker complexion, whereas Robin's grooming had become indifferent.

Robin had deliberately distanced herself from Electra, trying to become less dependent. She was the only person who knew that Electra and Christi had been lovers, and after Christi's mysterious death, she had hoped she could take Christi's place, but Electra's feelings towards Robin expressed love rather than a sexual intimacy. Robin could live with that as long as Electra was nearby. She rose to give a hug when Electra came to the booth while Sunshine wagged her tail.

"I haven't seen you for too long. And what happened to you? You've got scratches on your face." Electra slid into the booth before answering.

"I tripped while running and slid down a slope, but I'm on the mend. But I do have one surprise to show you." Electra glanced around to make sure no one was watching, then discreetly pulled down the top of her blouse.

"Holy Shit, you got a tattoo."

"Accidentally. Some rocks cut me when I fell. How does it look?" "Like an inverted cross. If Christi were here, she'd say it's totally sexy."

The waiter came by to say hi, asking if they would order the usual. After they did, Robin continued.

"Today's almost the anniversary of you and me and Holy finding Sunshine. I try not to reminisce too much, but I still miss him. Do you sometimes think about Christi?"

"Do you want my Alisha or Electra answer?"

"I'm not depressed today, so please give me your Alisha answer. I love you both, but Electra too often gives too much info."

"I've put Christi in the past and have moved on. Let me quote a verse from Indira:

> 'The past is but a memory, The future a dream unknown.
> But your present is a gift you see, It's meant for you alone.'
> This works for me, and it should for you too."

Electra paused while the waiter brought their order. They ate in pleasant silence until Electra spoke again.

"Why don't you show me your surprise."

"You're looking at it. Does it look like I've gained weight?" Electra studied Robin's appearance before replying.

"Your clothes are too loose-fitting. But you do look radiant. What gives?"

"You're the one who likes guessing games, so here's a clue. Pretty soon I'll have to take care of someone else, someone at the opposite end of the age spectrum."

"Are you pregnant?"

"You're the first person who knows; you can't tell anyone until I give you the OK." Electra slid to Robin's side of the booth.

"I didn't know you found a significant other. Congratulations." "I haven't. I want to be a single parent."

"I won't pry, and don't tell me who the father is unless you want to. But may I tell our friends in Washington? I'm going there next week. Zoe and Matt will want to know, as will Jennifer and Russell; so will Carter."

"Don't say a word, I'll tell them after the baby's born, but I'm going to tell Hud and Su the next time I see them. And don't start planning my future. I've already thought it through. I'm in good shape, thanks to your exercise program, so I'll work up to the week I deliver. I'll expand my caregiving business to include young children. It'll be a combination eldercare and daycare. And I'll train more border collies to be therapy dogs."

"What's the due date?" "September 9th."

"What a coincidence. That's 9 months after Zoe and Matt's wedding. When I see them, I'll diplomatically ask when they plan to start a family."

Robin smiled generously.

"I'm glad they got married. Zoe's a much better match for Matt than I was. And Carter's string of girlfriends suits him better than you ever did."

Robin checked her cell phone.

"Time's up. We both have places to go and things to do. But I still need you to be my best friend, please call me when you get back." "I promise. Electra and Alisha want us always to be ever the best of friends."

As they got up to leave, Electra hugged Robin, kissing her full on the lips. Sunshine wagged her tail.

As the Electra-Alisha duo reviewed that evening for the upcoming trip, Electra spoke first.

"We leave Friday for Washington after meeting tomorrow with Tim and Kwame, then briefly on Thursday with Hud, Woolly, and Sam. Then we'll use the weekend to socialize. Why don't you be in the foreground when we arrive in DC?"

"Good idea, but you take over when we meet with Professor Ravenhill on Monday. Then I'll come back Tuesday when we network with the politicos we've met at the National Governors Association. And then we fly to Hollywood Tuesday evening. Trust me, I'll have Hollywood details lined up. We can rehearse en route. After all, we're quick studies and have been acting our entire lives. And don't worry, that flight should be much more comfortable than the last. Hazmat uniforms won't be necessary."

Chapter 4
April 2126

"On the Road Again"
(Thread 2 Chapter 2)

Though Electra never asked for favors, Carter always met her at the airport because he was house-sitting for her. She much preferred an attentive presence by her erstwhile, almost co-friend rather than renting to an indifferent occupant.

Though not one of his virtues, Carter had disciplined himself to appreciate patience, which he now practiced while waiting at the baggage claim.

Five years ago, I wanted to marry her, but it's good we morphed our red-hot love affair into friendship. She's too intimidating, mentally and physically, even though my brain and body are better than most. I stand six feet, and she's only an inch shorter. I couldn't beat her in arm wrestling or mental gymnastics when we first met, and I certainly can't match her now. And though I'm five years older, she's more mature. Even her Alisha personality that emerged four years ago as she recovered from the T-Plague can be too much to handle. I see her coming. She's even better looking than before. Her clothes and makeup make her so sexy and cosmopolitan. But I've moved beyond all that. It's better I simply enjoy being her friend, especially when glimmers of her carefully concealed skills break through.

Electra returned Carter's wave, kissing him on the cheek as he hugged her when she reached his side.

"Thanks for picking me up. You're always so punctual. And there were no flight delays, so you didn't waste too much time waiting."

"You're right, as usual. Let's grab your bag and I'll treat you to pizza. I thought we'd get one at the place you and Robin liked. And should I call you Electra or Alisha?"

"I'm ready for fun, so call me Alisha. Which car did you drive?"

"My Vette. Tomorrow, we'll take your Mustang. I'll tell you as we drive what Zoe and Matt have planned." Alisha chattered as they walked before making Carter say more.

"They had a great Caribbean honeymoon cruise and are back to work. Ask them when you see them, but here's something for your ears only. About a month ago, Matt found her unconscious when he came home. She was all confused, didn't know how she ended up on the family room floor, or how she managed to spill two jars of spaghetti sauce. Maybe the cold medication she was taking caused a problem. No permanent damage, other than stains on the rug. Please don't tell them I told you."

Electra nodded and said nothing but already knew. I'm the only one who knows I did it, I'll make sure it stays that way.

"So, what's the plan for tomorrow?"

"You know Zoe. She's always finding new activities; she signed them into a bowling league. Tomorrow evening they'll take you and me and Hannah bowling. Russ and Jennifer Conklin will be there too. Have you ever read Bowling Alone, by Robert Putnam?"

"Why yes. He was a Harvard political scientist who published it in 1995. It analyzes the collapse of social capital in America and the steps people took to rebuild it. In fact—" Carter interrupted her mid-sentence as he pulled into a parking space.

"Please stop. I don't want an Electra lecture. I'll pick a different subject when we get seated. And I'll bring my laptop for self-defense."

The restaurant looked the same as she remembered, although none of the crew did. Carter ordered a beer while Alisha chose a Coke, and he let her choose the pizza: a large pepperoni and cheese.

"You must be hungry. You'll have to eat more than half. How do you stay so thin? Zoe stays pretty fit, and both Matt and I take pride in our athletic ability, but you look thinner and in as good a shape as you did when you played in the Co-NFL. I guess you're training for Hollywood."

"In a manner of speaking. But tell me about your love life. How's Hannah? I met her at Zoe's Gal Party. I like her. She's a smart lady." Carter took a small sip before answering.

"That she is. She teaches history and poli-sci at Howard University. But she likes me more than I like her. We got into a big argument. She told me I worry too much about happiness and still don't know much about sex versus love. She told me to read some Schopenhauer and then decide if I want to become a Buddhist monk." Alisha interrupted Carter for pen and paper, which he gave her from his laptop bag before continuing.

"I don't recall what Schopenhauer had to say about happiness, but I told her that we economists are interested in it because our goal is to maximize utility functions, which measure happiness. And today, neuroscientists can actually measure brain state happiness. It's rather complicated, but let me explain..." Electra scribbled notes while he summarized what he knew about correlations between biological markers and neural activity in brain areas associated with pleasure.

"So there you have it. And in the future, people might wear a device that displays numerically how happy they are. What do you think?"

"Take a look at my sketch that summarizes Schopenhauer. I can explain why he's so pessimistic about finding lasting happiness if the focus is only on sex." Carter studied what she had drawn before rolling his eyes.

Schopenhauer, Sex, and Happiness Summary

Schopenhauer, Sex, and Happiness Summary

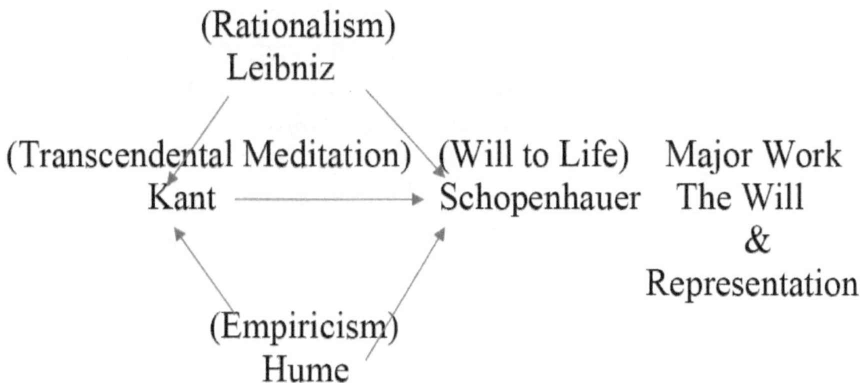

Schopenhauer:
* First Western Philosopher to incorporate Buddhism
* "The World is Wretched" "Life is a Tragedy"
* "Man is not meant to be Happy" Human Condition plagued with:
* Boredom Suffering Death
* Man is driven by: Will to Life Sex

- Intellectual Persona deceived by Emotional Persona
- Can Achieve Temporary Happiness in only two ways:
- Be a Sage/Monk
- Be a Philosopher or Artist
- His Philosophy foreshadows Freud
- His meditations on Space, Time, or Causality lack the precision Modern Physics provides

"Jesus, please don't pull an Electra on me. I'm not in the mood to wade through this information overload. I'll file it away for another time. And here comes our pizza, so let's eat first before I show you my latest white paper presentation."

The pause and pizza replenished Carter's patience; fifteen minutes later he positioned his laptop so both could see the screen.

"You're the first person to read what I'm going to explain to Angus. And please notice, I reference Putnam's book."

"I see that. And I suppose your recommendations can help Angus keep Jared inbounds. I like the James Madison quote you mention about men being angels. President Jared Gardner is certainly no angel. Please walk me through it."

"I cover policy recommendations for socioeconomic and political issues. And let's give Jared some credit. He understands how the turbulent time period – 1960's to 2020's – segued into America's great awakening that led to improved income and social equality, as well as political civility and compromise towards the middle. And his programs do repair some of the damage done by T-Plague and Middle East Terrorism. Thanks to his Guardian Party, T-Plague and the Middle East are under control..." Carter marched through the remainder of his presentation. Twenty minutes later Alisha gave her opinion.

"I like your recommendations and how you identify new threats that are outside your scope. The big three are Cyberterrorism and False Information, Automation and Artificial Intelligence, and Genetic Engineering and Transhumanism. They'll require techno-scientific solutions implemented via Normative Ethics. I must hire you to help forge my platform when I run for Congress."

"Ho-ho, I'll vote for you when you do, but the odds of that happening are less than Quantum Computers achieving the Singularity. Why—" Alisha interrupted.

"Please let me tell Angus first, but I'm going to run for a Texas Congressional seat and if I get elected, I can push for some of your recommendations."

"You're serious, aren't you? This must be Electra talking."

"I am, and it'll take both Alisha's bubbly personality and Electra's rational thinking. What do you think?"

"I'm all in for your campaign. And I'm all in mentally. You've worn me out. Let's go home. We can talk more tomorrow."

Alisha experienced once again the joys of running in a temperate climate on a morning whose zephyr-like March breeze warmed by sun rising into a cloudless sky heralds the promise of spring. Familiarity of running on the same bike path ever since adolescence allowed her to alternate thinking among different people and places. The years have been kind to Carter. He still has most of boyish good looks and only a few strands of gray in his light brown hair. Too bad his introspective nature complicates close encounters with the opposite sex, even with someone as well-balanced as Hannah. And how different for Matt. He resembles Carter physically, but not emotionally. Both he and Zoe are much more practical and outgoing. Tonight, I'll just observe and keep my mouth shut.

Alisha's pace accelerated as she reached the five-mile turnaround tree.

I took the scenery for granted when I ran here every day, but today I notice even the little things, like how sharp the shadows are that are cast across my path. I must remind Electra to look more at Nature than numbers.

As she cruised the final mile, a pleasant thought came to mind. How fortunate I've been to rotate living locations among Washington, Austin, and Hollywood. And I may have to add Japan to the mix for cloning work. But maybe I can set up a stealth lab in Austin. Time's tick will tell…

Time ticked calmly for the remainder of the morning. Carter and Alisha worked independently until he announced it was time to have an early afternoon lunch at Zoe and Matt's. The foursome would visit until it was time for bowling, then Carter would pick up Hannah while Matt drove Zoe and Alisha. Carter listened passively as the other three chatted after lunch.

"Carter tells me your holistic healthcare business is keeping you

two and Jennifer busy. When do you think Russell might join?"
Zoe let Matt talk first.

"I don't think he will. Health issues have slowed him down. That's one of the reasons the Conklins are bowling with us tonight. He's 15 years older than Jennifer, and she's trying everything to keep him active, physically and mentally."
Matt signaled for Zoe to pick up the conversation's thread.

"Jennifer tells me more than she does Matt because he's usually doing physical therapy at patients' homes, but you'll see for yourself tonight."

Carter spoke after checking his cell phone.

"I think I should go pick up Hannah. We'll rendezvous at the bowling alley. And since your drive is shorter than mine, you can talk a bit longer if you like." He left abruptly. Alisha was the first to speak after the door slammed.

"Do you know what upset him?"

Matt answered, "It's an issue between Hannah and him. He told me she wants more sex than he does." Matt stopped, not wanting to offend either of the ladies, but Zoe's giggles along with her words said he wouldn't.

"I'm now a married woman. I know all about sex, so keep talking, unless Alisha feels uncomfortable." Alisha smiled but said nothing, so Matt proceeded.

"Everyone has different turn-ons or offs, and Carter told me some of Hannah's idiosyncrasies annoy him, but he didn't elaborate." Alisha filled the pause by asking Zoe a question, leading to a safer subject.

"Carter told me you're the one who picked bowling for your next social activity. Why that choice?"

"As a poli-sci major in college, I read the gold standard social capital book, Bowling Alone. Social capital is a nation's network of people-oriented relationships, and it bridges the gap between people on opposite sides of income, political, or racial divides, as well as binds people to their cause or country. Bowling leagues are classic examples of how people increase social capital by getting together, so that's why I chose it."

Alisha added, "There've been decades in America's history when economic and sociopolitical trends depleted its stock of social capital. Late in the twentieth century, suburban sprawl, increases in low-tech unemployment, income inequality, women in the workplace, and divorce all joined forces with accelerating technology to stress people so much they stopped reaching out. But the country figured out how to reconnect using new tools like cell phones, the Internet, Social Media, and Crowdsourcing. Matt, what would you like to add?" "If Carter were here, he could speak for me, but since he's not I'll just say that Zoe's grasp of the subject impresses me. I'm sure she's seen examples in action because of her previous sociopolitical consulting and public relations careers. Maybe she can add something to what's already been said."

"I can add a warning that T-Plague and Middle East Terrorism drew down our social capital, and if we don't plan ahead, biotech and artificial intelligence might do the same. I'm sure Carter can tell us about that." Matt checked his cell phone.

"Time to go so we get to the bowling alley first."

Zoe described as Matt drove what she had organized.

"We'll set up two teams bowling on adjacent lanes. Me and Matt and Hannah and Carter are one, and you and Jennifer and Russell are the other. The team with the highest average score is the winner. And we'll all sit at the big table set up between our two lanes. Matt's a great bowler, and I'm getting better. And I bet you're good too."

"I can't recall when I last bowled but whenever it was, I wasn't very good. I'll count on Russell and Jennifer to make up for what I miss. Have they bowled with you before?"

"Russell's not very good, but Jennifer bowls a lot better than I do, and she looks great. You'd never guess she's our parents' age. She could reactivate her modeling career anytime she wants to, and she'd be in demand because ads and clothing designers are catering to older women. And from the pictures I've seen, her daughter Christi was almost as pretty. Too bad she died in an auto accident. Weren't you in it?" Alisha didn't have to revisit that part of her past because just then Matt parked the van.

"Okay ladies, let's roll out, roll in, and get ready to bowl."

Zoe took charge signing in and setting up; the trio had been sitting for only five minutes when Jennifer parked Russell across from Alisha and greeted everyone. Alisha smiled, waiting for Jennifer to finish, but her thoughts were the opposite of her expression.

Gads. Russell looks terrible.

Carter brought Hannah to the table a minute later. Zoe explained her rules so everyone knew where to sit and which lane to use. A waitress brought the drinks Zoe had preordered while Matt led off the conversation.

"Did Carter drive patiently today?" Hannah smiled faintly before answering.

"He always does. He pampers his Vette. I think he likes it better than me. And he's never at a loss for what to say about what makes him happy."

Sensing a pregnant pause coming, Alisha brushed it aside.

"I think that's why he's such a great discussion leader. We were just talking about social capital, so perhaps he could carry on."

He did, but with less than his usual enthusiasm.

"Social capital is to social scientists what the sum of the capitalized value of plant and equipment and employees is to economists. Today, an economy needs social and physical capital if it wants to maximize utility functions be—" Hannah glared at Carter as she talked over him.

"Why don't you stop obsessing about utility functions and happiness. Pick another topic."

"Well, since you know so much, why don't you tell us something about religion? I'd like to hear how you'll connect that to social capital."

"That's easy. We all know that society has become more secular, but America is the most religious nation in the Christian world. Christian ethics are woven into the nation's fabric, and social capital increases the number social networks, which is positively correlated with church attendance. Carter can tell us all about correlation coefficients."

Zoe interrupted before the arguing escalated further.

"Why don't we start our bowling contest. We can talk and bowl at the same time." There was a collective sigh of relief as the teams followed Zoe's instructions.

Alisha was happy to be more of a watcher than talker. Russell had trouble rolling anything other than gutter balls; he was the only bowler worse than Carter.

It doesn't look like Carter's eye-hand coordination carries over from tennis. He's becoming moody and silent. Well, it's my turn again, so I'll focus on the pins instead of their squabbling.

Her first ball left four standing, the 2-4-5-8 bucket, a common spare for mediocre bowlers. Alisha's form as she was about to release the second looked good, but Hannah's yell forced a gutter ball.

"Stop watching Alisha's backside, you should be watching mine, not hers or Jennifer's." The outburst turned heads on adjacent lanes. Carter stuttered to defend himself.

"I, uh, I watch everyone. You have good form too."

"That's baloney. That's game, set, and match, you ass." Hannah stormed to the locker room. Carter blinked while staring at Hannah's disappearing act, gobsmacked to the max before turning to his friends.

Alisha tried to lighten the mood.

"She should have said frame, game, and match. That would strike a better note. And she should have spared using one of Richard Feynman's favorite words. Baloney is what the great physicist used to describe most of post-modern philosophy."

"Oh shut up. Look what you've done. Now she's mad, thanks to you." Carter grabbed his gear, then bolted to the locker room. Zoe tried to salvage what had turned into a disastrous outing.

"He didn't mean that. It's his fault, not yours. Well let's keep bowling. The team competition is now Matt, Jennifer, and Russell versus Alisha and me. And we shouldn't worry about Hannah and Carter. I'm sure Carter will know what to say."

Alisha didn't see an apologetic Carter until she came in from her run late Sunday morning; he was sitting in the kitchen, having already placed one of her favorite breakfast treats on the table. "Thanks for blueberry muffins and extra butter sitting next to my Coke. When did you buy them?"

"On the drive back from Hannah's, and I won't make that trip again."

"We're good friends, so it's OK for me to pry. Besides, I've witnessed some of your previous lady-friend spats. I know that you and Matt understand what makes relationships work, so you don't need advice from me. But it's better to end a relationship sooner rather than later if the chemistry doesn't work."

They sat in comfortable silence while Alisha buttered a second muffin, waiting for Carter to reply. He poured another cup of coffee before speaking.

"I finally realized last night that you're the adult version of my very first love. When I was in 8th grade, my heart went boom for a girl named Darlene. She became the standard of comparison for all girls I dated until I got to college. That's when my approach to dating matured. I started enjoying each female on her own merits and found many I liked. But I found only one that made my heart thump, and that was you.

"Odd, isn't it? I'm a cerebral type, but even for me primal passions broke through because of you, and to this day I never tire of being around you. But it's good you backed away, and though you still can stir my emotions, we should keep it in the past tense. I now realize I've subconsciously been comparing my dates to you. I have to work through this issue on my own by first deciding what I want from a partner." Carter paused, glancing away for a moment, sipping his coffee and leaving space for Alisha.

"I don't think it's odd. What people want from a relationship evolves as they grow. But I do think you need a break. Why don't you get away from emotions and do something different for the rest of the day?"

"That's not a bad idea. What are you going to do?"

"Prepare for a Monday meeting with my GWU advisor, Professor Ravenhill, and a Tuesday meeting at my National Governors Association office. And before I fly to Hollywood, I'll contact Angus."

"You'll be busy the rest of the day, so I'll stay out of your way. And I'll be happy to drive you to the airport."

"Thanks for the offer, but I'll have one of my NGA contacts do that. People in politics practice reciprocal altruism, a subject you know about, but I won't bore you with a lecture because right now I'm Alisha." For the first time that morning, Carter cracked a smile.

It was Electra, not Alisha, who prepared diligently for Monday and Tuesday meetings. Late Sunday afternoon, Alisha suggested they take a break.

"You've worked long enough. Follow my advice, as well as that of the great mathematician Paul Erdos. He coined the term 'incomplete learning,' which means your subconscious fills in the gaps while you work on something else. So, why don't we let the lightning brain fill in any gaps while we have some fun. Let's treat Carter to some desserts at a sensual pleasures café. I'm certain that will make him smile again."

Carter perked up when he heard; he explained while driving why he picked the Couquelicot Café.

"This is the last place I took Rachel before I flushed her, and you were my only friend who had the nerve to force me to do what I needed to do. In retrospect, what you said to her that night is hilarious. A couple of days later, Matt laughed till he cried when he gave me his version of how you stomped all over her. But enough about her, or Hannah for that matter. They're both past-tense." Carter's mood became even better after sampling marijuana brownies and absorbing some of the mood-elevating fragrances floating about, so Alisha let his expansive thoughts lead the conversation.

"I'm glad my parents forced me to study religion at our synagogue because I came away knowing more than most people about Judeo-Christian beliefs and how they compare to Islamic and Oriental religions. I can counter all those books or articles pontificating about seven types of atheism, 36 reasons for the existence of god, or why Scandinavia is such a great place to live, even though most Scandinavians are atheists. Religion in general, and Christianity in particular, contributes much to the greatness of America. Many atheists agree. In fact, some atheists label themselves humanitarian agnostics. My beliefs haven't changed much, other than becoming more ecumenical as I get older. How about you?"

"I learned long ago it's a waste of time to argue faith versus reason or God's existence versus non-existence. People should respect all religions and choose what works best for them. That and America's acceptance of racial, ethnic, and gender diversity all contribute to American exceptionalism. They'll be part of my political platform, and I'm counting on you to help hammer it into place."

Carter had mellowed so much that Alisha didn't know if she could trust his driving a nail, let alone a car.

"Why don't I drive us home? I'm not wearing stilettos, so I can handle your Vette's stick shift."

Carter yawned while smiling, then said, "I never worry about you anymore. You and Electra can handle anything."

From the very start of her biotech graduate career at GWU, Electra had the knack for handling her advisor, initially holding him at a distance to prevent his meddling. But over time he had become an unwitting ally, gradually transforming from a brusque skeptic into a provider of grad students for her projects while she gave him ego-boosting credit for her accomplishments. Professor Ravenhill rose from behind his desk to greet her when she knocked on his office door.

"Hello, Professor Ravenhill. How are you?"

"Yes, yes, Kittner. I'm always fine. Come in and sit down. I have plenty of good news for you." Sitting opposite, she listened to his unexpectedly animated words.

"I knew I was onto something when I accepted you into our biotech grad program. You're smarter than you let on. And you've proved me right. That Smart Clothing Project you manage for GWU is churning out all sorts of patents. Now I know why you put a business grad student on the team. She's finding innovative applications for making clothes out of interactive fabrics. I'm certain you'll be appointed as an assistant professor starting the fall term. So, congratulations, but there's more.

"I've been asked to review a paper for the Materials Science Department that talks about rare earths. I want you to read it and write up a description of new commercial applications. I'll add what I can to it so both of us get our names listed as contributors, and that way we can add it to our published articles' bibliography. I always like seeing my name in print."

"Please send me a copy and I'll get after it."

"And I'd like you to look into something else. You know more about high-energy physics than I do. Some of my associates brag about all the imminent breakthroughs just over the horizon, but frankly, I think they're blowing smoke. Could you send me something that'll tell why I'm right and they're wrong?"

I already have just what he wants. But I better under-promise and over-deliver. That's what smart marketers do.

"I might have some notes that can help. And I know you like the Star Trek series. It's better than any other sci-fi for stretching actual science into science fiction. If you'd like, I can send you an explanation for how it connects to actual science."

"I never thought about it, but I like the idea. Can you give me an example?"

"Here's one that's a real stretch, the starship Enterprise has warp-drive engines that use antimatter to focus energy that creates black holes and wormholes to pull it through space faster than the speed of light. But here's one that's achievable today; directed energy barriers can be built. A hundred years ago, the President shut down the government because Congress wouldn't fund a five-billion-dollar border fence between Mexico and the United States. Today, we could erect a heat or sound barrier by focusing microwaves or sound waves that would repel anyone trying to cross. It would be easy and economical to build."

"Please write up something I can use. You are indeed clever. I like how you put grad students from GWU and UTA on the same team. Well, I have work to do, so carry on and be on your way."

Electra decided while driving to call Angus as soon as she got home. Alisha reminded her how useful he had been for her and vice versa.

"Thanks to your manipulations via his brain trust, Angus became President McTear. And you were the brains behind his throne until you accidentally poisoned yourself when taking out Jared. Now that Jared's back, Angus is sidelined but still runs Gardner's team of rivals advisory committee that you cleverly put in place to keep him inbounds. By the way, which Hollywood actor from the past does Angus look like?"

"I never considered that. How about giving me a clue?"

"You're the smart one so I won't, other than tell you to think about a submarine colored other than yellow. But do that after you call Angus."

The call gave Electra more to think about.

He's worried about Cyberterrorism. I know how to help him there. And he's going to resign from Jared's team of rivals as soon as he announces that he'll be the Democratic Presidential Candidate. And I'll resign too. That's all to the good. We can help each other plan our political campaigns. And that will rattle Jared. I'll have to give Mr. President new marching orders very soon.

After spending the next hour planning tomorrow's NGA office activities, Electra shifted gears.

I'll steal a march on tomorrow by calling Woolly right now, so I can devote more time tomorrow preparing for Hollywood. Alisha chimed in.

"That's an excellent idea because the extra time will help me. And by the way, what is the genesis of the idiom 'steal a march?' You must know it because you always tell your grad students to know words and phrases before using them."

"It means to gain an advantage over an opponent, and it comes from the military maneuver of moving troops secretly. It has been used since the early 18th century, when it was cited in the London Gazette in 1716."

"You are a fount – bordering on a flood – of knowledge. Some of our friends accuse you of dumping too much. But keep doing so when we talk and let me determine when you should dial back the quantity. Now please make the call."

This call, like the previous, added to what Electra needed to think about.

Woolly likes how I'm using my NGA connections to jump-start campaigning, but he wants me to meet with Sam as soon as I get back to Austin so I can take advantage of a sports-related stunt guaranteed to get me noticed. Even I'm beginning to feel stressed out. I'm experiencing a case of the news. Even if the news is all good, too much at one time is bad. I need to run; that always helps me center myself.

It did. She could feel the stress dissipate as she gained her second wind, becoming immersed in the immediate. By the time she reached home, the primal pulsation of blood surging magnified all sensations as she coasted to a stop.

I love how exercise makes me feel, tired physically but refreshed mentally. I hope I can always run or find another way to generate endorphins. If I can do that, I'll always be ready for tomorrow and tomorrow and tomorrow. And unlike Macbeth, I won't let them creep in at a petty pace. I'll seize each one and make it race, and welcome madness and the most.

Chapter 5
April 2126

"The Hollywood Connection"
(Thread 2 Chapter 3)

The Electra-Alisha duo would engage in only two of their three Hollywood adventures on this trip because Tim had the Cyber-Theater's rollout on schedule. This theater is a beyond state-of-the-art- art home entertainment system using line extensions of Electra's Brain Probe to build what the promotional material labeled a "Star Trek Holodeck for Virtual Reality Adventurers." Tim had equipped it with Kwame's 3-D GUI, making the Cyber-Theater an immersive experience beyond what the authors of Brave New World or 1984 could have possibly envisioned.

Alisha summarized during the flight what they would do this week and next.

"First order of business is filming episodes for the second season of the Superman series. I was a such a big hit playing my Supergirl role that the fans picked me to take the role of Chameleon in a new Mission Impossible movie series. We'll have dinner tonight with our mentor, Kathi Lauret, who will tell us about the filming schedule. "And after filming wraps up, we can visit Winona Kota and her daughter Carley. I hope Winona can tell us more about Indy, but if her Alzheimer's is worse, that will be impossible. Anything you'd like to add?"

"We never knew that Indy and Winona were roommates during their undergraduate days at Harvard. And Carley's American Indian features make her look like our kid sister if we had one. She has her hands full playing the caregiver role, but she doesn't complain."

"Then it's settled. I'll be in the foreground and you can observe from the shadows. But please, jump in if I get into trouble."

Alisha spotted the limo driver waiting at baggage claim; ninety minutes later she called Kathi from her room to confirm they'd have a 7 p.m. dinner at the hotel. Then she took a light workout in the fitness center, followed by laps in the pool. The lifeguard waved as she glided to the ladder.

"Welcome back, Ms. Kittner, and best of luck for the new season." Alisha walked towards him after grabbing her towel.

"Why thank you. I'm flattered you recognize me."

"Hey, even in Hollywood, your physique makes you special, and you're featured in a couple of promotional trailers. I like how your name, Kimberly Kitchner, jibes with your Chameleon codename. But I gotta know, do you actually do your own stunts, or are they virtual reality simulations?"

"That's part of the intrigue. Please watch more of them and then you tell me."

Alisha arrived at the restaurant ten minutes early but Kathi was already there. She rose to kiss her on the cheek when Alisha reached the table.

"Ah, you look alert as always. I've ordered Chardonnay for me and a Coca-Cola for you because you have a full slate of filming coming up. You can have the good stuff at our wrap party before you fly back to Austin. Did you bring your associate, Tim Godfrey? From what I've heard, he's been doing a great job coordinating Cyber-Theater launch with our studio."

"No. So far, virtual meetings have worked well, but he would like to come back for our parties to play the role of my chaperone."

"I'm not sure you need one, but he's welcome anytime. Now let me tell you the drill for this week and next.

"Vincent Valdez and Tyger Riddley will meet with you first thing tomorrow because you'll have alternate days filming Superman and Mission Impossible. Then Vince will take you for a briefing session with the Superman cast a crew. Tyger will do likewise the day after. And each will give you their filming schedule call sheets. Sometime next week there'll be a joint wrap party to celebrate all the filming completed."

"I'm glad you ordered me a Coke. I want to have a clear head so I can work hard tomorrow. I'm going to bed right after dinner."

"I seem to remember your Co-NFL motto, work hard play hard. Well, our PR people have come up with something more fitting for your new image. I hope you remember what it is."

"I do. It's sophisticated and intelligent virtue, cosmopolitan honesty in relationships, youthful yet elegant sexuality. And may I confide what will become known shortly?"

"Of course. I hope you consider me a friend, both professionally and personally."

"That's why I want to tell you. I plan to run for Congress this year." Kathi's expression scrunched but recovered a few seconds later. "Hmm. There've been only a handful of people from Hollywood who've combined acting and political careers, but you might have what it takes to join them. After all, politicians are great actors, but not vice versa. Hollywood publicity will add to whatever your campaign puts out. I'm pleased you told me. So, I propose a toast to your success and our friendship. And then let's get a light dinner and a good night's sleep…"

The ensuing ten days whirled by, and though Alisha was still considered a newcomer, both sets of cast and crew respected her effort to learn from their expertise. When she showed special interest in disguises because her Chameleon role used them, one of the makeup artists gave her a hands-on demonstration of wardrobe selection and facial mask 3-D printing. As the Friday wrap party approached, the directors congratulated everyone for jobs well done. And that included Ricardo Fonseca, an articulate and extroverted thirty-something who worked for both crews. He was good-looking too, but then every young male or female working in Hollywood seems photogenic. (Alisha observed that the same applies to the seasoned females; however, she didn't think the same could be said for many of the middle-age-plus males, a fact made obvious when comparing then versus now photos.)

Always the ladies' man, Ricky planned to use his charm and discriminating taste at tonight's party to hunt for a younger quarry who would play his game.

Alisha cruised in unescorted and fashionably late, wearing a lowcut red blouse and black slacks, both new and elegantly tailored. She chatted comfortably before heading to the bar where Ricky, casting a favorite line, tried to hook her.

"Well hello, Alisha. I'm sorry I didn't have an opportunity to coach you this week, but you didn't need my help."

"I remember your name, but not your role. Please tell me what you do and why I didn't need your help."

"I'm the Continuity Coach. Not many people know all the different uses for the word 'continuity,' but I do because the word figures importantly in linguistics and mathematics degree programs. And my eyes tell me you have nothing missing." Ricky's smile invited her into the game.

"You must be smart if you have those kinds of degrees. What does a Continuity Coach do?"

"I keep the actors role-centered by correcting any diction or gestures that don't fit the part. In other words, I eliminate any discontinuities, especially those occurring when speaking."

"Doesn't linguistics include phonetics, syntax, and semantics? How does that connect with mathematics?" As Ricky continued spinning lines, Alisha listened to her warning system.

This guy's smooth and sexy and would like to take me home. And my hormones are in the mood, so I'll use him to practice being seduced while he uses me to scratch his itch.

Ricky never gave his quarry too much information, so he stopped while Alisha wanted to know more.

"I'm impressed. I never knew that syntax has an X-Bar structure theory similar to mathematical logic. And I never considered how at the deepest level, linguistics is intimately connected to philosophy." "For an actress, you're pretty smart. Maybe you'll understand the connection Ludwig Wittgenstein made between philosophy and linguistics. Would you like to hear it?"

"I would. Please go on."

"Wittgenstein studied mathematics at Cambridge, where Bertrand Russell became his de facto mentor. Russell had already published volume one of his magnum opus, Principia Mathematica, and his celebrated 'Russell's Paradox' had shot holes in the consistency or completeness of Frege's axiomatic set theory. I won't confuse you with all the details, but the paradox goes something like this. Are you ready?" Alisha nodded, so Ricky unloaded.

"Here's the question it asks: 'In a one-barber town, where the barber is the one who shaves all those, and those only, who do not shave themselves, does the barber shave himself?' The answer results in a contradiction. The barber cannot shave himself as he only shaves those who do not shave themselves. As such, if he shaves himself, he ceases to be the barber. Conversely, if the barber does not shave himself, then he fits into the group of people who would be shaved by the barber, and thus, as the barber, he must shave himself."

Ricky paused, waiting for Alisha to surrender, but she surprised him.

"From the little I know about Wittgenstein, he abandoned mathematics to study linguistics because he wanted to eliminate logical inconsistencies by clarifying meaning. He spent the rest of his life developing Analytic Philosophy, which did gain a foothold among some Existentialists, but not long before his death he renounced it. A rather sad illustration of what can happen when a great mind becomes obsessive-compulsive. But I'm sure you know this, and even more."

"Uh, I do, and I have an idea. Why don't I take you to my place when the party wraps up? I can tell you more about how Semantic-Syntactic Theory is used in artificial intelligence for constructing listener responses to syntactically consistent, algorithmically filtered speaker input."

"I'd like that, but please go slow, at least when talking. And you'll need to drive me to my hotel afterwards."

"I can handle that. So, why don't we finish making the rounds, and then meet in the parking lot in half an hour? I'm driving a Porsche convertible. See you soon."

Alisha felt ready to seize the day after her early morning run and refreshing shower, but before she could call for her limo, Electra questioned her about last night.

"Weren't you rather careless? You didn't enforce your safe sex policy."

"Ricky's meticulous manners and grooming tell me he chooses his partners carefully, and I suppose he feels the same about me. But he didn't ask about birth control, so I guess he considered pregnancy my problem, even though we know that can't happen. However, I did remove what he had recorded on the videocam I spotted."

"I stand corrected. You weren't careless, but didn't you violate our pledge not to use people?"

"I think you're splitting hairs. Since no one got hurt, we were merely enjoying each other. So please, drop the inquisition and let me think about what to ask Carley's father. He might provide some new info about Mother. And I'm not using him because I'm treating him to lunch."

After a one-stop drive, the limo delivered Alisha to Carley's house, but when she opened the door, her expression spoke to a problem even before her greeting. Alisha could hear shouting in the background.

"Thanks for bringing a pizza. Mother will like it, but she's very quarrelsome today. I think it would be better if father takes you out to lunch while I feed Winona." The shouting stopped abruptly; a middle-aged, balding fellow about two inches shorter than Alisha appeared beside Carley.

"Hi, I'm Bob Carson. Gadzooks, Carley didn't exaggerate. You could be Indira's reincarnation. Come on, let me take you to lunch before Winona starts yelling again. We can walk to a place I have in mind." Electra did most of the talking as they walked.

I empathize with him. I'd be uncomfortable too if a person from my past stepped out of a time warp.

Bob became chattier after they sat at a booth in an uncrowded Mexican cantina.

"Even though we're near Azusa Pacific's campus, the food's upscale. You'll find it's real Mexican, not the Tex-Mex you get in Austin. Since Carley's already told me a lot about you, I won't ask a lot of questions. And I know why you're here, you want to know what I have to say about Indira, so ask away…"

For the next ninety minutes, Bob answered Alisha's delicately posed questions, but they added little to what she already knew from talking with Carley on a previous visit. She compared what he said to what she already knew.

Bob met Indira and Winona when they were summer interns at the film studio where he worked as a screenwriter. He liked Indy better, but she was dating a fellow from another studio so he started dating Winona, becoming co-friends after six months. Indy came back for a second summer, staying with Bob and Winona but she didn't date anyone that summer. Neither Bob nor Indy went to the party where Winona's boss raped her, and Indy left for Harvard grad school a couple of days later. I'll stop asking questions and let Bob just talk. People often say more that way. I think he wants to tell me his story so I'll say he's OK.

Bob finished the last bite of fried ice cream before saying more. "I hope you enjoyed lunch as much as I did."

"It's my treat. You've been so patient answering my questions, I'm sorry if I've been pestering you."

"Don't be, I feel better sharing a story almost nobody knows. The last time I saw Indy was just after the unfortunate party. And before your mother left, she made me promise to look after Winona. And I did, though we never married because I had trouble holding a job. I guess the saying that Life is what happens when you're making plans for something else applies to me." Alisha nodded but said nothing, instead sipping her Coke so Bob would fill the silence.

"Who knows how events might have turned out if I had been at the party, but I wasn't invited. But your mother insisted she and I visit Winona's boss the next evening. I volunteered to get to his condo first because I worked at his studio and I might be able to soften him up. But he was already drunk and he became even more belligerent when Indy showed up. We stepped onto the balcony after I suggested the cool air might settle him down, but all that did was add to his desire to punish Winona, who was now working full time at his studio as a graphics artist. I gave up and left. Your mother must have left soon afterwards because she was flying back to Boston early the next morning." Alisha left a sentence hanging. "When ifs and nuts are candy and buts..." Bob gave a whimsical smile and completed it.

"Oh, what a party we'd have. Well, the party continued for me two days later. Winona's boss had accidentally fallen from the balcony, and security video captured me coming and going, so the police paid me a visit. But the time stamp showed I had gone before he hit the ground right in front of people about to enter the building. And speaking of time, we better head back. Between now and your next visit, I'll try to come up with more stories about Indy. Maybe I can find another person you could talk to."

Winona had stopped yelling by the time they returned, but Carley looked exhausted. Alisha talked to her in private before leaving. "You're a dutiful daughter. I had a much easier time taking care of my grandfather."

"Mother's not always like this. And Dad pitches in when he can, so I'm getting by. Did you learn more about your mother?"

"I did, thanks to your dad. I'll make sure to call you on my next trip..."

Alisha asked Electra the 64 thousand-dollar question on the limo ride back to the hotel.

"What's your verdict? Did Indira pitch Winona's boss over the balcony railing?"

"I don't think so. There was nothing to gain but much to lose. What do you think?"

"I think Mother must have been very clever. Why didn't any video cameras catch her? She would have been a suspect too."
"But do you think she killed him?"

"She could have. We don't know the depth of their relationship, but Indira and Winona were more than casual friends. And I could argue that she did, using the 'Justice versus Mercy' paradigm. But we'll never know, so let's stop thinking about what no longer matters and do something that does. Let's take a workout and then pack for our early Sunday flight home."

The airport monitor reported on-time departure, so Alisha people-watched while sipping a Coke as she strolled the uncrowded concourse. When her cell chimed, she decided to take the call rather than shunt it to voice mail, even though she didn't recognize the caller ID.

Kathi blurted, "I'm so glad I reached you. There's a medical alert for everyone who attended the wrap party. Ricardo Fonseca's been struck down by the T-Plague. Everyone should be tested immediately to find out if he infected them. I can't talk longer because that's all I've been told and I have other people to warn, so please call me if you become ill."

Kathi disconnected before Alisha could stammer a goodbye, but she did manage to reach a restroom just before a feeling of dread gathering in the pit of her stomach made it turn. She collected herself as soon as a wave of nausea subsided.

Ricky didn't infect anyone, I infected him even though I'm taking my special meds and test negative. My dormant T-Plague has morphed into a sexually transmitted disease, and all I know for certain is that any guy not wearing a condom's at risk. I've turned into a black widow spider. This is my problem to solve alone if I ever want to have intimacy again. Alisha spoke from the shadow.

"Hold on. You're never alone. You've got me and the lightning brain. You and I should think happier thoughts on our flight home while we let the lightning brain worry about a solution. It always finds a way."

"You're right. No sense fretting about contingencies that might never happen. Let's hope for the best and let our brain handle the rest."

Each member of the duo mused separately all the way back to Austin.

Chapter 6
May 2126

"Double Play"
(Thread 1 Chapter 3)

"Didn't you hear the news? The Dow Jones plunged 10 percent late yesterday. You're not on top of events like you used to be. If you were, you might have told me or Angus that a Cyber-attack's coming. What are we going to do now?" Carter's early Tuesday morning call terminated Electra's troubled sleep, giving her something else to worry about.

"I've just come back from Hollywood and I didn't have time to catch the news yesterday, so I didn't know that most of the Federal Reserve and East Coast banking centers were taken offline. No wonder the stock market plunged. But it'll bounce back once the systems are brought back up. And how do you know Cyberterrorism's the cause?"

"Come on, Electra. That's not like you. What else could it be?"

He's right. Come on, focus.

"Sorry. Look, I've been preoccupied, so let me think things through and get back to you when I have something you can use."

"And I apologize for waking you at five and snapping at you. Please call me as soon as you have something."

"I promise. Bye." Electra stared into space after disconnecting, fighting her obsessive-compulsive desire to rush to her workstation and dive into the problem.

I worked nonstop yesterday coming up with no solution to my STD problem. I'm going for a run and think about something else.

That worked wonders. Electra could feel her worry morph into focus once she settled into rhythm. By the end of her run she knew what she could do for Carter and Angus.

These attacks have to be the work of the Iron Triangle, and I suspect Darla Tinibu's calling the shots. I put it out of action several months ago, but I haven't monitored it since. It's time to use my Network Security Suite and its Cyberweapons arsenal to do it again.

So, I'll have to work a double play. After handling the Iron Triangle, I'll work out an STD solution. And since I'm a great multi-tasker, I can handle both.

By late afternoon, Electra completed her first objective. She had tapped into Darla's Emails and hidden directories to trace all Iron Triangle correspondence since her initial retaliation. Then she unleashed two waves of Cyber torpedoes and nukes that turned its Cyber resources into useless bits and bytes. Afterwards, she even allowed herself a moment to savor the victory.

Kwame's 3-D GUIs make my Cyber-software better than any virtual reality game. And I'll assemble a military-strength security and weapons suite the CIA and DOD can buy from Hud that'll keep them ahead of all wanna-be Cyberterrorists. Now I'll stop for a snack and then return to my STD problem.

The peanut butter sandwich and Coca Cola restored her energy, but not even a 10 p.m. cookie break could help Electra break through to a solution. Near midnight she broke the pencil she had been using to doodle notes.Alisha, who had been watching from the sidelines, decided she could help.

"Carter had it partially right. Snapping a pencil is not like you, but it does show our cognitive persona is learning to show some emotion. And I think you've been looking too deep inside instead of staying on the surface. I have more experience with sex than you do, so allow me to explain.

"Looking for a genetic modification or a biotech drug solution is the wrong approach; it'll take too long for you to develop, so why not come up with a spermaticide-like T-Plague preventative. There are any number of dissolving vaginal films or sprays that make dandy contraceptives."

"That could work. All I have to do is suspend a T-Plague-killing chemical in a vaginal contraceptive. How did you figure this out?"

"Like I said, I have more experience in matters of the lower head, and I'm also getting smarter, thanks to your tutoring."

"I'm proud of you. And like you've been telling me, I'm becoming more empathetic, thanks to your assistance. Let's call it a night and go to bed." Alisha was on a roll so she made a final observation. "And to illustrate my increasing intelligence, may I correct your syntactical error? You should have said 'as you've been telling me' instead of 'like you've been telling me,' because 'like' is a preposition for connecting to a noun, and you should have used the conjunction 'as' because 'you've been telling me' is a clause." Electra had to agree, but did manage to get in the last remark.

"I think someday our dual personalities will merge. But until that happens, I'm the grammarian and you're the Hollywood star. But I have a question for you. What are your top three split personality movie picks? But please, don't tell me now. I've had enough of your cleverness for one evening, so goodnight."

Waking refreshed before the alarm chimed, Electra took a six-mile run before watching the news while eating a breakfast of oatmeal sweetened with organic honey. As she mixed it in, she reminded herself why she used it.

Organic honey contains phytonutrients that might make it an antioxidant as well as an antibacterial and antifungal. And it might also boost the immune system and reduce the risk of cancer. Do I believe these claims? It doesn't matter if I do or I don't because I eat honey for one reason only: it makes oat meal go down easier. And I remember a grade school rhyme about honey.

I eat my peas with honey, I've done it all my life.

It makes the peas taste funny, But it keeps them on the knife.

Whoever wrote the poem, and it might have been the 20th century American poet Ogden Nash, would have made a most interesting dinner guest.

Her breakfast-table humor made the gloomy Cyberterrorism news easier to take since she knew more than the reporters, but she did empathize with those affected and understood why reporting had taken a darker turn. One commentator's summary was particularly sobering.

"… And no one knows how quickly the stock market will rebound because this round of attacks hit more than financial assets. We've seen videos of malfunctioning revolving doors and elevators trapping and injuring occupants, and escalators speeding up and dumping people in a heap. All this is a stern warning that the 'Internet of Things' poses downside risks in addition to upside rewards. Make sure you can find the stairways and manual overrides on appliances, doors, and vehicles…"

Electra called Carter but he didn't pick up, so she called Angus. He didn't answer either, so she left a phone number for his DOD or CIA contacts that would put them in touch with a network security developer if they would call early next week.

Now it's time to work a double play with Hud.

He was already having a second cup of coffee when she cruised into his office.

"Howdy, Electra. You musta come back with a passel of projects. Su told me not to bother you, so I been waiting for you to bother me. What's up?"

"It's all good. First, you should expect a call sometime next week from DOD or CIA. They'll want you to develop a suite of proprietary Network Security Software and a toolkit of Cyberweapons. Tim and Kwame will have all the details for you to coordinate, but please keep me invisible and don't give them any insider information. "Second, we need to order some additional biotech equipment for my lab here in Austin and for Su's lab in Japan. I'll place my order immediately and let Su order hers when she's ready. And don't worry, the profit you'll make on the proprietary software suite will offset the equipment cost."

"I never have to worry when you get involved. You're always on top of things. But did you remember to call Sam?"

"I'll do that later today..."

Electra spent the rest of the morning collecting cloning articles and tabulating a list of online seminars she would binge-read or watch later, then she called Hollywood.

"Hi, Kathi, it's Alisha. Has the T-Plague scare gone away?"

"Yes, and thanks for calling. You sound chipper, so I assume Ricky didn't infect you. And no one at the party was either. I guess we're lucky. Ricky's condition has stabilized."

"I'm happy to hear that. And I'll be ready for the next filming session. Please call me when you want me back."

"I will. And please stay healthy and use stairways. I don't think terrorists have found a way yet to hack them. I'm swearing off elevators and escalators. Besides, I can use the exercise I'll get by walking. Bye-bye."

Electra brought a pizza to an impromptu lunch meeting with Tim and Kwame. Each of them had turned their high-functioning autism to their advantage by choosing hi-tech careers, but she always gave them special attention. They welcomed her as much as the pizza. Electra described a new project after everyone had consumed several slices.

"I'll carve out a set of what I'll call military grade network security tools and Cyberweapons that I want you to package. Kwame will assemble, using his 3-D GUIs, and Tim will write an instruction manual. And under no circumstances do you reveal my proprietary software or who we are. Let Hud be our liaison. He's expecting a call next week, so start working now but wait for him to ask. I'll give you a list by the end of the week. Any questions?" Tim asked the only one.

"Not about the software, but we will after Hud talks to us. But why don't you tell us about you latest Hollywood trip?" Alisha gave an edited version.

Electra took an afternoon break to call Sam, who said he had good news and offered to take her out for dinner. Alisha accepted immediately.

Sam brought his father, Sam Ryder Senior, and they reviewed while driving what they would propose. Junior spoke first.

"I'm glad I picked Trulucks. That's where Alisha's odyssey with us started. And look where it's led. She got us the Co-NFL title, and we got her started in politics when we brought Woolly into the mix." "Yessir, she's got the goods for sports or politics, and our plan contains both as well as connecting with Hollywood. And that's what I'd call a triple play. Do you think she'll go for it?"

"Sure. She likes sporting games as much as we do. You'll see." After gliding to the curb when she spotted Sam's car, Alisha folded herself into the back seat and waited for Sam to speak.

"You look even better now than when you were our T-Breds quarterback. And you've dropped a couple of pounds, replacing them with a more cosmopolitan gravitas. That must be Hollywood's magic."

"Perhaps so, and I have you to thank. You're the one who made Hollywood connections for me. And I'm counting on you and your dad to help me make more connections for my campaign."

"Well now, that's the dessert for tonight's dinner, so we'll start on it after we eat..."

As they chatted, Alisha noted that Truluck's ambiance matched many of Hollywood's upscale seafood restaurants.

The translucent curtains are just right for the floor-to-ceiling windows and lamp-lit white tablecloths. And Sam's not bragging about knowing the owner. The host placed us at a table giving us enough privacy to speak freely. I'm ready to hear what Sam has to offer.

Sam steered the discussion to his deal after Alisha finished one of Truluck's signature desserts, a three-layer double chocolate cake square containing thick layers of fudge frosting topped with a strawberry sauce.

"Well now, if that satisfied your taste for chocolate, Dad and I have something to satisfy your liking for sports and politics. What do you know about baseball?"

"It's the granddaddy of American professional sports, even though sports aficionados claim lacrosse to be the oldest. But fans would like it to be faster-paced."

"Right you are, and that's why Dad and I bought the Midland RockHounds. It's one of the eight teams in the Texas League and it feeds talent into the Oakland Athletics. The A's are the team that the book and movie Moneyball are based on. I convinced the league owners to let us install some new rules guaranteed to speed up the game. I won't go into all of them, but here are the biggies.

"There's no fixed number of innings because of a three-hour time limit, even though each team still gets 27 outs. They can use as many consecutively as they want. When the team with the lower score has used them all, the game's over. If the game ends in a tie, each team gets 6 more outs, and if the score is still tied when those outs are gone, each team gets half-a-win.

"And there are strict time limits for throwing pitches. Pinch runners can sub for men-on-base without pulling from the game the guy who got the hit. And for each game, fans can pay to download to whatever device they want a copy of the league's StatBall app that'll be activated for only that game. It accesses StatBall's databases and captures real-time data sent from stadium monitors to forecast probabilities for what might happen as an inning unfolds. Fans love it because they get a window into what players and managers are thinking, and of course they get a leg up when placing bets on outcomes."

"How do I fit in?"

It's a win-win because playing ball on our team will add to your campaign publicity. The RockHounds are in the heart of your Congressional District. And it's a win for Dad and me because you'll be a big draw. The fans loved you when you played in the Co-NFL, and they'll want to see how you do in baseball. Only a handful of pro athletes in other sports could handle it. What do you think?"

"I'll tell you after you describe my role."

"OK, now think about this. Baseball's a thinking and skill sport rather than a brute force contest. There's less risk of injury. And here are the skills you need. You gotta run, catch, throw, hit, and hit with power. We know you can run and catch, and probably can hit because you have good eye-hand coordination. But you won't be able to throw long or hit with power like the guys because female throwing and hitting biomechanics aren't as good. But that's OK because you'll be sort of a novelty, the first female to play professional baseball at the Double-A level. We can have you run bases and play second base, which is the easiest position. So, do we have your attention?" Alisha didn't talk to Sam until she did to herself.

This has possibilities, but I'm not going to be a novelty. If I've got the goods, I want to go all-in.

"You do, but think about this. I want to play center field, so invite me to a tryout where I can show you and the team what I can do. If I have what it takes, I'll play." Sam let Sam Senior wrap up the evening.

"We rolled the dice when you played football, and they came up a winner. We'll do it again if, after a tryout, you think you can play ball. Junior will schedule a tryout for next week…"

Electra kept busy researching biotech topics related to cloning, putting baseball on the back burner until Sam called on Friday. He had arranged a tryout next week, Tuesday at the RockHounds' recently renovated Security Park Stadium located in Midland. Midland is 340 miles west of Austin, so Sam had convinced Hud to fly them, using the H&H helicopter.

Electra went to Hud's office immediately after the call. She spoke just as soon as he looked up from the pile of papers he was sorting through.

"I'm pleased you're coming to my baseball tryout."

"Sure thing. I used to play ball in high school and never lost my love for the game. Maybe I can help."

"I understand there are seniors leagues. Do you have any buddies nearby who still play?"

"No, but one of my gambling partners coaches in the Austin Metro Baseball League. Whatcha got in mind?"

"I'd like some coaching and practice over the weekend. Would you be able to arrange it?"

"Sure thing. Do you want me to tell Sam?"

Electra smiled impishly as she replied, "No, this is a game for just you and me." Hud grinned as he made the call.

Electra watched videos on baseball fundamentals that evening, memorizing the 'seven absolutes' for a perfect swing as well as a technique for not hitting ground balls (get the bat ASAP into the plane of the ball and don't roll the wrists when making contact), but the one explaining how outfielders track fly balls instantly became her favorite because it used principles of physics. The coach explained three possible techniques (trajectory projection, optical acceleration cancellation, and linear optical trajectory) but he said all outfielders run instinctively when tracking a ball. Then he diagrammed the path outfielders run to catch it. After adding the sketch to her notes, Electra knew which method to use.

Trajectory projection works for me because it yields the most efficient path. The lightning brain will tell me where to run.

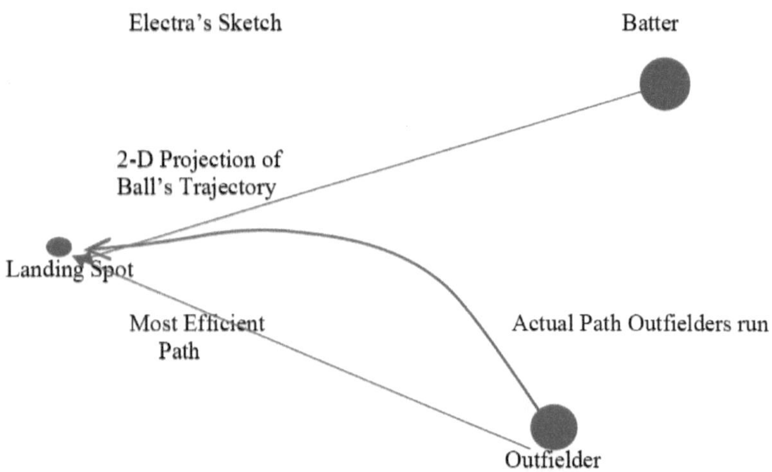

I'm ready to have fun practicing this weekend, but come Tuesday I'll have my game face on.

Ronnie Logan liked his 'Coach P' nickname because it fit him even better than his Midland RockHounds manager's uniform. One look and you knew what a baseball purist looks like. He had gained weight and lost most of his athletic build that had made him a three- sport starter at Midland College where he had earned an engineering degree and oilfield certification. Now in his mid-fifties, he fit the image of a seasoned coach-manager and was glad to have the job because it helped fill gaps in his less than fulltime employment. He knew his oilfield service career was winding down, but he didn't want to move away from his lifelong home in the Permian Basin, so he did the best he could for his wife and high-school-age daughter.

Today he would supervise a tryout for the new owner's "pet project." And though a purist, his engineering background always kept him looking for ways to improve his team or the game. That's why he liked Sam Ryder and would give the female a fair shot. Ronnie respected all athletes who made an honest effort, but he told Sam he wouldn't let the girl play if she couldn't cut it on the field. Sam had replied that she might surprise everyone because her football training and athletic ability might carry over. Ronnie scheduled the tryout for 3 p.m. so he could see how the girl did in sunny and windy conditions.

The girl and her two escorts were already on the field when Ronnie led his starters out of the clubhouse. As they joined the trio, he wasn't the only one to notice how well she wore a uniform. Ronnie shook hands with all of them before giving commands.

"Hello, Missy. We're gonna do some drills that'll test the five skills we look for in a player. We'll start by hitting fungo flyballs for you to catch. Then we'll put you through a drill for you to throw out runners. And we'll wrap up by having you try to hit pitches. Sam and his friend can watch but they have to stay out of my way. And I'll put some of my players alongside to help you get acclimated. Any questions?"

"No sir."

By the way, I forgot to ask. What should I call you?"

"Please call me Alisha when we're having fun, but call me Kit when I'm wearing my game face." Ronnie flickered a smile.

"I like your attitude. Now, let's see how you handle yourself in action."

Ronnie let Hud and Sam stand with him as he barked orders to the player hitting flyballs.

"Start with cans of corn, and make the drives harder to catch as you go." The hitter did as told. Ronnie turned to Sam as the drill proceeded.

"I don't get it, but she sure can. She runs different than everyone else. It's like she knows where the ball is gonna land and heads right to the spot. And she's fast. She ranges better than our center fielder."

Ronnie ended the fielding drill and started one for throwing. Kit had to throw from straightaway center field to home plate, trying to cut down a runner from second or third. After five throws, each successively deeper, he stopped the drill.

"Jesus, when she catches the ball she's already running like lightning towards the plate before letting it go. That makes up for lack of arm strength. She's pretty damn good." Ronnie waved everyone to gather, then announced the last drill.

"Time for the test of truth, hitting. We'll start you off easy, throwing lazy curves and mid-speed fastballs, but we'll go up from there. Are you lefty or righty?"

"I'm a switch hitter. I have more power batting righty but I get to first faster when I bat lefty. If it's OK, I'll start lefty." Kit's matter-of-fact answer drew snickers from a couple of players.

"You got it. Now go try to hit the ball."

Following Ronnie's orders, the first pitcher lobbed easy-to-hit pitches, but soon started bearing down as Kit peppered line drives into the outfield. As the velocity increased, so did the distance the ball traveled. And she nailed every single curve ball. Ronnie stopped for Kit to bat from the right side and put in another pitcher, who began throwing hard right from the get-go. She timed her swing perfectly; the ball literally exploded off the bat. As the drill continued, Ronnie yelled to his players.

"Watch her swing. It's practically perfect. Her mechanics and timing compensate for lack of arm strength. OK, one more pitcher to go." Though Ronnie didn't know, the players had conspired yesterday to test the wanna-be rookie under fire. The new pitcher mixed brush-backs in his assortment of throws. Kit had to dodge out of the box several times, and one throw plunked off her helmet. She said not a word, instead dusting herself off and digging in again. But she appeared rattled. She fouled off two pitches and lost her grip on the bat as the next pitch zinged past. She trotted towards the mound to retrieve it; the pitcher swaggered towards it too. Big mistake.

Kit charged, her leg tackle bringing him down and herself on top. She pummeled her stunned victim with several punches before two players dragged her off. Yelling instructions, Ronnie joined the group that had gathered near the mound.

"OK, shake hands. We gotta have solidarity. And I declare, we got us a player." Kit was the next to speak.

"I apologize, but I've been trained to watch my back." The pitcher grinned sheepishly after wiping away a smudge of blood.
"I'll watch yours if you'll watch mine."

The other players huddled around Kit, welcoming their new teammate while Sam and Hud looked on. There'd be more to say on the flight home, but those words would wait so all could enjoy the moment.

As Alisha headed to the locker room, Electra made a comment she couldn't hold back.

"You showed we've got the goods, so you can strut our stuff. And let's make sure we get a tailored uniform because we want to look good, on or off any playing field."
Alisha agreed wholeheartedly.

Chapter 7
June 2126

"Enemies Within or Without"
(Thread 3 Chapter 1)

Darla Tinibu, president of Cybergard Security Systems, watched one back only: her own. Events that had unfolded during the past three years caused her to change directions, making it even more critical to cover her tracks while covering her backside. Smart, manipulative, and greedy, she could be dangerous to allies and enemies alike, especially if they became impediments to her ambitions.

Her plan to leapfrog beyond state-of-the-art network security software required she pirate algorithms from a tightly controlled Texas company, but the attempt had been botched. Her failure to find a viable alternative jeopardized another plan that she shared only with her Iron Triangle Alliance partners– China, Russia, and Isilabad. Adding to that, the Cyberwar and its crippling Cyberterrorism she had escalated had become pyrrhic: she and the IT Alliance absorbed more damage than they dispensed. She needed to develop a contingency plan that would work regardless of what enemies from within or without intended to do.

Darla had begun building her grand plan years ago when she envisioned an African Silicon Valley powerhouse headquartered in Harare, the capital of Zimbabwe, her parent's homeland. She had made political connections that gave her Cybergard spinoff company, also headquartered in Harare, a running start for becoming Africa's hi-tech leader. The patents and algorithms she stole from the parent company made Pan-Africa Network Systems (a virtual and untraceable umbrella Cyber-company containing three units: network security software, A.I. software, A.I. Robotics) profitable from day one, but growth had slowed because additional pirated software was no longer forthcoming. But she used her quantum computing knowledge to find another business opportunity that would be good for herself and her favorite country: Zimbabwe. (She had used her Big Data Infiltration apps to adjust all confidential data so she qualified for citizenship in Zimbabwe and the United States.) And it could be a win for her IT Alliance partners if they would follow her instructions, for if they did, she would build a 22nd century cartel even more powerful than OPEC had been. She would present her master plan tomorrow when she convenes at her office in Harare the last Iron Triangle Alliance meeting ever, even though her encrypted Email gave no details other than ordering her partners to pack only one bag and meet her for a 6 p.m. dinner in the restaurant at the Hotel Avenida in Maputo, the capital of Mozambique. She deliberately excluded mentioning it is 570 miles southeast from Harare because she would tell them at dinner what they needed to know. Even though it was only 5:30, she was already sitting in the restaurant, scheming and role-playing before her partners trickled in. Darla's energy level showed the benefits of arriving early; she had flown in yesterday to make all arrangements.

Walking softly and uncertainly, accompanied only by growing trepidation, Ziarmal Thaqaf approached the restaurant. He knew what his Exalted Ruler wanted him to do: use the Iron Triangle to hold the West at bay while Isilabad becomes a more enlightened Caliphate of Islam. But he hadn't a clue why Darla had become so assertive, so secretive. She had been willing to let him lead until early this year, but that had abruptly ended.

His Chinese and Russian counterparts, Chen Xu and Sergei Zaitsev, were more transparent. China wanted to dislodge America from its top spot in world economic pecking order, and Russia wanted to shore up its declining raw materials economy by seizing a larger share of the international financial market. They couldn't defeat America on land, sea, or in the air, but if they pooled their Cyber-resources, a Cyberspace victory might be theirs, so Chen contributed weapon arming and launch apps, Sergei guidance and triggering apps, and Ziarmal network infiltration and disruption apps, while Darla dispensed network security software containing built-in trapdoors only she knew about. The IT Alliance won early skirmishes, but as the battles escalated, so did IT's collateral damage. Neither she nor her partners knew who or what was mangling their hardware and software.

Darla's fire hydrant build and intense expression made her visible in any crowd. Ziarmal waved when spotting her sitting alone as he entered the restaurant at 6:15, but she merely stared at him. Chen and Sergei caught up to him as they approached their new leader. Darla motioned for them to sit before she began talking. Unlike Ziarmal or Sergei, Darla always skipped introductory pleasantries, instead boring into the guts of the issue.

"Starting immediately, we're going dark. There will be no more Internet or cell phone communications because some organization has hacked into even our encrypted channels. And we are terminating the IT Alliance immediately, replacing it tomorrow per my plan. We will fly directly after dinner to another location. So if there are no questions, eat what you want and then get ready to go." Chen nodded while studying the menu, as did Sergei, but Ziarmal appeared ready to argue.

"If you want to be the leader you should not disrespect your partners. Show us more courtesy, more civility. If you cannot do that, I do not wish to be part of your plan. What entertainment and relaxation have you arranged? I had hoped to observe some of Africa's large animals roaming in a game preserve." Darla softened her tone.

"I apologize, I'll add your request to our agenda. Now please, order something to eat."

Arduous plane flights had sapped everyone's energy, so Darla prodded a conversation to elicit additional concerns. As expected, she noticed Chen's and Zaitsev's more open-minded attitudes, but Ziarmal became increasingly skeptical. She decided to take the next step when dinner ended.

"I empathize with you, but please trust me. All will become clear shortly. And for added precaution, we'll take two jeeps to different airports. Ziarmal, we have been friends since our Silicon Valley days, so please ride with me. Let our drivers carry your bags. I see them coming, so I think it is time we leave. All of us will be settled in our destination hotel by midnight, and we'll start fresh tomorrow at an 8 a.m. breakfast meeting. Travel safe and sleep well." Darla spoke in an African dialect to the drivers. Smiling politely, they escorted their guests to awaiting jeeps.

Darla's jeep turned south while the other headed north. Though dusk had already fallen because Mozambique is south of the Equator, Ziarmal enjoyed the ride into the country, expecting to see airport lights soon. Suddenly, the jeep swerved onto a rough side road, bouncing him from side to side in the cab. He grabbed a support bar but was a jumbled wreck by the time the jeep slid to a stop. Two burly men dragged him from the vehicle, one beaming a flashlight in his face as the other pummeled him to the ground, then began ripping off his clothes.

"Darla! Help me!"

"I am. I'm granting your final wish. You're about to meet some of the big cats at Kruger National Park."

Darla played the role next morning of an attentive hostess when she cheerfully greeted her still-fatigued partners in the lobby, explaining why she had changed the meeting location.

"We'll have more privacy at my office, and I assure you my company's security is unrivaled, as is my planning. And Ziarmal agrees. To settle his nerves, I showed him a summary of what we will discuss today. He endorses my plan, but I was unaware that his country doesn't have enough resources to be of use, so he departs this morning for Isilabad. However, I have adjusted my plan to cover Isilabad's shortfall. I am certain you will approve it." Chen nodded as Sergei replied.

"Yes, maybe we will be better without Ziarmal. His software contributions were marginal, and we don't need him to coordinate encrypted communications anymore." Sergei's words provoked more from usually reticent Chen.

"I glad he's gone. I think he not believe in Islam. Ho-ho, I make joke. He is faker, not fakir."

Darla said, "Yes, his rants about religion were beginning to bother me too. Ah, here come our security escorts. Let's go to my office building."

Twenty minutes later Darla had the trio sitting in a typical conference room. There was a selection of sweet rolls, muffins, and beverages on a credenza next to the table. She waited for Chen and Sergei to grab breakfast, then launched into her presentation. Her first slide, prominently displayed as she began talking, was as bold as her delivery.

TRIUMVIRATE TEAM TOTAL PLAN
(AKA T-CUBE PLAN)
FOR TOTAL DOMINATION

OUR TIME HAS COME!

- CHINA POSITIONED TO DOMINATE WORLD ECONOMY
- RUSSIA POSITIONED TO DOMINATE FINANCIAL MARKETS
- AFRICA POSITIONED TO DOMINATE SUPERCOMPUTER MARKET
- ALL POSITIONED TO DOMINATE CRITICAL RAW MATERIALS MARKET

IF WE WORK TOGETHER TO ACHIEVE VICTORY WHY HAVE OUR PREVIOUS ATTEMPTS FAILED?

- T-PLAGUE TERRORISM HAS RUN ITS COURSE (EFFECTIVE VACCINES MINIMIZE THREAT)
- APOCALYPSE CLOCK "DECOMMISSIONED" (SOMEONE OR SOME ORGANIZATION HACKED INTO IT)
- UNABLE TO LEAPFROG CURRENT SECURITY SOFTWARE
- THE WEST COUNTERED IRON TRIANGLE CYBERSPACE ATTACKS
- SOMEONE OR SOME ORGANIZATION HAS HACKED US!

"We are the new triumvirate because we don't need Ziarmal's Isilabad contribution to dominate the world. Ancient China had its Three Excellencies, Ancient Rome had its First Triumvirate, and post WWI Russia had its Troika. Now it's our turn if we work together. "And our failures are in the past. My plan has all the workarounds we need." Having captured her partners' attention, Darla showed the next slide.

THE NEW PLAN:

- REPLACE IRON TRIANGLE WITH T-CUBE FORCE (CHINA RUSSIAAFRICA)
- GO DARK
- CONTINUE CYBERSPACE ATTACKS AS A DIVERSION (CHINA:
- U.S. INFRASTRUCTURERUSSIA: MAJOR MONEY CENTERS AFRICA: REGIONAL BANKING CENTERS)
- ESTABLISH COVERT SUPER SOLDIER STRIKE FORCE
- DESTROY HARD ASSETS IN 3-D SPACE, NOT CYBERSPACE, VIA SUPER SOLDIER STRIKE FORCE

- CREATE AND DOMINATE THE RARE EARTHS CARTEL (CHINARUSSIAAFRICA)
- MARGINALIZE (VIA STRIKE FORCE) ALL OTHER RARE EARTHS SUPPLIERS (AUSTRALIACANADAAMERICA)

"Here is a listing of our plan's most important components. I've branded us 'The T-Cube Force,' or 'T-Cube,' for short, but we tell that to no one because, for security purposes, we are going dark. We will never communicate anything to anyone outside this room, and we three only communicate in person." Sergei's question interrupted.

"If we don't talk, how do we coordinate diversionary attacks?"

"We don't have to. Each of us acts secretly and independently. That will keep all our enemies confused, and there's no risk of being hacked."

"Chen said, "I like it. And China has head start making super soldiers and grabbing rare earths market."

Darla clucked, "I knew you would." Now let me explain who contributes what. Take a look at the next slide."

WHO CONTRIBUTES WHAT:

- CHINA: DNA/GENETIC ENHANCEMENTS TO SUPER SOLDIERS EXOSKELETONS ROBOTICS
- RUSSIA: ADVANCED MILITARY-GRADE WEAPONS (DIRECTED ENERGY THERMOBARICS)STEALTH VEHICLES
- AFRICA: RARE EARTHS MINING EQUIPMENT MORE POWERFUL QUANTUM COMPUTERS A.I. APPS
- ALL PARTNERS CONTRIBUTE HUMAN ASSETS TRANSFORMED INTO COVERT SUPER SOLDIER STRIKE FORCE RUSSIA BUILDS IT CHINA FUNDS IT

"Each country contributes what it does best. And let me answer the question before you ask. I can contribute more software apps to cover for Isilabad, and all of us can contribute recruits to our super soldier strike force from our countries' elite special forces. Notice that Russia builds it and then turns it loose. Its codename is 'S- Cube.' Hold the rest of your questions until I finish." Darla proceeded to the final slide.

HOW TO IMPLEMENT:

- EACH PARTNER AGREES TO THE PLAN BUT WORKS INDEPENDENTLY TO STAY INVISIBLE

- STRIKE FORCE AGREES TO THE PLAN BUT OPERATES AUTONOMOUSLY TO STAY INVISIBLE
- PARTNERS HOLD ONLY COVERT ANNIAL IN-PERSON MEETING TO STAY INVISIBLE
- STRICT CODE OF SILENCE

"And this is how we launch the plan. After we finalize all the details–and we have to do this before we leave – each of us operates on our own. And that includes S-Cube. Only we three and a military person Sergei chooses to lead S-Cube will meet in person once a year at a time and location I will communicate to you. Sergei will communicate that to his S-Cube commander."

Sergei asked, "If you're afraid of messages being intercepted, how can you communicate with us?"

"I'll use an encryption algorithm built on the only method that still can't be hacked by quantum computers: RSA. And I'll use untouchable communications channels that route through the Deep- Dark Web." Darla saw Chen's scowl forming so she pointed to him. "What's bothering you?"

"You give maybe too much power to Sergei. Only he knows all details about S-Cube, and only he talks to its leader."

Darla snapped back, "It's in Russia's best interest to stick to the plan. I'm sure Sergei agrees."

"Of course. Our three countries share the same path into the future. My only concern is America's reaction if it finds out. Ziarmal knows our intentions and might turn against us by leaking our plans because he is no longer a partner. If things turn out badly for Isilabad, he might not take it lying down."

"There's a Biblical metaphor about the lamb lying down with the lion and living happily ever after. I'm certain it matches Ziarmal's position. Rest assured, he won't divulge any details. Why don't we grab another snack? Then I'll take you through my rare earths primer."

Needing only one slide, Darla dived into her rare earths presentation while Chen and Sergei were still eating.

RARE EARTHS PRIMER

- Rare Earths: Seventeen chemical elements found together in Earth's crust sharing important metallic properties. Includes the 15 Lanthanide Series elements plus Scandium and

Ytterbium.

- Found in uncommon igneous rock formations: alkalines and carbonatites.
- Primary Producers: CHINA RUSSIA Secondary Producers: AFRICA Australia Canada USA
- Important Properties: ElectricalMagnetic
- Important Uses: Military Electronics Solar PanelsQuantum Computers Electrical Storage Batteries
- Why Important: Raise Superconducting Temperature Increase Energy Conversion Efficiency Stabilize Material Substrate
- Latest R&D confirms breakthrough Quantum Computer applications for previously ignored rare earths
- Demand growing because of electrical and magnetic properties.
- How Produced: Low-Tech Mining and Smelting produces Bulk Waste often containing low-level Radiation Creates Jobs
- Rare Earths Mining/Processing and Materials Science technologies primed to piggyback on A.I. currently in use

"You can read between the lines to connect rare earths to our plan for building a Rare Earths Cartel. Our countries already mine them; military and computer applications are driving demand growth. And African miners have recently discovered additional mineral beds containing rare earths important for next generation Quantum Computing chips.

"And there's more good news. Rare earths mining has lagged behind other raw materials industries, like oil and gas, for using A.I. to modernize operations. My company has that A.I. expertise, and I'll share it for a bigger cut of rare earths mining profits. So, we all win. And now that you have my plan, does it have your approval? Can we call it our plan?" Chen and Sergei looked at one another, nodded, and smiled. Sergei spoke for both.

"I believe so. What do you want us to do?"

"Before we fly home, we need to put our plan in writing. I know all about writing plans, so we'll use my templates, which include task lists that get converted into PERT/CPM diagrams. We'll make one hard copy for each of us but create no electronic documents. And do not give a copy to anyone. Sergei will give only those parts that his S-Cube commander needs. I will order lunch and we can start now."

By the time Darla's security guards delivered the new triumvirate to Harare International Airport (long ago renamed from Robert Gabriel Mugabe International Airport), the plan had been completed and goodbyes said. Darla's flight to San Francisco would take a day, but that didn't bother her because she would use her devious mind during the trip to add tasks to the plan, tasks that would be for her benefit only.

Though Darla had no worries, Jared Gardner did. His latest invisible blackmailer's Email had arrived two days ago, and he continued floundering for a Divinely inspired solution. Jared muttered to himself while awaiting in the Oval Office for a trusted security agent. Damn that Angus. He's bailing out of the team of rivals that damn blackmailer made me put in place. Now there's only one person left on that team, a Mr. Carter Quavah, who I'm supposed to put in charge. But I have to give Quavah some credit. He does endorse some of my projects because they do help the economy, even though in a heavy-handed way. I'll have to figure out a way to use him.

Jared's chief of staff, Dean Corfu, interrupted his private thoughts. "Mr. President, Greg Unger is here. Shall I bring him in?"

"Yes, and make sure we're not disturbed."

Yes, Mr. President." Dean brought Greg to Jared, who walked around his desk to shake hands. Dean left as soon as introductions had been made. Jared sat on a sofa positioned perpendicular to his desk while Greg sat at attention in a side chair. Time and T-Plague might have dulled Jared's wits a bit, but his people skills could still be charming. He smiled while leaning back.

"Ever been in the Oval Office?"

"No sir. It's even more impressive than the photographs. The blue rug emblazoned with the Presidential Seal is impressive. Very fitting for a president of your stature. Your policies are certainly making a difference."

"I'm glad you feel that way, because you've touched on why you're here. I have an assignment for your eyes and ears only. What I'm about to tell you must stay between only us. Kapish?"

"Yes sir."

"I want you to find someone. I have an invisible blackmailer who interferes in my decision-making. Your predecessor snooped online to uncover the source of the Emails, but came up empty, so I want you to take over."

"It would help if I talk with my predecessor. May I contact that person?" Jared had a bogus reply for why that person went missing. "No, Kay Klatterbuck retired. But I know you have better people skills for finding enemies inside or outside my inner circle. How might you start?"

"By any chance, do you have a list of possible suspects that you gave to her? I can build from there."

"I think I do. If not, I'll reconstruct it and give it to you in person. I have to be careful what I send electronically. My blackmailer seems to follow everything I do in Cyberspace."

"I understand. Please have Dean contact me as soon as you are ready for me to come back." Jared glanced at the grandfather clock ticking patiently nearby.

"I'm a busy man and have another meeting in ten minutes, but I like to take a moment every now and then to savor being president. And just like that heirloom grandfather clock, I want to keep standing tall and ticking off programs that will keep America great. Can I count on you?"

"Yes sir. I know what to do and won't stop until I deliver what you want."

"Good. If you do, I'll take care of you. But remember this. I don't want to know what you do or how you do it, and I don't want anyone or anything pointing at me if you screw up. Now be on your way. I'll bring you back as soon as I find that list of suspects. And that'll be soon because my memory is still pretty damn good, especially for remembering my enemies or those who disappoint me. Make sure you stay off those lists." Greg's silent nod was as good as a salute.

As if on cue, Dean returned to usher Greg out, noting to himself that Jared looked satisfied. That always made his job a little easier and the odds for staying on Jared's good side a little better. He knew that was the best place to be.

Chapter 8
July 2126

"Serendipity's Kiss"
(Thread 2 Chapter 4)

Electra had only mixed success combatting her T-Plague STD problem. The spray containing virus-killing chemicals worked 80 percent of the time when used in tandem with a condom, but computer simulation and in vitro testing concluded that the strain of vaginal virus she carried could erupt in anyone exposed, causing incapacitating side effects within two hours. The Electra-Alisha duo understood that only by curtailing their sexual activities could partner risk be reduced to zero. Alisha complained more than Electra, but she too agreed to do the right thing.

However, serious problems plagued other pieces of projects, which Electra summarized to herself as she studied notes.

Both labs are equipped for cloning, so Kameyo and I can work independently. She'll share her results, but I won't. And I can improve on the protocols I've pirated from China and Japan when I start cloning myself. But growing an egg in an artificial womb poses major challenges. I'll have to modify my Big Data Genetic Analysis apps to simulate a wider range of gestation parameters for confirming which combinations have a higher probability of success. And I have similar challenges when editing genes, but I can make faster progress by working alone because I control all steps.

Too bad I don't control all details for other activities. Case in point is politics. Accurately forecasting Alisha's voter approval rating will be a tough call, but she's practiced her pitch and Woolly has her schedule organized. All she needs to do is stay focused on campaigning.

As they boarded Hud's chopper early on the last Wednesday in July, Woolly announced what Alisha should do.

"Latest voter interviews confirm Texans like you, and all the PR we're doing is building your brand awareness, but your Democratic and Guardian Party opponents are going negative. Start talking more about why voters can trust you. And you gotta convince them you're serious about politics. Some of your constituents think you treat politics like a hobby. Hud, what can you add?"

"My contacts got you a place at the Midland Oilmen's Roundtable Dinner Meeting before we fly back Friday. Tell 'em all the great ideas you have. I can vouch for you, and—"Alisha interrupted.

"Don't ever mention anything about our business relationship. I don't want anyone connecting you to me. I've heard enough, please be quiet and let me practice my delivery during the flight."

Alisha's pitch improved during the tour. Hud drove them from one rally to the next, where most of the people practiced common courtesy when asking questions, but a doubting voter's gruff complaint raised late Friday afternoon voiced a common concern. "Yeah, so you can act and can play ball and can do biotech and computer stuff. But why do you think you can play politics? You don't know what us West Texans need, and you flit from one thing to the next. I bet you don't even know Midland's the ostrich capital of Texas." Alisha smiled, pausing for a sip of water to re-group.

"You're right, I didn't know until you told me. Just goes to show no one can ever know it all. And I don't flit from job to job. The skills and experience I gain carry over, and I'm always thinking about how I can make West Texas better economically. I'll explain more details this evening at the Oilmen's Roundtable."

There was nodding agreement among the oilmen that Alisha knew what she was talking about. Several had already thought about solar panel and environmentally enclosed crop farms but didn't know how to start. Alisha offered a way forward.

"I'll come up with contacts who are interested in having you construct already-proven businesses. And I believe that Mr. Haller knows how to coordinate building all supporting infrastructure. And I also know we Texans don't want government handouts, so I'll connect you to venture capital groups when I become your representative." Woolly concluded the discussion thirty minutes later. "Well, I think Alisha has shown you she has the right stuff to represent you. And she'll be back soon for another round of 'Meet the People.' Thanks for your support."

A welcome silence rode in the chopper on the return flight. Only Woolly's attempted humor lifted the collective fatigue.

"Anyone who likes heat and wide-open spaces should come to Midland. The blast of hot air nearly bowled me over when I opened the car door, And if it had, it would have rolled me over the horizon. When I scan the terrain, it's like I'm standing in the middle of a shallow dish. Everywhere I look is up at the sky." Alisha perked up. "Yes, but it's a dry heat, not like in Houston where August humidity feels like you're breathing liquid air. But I like Texas atmosphere better than DC's. And Texas, just like Main Street, is where Congress must stay in touch. I think I can do that, but I'll have to find better words to say it."

Alisha awoke at sunrise next day.

I think I'll run on Walnut Creek's bike path. It won't be crowded at 6 a.m. and it'll bring back memories of the day Robin found Sunshine. And that reminds me, she and I are having lunch today. I'll ask her to meet me at the pancake house and bring Tim and Kwame so I can drive them back to the lab for our monthly Saturday meeting. I'm sure a change of plans won't bother them.

Change of appearance, not change of plans, was bothering Robin. Now well into the third trimester, bloating and a sizeable baby bump had distended her shape, making her physically and emotionally uncomfortable, but she refused Electra's advice to see an obstetrician. Ever since contracting the T-Plague years ago, she had lost confidence in traditional medicine, preferring to treat herself or, as a last resort, relying on Electra. But she usually felt better as soon as her busy caregiving day began.

Today, however, was an exception. Electra read Robin's out-of-sorts expression as soon as Tim and Kwame escorted her to the table, Sunshine trotting behind her alpha female. Electra tried to inject some humor into her greeting.

"I like this audience even better than what I faced in Midland. Too bad you people can't vote in my district. And if Robin could, I'm sure she would recruit many of her caregiver clients. Do many of them comment on how good you look?"

"Most of the women, but the men are embarrassed to talk about female issues, I guess because they know I want to be a single parent." No one spoke until Electra filled the silence.

"They know you're strong, but older men don't understand us women of Modernity. But they might feel better if you told them you had an ob-gyn."

"Stop telling me what to do. Let's change the subject." Tim was happy to do so.

"After lunch, I want Electra to tell us all about encryption algorithms. Kwame and I use them to protect all our device control software."

Kwame and Tim peppered Electra with questions until the waitress served lunch. As they started eating, Electra directed the conversation back to Robin.

"I think Robin's baby bump is attractive. And she's self-medicating, using holistic remedies to handle some of those morning sickness symptoms. How's that working?"

"Didn't I tell you to change the subject? Try listening to me for a change instead of telling me what to do."

"I apologize. I hope you're in a better mood when visiting your clients this afternoon. Maybe you should hire an associate to help carry the load. It must be getting harder, now that you're into your third trimester."

"Sometimes I hate you! You're always telling people what to do. Why don't you tell us how you like my lunch?"

Robin plastered her plate of butter-and-syrup-soaked pancakes directly into Electra's chest, then rushed for the exit. Sunshine trotted happily behind, wagging her tail as if Robin were playing a game. The plate fell into Electra's lap before she could react. No one filled the awkward silence until she returned from the restroom.

"I hope neither of you have plans to get pregnant. Come on, please finish and I'll drive us to the lab."

"Kwame said, "We left our laptops in Robin's van. Will you get them when you see her later?"

"I'll do that, and by then I hope she's in a better mood."

Tim and Kwame forgot about Robin's outburst once Electra began explaining her RSA encryption write-up, which she summarized two hours later.

"So you see, RSA public-private key encryption uses some of the basic algebraic theorems found in number theory. Computer security uses them because even today, Quantum Computers are unable to find prime factors of large numbers fast enough. There's always hype that a new algorithm can do so, but none of them can do it fast enough to crack into computer systems if you generate big enough keys using the procedure I listed. So, you can rest assured that the software suites you're building won't be hacked as long as you keep using the encryption algorithms I give you. And that reminds me, I better retrieve your laptops. Carry on."

Electra called Robin's cell number after returning to her lab, but the call went to voicemail.

Maybe she spotted my caller ID and is still mad. I'll try later.

Robin's anger directed at Electra had faded but was now replaced by anger directed at a flat tire. She had taken a wrong turn while driving to Webberville's assisted living center and had dented a rim when banging into a pothole on a rutted road. She shoved her phone into a pocket because she always struggled reading instruction manuals over the Internet; then she yelled to Sunshine. "I know where the jack is. You and me can figure out what to do."

Roberto crowed to Juan as soon as he slowed his pickup truck.

"Ain't that a sight. How'd that lady get so lost? Hardly no one comes this way. Let's go help ourselves to what she's got."

Robin didn't stop jacking down the van until Sunshine started barking. As she turned to face a couple of tough-looking thirty-somethings, the pain in her abdomen turned as well. One of the fellows poked his head into the van while the other walked closer. "Whatcha doin here?" His partner spoke before Robin.

"Hey, I see some hi-priced laptops. I know where we can fence them." Rising awkwardly, Robin screamed into the face of the closer fellow.

"Get away from me or I'll zap you on my cell phone!"

Roberto clubbed her with his gun before she could push him away. She crumpled to the ground, her screams now tinged with pain.

Both fellows stared mutely at Robin, who had curled into a ball as she shrieked even louder, her face contorted. Suddenly, Roberto blurted when he spotted a wetness spreading on Robin's slacks. "Jesus, she's pregnant." And then Sunshine attacked, biting into his leg, tumbling him backward.

"Get the damn thing off me!"

Juan kicked brutally, sending Sunshine flying, but the little dog charged again. Juan fired twice; two bullets jerked Sunshine into a whimpering heap. Roberto struggled to his feet before yelling.

"Let's jack down the van and take it." Juan wasn't so sure. "What about her? We can't leave her like this."

"Sure we can. She can't I.D. us. To her kind, we all look alike. Let's do it."

Electra was ready to drive home at five but still hadn't been able to contact Robin.

This isn't like her. She would have answered by now or called me unless there's something wrong. Good thing I can track her cell phone.

Electra punched in the commands. Three minutes later she ran to her car as winds blew uncertainly.

She's in the middle of nowhere. I better reel her in before something bad happens.

Ninety minutes later, Electra was kneeling in a pouring rain next to Robin, who was now exhausted from hours of labor contractions. Panting disoriented words, she clutched Electra.

"I screwed up… my fault…not yours…" another wave of cramps racked Robin's groin, causing shrieks like those of a tortured animal. "Oh, god, the pain, do something." Electra ran to her car and returned with a large blanket she spread on the ground before pulling Robin on top. Then she removed Robin's slacks. The sight made her gag.

"I have to make a call from the car, hold on." Electra yelled instructions as soon as the dispatcher answered.

"Medical emergency. Breech miscarriage in progress. Significant blood loss. I don't know where we are. Track my cell phone location."

Thirty minutes later, two EMT's swerved to a stop. They were about to load Robin into the ambulance when she cried out to Electra, her eyes filling with panic.

"Take care of Sunshine. You can't leave her here. Promise me." Electra rushed to Robin's side, clutching both sides of her head. "Look at me, look at my eyes. I'll take care of Sunshine, and the EMTs will take care of you. I'll come as soon as I can." The closer EMT needed patient information before they could speed to a nearby clinic.

"What's her name? Will you follow us?"

"It's Robin Setdarova. Call Hudson Haller. Here's his number…" Electra stared into the growing gloom as the ambulance raced away and gusts blew rain in her face. She collected her thoughts, then carefully placed Sunshine on the blanket, her once-alert prancing manner now frozen in lifeless repose. The rain had matted the coat on the dog's stiffening frame, making the undersized body look even emptier. Electra was unaware of tears coursing down her rain-streaked cheeks as she mechanically bundled the little dog for its homeward journey, but as she placed the lifeless package in the trunk, the lightning brain shifted gears, causing a change in destination. She wrestled into different clothes, then raced away as lightning flickered and thunder rumbled and tumbled in the distance. Neither Roberto nor Juan spoke much after pulling into the parking lot of the scrap metal recycling plant where they worked second shift. Fully automated, it needed only two to operate, which suited them tonight. They didn't want to be bothered and were certain the rains would keep anyone away, so they were startled when an unrecognizable, black-hoodie-clad person entered the office a little before midnight. They had just restarted the conveyor system after adjusting settings and were now monitoring via computer screens the inclined portion of the belt dumping large pieces of metal into a combination grinder-furnace. Roberto glanced out the window, expecting to see a third vehicle but counted only pickup and van. He neither smiled nor frowned as he spoke matter-of-factly.

"If you need a ride, we can't help you."

"Say, that's a nice van you've got. Where'd you get it? I want to borrow it."

"No way. My buddy and I just bought it and we aren't gonna part with it so soon."

"Perhaps I can change your mind."

Electra had been fighting mightily to keep her Monster from the Id from breaking through, but she could feel it emerging. Without warning, she whipped out a Traser and zapped her victims. By the time they could move, she had handcuffed one foot of each to an immobile piece of scrap positioned at the base of the stationary belt after cuffing one hand of each together.

"I took a hack saw from your workbench, and a gun and some handcuffs you left in the pickup. Here's the hacksaw. And I'll put the keys just out of reach. You figure out what to do. But you better hurry, because you'll reach the mouth of the grinder very soon."

Electra's Monster activated the belt and watched gleefully as her victims approached the mouth of the hungry grinder. One of her victims had kayoed the other and was frantically sawing away, but time had nearly expired. Electra's rational persona abruptly regained control.

This is not a drill, soldier, you're better than your enemies. No need to kill. You've inflicted enough pain and you've got what you came for. Shut down the belt and go.

Electra followed orders, then drove Robin's van to her car so she could load Sunshine, thinking all the way.

I wouldn't be here if I hadn't planted tracking chips in the laptops. I'll call Hud tonight. If he yells at me for not being at Robin's side, I'll tell him I had places to go and things to do. And it's true, though I can only give him a redacted version. And I'll bury Sunshine at first light.

Hud answered on the third ring, speaking harshly in hushed tones. "Jesus, where are you? You let me down, and Robin too. Why didn't you tell the ambulance guys your name? She was hysterical. The doctor had to sedate her before she'd let me take her home." "I'll tell you tomorrow. Goodnight." Electra disconnected before Hud could complain further.

Electra awoke just before sunrise, feeling more rested than she thought she'd be. The sky had cleared, promising a better day than yesterday and giving enough light to find a shovel. She placed it next to Sunshine, then drove to a fitting burial spot: the place in Walnut Creek Park where Robin had found her precious companion two years ago.

She parked as close as she could, then walked on the tranquil trail as the rising sun sent sunbeams dancing through wind-rustling leaves. She dug deliberately after reaching a spot she thought Robin would like. Thirty minutes later, after completing the task Robin had made her promise, she surveyed her handiwork and surroundings.

Alisha shows emotions better than I, but this moment has brought mine to the surface, putting them in touch with the finality of death. How I take for granted those possessions I think are built to last until suddenly they are no more. And I know why. One of Mother's poems points to me. She named it No Shows, and I can recall it now:

> Do Emotions give embarrassed fright?
> Reluctant to show what's inside me.

The flaws I want no one to see,
I try to keep them out of sight.
But think what those emotions add,
Helping navigate the days.
Steering clear of barren ways,
Nudging me to good from bad.
So do not banish from the mind,
Let them sing a heartfelt tune.
Turning March to glorious June,
This better part of humankind.

I'll come back here only one more time. I'll bring Robin when she wants to be friends again. But now I should go. I have places to visit and people to call."

Electra went first to Austin's border collie rescue shelter, explaining to the custodian why Robin's tragedy should put her at the head of the line. She agreed, and serendipity kissed Electra; there were two tiny female puppies remaining from an abandoned litter. The custodian offered to waive the adoption fees, but Electra insisted she pay the normal $200 fee for each. Two hours later she had them wriggling in a blanket-lined box.

Electra then phoned Tim, who even on a Sunday was already at the lab. He agreed to meet at Hud's house and then drive to her car. In return, she would give him the errant laptops.

Electra decided not to call Hud because she knew he'd be home taking care of Robin. Though bleary-eyed, he perked up when he saw what she was delivering.

"Those pups look as soft and cuddly as two-minute eggs. If they can't jostle Robin up, I don't know what can. Why don't you come in and give them to her?"

"No, you should. I want to get my car. I'll leave Robin's van parked in front." Hud gave her a Texas-sized hug before she ran.

After retrieving her car and returning to her apartment, Electra used a late afternoon run to drain away the stress that had accumulated. By 8 p.m. she had showered and just finished eating a cheese omelette when her cell phone chimed. She knew who it was but pretended she didn't.

"Hello, this is Electra." She could hear the tears in Robin's voice. "It's me. Please don't be mad anymore. I didn't mean what I said yesterday. I don't hate you, I love you. Please say something." Electra's emotions burst through.

"Me too you too. I didn't follow the ambulance because the EMTs didn't need me, and I wanted to find your van."

"You did much more than that. You found two reasons for me to ditch my depression, and I already gave them names. Please stay with me at Hud's tonight so you can help me take care of the new Electra and Alisha." Robin heard a girlish giggle.

"How do you know they're females?" It was Robin's turn to laugh. "Oh, I know what to look for, and we'll train them to be two smart and well-behaved ladies. Please come over so we can start."
The old Alisha obeyed.

Chapter 9
October 2126

"Rolling Their way"
(Thread 2 Chapter 5)

The Electra-Alisha duo could remember few times when so much progress on so many projects was rolling their way, all resulting from so much team effort. Electra had invited Hud to join her and her Neuro-Device team in the lab for a Cyber-Theater demonstration that Tim would lead. Kwame stood alongside as Tim pointed proudly to the latest improvements.

"Kwame's installed his latest VR-GUI modification. When you strap yourself in and put on the helmet, the image is even sharper because of increased pixel density. And all the sensory channels embedded in the CD are now fully functional. Get set to be blown away... uh, virtually, that is."

Always adventurous, Hud buckled into the Cyber-Throne and gave Kwame a thumb's up after locking the helmet in place. Tim inserted a demo CD and activated the theater, then stood with Kwame and Electra as the Throne vibrated in three dimensions. Kwame rattled off details when Electra asked about the demo CD.

"This is my favorite. The studio retrofitted the Jurassic Park CD to run on our Theater, even adding an aroma track. It captures the chase scene where the T-Rex pushes the jeep over the edge." Hud gave it a five-star rating five minutes later.

"Well, if that don't beat riding a bull nothing will. Now I know what you mean about the helmet being a 360-degree screen. I see different angles of 3-D reality when I turn my head. And how do you get the aroma matched to the scenery?" Tim explained.

"The CD contains a digital fragrance track that controls a mix of orthogonal fragrances that duplicate whatever smell is programmed in. The public loves it, and so do sensual pleasures cafes. The studio's getting orders from some of the bigger cafe chains and fantasy clubs, so there's a commercial as well as private market, which means manufacturing economies of scale. And demand should grow even faster when we launch the interactive line extension because chip implants will make viewing even more immersive."

"I don't know what orthogonal fragrances are and I don't want to as long as our royalty checks are gonna grow. You fellows have done great work on the Cyber-Theater. And I'm sure your security software is just as good. The military folks Electra found seem real interested in what we can do. I told'em I'd call when we have a prototype suite ready. When will you be ready to demo it?" Electra answered for her team.

"Give us another week to complete our initial integration test. Tim will let you know."

Tim added, "And tell them we'll demo at one of their locations. Electra has told us never to bring people into our lab."

"I guess our computer guys don't consider us people. Come on, Hud, let's go visit Su and Kameyo. They know we're for real."

"Nope, I'll let you chat with them. You can tell me what they say when you're ready to explain what they're doing."

"I'll do that when I come back from DC. And I might bring back more good news for you when I do."

Leaving together, Hud walked Electra to her lab before heading to his office. Electra then powered up her workstation so she could start an online meeting that Su and Kameyo would join from their rebuilt lab. The first item on Electra's agenda would be cloning activity. Electra asked Kameyo for a summary.

"I am pleased to report we are fully operational. We have secured a supply of donor eggs and tissue samples, and have installed four Neuro-Life Vessels for in vitro donor egg gestation. I have cultivated ample cells from the tissue samples and have practiced removing and inserting DNA into donor eggs before shocking them with the electro-cell manipulator. And as requested, I sent you last week my priority list of multifactor combinations and nutrient timing that may determine cloning success probabilities."

"I read it. Please operate from what you've recommended. I'll run simulations on others. When will you begin placing donor eggs in your NLVs?"

"I shall start incubation tomorrow."

"Excellent. At our next meeting, please report what success you have maintaining post-ignition heartbeat and nutrient-hormone circulation. And now, it's Su's turn. Would you please summarize gene editing results?"

"You've assigned to me the task of finding several elusive genetic engineering Holy Grails. I'm not as quick as Kameyo, but I will send you before our next meeting you roll into combination of genes must be edited, and how, for the factors you have selected. And I assume the factors remain the following: intelligence, growth rate, and longevity."

"Yes, and only I will actually edit, using your Crispr-Cas9 modifications. Use the rest of your time to develop the next generation of T-Plague vaccines because that will be the foundation for our Alzheimer's vaccine."

"Very well, but we may soon need your help identifying more combinations if our list doesn't work. We'll know more when you finish editing. When should that be?"

"I should complete my simulations by the end of the year. Depending on Kameyo's findings, I hope to begin in-vivo editing no later than next-year March. Both of you should be pleased with your results-to-date. I know I am. I'll schedule our next call for mid-December. Do you have any questions before we end this one?" Kameyo signaled for Su to speak.

"Yes. We would like to discuss ethical ramifications of what we are attempting, which is a topic best handled in person."

"You are correct, so expect me to visit before next-year June." Everyone seemed satisfied, so Electra ended the call. Afterwards, Alisha complimented her alter ego.

"From what I've just observed, you are quite the leader. You've built two high-performance teams by constructing thorough plans and then bringing your people into the decision loop so they take ownership. And then you apply situational leadership principles. You manage each person individually. That's a lot of work, so why don't I call Robin after I do the packing? And I must say, I've done a fine job making our travel pleasant. Not only do we have clothes at the places we stay, but we have airport pickup guaranteed, thanks to Carter and Kathi."

"You've done all that and more because you are our 'Miss Personality,'using your people skills to keep our Hollywood and political careers blossoming. Just don't run yourself ragged juggling filming and campaigning. Keep the campaign slogan 'Run Girl Run' inbounds. It worked in the Co-NFL. No reason you can't make it work in Washington. Now go check on Robin."

Robin answered the call as soon as she recognized the caller ID. "Hello Electra. Or are you in the Alisha mindset?"

"Call me Alisha. I'm about to leave for DC and then Hollywood. How are you?"

"I've bounced back. I'm feeling good again, and thanks to some of your advice I've lightened the load by hiring an assistant. Her name is Hope, she's in her mid-40's, plays a guitar, and trained her German Shepherd to be a therapy dog. If she can help me grow the business, we'll be partners."

"I'm sure she will. And how are your puppies doing?"

"They're growing so fast. Border collies practically double their weight every ten days, so the next time you see them, Electra and Alisha will be even bigger girls. And smarter too. I'm following some of Hope's training manuals."

"I'm happy for you, but I won't say anything to our Washington friends. You can call them when you're ready. And I'll call you when I get back."

Alisha waved as soon as she spotted Carter. As he walked to greet her, a stream of thoughts tumbled into words he spoke only to himself.

Tonight's the last time I'll ever pick her up at the airport. She hasn't visited for six months, and since then we've talked only once. I guess we're going separate ways. I've made several career-enhancing moves so it's good I put distance between us. And I'll keep the details to myself. Ah, here she is. I'll always love the way she looks and thinks, but not like I used to. I've found other things to move me.
Alisha spoke first after kissing him on the cheek.

"Thanks once again for picking me up. And please call me Alisha. I'm here to have some fun. How are you?" Carter smiled but didn't say anything until he grabbed her bag off the carousel, giving Alisha time for private thoughts.

He looks the same but his body language tells me his feelings have changed. I better pay attention.

"I thought we'd have dinner on the way home, so let's stop for pizza. I'll feel more comfortable telling you my story there, but please tell me yours on the way. And you might want me to call you Electra."

Once in Carter's Vette, Electra chatted about political campaigning because that would be her primary activity on this trip. She would work from her NGA office as well as visit some Congressional staffers. She would also visit Angus at his campaign headquarters. By the time they were eating a second slice, Carter decided it was his turn to talk.

"I'm paying close attention to midterm elections because you're running for a Texas Congressional seat and Angus hopes to become a senator from Maryland. The polls show him ahead and you behind, but you're within the margin of error. Since there are only two weeks to go, I should think you'd want to be campaigning in Texas rather than visiting Washington."

"Actually, my campaign has featured online tours and rallies because I need to split time among research, acting, and campaigning. But enough about me; how are events moving in your life?"

"That's a very appropriate question to ask, because come January, I plan to move back to my condo. But I'll have your place spic and span before I leave."

"I never worry about how clean the place is. It's usually neater than a five-star luxury hotel room at check-in. But may I ask why you're moving out?"

"I've decided to redirect my career. I'm taking a leave of absence from my position at the Fed. I'm emphasizing public sector policies, thanks to all the staff assignments I have on economics-related Congressional committees, and I've been appointed to the President's Council of Economic Advisors. All this has come my way since President Gardner appointed me head of his Team of Rivals brain trust." Carter could see Electra preparing a queue of questions, so he answered before she asked.

"Look, I don't want you to dump a lot of questions on me. I'll just say we've misjudged Jared. He's a different person now, and he's giving me free rein to develop Guardian Party economic programs. I can't go into the details, but trust me, I know what I'm doing."

"Let me ask just one. Who's in the brain trust? Angus and I resigned because we're running for office, and Conklin dropped out for health-related issues."

"Jared gave me the authority to recruit an entire set of new members. I used his contacts and mine to select two. It's not important you know who they are, but one knows the law because she's a lawyer, and the other knows social issues because he works for a Beltway think tank. Jared likes most of our new programs, but I shouldn't divulge any details until he announces them."

Though still puzzled, Electra extricated herself from what was becoming uncomfortable.

"Let's talk about what's happening tomorrow. I'll be working out of my NGA office."

"Do you need me to drive you tomorrow?"

"No, but thanks for offering. I'll us my Mustang. And please let me make my own breakfast. Our schedules tomorrow may not mesh." Carter nodded, remaining silent.

"I'm tired, so I'm going to bed as soon as we get home. We can have the leftover pizza for a snack tomorrow night and continue our political discussion then."

Alisha left early the next morning, arriving at her NGA office after an abbreviated workout. First order of business was placing a call to Matt, who picked up promptly.

"So, you're in town. Are you staying long?"

"Only a couple of days, and I'm pressed for time, but I'd like to talk with you and Zoe before I leave. May I impose on you for a ride to the airport? I'll treat you to breakfast."

"That'll be fine. Please call when you have flight details confirmed."

"Will do. Bye till then."

After the call, she met with the staffer who had agreed to walk her later that morning through the underground tunnel system connecting all the Congressional office buildings. Then she called her Midland campaign headquarters to talk with the lead organizer; his frustration came through louder than all the background noise.

"I wish you were campaigning in Texas. The Guardian incumbent has been running a lot of negative ads, and Social Media is amping up some of the fake news. We're countering it, so make sure you view what's being said and what our rebuttal is before you roll into the virtual campaign rallies we've set up. They should help get your message out, but meeting voters in person is still a better option. Anyway, the polls show you're close enough, the race is a toss-up."

"Thanks for all you've done. I'm going to meet with some ofTexas House Rep staffers so I can navigate the halls of Congress before I'm sworn in. I'll call you later today."

Alisha's last call before hiking through the underground tunnels was to Woolly.

"I'd rather you be in Texas instead of heading to Hollywood. Texans prefer talking to candidates in person, not in Cyberspace, but you're poised and photogenic, and that helps. But your opponents are calling you a gadfly that flits from one thing to the next. Make sure you watch what they're spreading. You're a great wordsmith, so I'm sure you'll make a witty reply."

"I'll try. And I'll call you before I fly to Hollywood. Bye for now." Electra tried to buck up Alisha's spirits as she walked mid-afternoon back to the NGA office.

"Don't fret about being called names. Stay on the high road. And all our training will pay off. Not only are we fast on our feet, but we have the endurance to go the distance. And we'll use our combined smarts and diplomacy to make clever responses to some of the negative hype. Let's be sure to call Angus before we wrap up the day. He's expecting your call."

Angus picked up the 6:30 call after the second ring. His booming voice came through loud and clear in spite of background commotion.

"Glad you called before I go to a local rally. Are you still good to meet me at my campaign headquarters tomorrow?"

"Yes. What time works for you?"

"Be here at 8 a.m. We have lots to cover. Bye."

Alisha needed to decompress and assess the day, so she changed into a running outfit after returning home and then sailed away, noting that Carter was somewhere else.

I'm a better campaigner than Electra. She sometimes gets frustrated with all the sidebars and soundings that are necessary for politicking, but since I like the schmoozing, I'll take care of the lighter stuff while she does the heavyweight thinking. What a team we are as long as we act our parts. Ditto for Hollywood. And I'll remind her to put in a cameo appearance tomorrow afternoon at Professor Ravenhill's. That'll be a pleasant pause from politics.

Even at 8 a.m., Angus had his campaign staffers hustling. There was no wasted sound or motion. Even when sitting at his desk, he projected a leadership style that made people look up. Angus motioned for Alisha to shut the door before sitting across from him. His no-nonsense words got right to the point.

"I've been watching poll numbers. I'm leading, and if I were a betting man, I'd put my money where my mouth is. You're behind, but close enough so you can close the gap, but you have to make the next two weeks count."

"I will." Alisha waited for Angus to get to another point.

"Too bad we couldn't count on Carter. He decided not to work on my platform and has put some distance between us. He's had a change of attitude now that he's working for Jared, but I did manage to get a copy of what economic programs he'll recommend. Did he show them to you?"

"No, but I think his intentions have shifted." Angus reached into a folder for Carter's bullet point list.

"I won't make you a copy, but take a look while I give you my comments. It's a damn good list, containing some of the items he already told us about, but it includes a number of new ones that are pretty damn harsh, even though he can justify their economic benefits. I'll point out one that's particularly troubling. I'm sure you remember the retro sci-fi action movie series, The Hunger Games. Well, he's come up with 'The Hunter Games.' Death row prisoners are set free in a fenced-in forest preserve. The government awards hunting licenses to the highest-bidding hunter team and televises the hunt on a cable channel that subscribers can watch. He says it'll generate a lot of revenue and reduce the number of inmates."

"I imagine he has the stats to support his claim. And as he always says, his economics programs are positive, not normative. That's why he discounts the moral angle."

"But there's more to it than economics. Let me jot down some bullet points that pinpoint the President. I'll draw a 'Benjamin Franklin Close' argument. You know what that is: list the pros and the cons and whichever list is longer is the winner." Angus didn't talk again until he had penned the list.

Benjamin Franklin Close for Jared

Pro's
- Committed to America #1 Practices Pragmatic Realpolitiks Stopped America's Decline Reduced Budget Deficit Generates Jobs
- Connects with Main Street Shored up Military/Security Rebuilds Infrastructure
- Streamlined Government Bureaucracy Reduced Crime
- Con's
- Pushing Harsh Programs
- Acting on his own
- Overstepping Presidential Limits
- Damaging America Long-Term
- Alienating International Friends
- Ignoring T-Plague Victims
- Believing he's been "Chosen"
- Sidestepping Hi-Tech
- Disrespecting Grounded Intellectualism
- Polarizing the Public
- Did we act for the right reasons? (What tangible evidence?)
- Prostitutes in the Oval Office
- Sexual Abuse
- Hidden Agendas
- Fake News
- Trumped-up Terrorism Charges
- Racketeering

"I've got ten items in the plus column and ten in the minus. You want to add any?" Alisha answered a minute later.

"No. You've been very thorough." Where's all this leading?"

"Carter said we misjudged Gardner. I'm inferring that he thinks you acted too hastily when six years ago you masterminded using the T-Plague to take him out. All the reasons you rattled off way back when scared us into going along with your plan after it was already fait accompli. And it's lucky all of us destroyed any Cyberdata that could incriminate us." Alisha squinted as she spoke carefully.

"Your Ben Franklin reference is appropriate. I'm sure you know this quote, 'We must all hang together, or most assuredly we shall all hang separately.' You and Carter are the only ones still alive, other than Russell Conklin, who are smart enough to connect all the dots, and Russell no longer counts. Where do you plan on taking this?" Angus ripped the list into tiny pieces, then dumped them into a waste basket.

"I'll let the trash collectors dispose of it in the usual manner. Let's never talk about this again. And if both of us get elected, we can talk about corralling Carter if we don't like his ethics." Alisha took the hint when Angus glanced at the wall clock.

"Perhaps, but only time will tell. And the clock's telling me it's time to leave."

Electra took over as the duo drove to meet Professor Ravenhill. He waved her into his office, pointing to a chair on the other side of his desk.

"So Kittner, how do you like being an assistant professor?" "I like the title, but I feel the same as I did before."

"You're right, but it's important when playing the academic game so display your title proudly. Besides, you earned it. And that was a dandy rare earths summary you sent me. The extra info describing geology and current market conditions made me sound smart when I talked to colleagues, and I particularly like how you connected electromagnetic properties to military applications. And if I were a business person, I might look for a way to corner the market. Do you think that could happen?"

"That's one possibility, but I haven't considered it."

"Maybe you should have that business grad student you put on one of your teams look into it. She's uncovered a lot of applications for the patents her team is churning out."

"I'll think about it."

"Yes, yes, but you're probably way ahead of me. You know more than you let on, but that's OK. Just let me in when you come up with more surprises."

Alisha used the front porch waiting time to enjoy the burnishing glow from the early morning sunlight bouncing off autumn leaves. That and the unusually warm late October weather pushed campaign concerns into the background as she began posing questions for Matt and Zoe. She had them at the ready when Matt's van pulled up. Zoe twittered a greeting in her typically breathless manner.

"I love the coat. That's the latest fall Gucci design. It's too stylish for campaigning, but great for Hollywood." Alisha led the conversation from there through breakfast, keeping it light until she asked about Carter.

"Did Carter mention he plans to move back into his condo before the end of the year?" Matt shrugged before answering.

"Not in any detail. We don't see him as much as we did earlier in the year. I think he's preoccupied with work. And we haven't seen much of Russell either. He lost a lot of mobility after taking a bad fall last summer. Jennifer asked me to give him stretching therapy and it helped, but he's reluctant to go out much. I think he spends most of his time reading or on the Internet. And he's not as sharp as he used to be. Jennifer told me he lost a big chunk of money when an Internet scammer contacted him. I didn't pry, but I could tell she's getting frustrated that he's slowing down faster than she expected. But that usually happens to everyone as they age, and I see it in many of my patients, but not as fast as what's happening to Russell." Zoe poked Matt.

"We better speed up or Alisha will miss her flight. And we don't have to worry about her slowing down. But I do hope she lets the voters catch up to her at the polls, because we'll see her more often if she wins."

Alisha used her cell phone to pay for breakfast in spite of Matt's protest.

"Next time you visit, I'll pick up the tab for dinner and you can pick the restaurant. And now, let's roll out of here and get our favorite Texas politician airborne. I'm sorry we can't vote for you, but I'll post some good Social Media comments for you. Do you want me to say something bad about your opponents?"

"No. My campaign is staying positive. I want people to vote for me if they like what's good about me, not what's bad about my opponent. And that's how I intend to stay, no matter what rolls my way."

Chapter 10
November 2126

"Hollywood Shockers"
(Thread 2 Chapter 6)

I'm on the edge but I've driven like this before. Brake now and I won't lose control.

Only Alisha heard what she was replaying in her head. Her SUV spun madly, barely staying on the coastal road; as expected, the chase car was not as lucky. It smashed into the wall, bursting into a fireball that hurled shards of metal that blasted open the SUV's read door. Centrifugal force took control as the vehicle spun into a tight curve ahead.

Her partner screamed, "We're going over!" just before the SUV flipped down an embankment, sliding to rest upside down and dangling over the edge, the pungent smell of gasoline filling the vehicle.

"Get out get out!" she yelled, but her partner couldn't. Blood gushed from the gash on his head.

I can do this. I've done it before and it's easier the second time. Alisha struggled to free herself, only to find the door wouldn't budge. She dragged herself through the van to the rear where she stared at a forty-foot drop to the ocean below. With every ounce of remaining strength, she swung herself out and up to safety, then scrambled to drag her partner from the SUV just before it exploded. Her partner was safe, but she was not quick enough to save herself. A large chunk of metal slammed into her, knocking her over the ledge. She plunged to earth head first, then tumbled forward, faster and faster, toward an ominous, infinite ocean. An image more vivid than the desperate reality now whirling about flashed inside her brain. It was that of the Chameleon transforming into the Phoenix, triumphantly soaring skyward.

Tyger shouted, "That's a wrap, it's in the can. That final scene's gonna be an audience shocker. Let the weekend begin."

The film crew and bystanders cheered; even the stand-in stunt driver standing next to Kathi applauded.

"That Alisha Kittner sure can handle a vehicle."

Kathi said, "Please bring Alisha with you and Vince when we have dinner at the studio cafeteria. See you at six."

Alisha couldn't be happier. The crew assistants took her to the off-set base camp where they helped her change into sweats and a robe for the ride back to the studio. Four hours later, Electra applauded her alter ego while still in the dressing room.

"You drive like a guy, which is the best compliment I can think of." Alisha nodded, but downplayed today's victory.

"Yes, but we lived through today's stunt when we were chased after our Fukushima lab blew up. How nice that the lightning brain remembers everything."

Kathi and her two directors were already at the table when Alisha cruised in. Vince and Tyger hugged her while Kathi filled the champagne glasses.

"Let's toast Chameleon and Supergirl, then talk about what's to come." The directors did most of the talking through dinner and dessert.

"All those Supergirl stunts helped train you for doing the more exotic ones audiences look for in Mission Impossible movies. I'm sure Kathi can add to that comment."

"Each series helps the other. We make great action scenes as well as insert character and plot complexity that take viewers beyond typical action adventures. But what if the election takes Alisha to Congress? We have three months to decide because we don't start filming until late January. And no matter the vote, let's toast our future success…"

Alisha awoke pressure-free early Saturday because she had no more lines to say for filming or campaigning. From now until Tuesday, though her opponents might be stumping for last-minute votes, Alisha would follow her own plan: rely on pre-recorded messages that would be blasted online from Saturday through Monday. So today she would visit again with Carley Kota and her mother. And afterwards, she would meet a person Carley's father had found who would chat about Indira. They would have dinner at Hollywood's Brown Derby Restaurant, a location most fitting for

Alisha's attire, a scalloped red dinner dress that displayed just the right amount of thigh and cleavage.

Alisha's regular limo driver knew all about the place.

"The Brown Derby anchors one end of a Hollywood Boulevard stretch that preserves all the glamour of Hollywood's golden age. It's famous for lunches between the famous and the powerful, and it's particularly special because it's on Disney studio grounds. My parents took me there when I was a kid, and I never forgot the derby-shaped sign. Well, here we are. And I must say, your dress would catch anyone's eye. Please call the usual number thirty minutes before if you want a ride back to the hotel."

Alisha ambled towards the maître de, absorbing as much of the ambiance as possible. The high ceilings, mahogany paneling, and patterned carpeting showcased art deco booths lighted by Tiffany-type lamps that gave a warm glow to the gallery of signed photographs. When he asked for the reservation name, she asked for the Brandon Marshall booth.

"Oh, yes. Mr. Marshall is waiting. Please follow me."

As she approached the booth, an impeccably groomed aristocratic aristocratic-looking, silver-haired gentleman rose to greet her, smiling cautiously. "I'm Brandon Marshall. Please join me." Brandon's manners and small talk matched his appearance.

"Since I know nothing about you, other than you are Indira Ramanujan's daughter, I thought you might like meeting here. I came here often for business and still meet some of my associates. And the food is as good as ever. Long ago, a previous owner created the Cobb Salad, so you might enjoy that and Brown Derby's signature dessert, Grapefruit Cake."

Brandon paused while the waiter took orders. Afterwards, Alisha explained why she wanted to meet.

"Mother died during childbirth, so I never got to know the real Indy. Relatives have told me about her early years, and Indy's friends have told me about her life during and after grad school, but what she was like and what she did during her undergrad years at Harvard are unknown. Winona is no help, so anything you remember would help me fill in the gap. My grandparents told me she was a practically perfect child, and her friends said she was peerless, a genuinely nice person who had it all, brains, looks, and personality, of practically mythic proportions, no faults."

Brandon took another sip of his martini before replying.

"How much truth can you handle? You look mature enough to deal with it, but sometimes we prefer to keep the image of our parents pristine. And that's for you to decide."

"I'm a big girl now. The more I know about Indy, the more I understand why I'm the way I am."

"Yes, I see that. Indy came into my life when she was twenty. You're older and wear designer clothes, but if we made those adjustments, you'd look almost the same. I'm twenty-five years older than your mother, and I last saw her forty years ago, but I remember nearly everything she revealed to me. So, let me tell the tale and you can ask questions when I'm done." Alisha nodded.

"I met Indira the first year she and Winona came to Hollywood for studio intern positions. They didn't work at my studio, but I noticed her at a party. I had recently divorced and wanted something different, and Indira gave me even more than I was looking for. It took a long time to realize that she seduced me. She liked to party and was great in bed. And she was a great actress. I thought she was a genuinely nice person, but I saw different facets every now and then. She could be cruel and ruthless. And I saw a completely different persona two months later. She was back at Harvard, ready to graduate after the fall term, when she told me I had made her pregnant. She insisted I fly her to Hollywood where she would stay until giving birth. Then she'd live with Winona, leaving the infant in my possession, and working as a summer intern until going to grad school in the fall. And I was to tell no one, not even Winona, about her pregnancy. If I didn't agree to all this, she claimed that DNA testing and the videos she had would prove I'm the father. So, you could say she blackmailed me into doing the right thing."

By now, Alisha's appetite had disappeared; she stopped picking at the salad as Brandon continued.

"The last time I saw your mother was early April 2087 when she left the hospital by herself and me with an infant daughter. And she never visited or wrote until ten years later when she sent me a letter, a poem, and a pair of earrings like the ones you're wearing. She asked me to give all the items to my daughter, whose name – Cassandra – she had chosen. I wrote back once, but never got a reply so that ended our correspondence."

"Did Cassandra like what was sent?"

"She liked the lightning bolt earrings, but I didn't give her the letter or poems because she was only ten. And later, I decided never to give them because she had a troubled adolescence. I apologize if my story shocks you, but you asked for the truth."

"I didn't expect it, but I'm glad you told me. And may I ask, why did you agree to meet me?"

"A bit of a selfish motive. You're my daughter's half-sister, and I wanted to compare you to her." Brandon paused to give Alisha an envelope.

"I'm giving you the letter and poem. I never shared it with anyone, not even with my second wife, whom I married when Cassandra turned three. She was a devoted stepmother even though Cassandra's addiction issues and subsequent therapy strained all relationships. Cass did pull through, but she and Bess never fully reconciled, even by the time Bess died five years ago. By the way, when were you born?"

"February 11, 2097."

"Then you're ten years younger than Cass. Her birth date is April 15, 2087. And that explains why Indira never replied. Her letter came a couple of days before you were born, and I replied a week later, but by then Indira was dead. May I ask how she died?" Alisha told the truth, but not the whole truth.

"As I said, she died in childbirth. Many women die of natural causes when giving life to their child."

Brandon and Alisha groped for something else to say. Alisha finally spoke.

"Well, I hope our conversation has been as eye-opening for you as for me. And thanks to you, I get to taste the Grapefruit Cake. I'll take it with me because it's time to call for my limo."

"Please let me drive you. Meeting you has helped me too." Alisha accepted the offer, but neither spoke until she was about to exit. "After you read the letter, you might wish to call me. Use the number on the business card I put in the envelope. But I leave that up to you."

Alisha lacked the emotional energy to open the envelope that evening. Nor did she open it after her early Sunday run, or before she left for the airport. Not until midway to Austin did she read what Indira had written thirty years ago. First the letter:

Dear Brandon,

Ten years have elapsed since I last saw my first child and you, so I imagine this letter comes like a bolt from the blue. Or it may never come to you; the address is ten years old. But no matter, because writing this letter allows me to express my feelings.

I have matured, as all people do after leaving home. I've earned multiple degrees and started a career. And I have developed more empathy and no longer use people. But please remember: I have always been honest with others and myself. I have never pretended to be more than I am. I never claimed I was perfect, as you so rudely pointed out when we parted. Perhaps I deserved some of your anger. Maybe I did use you, but I didn't hurt you. Both of us enjoyed what we had.

Yes, I did leave you with my first child because I was ill-prepared to raise her while acquiring what I needed to become a "woman of modernity." Even though I did not develop a "mother's love" at any time during my pregnancy or after delivery, I did not abandon Cassandra. We agreed that you had the resources and emotional maturity to care for her. Perhaps I did threaten, but the threat convinced you to do what is right. You were willing to assume responsibility for what you helped create.

I am writing to you because I will give birth next week to my second child, a daughter I will name Alisha. And this time, I have a mother's love, no matter what she is or becomes.

I would like to know how Cassandra is. She may provide a glimpse into what Alisha's three personas may become. Perhaps you and I could have them meet at a time and place to be determined. They might be able to help one another.

Did you marry again? If so, did Cassandra bond with your second wife? I have no desire to come between you or a stepmother and Cassandra (she's your daughter too.) In fact, it might be better for just the girls to meet. I can enter the mix later if that would help them.

Did you tell her about me? No matter; I am enclosing a poem I wrote that describes some of my feelings that made me do what I did. I am also enclosing another pair of my favorite earrings, identical to the ones my mother gave to me when I left India for America.

Mother found another pair for me to give Alisha when she's old enough to appreciate them. But I would rather give them to Cassandra. She is old enough today to wear pierced earrings. And their design obviously connects with the poem.

Please correspond if you wish… Indira Ramanujan
And then the poem:

Lose the Sadness
Sometimes I feel so sad for us,
Great expectations lead up to a fall.
Our history casts a similar pall,
Ashes to ashes dust to dust.
But then I simply must recall,
Think of life as comedy.
Humor-filled not elegy,
We bounce no matter how we fall.
So lose the sadness make it gone,
Life like lightning bolt is flow.
And like it we come and go,
The Phoenix rises from ashes anon.

Alisha invited Electra to comment. She carefully read again, considering yesterday's revelations as well as today's, before making a terse reply.

"Jesus, Brandon's story and Mother's letter shock me too. Let's discuss this after we've calmed down. You need a diversion, so why don't you do something else?"

Alisha took the advice and called her lead organizer as soon as she could. His words shocked her too.

"We've got a big problem. The Guardian Party candidate gave a live interview last night, connecting you and that tattoo on your chest to a devil-worshipping cult, claiming that's what you were doing in Hollywood instead of connecting with voters. You better get back here and help me set the voters straight."

"I'll be at headquarters first thing tomorrow morning. Please handle issues as best you can until then." Alisha ended the call, not knowing what to do. Electra butted in.

"We've had three shocks, but politics is not like baseball, where three strikes and you're out. Why don't you rest and regroup, and let me decide how to strike back. I'm good at that."

Chapter 11
December 2126

"Winners and Losers"
(Thread 3 Chapter 2)

"You can't win 'em all. Besides, a little failure now and then keeps us humble." Alisha grimaced as Woolly continued his homily on politics. "And consider what you've learned. Winning an election isn't rocket science; the formula is to show up and talk to the people you'll represent, always remembering they're your boss. You need a little more political seasoning, which you'll get as our NGA liaison. By the way, the Governor thought your concession speech was most gracious, and he particularly liked how you turned that devil worship fake news to your advantage. I never realized that an inverted cross is a symbol for Saint Peter. So, don't be discouraged. In the long-run you can be a winner if you run again. Just don't drop out of public sight. You have to meet your constituency in person, not in Cyberspace."

"You're right. Even though we live in a high-tech world, people still like high-touch. I should have remembered better what John Naisbitt wrote about in Megatrends. And according to the exit polls, too many voters thought I spread myself too thin. One comment said it pretty well: I should play ball in one game at a time."

"Will you play next season for the Midland RockHounds? You became much more than a public relations gimmick."

"I don't know, but I do know I'll be ready for January's NGA session. Please thank the Governor for reappointing me. And I have a full slate of R&D projects to manage, so I have plenty to do between now and the end of the year. I better get after it. And thanks again for all you've done."

Electra asked herself a pertinent question while driving to the lab. How disappointed am I? Even when Alisha's in charge, acting like a politician can be a drag. And neither of us might like all the responsibilities that come with holding office. Even for dedicated politicians, the demands can be draining. Perhaps that's the lesson I learned best.

That afternoon, Electra found articles and online videos covering linguistics, a subject that might help when developing A.I. apps. Ricky Fonseca had touched on last April, but only now did she have the time to investigate. When she finally stopped for a dinner snack, she had written enough in her white paper to conclude she needed to develop additional software that Tim and Kwame would integrate into GUIs. The apps she would give them would be just the simpler ones. Only she would use those that accessed deeper A.I. levels. She reviewed her work one more time, summarizing it before shutting down her workstation.

Linguistics is the linchpin for reaching A.I.'s Holy Grail – computer cognition –, which is the First Order Singularity. A.I. apps must communicate in written or spoken language much better than the current crop of apps mere mortals have developed. And only mathematically grounded Linguistics can be the foundation. I need to build two machine-learning apps, one for syntax and another for semantics so I can handle two-way speaking or writing recognition and translation. The syntactical piece is easier because Extended Syntax X-Bar Theory has enough precision for me to extend it using Modal Logic Programming. The semantics piece is much harder because its X-Bar Theory contains embedded sub-theories lacking the precision needed to handle indirection or infinite regress.

But I can code both because I've already outlined an Input Process Output Model that will feed on Big Data. And after I do that, I'll decide how best to train these new modules via neural network learning loops. And I'll embed routines guaranteed to keep me in control if they get out of line.

I could work until midnight but I better stop now before my obsessive-compulsive tendencies start controlling me. And if don't stop, Alisha will remind me, but she knows not to say slow down and smell the roses because roses have no fragrance. People mistake the smell of chlorophyll and soil for rose fragrance. However, the sentiment is correct. I'm learning to slow down and appreciate the beauty that's all around. And when I do that, Alisha can come out to play.

Maksim Popovitch, best of the best among all elite Spetsnaz-like troopers churned out by the Russian Defense Ministry, never slowed down, nor did he ever lose. His codename – Max the Popper – had been earned in countless firefights where his unerring accuracy using any weapon in Russia's clandestine arsenal always eliminated opponents. Teams he commanded would follow him into battle anywhere because he led from the front and covered their backs. And last summer, he won an assignment he would have killed to get: first build a team and its base of operations, then mold his troops into an elite, rogue covert strike force codenamed S-Cube, reporting only once a year to an anonymous contact codenamed T-Cube that he had met only once.

Maksim neither knew nor cared how he had won the assignment because he considered that a dead subject. He and his team had labored for six months to repurpose their base camp. But only Maksim knew precisely its location or ultimate mission.

T-Cube had given him all necessary contacts: one contact for obtaining transport vehicles and communications gear, another for recruiting personnel, and a third for supplying beyond state-of-the-art- military hardware. T-Cube communications would come via an encrypted communications channel embedded in the cell phone T-Cube had given him. And the most important piece of information: a target list. Maksim could strike whichever and whenever he chose. And he didn't care who his targets were, because his Swiss bank account now contained $10 million.

Locked and loaded and training each day, Maksim transformed his team into super soldiers who were eager to follow him into battles that only he planned, confident that next year would hold many victories.

Greg Unger's victory plans weren't as extensive; he had but one target who he had analyzed meticulously, relentlessly tightening a circle of diminishing radius. The midterm election campaigns he had followed helped to narrow his focus even more, and though the timing of when to strike was still to be determined, he too believed that he would grasp the brass ring next year. That's what he would tell Jared Gardner when next summoned.

Before declaring a Holiday break for all her teams, Electra had one more meeting for Tim and Kwame to present a year-end report summarizing recent accomplishments and goals for next year. Tim talked first.

"That last Brain Probe teaching session you gave me helped clarify how I'll make our Cyber-Theater more interactive by putting additional computer chips in the Cyber-Throne. Those will be the same chips for interfacing with chips embedded in people, but you'll need to show me how that works. Will you do that next year?"

I haven't finalized next year's task list, so please keep working as you are." Tim looked at Kwame before changing subjects.

"Kwame and I have a favor to ask. Could we postpone the rest of the meeting so you can help us?"

"What do you have in mind?"

"We want to play a game that starts on the Internet at noon. We're one of the first 100 teams that responded to the NGA flash announcement. Teams consist of three or fewer and—" Electra interrupted before Tim could blast out more words.

"Do you mean the National Governors Association?"

"No. Sorry. It's from the National Go Association. Kwame and I are members. Here are the rules for today's game: each team connects to a two-way audiovisual session, teams can see the identity of the host but not the judging panels, judging panels can see teams to make sure they don't cheat. The host will ask four questions, and judging panels will listen for a maximum of five minutes to each answer, so teams must already know the answer or solve it immediately. Scoring is instant, each question being worth 15 points.

here is only one winner, and that team gets automatic and fully paid entry to the NGA Team Go Speed Tournament that's held annually during the Las Vega A.I. Expo. And the winner has five years to claim the prize. You gotta be our third member."

"I've never played Go. Isn't it the Holy Grail of A.I. software developers because it has even more scenarios than chess? I won't be of much help." Electra's response stopped Tim but not Kwame. "NGA flash games always ask surprising questions, often unrelated to Go, so play with us."

"OK, you win. Consider it a Christmas present for preparing your year-end report."

The trio huddled on one side of the conference room table facing a wall monitor when Kwame logged on at 11:55, and at noon, the host appeared.

"Hello, you brave Go Gamers. One hundred teams are logged on and ready to go. I won't repeat the rules, so let's get started. Question number one, Why is the Union of an Empty Collection of Empty Sets the Null Set, whereas the Intersection of an Empty Collection of Empty Sets is the Universal Set? You have five minutes to answer."

Tim and Kwame stared at one another, then looked expectantly at Electra, who announced, "This is the kind of question only computer geeks will like because answers might show how smart they are when considering questions few people care about. Come on guys, chop-chop. I'll help when I'm needed." Three minutes later, Electra rattled off an answer.

"An explanation for why the Union of an Empty Collection of Empty Sets is the Null Set, whereas the Intersection of an Empty Collection of Empty Sets is the Universal Set, takes us to the edge of a slippery slope whose first step slides into Russell's Paradox. The explanation hinges on linguistics, not numbers, and has two parts.

"First, the Union is formed by finding elements contained in sets and then putting them together. Since we can find no elements in any empty set, the Union of an Empty Collection of Empty Sets is vacuously true.

"The second part, dealing with Intersection, takes more finessing. Here's the logic for it. For an element not to be in the Intersection, you must find a set that does not contain the element. But because our collection of sets is empty, we can find no set that doesn't contain any chosen element. Thus, the Intersection of an Empty Collection of Empty Sets must contain all elements, which by definition is be the Universal Set.

So, QED. Pretty tasty apples for math types."

There was a minute of silence before the host spoke again. "Question number two: How can you trisect an angle using only a straightedge and compass? You have five minutes to answer."

Tim and Kwame's reaction mirrored question one's; so did Electra's words.

"This is a trickier question that is also of interest only to a subset of IYIers. here's an answer.

"Euclid, the great Greek philosopher and mathematician, founded the study of plane geometry. He was a master of angles and triangles, proving many congruence theorems and establishing constructions using straightedge and compass.

"Among the most famous is the impossibility of trisecting an angle using only those tools. He showed how to bisect an angle and claimed that angle trisection is impossible but never proved it. The Greeks didn't have a 'limit concept.' If they did, a clever Greek mathematician might have used the following argument for trisecting an angle.

1. Take an angle and bisect it. Keep bisecting the bisection for as many times as you like.
2. For example, we can split an angle into 2, 4, 8, 16, 32, 64,
3. 128, 256, 512, 1024, etc. equal pieces.
4. I'll stop at 1024 to illustrate.
5. Divide 1024 by 3 and discard the remainder. We get 341, remainder 1.
6. Put together 341 of the original angle's pieces. The sum is a lower limit of its trisection.
7. Add one more piece, the remainder, to the sum. That's an upper limit.
8. Stop here, or repeat until you cannot distinguish lower from upper. The result is a trisection, accurate to as fine a measure as you like.

By the way, there is a formal proof that angle trisection is impossible for all except a small set of special angles, but that's not the answer judges should be looking for. Peter Wanzel proved it in 1837, and when stated in a modern mathematical context, it relies on extension fields, a topic included in Galois Theory. Don't try reading it unless you seek a cure for insomnia."

Only Tim broke the silence. "Jesus, it sounds like you're reading from a textbook embedded in your brain."

The host spoke again.

"We're changing the rules for the next two questions. Here's Question three:

Why is each question worth 15 points?

You have two minutes to answer." Electra spoke immediately. "Wow, each question is more and more feckless. There are numerous answers to this one, all unimportant. I'm leaving our answer up to you, but make it quick." As time ticked away,

Tim blurted his best guess.

"Because a perfect score for the contest equals 60, which is the smallest whole number less than 100 containing the most prime factors 2 and 3 and 5."

Five seconds later, the host came back. "Question four:

What percent of the judging panelists are computers?

You have two minutes." Electra liked this one.

"Finally, a question people might be interested in." Tim yelled an answer before Electra could say anything else.

"I know this. It's gotta be a trick question. The answer is 100 percent. And I can use contest rules, Turing's A.I. test, and current state of computer intelligence to support it. Here's how. Turing's test says you can't tell the difference between a human and a smart A.I. computer, so that's 50 percent. And experts say the best A.I. computers today are only a quarter of the way to matching human intelligence. So the product is 12.5 percent. But the contest is scored instantly, and only computers can process 100 scores that fast. So, our answer is 100 percent."

Two minutes later, the host returned for the final time.

"Thanks to all teams for playing. The winning team is team number 97. Check your logon screen for your assigned number. All teams will be emailed their graded answers. The winning team will also be emailed the prize voucher. This is your host signing off and wishing you Happy Holidays. Please go play, and of course, play Go."

Tim shouted, "We're number 97. We won." Kwame shared the results after printing out their email and electronically storing the prize.

"Look at this. Judges took off one point for each question. And listen to the comment: No one is perfect, so we had to subtract one point from each answer. But you are impressive. You possess brains that think as fast as computer chips."

While Tim and Kwame started babbling about Go tournament plans, Electra commented to herself.

The semantic processing apps running on those judging computers are primitive because they failed to recognize the whimsical humor in my answers. Nor did they figure out what IYI refers to: people who are intellectual yet idiotic. If they had, their comment would have been more like a person's reply. My semantic app will do much better.

Following their Holiday Break tradition, the Electra-Alisha duo divided next year's tasks into a list for each, and they would further subdivide each task into events containing assigned completion dates. As expected, Alisha postponed her work until January while Electra took few breaks until completing hers by late afternoon on Christmas Eve. Reviewing her work one more time before putting Alisha in charge for the Holiday, she cautiously commended her effort.

I can start cloning my cells within a month because I've adjusted my cloning protocol parameters per Su's findings. That's when I'll discover if I can use the Electro-Cell Manipulator to correct any heartbeat ignition issues or must instead tighten the focal aperture on my Brain Probe. And I'm ahead of schedule on gene editing, so I'll know by April what DNA segments to edit. But I must carefully control what I'm doing or I run the risk of unintended actual or ethical consequences. And the same applies to my A.I. apps. That's why Tim and Kwame get only my dummied-down releases. And ethical issues also surface in politics, so perhaps I'll need to use Angus here. Correction, I mean let him help me as I help him.

I've reached my point of diminishing returns, so I'll break away and have Alisha break in.

Alisha much preferred Austin's Christmas weather to DC's. She didn't need gloves or face mask when running; she could let her thoughts ramble rather than focus on slippery snow-covered sidewalks.

Running today is deja vu. Weather and route are identical to last year's Christmas morning run, but I appreciate today even more. How splendid the sunrise now splashing off shrubs and trees. How nice it is just to be alive. No worries until next year gets here. But when it does, Electra and I will have issues to resolve.

Alisha scaled back this year's post-Christmas partying, picking just one. Hud took her and Robin to a party hosted by Sam. Alisha left soon after toasting in 2127, telling Robin she had promised herself to write up plans for the year. By 2 a.m. she was asleep.

"Alisha… Alisha. Please awaken and pay attention to me. In the coming year, you'll have much to do that will be new. And to help you, I have two questions for you to answer."

Bolting upright, she saw the softly glowing apparition of Indira standing beside the bed.

"Mother, the lightning brain has conjured another visit. You must know what's troubling us."

"I do, and I shall help you talk them through. And here is the first, how did visiting Brandon and reading my very last letter alter what you think of me?"

"They make me love you even more. Your flaws were minor and as you matured you tried to correct them. And you never pretended to be anything other than yourself, always open and honest and caring for others. You did what you thought best for Cassandra. Don't you agree?"

"Perhaps, but what matters more is what agrees with you, so accept your feelings and move on to my next question. How have last year's adventures altered your understanding of relationships?" "They have shown me that the combination of human language and the complexity of relationships is the hallmark of humanity. And I now know even better that I must constantly work to keep relationships healthy, and not to place unrealistic expectations on partners, or turn them into myths, like most people do to their parents. And my T-Plague STD issue has forced me to adjust how I balance sex versus love. I'm still adjusting, trying to balance commitment against constraints."

"Yes, love is the most enigmatic and of all human emotions. And even though cognitive psychology dismisses the Romantic Love notion, mere mortals – no matter their age – shall always be swayed by their passions. But heed my warning that a life lived without commitment, though it may give unconstrained freedom, may ultimately not be worth living.

"But be pleased that you and your alter ego achieved many new insights last year because of all your adventures. Now rest until dawn so you can plan what next year may hold. And always remember, life is supposed to be your thoughts-in-action. Don't agonize or over-analyze. Think enough then do your best. Make a decision and act on it instead of endlessly debating or questioning yourself.

"It is time for me to follow my own advice. I have questioned you enough, so I shall leave you now. But always remember: I'm always with you."

Indira vanished before Alisha could say another word, but there was no need for even one more, so she let her thoughts take her into a dreamless sleep. She awoke at dawn, ready to seize the day, seize the year. No matter what challenges lie ahead, she and her alter ego would persevere.

Chapter 12
March 2126

"Hearts of Darkness"
(Thread 3 Chapter 3)

Electra hoped the mid-March video conference she was about to conclude hadn't left Su and Kameyo in the dark.

"So, I've successfully cloned and grown cells in an NLV, reaching the edge of the fetal state, but I'm unable to maintain heart ignition and normal growth rate. That's why I've given Kameyo a list of combination parameters I want her to use when incubating fertilized eggs. I'll work from a different list. Let's compare results in three months."

"You might need to visit us if Kameyo needs you to shed more light on what we're trying to do. Kameyo, what would you like to add?" "Your explanation today cleared up some of my concerns. I hope you will do that again on our next call if I don't get the results you want."

"I'm confident you will. And depending on progress, I plan to visit no later than the end of the year. So, let's carry on and see what you need."

Though she was satisfied when she ended the call, Electra wouldn't be if she were to compare her progress with that of Darla Tinibu. In less than a year, Darla had pirated enough of what she needed to upgrade drone mining extractors built by Pan-Africa's A.I. Robotics unit so they exceeded the competition's. She had every intention of equipping the African Big-6 Diggers Cooperative so their mining efficiencies could reduce selected competitors' sales while someone else used different equipment to reduce the output from competitors' mines. Today, she would meet in person with Kwanza, manager of Zaire's first rare earths mine using Pan-Africa's extractors, explaining as she toured the facility what she had in mind, while Kwanza explained some history of his country and this mine. Kwanza talked first as he began his one-guest tour from the comfort of a headquarters office in the country's capital, Kinshasa.

"It is fitting that I am manager of my country's first mine to use your extractors because my Swahili Bantu tribal name means first. And my country's name changed from Congo to Zaire in 1971, eleven years after gaining independence, because the name Congo has many ominous associations, such as with the dark novel, Heart of Darkness, penned by Joseph Conrad in 1899, and the Congo river, second longest in Africa and seventh in the world, populated by man-eating crocodiles.

"My country is quite beautiful, displaying lush rainforests as well as savannahs that are home to great herds of mammals, large and small. The Equator cuts through the country's heart; our climate's heat and humidity support thriving vegetation. Sometimes, I am saddened by the scars left by strip mining, but modern mining techniques have become environmentally friendly, eliminating predatory mining practices and creating jobs for nearly a quarter of our workforce." Darla, interested only in present and future plans, had heard enough about the past.

"And after our extractors finish scooping, our milling machines finish grinding, our furnaces finish smelting, and our conveyors finish delivering, our automated dozers will scrape away the debris. That's why the entire four-stage process, when fully networked with my A.I. software, is so effective. Worker safety and environmental damage are minimized. Output is maximized."

"Yes, I understand that, but I fear your bigger and smarter machines will scrape away the jobs my people need. Most are now well educated, but our economy is still dependent on agriculture, mining, and forestry. Smart machines and computers are removing more jobs than they are putting back." Darla's answer came from the hi-tech industry playbook.

"New technologies are always disruptive in the short run, but always lead to long-term improvements. It's economic survival of the fittest. Take me now to the mining location. I want to see the control room and extractors in action."

"As you wish. And unlike our protagonist in Conrad's novel, we travel ninety minutes by helicopter, not two months by steamboat. Please follow me."

Darla looked at the scenery below during the flight but didn't see the breathtaking vista of a lush forest canopy because her dark-hearted thoughts clouded her vision. But once inside the control room, she saw better than anyone how the drone operators used her company's 3-D GUIs for piloting mining extractors and other machinery. Her command of technology impressed Kwanza.

"Look how easy it is for your operators to drive the extractors. The GUI shows the avatar sitting in the cab, and your operators can talk or push virtual levers to control the digging. And just wait until we install A.I. software that links milling to smelting operations. The software avatars will trick you into believing real people are extracting metals from the ore. And if an avatar accidentally falls into a melting pot, he'll get recreated. No medical or insurance claims to fret about. And you don't have to pay any wages." Kwanza shook his head.

"You make it sound so foolproof. But what might have malfunctioned at competitor locations? Did you see the Internet videos? Several mines in Australia and Canada blew up. No survivors. A total loss. The aerial drone videos were shocking, as if atomic bombs had closed the mines forever. Maybe their machines were too big and powerful, or maybe their software ran amok." "That can't happen at any Big-6 mine. That's for our competitors to worry about, not you. I've seen enough. Take me back…"

Darla wasted no time looking out any window on any leg of the trip back to Cybergard headquarters in Milpitas California, preferring instead to peer straight ahead, into her laptop where her devious plan of attack against other mining operations lurked, but these operations weren't like Kwanza's. These were Cyberspace peer-to-peer financial networks whose mining apps earned Bitcoin or other cryptocurrency payments whenever their algorithms correctly verified and transmitted blockchains that must accompany every financial transaction.

Darla knew why cryptocurrency networks dominate. They are faster, cheaper, and most importantly, keep all identities anonymous. Nor can transferred funds be stolen because they are protected by cryptographic security hashing algorithms that are hackproof. Every time a network security expert thinks he's found a way to hack in, developers prove otherwise by adding more bits to the RSA public-private key computation, staying a step ahead of the fastest Quantum Computers.

But Darla's dark thoughts found opportunities for her apps to unlock trapdoors built into Cybergard's suite of security software it sold to the banking industry. Not only would she get paid to protect transactions, but trapdoor software would steal transmitted Bitcoins, and network anonymity would keep everyone in the dark but Darla. And her dark humor found a snappy reply to any mining industry employee whose job might be eliminated by A.I. mining technology: Just retrain to become a Cyber miner. Great salary, working conditions, and fringe benefits if you're smart enough. And Cybergard will be happy to retrain anyone if they pay for certification.

By the time she elbowed away from the baggage claim carousel, Darla had outlined another piece of her Cyberspace disruption plan. She need only train a hand-picked development team that would then start digging for Cybergold.

As Darla's team labored to meet a July deadline, Max the Popper was about to brief his for a sortie to retrieve a different form of gold. His team would seize gold reserves held at one of the European Central Bank's storage facilities while eliminating all physical and human assets found there. All eyes trained on Max.

"My super soldiers, your performance on previous missions proclaims our superiority, and our enemies are in the dark because we are an invisible enigma, leaving no trail or traces or open eyes. Soon we shall deploy to destabilize an enemy's banking system, because even in the age of cryptocurrency, gold bullion backs up a country's international financial transactions. So we, world's superior strike force, will use assets given to us by our backers to deposit fear while withdrawing gold." One of the Russian soldiers gloated. "Mother Russia must have known this day would come. How else could she have built, back in the glorious days of the first Cold War, an underground site of this magnitude? Today it would be impossible to go undetected, even in the middle of a Middle East desert." A second chimed in.

"And from this home base, rapid deployment anywhere is assured, thanks to our stealth aircraft that can rendezvous with existing Russian military support systems."

A Chinese trooper gave additional plaudits.

"Even the best of our enemies' special forces cannot match us. Russian weapons and Chinese wearable robotic modifications make us unstoppable." Maksim let the bold bragging go for another minute before bringing everyone back to training.

"And every victory we achieve adds to our enemies' fear of the unknown. So, now we continue our perfect practice for our next victory."

Greg Unger needed no practice because he had already mastered the art of snooping in the actual world of 3-D Space, not in a virtual Cyberspace. He was having better success hunting for President Gardner's blackmailer than any of his predecessors. Greg smiled as he strode towards his Oval Office meeting, practicing his punchline: Soon your blackmailer shall be as white as a corpse. Greg was confident that Jared would grant him two more months to deliver.

Unaware of new enemies lurking just over her current events horizon, Electra kept fully occupied working on Cyberspace software and cloning. Tim and Kwame's efforts kept the software timeline ticking forward but they needed guidance, so she dived again into the darker places of Cyberspace and sketched a summary of information that would help them avoid mistakes. She reviewed it one more time before powering off her workstation.

The Deep-Dark Web: Network Security and GUI's Darknet or Dark Web:

- Restricted to special browsers
- Not indexed for Search Engines Large scale illegal activity
- Unmeasurable Deep Web:
- Contains Dark Web
- Accessible by password, encryption, or gateway software
- Not indexed for Search Engines
- Little illegal activity outside of Dark Web
- Huge and growing exponentially Surface Web:
- Accessible
- Indexed for Search Engines
- Little illegal activity
- Relatively small

The Internet is a collection of Websites linked together to form "Markets."

Surface Web is "Visible" to "Honest People."

Deep-Dark Web is for those who wish to
be "Anonymous." It is four times larger than Surface Web.

Marianas Web named after deepest part
Of the Ocean. Place to buy debauched items.

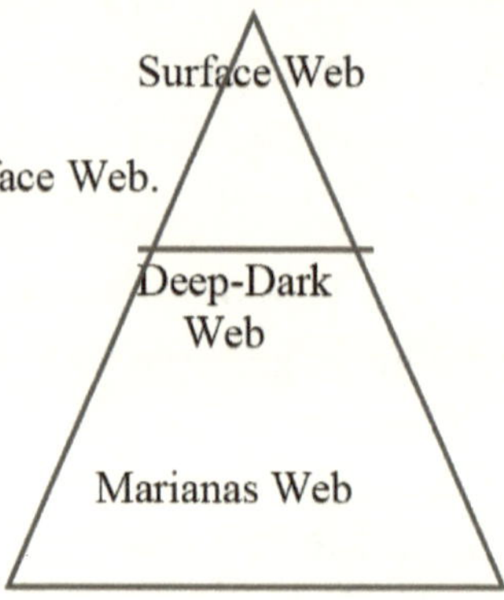

Marianas Web

Need special browser (TOR = The Onion Router) to access Deep Dark Web. It links Source (Seller) to Destination (Buyer) via convoluted Proxy Server Path to keep IP addresses, etc. hidden.

Uses Cryptocurrency so there is no $ Transaction Audit Trail

Uses Blockchain to guarantee Data Reliability and detect tampering Provides "Secure Message Features" (SMF) to guarantee communications privacy

For Sale in the Deep-Dark Web: Murderers Terrorists Malware Drugs Slaves Sex etc.

Though deep and dark, Web hardware/software is "conventional." Utilizes current Network Security Services and hacking techniques to: Snoop Corrupt Destroy, Change Hijack Blackmail

MMORG (massively multiplayer online role-playing games) and Persistent State World Player's Sandbox have addictive GUI's. Players vanish into Cyberspace.

For Sale in the Deep-Dark Web: Hardware, Software, Chips for embedding into Humans or Hardware. Build your own interactive Cyber-Theater for a Virtual Reality World of extralegal Drugs, Sex, Gambling, etc.

I've built for my use only Network Defense and Network Offense Security Suites equipped with 3-D Augmented VR GUIs that turn my apps into video game-like software in which I can insert Personal Avatars to battle enemies, but many Dark Web videogame GUI's are even better than mine. Players can buy hardware and software, and even hire someone to implant chips and ports into themselves for connecting to a Cyber-Theater. This is Huxley's "Brave New World Revisited." Society better be careful of unintended consequences.

Electra put those gloomy thoughts away as she prepared for an early evening run.

What a glorious time to hit the trail. We're on the cusp of the Summer Solstice. I should be overjoyed, but instead I feel troubled. Maybe running will lift my spirits.

As she settled into a comfortable pace, her brain searched for the right words, bringing to mind a poem from Indira.

Mother's poem, the one called Summer Solstice, speaks to me. I know it by heart.

Ephemeral Summer Solstice,
Spring ends with most daylight.
Our westward gaze absorbs last rays,
The Sun submerged from sight.
Thoughts dwell on past encounters,
When other orbs shone bright,
But like the Sun their day is done,
They've passed to that good night.
Try not to wax nostalgic,
To melancholy do not cling,
It is the same for everyone,
No matter pawn or king.
Sadness seeps inside us,
Loved voices no longer sing,
We missed our chance for one last dance,
And peace of mind it brings.
Many things taken for granted,
Many things left unsaid,
It's but a meager substitute,
When eulogies are read.
But on this evening hear them,
It happens in your mind,
Rendezvous with those now past,
Let calendars rewind.
How melancholy but true.
And just like Mother,
I have darker moments too.

As the lightning brain freewheeled, an odd thought brought her to a halt.

My research reaches toward both poles of the cognition spectrum: all the way from Neuroscience and DNA manipulation to the Singularity and Quantum Computers. And Modernity has eliminated what used to be mankind's only pole, Religion. And even I sometimes miss the comfort Faith provides when trying to believe humans are more than complex electrochemical reactions. Are we more than emergent phenomena? I fear these deep questions may stay forever beyond my grasp. Perhaps Robert Browning's couplet says it better: Ah, but a man's reach should exceed his grasp, or what's a heaven for? It comes from his poem Andrea del Sarto that expresses his struggle with religion. I'm not the poet, Mother is, but at least I can empathize with Browning and Indira.

Satisfied with her contingent answers, Electra sped homeward in a twilight glow, anxious for Alisha to take command of those activities needing her brightness and light touch. She knew she could depend on her alter-ego to keep darkness at bay, night or day, no matter what might come their way.

Chapter 13
August 2126

"Hollywood Mishaps"
(Thread 2 Chapter 7)

THIS IS GONNA HURT!

Only Alisha heard the words she screamed inside her head, twisting as she closed her eyes just before crashing into the ground, the force knocking her unconscious. Coming to with eyes still closed, she heard a worried voice.

"Can you hear me? Can you talk? Where do you hurt?" Her eyes stayed open after blinking several times, spotting Vince and two EMTs hovering above. Alisha winced as she answered.

"I think I broke a rib. I get a stabbing pain in my right side when I try to breathe." An EMT took over.

"Try to relax and take shallow breaths. We're positioning a slider board underneath so we can get you onto a stretcher. It'll be a quick ride to the ER. You'll be OK."

Two hours later, one of the ER doctors briefed Alisha as Vince and Kathi listened.

"X-rays show you broke the two floating ribs on your right side. You have twelve sets, and the two you broke should heal in 4 to 6 weeks, though in your case I expect them to heal much faster because of your physical conditioning. We no longer apply flexible wraps because they force shallow breathing, which increases the risk of pneumonia. Do deep breathing exercises and take pain meds if you need them. I'll write you a prescription. That's it, you're free to go." Kathi thanked the doctor and did all the talking as she and Vince walked Alisha to his van.

"Why don't you stay with me until you fly back to Austin on Sunday? Vince can check you out of the hotel after I help you pack. Then we'll grab a fast food snack before going to my condo."

"Are you sure? I don't want to be a bother."

"I am, and you'll meet one of your fans. Now please, let Vince and me do the talking." Vince started as soon as they drove away.

"We're lucky your misstep didn't turn into a major mishap. I think we'll want to start using a stunt double for your own good on all action scenes. So far, you've handled them, except those that Kathi nixed, and we've been making them more and more demanding because fans have ratcheted up expectations. Maybe your double wouldn't have slipped off the ledge." Kathi said more.

"I mentioned this to you way back when. Maybe you tripped over a Biblical proverb, Pride goeth before the fall. No one's indestructible." Alisha nodded but said nothing.

Two hours later, she was ensconced in Kathi's third bedroom, now containing two additional ladies. Kathi introduced a little girl who was peering hesitantly from behind a nattily dressed early-twenties young woman.

"I'd like you to meet Zabian and her Nanny, Abila. Both are from Lebanon." Alisha felt an emotional ping as she spoke.

"What beautiful names for two beautiful ladies. What do the names mean?"

Abila said, "Zabian means a worshipper of heavenly bodies. I guess that's why she's Supergirl's biggest fan. And mine means beautiful and healthy. Come, Zaby. It's late." Zaby squirmed free to ask one question.

"Did you really come from another planet where everyone has superpowers and is super smart. But here on Earth you have to pretend to be like everyone else because even though you do good things, people would be afraid if they knew what you are?" Kathi spoke before Alisha could answer.

"I'm sure Alisha will tell you tomorrow she's just like everyone else when not wearing her Supergirl costume, but she just had a bad fall and needs to rest, just like you should. So, let's all say goodnight and talk at breakfast. And since there's no school on Saturday, you can ask her lots of questions."

Alisha gingerly crawled into bed after Kathi herded everyone out of the room. A peculiar thought came to mind before she fell asleep.

This is the third time a wild guess has come close to my secret. And this time, how ironic, Hollywood advertises what I am.

It drifted away as quickly as it had come. Alisha slept worry-free. She awoke nearly pain-free, happy to share the news at breakfast with Kathi.

"I'm feeling much better. My ribs hardly bother. And I'm glad we've finished filming all episodes for next season. Do you know when shooting for the next Mission Impossible movie begins?"

"Tyger and I are planning for November, so you have three months to do all your other things, and maybe Zaby's right. Maybe you do have superpowers to juggle all that you do."

"I might say the same about you. I didn't know you have a foster child. That must keep you busy too."

"I'm fortunate to have an income that lets me hire a nanny so I can focus on a career that pays well. And Hollywood might be one of the last bastions for protecting jobs against artificial intelligence. Jobs here are pretty safe until computers or robots learn to be creative. Do you think that's going to happen in our lifetimes?"

"Experts say it will, but they're often wrong when projecting technology into the future. They always overestimate what actually happens short term and underestimate long-term. And speaking of the short-term, I had planned to visit someone today. I better call the limo service for them to pick me up."

"Would you please chat with Zaby before you leave? She wants to show you how smart she is. She can use all the electronic gizmos I can't handle. Here she comes..."

Alisha's regular driver acted like an experienced tour guide whenever taking her places. This time, he gave her a little-known fact when dropping her off.

"Yes, ma'am, this section of LA has lots of bungalows. It's not the best neighborhood, but the afternoon sun and low humidity sure make it look and feel good. Do you know that 'bungalow' is a Hindi word describing small houses in the Bengal region of India? And Jim Morrison made LA bungalows famous by mentioning them in the lyrics of one of the Doors' big hits, LA Woman. Now be sure to call me a half hour ahead of when you want to be picked up..."

Alisha listened to her own thoughts after exiting the limo. Cassandra's call a couple of weeks ago surprised me, but its timing was good because I can visit her on this trip. She postponed answering some of my questions, saying it's better if we talk in person. She seemed somewhat distracted, so I'm not sure what to expect, but I'll find out soon enough. I hope she likes the pizza I'm bringing.

Cassandra's only preparation for Alisha's visit was to wear the lightning bolt earrings Indira had sent thirty years ago. Six months ago, her father told her she had a half-sister named Alisha, even giving her phone number. She ignored her father's plea and didn't call because she knew she would hate Alisha more than she hated most others. But Cassandra's curiosity stirred enough to make the call. She remembered that Alisha would arrive sometime this afternoon, but until then, she would play around with one of her favorite males.

Alisha noticed as she walked up to Cassandra's porch that neighboring houses looked better cared for. Then she noticed a broken doorbell, so she knocked. When no one answered, she turned a wobbly doorknob and crept in, hearing a woman's screams and a man's laughter coming from just beyond the living room. Alisha's warning system escalated as she tiptoed forward, stopping when she reached the source of the sounds, a middle-aged woman sitting in front of a monitor. Both the woman and the monitor were attached to a computer-like device. Alisha knew instantly what Cassandra was doing.

She's plugged into a Cyberspace VR game.

Cassandra must have noticed Alisha's flickering shadow. She turned her head to face her guest.

"Hello, Cassandra. I'm Alisha Kittner. Your front door's unlocked, so I came in." Cassandra paused the game, her eyes reflecting dull surprise.

"So, you're my half-sister. Let's go sit in the kitchen. Follow me." Reaching the table, Cassandra brushed onto the floor wrappers and paper napkins as well as a crumb-filled plate. Alisha grimaced when spotting a roach zigging toward the landing spot, then reluctantly placed the pizza on the table and sat across from Cassandra, who opened the box and slapped two slices on paper plates she had grabbed off a nearby counter. Alisha broke a tension-filled silence. "Your father tells me you're a talented multi-media digital arts designer. Which studio do you work for?" Cassandra stopped chewing.

"At whichever one needs a contract artist when I need money. I can code apps for music, speech, and graphics." She resumed chewing; Alisha struggled to keep the conversation going.

"Were you a computer arts major in college?"

"No. I despise computers. I studied liberal arts as an undergrad and got a masters in Multi-Arts."

"I don't know much about contemporary multi-arts programs. What are they like?" Finally, Cassandra's interest flickered on.

"The good ones explain how music, poetry, and painting are all integrated expressions of cultural values, each using a different communications channel meant to convey the essence of a liberal education. The bad ones churn out programmer drones who know nothing beyond bits and bytes."

"Do you know how a liberal arts education started?"

"Uh, no. Tell me."

"It started with Plato's Trivium: Arithmetic, Logic, and Rhetoric. Students master these disciplines to understand the world around them. It forms the foundation for continuing into the Quadrivium, where those who qualify study Algebra, Astronomy, Music, and Geometry. And from there—" Cassandra interrupted.

"You talk too much. I'm not as dumb as you think. I see where Plato's heading, but none of that stuff helps get a job today. Schools push nothing but STEM stuff that turns students into mindless data crunchers who can barely read or write."

"You're not dumb. I think you understand the challenge facing students. They need to get some sort of job certification while getting enough liberal arts to understand the emotional side of life. You must have graduated from good schools."

"How could you possibly know? We've been talking for only ten minutes and you think you know me? Brandon had to pay for me to finish a ten-week computer graphics certification program so I could finally get an intern position."

"Well, it worked, didn't it? I imagine you've built a nice resume listing a number of good assignments."

"No. And I can't hide my addiction issues or aborted therapy cures. Big Data's got it all. Brandon should have given me more to make up for what our mother didn't."

"You're beginning to sound like a whiner and a complainer. You had a stepmother. Didn't that help?"

"It might have, but I was too angry. She did all she could, but I was a bad teenager. I was nicer to her when I finally outgrew adolescence, and we sort of became friends, but then she died."

"I'm sorry for your loss. I've had them too and I empathize with you, but you have to make an effort to engage."

"Why should I? The world hasn't treated me well. Sometimes, I wish the world would go away."

"Uh, I don't want to pry, but when I came in you were in your own Cyberworld. I wouldn't imagine that's a good place to go."

"How can you possibly know what's good for me? I'm better off plugging into my virtual reality Cyberworld where I can play games and get high on virtual sex and drugs instead exposing myself to the dangers of STD, needles, and other street-supplied perversions. It's the real world that put me into therapy, not the Cyberworld. It's better for me to withdraw into myself than to venture out and get slammed by life."

"But life is supposed to be reaching out to others, not turning inward to a make-believe fantasy. You'll wither and die if you do." "You don't know what you're talking about. You think death is a tragedy. Well, here's a quote from Jim Morrison, lead vocalist for a now classic rock group that spoke to his generation, 'Death makes angels of us all and gives us wings where we had shoulders smooth as raven's claws.' The guy was a genius. Wrote his own poetic lyrics. Had an I.Q. of 140 and is compared to Lord Byron. Listen to some of the Doors music and maybe you'll understand. You're probably too arrogant to know who they are. Their music is much better than the pap dished out today." Alisha came to her own defense.

"I might not have the artistic ability you do, but I do study different art forms and periods. I might agree that music from the 1960's had greater complexity and timbre, which add so much to its driving rhythm and beat." Cassandra's tone softened slightly.

"Look, I wanted to meet you so I could hate you, but you're actually a nice person, much nicer than me. Both of us missed out having a mother, but you were able to make a life for yourself. You're a somebody and I'm a nobody. But don't criticize me for choosing to live in Cyberspace. And don't tell me I should go through more therapy to cure my Cyberaddiction. It's a better kind of addiction than I had before. And I think it's time you go."

"I'll call for my ride. Until it gets here, could you show me your Cyberworld? I've never plugged into it like you have."

"Sure, but if you don't have an implanted chip, the experience won't be as vivid. You can be an observer on a one-way channel while I control the game." As they rose from the table, Cass said, "You can take the pizza if you want to."

"No, I bought it for you. I'm sorry I didn't bring you something to drink. What do you like?"

"I stopped drinking hard stuff once I got a chip implanted. The computer generates signals that stimulate my brain better than booze, and I don't get a hangover. If you ever want to get a chip implant, call me when you're doing your Hollywood gig. I gotta guy that does it on the cheap..."

Luckily for Alisha, her usual driver had been assigned to a different pickup, so she didn't need to talk on the ride back. And she said little to Kathi before going to bed. Only then did Alisha recap to herself visiting Cassandra.

Now I see why Cyberspace can be addictive. But I better not meddle in Cass's life. She's smart and knows the consequences of what she's doing. But I feel sorry for her. And that Doors' song she played for me, LA Woman, fits her to a T. She looks lost and lonely. She does have some of Indy's DNA and features, but she looks worn out. It shows that DNA is not destiny. Half of what we become comes from how we handle what comes our way.

I don't want to see her or Brandon again. I feel bad that I can't help her, but she doesn't want it from me. They'll have to figure out what to do.

Alisha's early Sunday run helped lift her spirits, and Zaby's cheerful early-afternoon goodbye helped even more, as did her suggestion to Kathi as Alisha was about to climb into a small limo.

"Why don't you let Supergirl leave her suitcase with us? Then she'll stay again." Kathi put her hands on Zaby's shoulders as she spoke to Alisha.

"That's a good idea, because then all you'll need to carry on the plane is your cell phone and laptop."

Alisha knelt next to Zaby and said, "You can be Supergirl's helper, but you and Momma-K and me must always keep it a secret. Do you promise?" Zaby's giggle needed no additional words, so Alisha hugged her and Kathi before climbing into the back seat.

"Hello, Ms. Kittner. Your usual driver and limo are not in service this afternoon, but not to worry. I know all the routes to LAX and traffic should be light, so please sit back and relax. Go ahead and turn on the radio if you like. And I'll slide the partition window closed so you won't hear what I'm playing, and vice versa."

"I think I will. I'll work on my laptop when I'm in the terminal. What classical music station would you recommend?"

"Try KUSC FM 101. It's owned and operated by the University of Southern California, so I guess it's highbrow music. No wonder it puts me to sleep. Careful, or it might do the same to you."

"I'll be fine, but if it does, I'll open the window."

As the limo rolled along LA's freeways, Alisha played the radio and acted like a tourist, paying attention to the scenery and traffic flow.

Driverless vehicle lanes have little traffic, even here on the most extensive freeway system in America. It shows that the public doesn't trust autonomous vehicles. I heard a news report about a robo-vehicle pileup and multi-aero-drone collision that occurred during a safety demonstration at a recent driverless vehicle show. That's bad publicity for promoting what the public already fears. Maybe the robots fell asleep, like I'm about to. I'm getting drowsy. I think I'll nap until we get to the airport.

The driver contacted his handler as soon as Alisha was unconscious, removing a compact air filtration mask before reporting in.

"Knockout gas worked. The package is out cold. I'll deliver to the storage location. Should be there in twenty minutes…"

By the time Alisha came to, she was tied to a chair in a dimly-lighted windowless storage unit at an industrial complex near the airport. The only furniture she saw consisted of two chairs behind a narrow table placed in front of her, and a bed in the corner opposite the entry door. The limo filled the rest of the space. Shaking her head to clear her thinking didn't help, but she tried her best to confront two large men sitting behind the table and wearing dark glasses.

"Why have you kidnapped me?" The longhaired fellow looked at the bald guy, who did the talking.

"There's a guy who knows a guy in high places who's interested in you. He's on his way, so relax. And until then, let's have some entertainment."

As if following a script, the longhaired fellow carefully pulled on a pair of black leather gloves before walking toward Alisha. He freed her from the chair, though her arms and legs were still bound. Then he yanked her to a standing position while the bald guy watched. "This is gonna hurt, but Supergirl's supposed to be tough, so let's see how she handles pain."

He started by slapping, at first with the left hand, but adding the right when Alisha tried blocking the blows. Pausing briefly between each strike, he increased tempo and force until his victim's reddened cheeks swayed back and forth like an erratic metronome. When he stopped, Alisha showed no emotion, staring straight ahead while ignoring the blood trickling from her nose and mouth. Then he hammered a short left into her ribs. Alisha crumpled to the floor, gasping. He pulled her by the hair to a kneeling position.

"Come on, show me what you've got." Alisha saw another blow coming; she twisted to her right to avoid a direct hit, but instead it landed directly on her left eye, its vision exploding into a shower of lightning bolts. She toppled backwards, crashing her head onto the concrete. Her attacker came on, kicking twice into the midsection, sending lances of pain into more cracked ribs. She rolled onto her stomach, fighting to push herself up so she could defend herself, but the pain was too great. Suddenly, a soothing sensation enveloped her. She stopped fighting and relaxed as all senses faded. The last she saw before blacking out was the bald fellow puffing a cigar while putting his gun and glasses on the table as his partner dragged her by the hair towards the bed.

Alisha's alter ego came to ninety minutes later.

I'm hurt, but I don't know how bad. I'll pretend I'm still out until I know how bad it is. And bad it was. She was lying naked on the bed, arms and legs unbound but left eye swollen shut, stabbing pains making it nearly impossible to breathe, and blood still oozing. Don't move. Just listen. Her kidnappers were eating and drinking while bragging. Electra guessed the bald one was doing the talking.

"I'm glad you ran out for some Mexican chow and beer. I'm all energized again, so if she comes to before Unger gets here, we'll have another go. Damn, that was fun. We really worked her over good, but too bad she didn't put up a fight. I guess Supergirl ain't so tough." The monologue stopped when she heard bottle caps jingle on the concrete, soon replaced by noisy gulping. Electra's brain worked feverishly.

Who's Unger? What's next? I'm SOL unless I find a way out. Nothing came to mind until she heard more words from the bald guy.

"Where'd you get the Mex from? My stomach's starting to turn. It's not that ptomaine poisoning chain, is it?"

"I feel fine. You just ate too much. Have another beer to cleanse the palate. That's what I hear fine diners do. And we're a fine pair, ain't we?"

The bald guy didn't talk, instead swigging more beer. But that didn't help, as he complained again ten minutes later.

"Jesus, my stomach is churning and I gotta take a dump. Oh no! Aagh." Electra pieced together a picture from the commotion.

Baldy just toppled out of his chair and onto the table. And now his partner's doing the same.

She propped her head just enough to see the action. Both bad guys were writhing on the floor, gagging and squirming. Suddenly, the cause of their problem crashed into her head.

While they were working me over, I infected them with T-Plague. Now it'll be more of a fair fight.

Electra rolled from the bed to the floor, unable to stand because of blurred vision and excruciating pain, so she crawled on hands and knees towards the gun that had spilled off the table. The bald guy saw her and yelled.

"Hey, she's moving! Go get her before she gets my gun." His partner tried to follow orders, but a trifecta of diarrhea, dizziness, and nausea slowed him just enough for Electra to arrive at the same instant. Grabbing clumps of hair with both hands, she pounded his head on the concrete as many times as pain would allow. It was enough to put him out, but she didn't have the strength to twist his neck so she grabbed the gun and clubbed him until she collapsed from the pain.

The bald guy, seeing that she was about to pass out again, struggled to reach the gun, but suddenly a singular clarity engulfed Electra. The lightning brain shifted to its highest gear, unleashing her Monster from the Id, not some mindless beast, but the lightning brain in full control, wielding all its powers. It lusted for the blood and the pain of others, or for its own if necessary.

Electra sprang forward and used the pistol to hammer dents in the bald guys skull. Both adversaries were now permanently out of action, but she couldn't rest because she heard a car door slam.

Unger's coming. There only one place to hide, next to the hinged side of the door.

She scrambled into position just before Unger entered, and when he did, what greeted his eyes froze him in spacetime. Electra slammed the door and shoved the gun into his ribs.

"Walk slowly to the chairs. Set them up facing each other, and sit down slowly. And don't talk until I tell you. I'll kill you if you don't follow orders." Unger obeyed; Electra began an inquisition.

"Slowly, give me your I.D.s and keys." Two minutes later, she spoke again.

"So, Mr. Unger, why are you and the CIA after me?" Unger's glare was as hard as his words.

"Someone who doesn't like you asked me to find you. That's all I'll say." Electra shot him in the right kneecap. Unger screamed harsh words before she spoke again.

"I checked the magazine. There are plenty of cartridges left, and no one's going to hear what you're saying except me. So please tell me more."

"OK! OK! Someone says you're a blackmailer. If you are, you can figure out who sent me."

"Who are the kidnappers you sent after me?"

"Local thugs-for-hire. They don't know anything other than my name and cell number."

"What makes you think I'm the blackmailer?"

"You might be untouchable in Cyberspace, but I'm pretty clever at tracking victims in brick-and-mortar places."

"What tipped you off?" "That's my secret."

Electra fired another bullet, this time into his left kneecap. Unger screamed like a sinner about to be baptized in a vat of boiling water. "Stop it! Stop it! You're hurting me worse than I wanted those stooges to hurt you." Electra checked the cartridge count again. "So, tell me."

"I combed through Gardner's list of everyone left after the Chinese tried to decapitate Washington by poisoning people on the Presidential succession list. And then I played hunches I found among staffers and politicos that Jared vaguely remembered, paying close attention to the last election. I can't prove it, but you came up in my gut-feel crosshairs as the only one capable of pulling it off."

"Now I know. Our meeting is over." Unger straightened his shoulders.

"At least give the condemned a moment of satisfaction. Are you the President's blackmailer?"

"Yes, and I salute you. If we had met under different circumstances, our relationship might not have ended like this."

"I'd do the same if our roles were reversed. Just do me a favor and—" Electra fired two bullets that fulfilled his last request.

The Monster submerged into the subconscious, but as it did the pain from her beating surged back.

I have to find shelter. I can't be found here. No one can ever know what happened. I'm dizzy and my vision's blurry. I don't know where to go. Come on, think...

I'll wear Unger's coat and my punisher's glovers, then take my laptop and cell phone and drive Unger's car as far as I can. By then I'll be feeling better. But I better take wallets and I.D.s and cover my tracks."

Electra stuffed cloth ripped from the bald guy's shirt down the limo's fuel tank filler pipe, then lit it with his matches.

The rest of Electra's escape plan worked for only a couple of miles. She couldn't see well enough to steer the car; she abandoned it and stumbled away, carrying her laptop and cell phone after pitching the I.D.s in a trash dumpster. There were few lights to guide her on the asphalt road, but she stumbled ahead for another mile before rolling onto the shoulder after tumbling to her knees.

I'm at my limit, I need help, but I can't call police. Who can I trust? One name flashed in her brain.

Kathi's angry voice blared when she answered after the fourth ring. "This better be important. It's 2 a.m. Who are you and why are you calling?" The stuttering answers snapped Kathi awake.

"Alisha, where are you?... You don't know and can't call the police?... You want me to come and get you?... How can I find you?... But I don't know how... Alisha, Alisha, I can't hear you." Kathi's yelling roused Abila and Zaby, but she calmed herself enough to explain the predicament.

"Alisha just called. She's injured and needs our help, but she doesn't know where she is. How are we going to find her?"

Alisha awoke wearing a hospital gown under clean sheets in a tiny room. Next to the bed were two chairs, the closer one occupied by a little girl. It was Zaby, who jumped to Alisha's side when she called out.

"Hello Zaby. Where am I?"

"Hi Supergirl. Momma-K took us to the studio clinic after we found you."

"How did you find me?"

"I tracked your cell phone location."

"Let me give you a big kiss. You saved Supergirl." Zaby burst into tears while Alisha held her as best she could.

"Please tell me why you're crying. You should be happy because you're Supergirl's helper."

"They hurt you bad. You're all beat up." Alisha rubbed Zaby's hair before asking another question.

"Do you like Batman movies?"

"Zaby dried her eyes before saying, "Yes, but not as much as Supergirl."

"Well,_ just_ remember what Thomas Wayne said to his son in a Batman movie when little Bruce broke his arm, 'Why do we fall? It's to learn to pick ourselves up.' So, you helped pick me up, which is what friends do for one another."

Just then Kathi and an EMT walked in. Neither were smiling.

"Hello Ms. Kittner. I'm the on-duty studio EMT. I need to record your accident. It'll be better if the little girl isn't here."

"Zaby honey, come with me. Abila wants to get you a snack." The EMT waited for Kathi to return before talking.

"Ms. Kittner, let me speak frankly. You've been badly beaten, and I am required to report these kinds of injuries to the police so they can collect evidence and apprehend your attackers."

Alisha stiffened as he reported all the damage but managed to speak.

"No, you don't need to report any of this to the police if I say I wasn't attacked. Suppose I say I was playing a Hollywood game that got out of control?" The EMT looked at Kathi, waiting for her to say anything.

"Alisha, please don't be afraid. Hollywood thought it got rid of its worst sex offenders, but it looks like some are still lurking. Let me help you, please."

"You are, believe me. I need to fly home right now. I feel good enough to travel, so I want to leave as soon as I put on clothes and eat something." Kathi looked at the EMT.

"She's right. We can't hold her against her will, and if she says she can travel we have to honor her wishes. But please, Ms. Kittner, you need to see a doctor as soon as possible. I've patched you best as I can, but it's only until you get a more thorough evaluation. Be sure to wear the eye patch for comfort, but don't wear it continuously because the moisture and darkness underneath make it a breeding ground for bacteria and certain types of viruses. You can leave anytime you wish…"

Only Kathi spoke on the drive to her condominium. Abila sat up front, while Zaby sat next to Alisha, who stroked the child's hair while listening.

"Please call me as soon as you get your doctor's report so I can reschedule the date for shooting. I wish I could think of something else to say, but I'm too upset." Just before parking, Kathi spoke again.

"We'll put you in the shower and then eat breakfast. Then Zaby will help you get ready to go while I reschedule your flight. And I'll take you to the security check-in. It'll make me feel better even if it won't get you home any sooner." Alisha was starting to regroup. She thanked everyone as they helped her out of the car.

After Kathi arranged an early afternoon flight, Alisha placed one call to Matt. He answered on the third ring and recognized her voice. "I'm flying to DC later today and will stay at home, so if you drive by and see the lights on, I'm the reason. And I want to thank you again for keeping tabs on my place now that Carter's out."

"This is good news. Please make time to fit Zoe and me into your schedule."

"That's the other reason for my call. I've been in an accident. I need Dr. Liefen-Liu and your clinic's eye specialist to examine me as soon as possible."

"Tell me your flight number so Zoe and I can pick you up."

"It's UA0783 but it lands at Dulles after midnight so I'll call for a rideshare. I need to leave now, so when can I call for an appointment?"

"Just go to the clinic as soon as you can. We'll fit you in."

"Thanks. Bye."

Alisha started feeling better on the ride to LAX because Zaby's trusting innocence lifted everyone's spirits. Kathi grumbled when Alisha asked to be dropped at the departure zone, and she told Zaby not to hug Supergirl, but Alisha hugged them both before resolutely trudging to the boarding gate.

Alisha followed Electra's advice on the flight home. She wouldn't fret about what was out of her control. The Electra-Alisha duo slept without stirring, taking comfort in believing that no matter what the doctors reported, tomorrow and the days to follow would be better.

Neurologist Henry Liefen-Liu broke the news as soon as he and the ophthalmologist had finished evaluating brain scans and acuity tests. "I know you like to face facts, so I shall give you the bad news first. Optic nerve damage to your left eye is irreparable, so you should not expect to regain much sight. But your concussion symptoms have abated, which means you can resume a more normal schedule, but contact us immediately if headaches or blurred vision in your right eye intensify, or if you feel dizzy or nauseous. And practice deep breathing until the pain in your ribs disappears. And finally, your occipital socket did not break. There is no need for any surgery or stitching. The swelling and discoloration should fade away within a week or two. Finally, we shall give you eye drops and a smaller patch as well as instructions for self-treatment. Please come back in one week. Would you like to ask questions?" Electra half-heartedly tried to inject a touch of humor into what had become a depressing prognosis.

"Only one. I know that any surgery Dr. Antar would perform would require minimal stitching, but wouldn't you agree I could find a better reason for seeing her again?"

"Yes. Even though her subcuticular stitching would leave little evidence, it is always better to avoid her persistent needle. But I shall say hello for you."

"And I thank you for all your help."

Alisha could feel her sense of humor trying to resurface. She joked to herself as she eased into her Mustang before driving home.

Avoiding a persistent needle is good advice. Even Indira's Buddhist Monk would have to agree. Now I go home and start healing and start planning. And the Monk would agree those are two of my specialties. Just wait and see.

Chapter 14
December 2127

"The Self-Controller"
(Thread 1 Chapter 4)

"And so, I stand before you, bearing the words of a victim whose self-control has overcome the physical and emotional scars left from a savage beating. She fears reprisal if she were to call out those responsible, so I speak for her. The greater good will be served by demonstrating that the love and support from those who care are stronger than the evil lurking in cowardly hearts. She will let her attackers suffer alone through her silent testimony."

Kathi's concluding words, spoken as the last person to appear at a Hollywood fundraiser for ferreting out any remaining vestiges of Hollywood's cult of sex abusers, drew applause from a sympathetic audience. The Electra-Alisha duo approved Kathi's performance while watching from their home in DC. Alisha spoke first.

"I must say, all your planning since that Hollywood mishap is paying off, and my words for Kathi hit the mark, as did my suggestion for the Superman scriptwriters to weave loss of vision into an episode. They've tapped into audience empathy, showing that even those who think they're invincible are fragile too, a wonderful lesson for everyone."

"Yes, and now you see clearly, if you'll pardon my pun, why I can close out this problematic episode by using the Buddhist Monk's answer. The eye patch makes a sexy fashion statement for you and a bit of cover for me."

"It looks good either way. And now, please tell me, where are we running to next?"

"To see a doctor when we launch my next plan, so please let me drive the action as well as the Mustang when we go." Alisha agreed. Electra had bounced back quickly after being beaten, concentrating on medical contingencies first, ignoring what doctors had said about her left eye. She knew more than they did and planned to extend the boundaries of current technology by using a technique they hadn't mentioned.

I know what regenerative medicine is, it's a branch of translational research in tissue engineering and molecular biology for replacing, re-engineering, and regenerating nerves and organs. And I know how to shock stem cells when injected into my optic nerve for better results by making adjustments to my Neuro-Knitter. And I can cultivate my own stem cells too. All that's left is to find the right doctor.

America's medical bureaucracy and its attendant lobbyists often support special interests more than the public by sometimes restricting access to radically promising therapies, forcing Electra, like many seeking better outcomes, to search the Deep-Dark Web for a sympathetic doctor. She would have paid with Bitcoins to ensure anonymity, but her search came up empty.

I have to find a legitimate doctor who'll be willing to work with me. I better search the Surface Web using different criteria. Thirty minutes later, she found an ophthalmologist who agreed to meet for lunch at the Mystic Kitchen Restaurant in North Stonington, Connecticut.

Doctor Betje Holbrook didn't mention it, but she must be a Native American Indian. Why else would she have an eyecare clinic situated on an Eastern Pequot Tribal Nation Reservation? I'm going to find out more about the name Betje and the Pequots.

Electra knew all she needed half an hour later.

Betje is an Indian name for the promise of God, but I'll settle for the promise of restored vision. And her tribe, the Pequots, is a sister to the Mohicans and a daughter of the Algonquins. Pequot means destroyers, and the tribe was supposedly the most dreaded of all South New England's tribes, but how ironic. The Settlers conquered them in the 1637 Pequot War. Too bad the Mohicans and Cooper's heroic characters Natty Bumpo, Chingachgook, and his only son Uncas, fought alongside the Colonists who later turned against the Pequots. And I empathize with the Pequots. They had to deal with the same conditions I've been facing, but I have much better odds. They faced a smallpox plague, terrorism at the hands of ruthless settlers, and harsh treatment by the Colonial government. Only King George's intervention prevented extermination when he granted them reservation land. But it took over 300 years for the reorganized survivors to win from the Bureau of Indian Affairs tribal sovereignty. I must turn our meeting into an opportunity for both of us.

Electra walked towards a mid-50's lady, whose brown eyes and silver-streaked dark hair complemented a trim physique. Rising as Electra approached the booth, she looked professional and sophisticated, her smile and demeanor matching her attire: black slacks and ivory blouse, accented with a bold red-and-blue-patterned scarf and decorative shell earrings.

"You must be Electra. I'm Doctor Holbrook. Welcome to the lands of the Eastern Pequot Tribal Nation. The restrooms are in the back if you want to freshen up after your drive."

"No, I'm fine. I stopped at a tourist center a little earlier. It had a video showing a number of picturesque historical markers."
Doctor Holbrook talked next after both sat.

"The early settlers called our land paradise because it offered abundant game and crops in a pristine forest setting. Even as we approach winter, the quiet meadows appear to be resting under a light blanket of sunlit snow, ready for the bounty of Nature to burst forth when beckoned by March sunlight." She segued to the purpose of their meeting after the waitress took orders.

"Your features are as attractive as our landscape. It's unfortunate you have suffered a mishap. Would you please remove your eye patch and lean forward?" She delicately touched the skin around Electra's left eye.

"The swelling's gone and your eye looks and moves as if your accident were minor. Can you sense light and dark?"

"Sometimes."

"Good. Your optic nerve is functioning. It's the pathway to restoring your vision. Technology today offers future hope for eye transplants or bionic eyes when optic nerve rewiring becomes more granular, more precise. But my therapy can work now. I suspend stem cells in a cellular matrix that I inject directly into an optic nerve so they attach to binding sites. Then the optic nerve self-controls repairs. Did you bring your own stem cells?"

"They're in a cryogenic container."

"Good. After lunch I'll perform optic nerve scans to measure damage and determine therapy options. And now, let's say blessing…"

Electra followed the doctor's van to a modest complex of freestanding houses converted into business offices. The exam started twenty minutes later.

"I'll examine all eye structures first, then I'll place your head in a cranial scanner to measure your optic nerve's cellular metabolic activity. You should feel no pain, so please relax while I do my work. We'll talk again in about an hour."

Electra sat stoically for the entire time and was now ready for the diagnosis.

"When did your mishap occur?"

"Four months ago."

"It's unfortunate you waited so long to contact me. I can't judge how much repair may have already occurred. If your accident was minor, little healing has taken place and my procedure might not help. But if you suffered severe trauma, my procedure might work. What caused your injury?"

"Perhaps you should know more about my background, but I never share it with people I can't trust." Electra sat motionless, showing no emotion, waiting to judge the doctor.

"According to my lineal descendancy that's recorded in our tribal records, I'm one-quarter Indian, and it traces through ancestors who practiced healing. Our healers are known for holistic medicine, which requires empathy and faith. I sense you're a good person too, one who can be trusted, as can I. I will honor your privacy."

"My full name is Electra Kittner and I play several roles. Currently I play Supergirl in a TV series. I tell anyone who asks that I injured myself falling while shooting a stunt, but that's not true. I was beaten unconscious by a Hollywood predator. I didn't report the incident for personal reasons. The specialists told me my concussion and blurred vision in my right eye would clear up, but I would be permanently blind in my left."

"Now I know why you look familiar. Several of our Tribe's children love to watch Supergirl. I should tell you that my friends call me Bea. And my last name traces back to the Pilgrims. Now to the business at hand.

"A severe beating to the head could have caused grave optic nerve damage. Let's try my injections. Stay the night at the Hilltop Inn, and come back tomorrow at 7:30. Follow me..."

After an abbreviated exercise session and light dinner, Electra spent the rest of the evening researching North American Indian history, recapping all she had learned before powering off her laptop.

Long before the Pilgrims arrived, an entire continent of flourishing Native American Civilizations claimed the land, a network of distinct Indian nations covering the continent, each building a sophisticated culture possessing all the trappings of a well-organized society living in harmony with Nature. The destruction caused by European conquerors angers me; how rapacious they were. But mankind's history is written in the blood of the innocent, unlucky, or ill-equipped. My poor Pequots. They reached out to help when the Pilgrims landed in 1620, only to be burned and massacred in the 1637 Pequot War. But they've risen from the ashes. I'll ask Doctor Holbrook about contemporary reservation life. Depending on how well my eye recovers, there might be more she can do for me and vice versa. But don't push to fast or too far. I'll remember to throttle back my obsessive-compulsive tendencies until I see a path forward. Doctor Holbrook had her procedure room already prepped when Electra arrived. Her greeting was brief.

"Before you lie on the reclining bed, do you want a local anesthetic or sedation? Many patients do. "What are you going to do?"

"I'll do two stem cell injections close to your optic nerve and monitor migration into damaged cells. And as you see, my equipment is computer-controlled, so you might say I'm the computer's assistant."

"Is your computer A.I.-equipped?"

"No. A.I. control is not yet precise enough for eye surgery, but who knows what the future holds? Would you prefer sedation?"

"No, I'd rather stay alert."

"Very well, but I must ask you a question. You brought a device. What is it?"

"It's my Neuro-Knitter. Another role I play is medical researcher. My Neuro-Knitter stimulates neurons by precisely focusing electromagnetic waves on target cells. I have adjusted it to do that for my left eye's optic nerve. Research indicates radiation accelerates healing. You might have read in the literature that Pulsed Electromagnetic Field Therapy, aka PEMF, is practiced on spinal cord injuries, and that repetitive transcranial magnetic stimulation, aka rTMS, is sometimes used to stimulate regions of the brain associated with muscle movement if spinal cord damage is light to moderate. Researchers have not yet developed equipment as precise as mine for directing radiation. I plan to use my Neuro-Knitter after you complete your procedure."

"How many times have you treated patients?"

"My company markets a line of Neuro-Knitter devices already approved to treat broken bones. And I will be my first clinical trial for optic nerve repair. You can help me determine safety and efficacy." The doctor said nothing, so Electra soldiered ahead.

"I've already paid for your treatment, so whether or not you want to help, let's get started. How long will it take?"

"One hour for treatment and a half-hour to assess results. We'll start now."

Ninety minutes later, Electra listened to the report.

"You have extraordinary self-control. You didn't blink or flinch a fraction of an inch. Measurements tell me injections can be effective. And I apologize for being so hesitant when you invited me to help. What do you want me to do?"

"I'm sure you know the rate at which nerve repair occurs after your treatment. I plan to irradiate my optic nerve twice a day until I come back for a second treatment, and when I do, I would like you to measure how much repair has taken place. I can measure it informally by judging any sight improvement. How long should that take?"

"I measure a sigmoidal S-shaped improvement curve. The tip of the 'S' comes in about four weeks. If your device works, your vision should be much better in a month. If it doesn't, your vision might be only slightly improved. We'll know by then."

"Good to know what to expect. I appreciate your help..."

Now that the serious business was out of the way, Electra could use the Interstate 95 drive time to let her thoughts meander, a perfect setting for Alisha to congratulate her alter ego.

"Your preparations paid off, and I'm certain you'll be just as thorough the next time. As your reward, let me take care of our Holiday schedule. I'll call Zoe and Matt first, and then Angus. Finally, I'll call Jennifer and Russell. Depending on what comes our way, I can add other parties to the mix, or we can relax and savor our blessings. Either way, I plan to enjoy the moment, and I'll remind you to follow my lead." Electra agreed.

Intent on following her plan, Alisha called Zoe and Matt the next evening. Zoe's always chipper yet breathless voice made it easy to recognize.

"Happy Holidays to you and Matt. I'm staying in DC for the next month and hope you and Matt will make time for me."

"That'll work. Matt told me about your accident, but I haven't called because I know you don't like people meddling. And your timing's perfect. My latest social activity is attending Shakespeare plays. Matt and I are treating Jennifer and Russell to Saturday evening's performance of Twelfth Night at DC's Lansburgh Theater. Why don't you join the four of us for dinner here before the play? And we'll listen to a lecture before the play begins. I'll get an extra ticket. And why don't you get here early so we can gossip?"

"I will, but please give me a preview of what's been happening."

"Here's the one closest to Matt and me. I just found out, and you're the only person we're going to tell until it shows. I'm gonna be a momtrepreneur starting next September, balancing a baby while assisting Jennifer and Matt and plugging away at my PR job. I'll save the rest until we see you Saturday afternoon."

"Congratulations. I'll save all my questions until then. And I won't mention your pregnancy unless you or Matt bring up the subject. So, I'll say bye for now."

One call down and one to go. Time to call Angus. His hearty voice boomed out when he picked up on the third ring.

"Damnation, it's good to hear your voice. You've dropped off the radar since we spoke last summer. No doubt you've been busy, and the same goes for me. I hope your to-do list has been happier than mine. Can you come over Sunday morning like you used to?"

"Is 8 a.m. still good for you?"

"Sure is. I'm usually up even earlier because of all I have to do. But I've learned from you to exercise as soon as I wake up. You'll see I'm keeping my man-sized frame pretty fit."

"Then I'll bring yogurt for you and muffins for me."

"And I know your favorite drink, so don't bring any. See you Sunday."

Alisha was about to power down her home workstation when she suddenly remembered there was another person to call, but decided to send Professor Ravenhill an Email instead and follow up with a phone call tomorrow because she didn't want to intrude so late on Thursday evening. He surprised her by calling immediately.

"Hello Professor Ravenhill. I hope all is well."

"Yes yes, Kittner. I'm always fine. And your timing is excellent. I have something you might like to do for me. I'll put you on my calendar for next week Tuesday at 10 a.m. Be at my office then. Oh, and by the way, Happy Holidays."

"Same to you, and would you please give me a clue what you want me to do? That way, I can start preparing."

"I need you to teach me about 'The Singularity.' I've been asked to insert a section in a paper explaining how it links to the integration of A.I. and biotechnology, and I remember you touched on that in your thesis. Whether or not you're doing anything in this area, I know what a quick study you are, so help me out and both of us get our names on the paper. Do we have a deal?"

"Yessir, and I'll meet with you next Tuesday. Thanks for considering me." Ravenhill's gruff voice didn't match his sentiments when he ended the call.

"Yes yes, but I should add a thank you too. Your cleverness always surprises me, so I'm sure you'll impress me again. See you then." Alisha mused while falling asleep that Voltaire's Doctor Pangloss would agree that the duo had done well this week.

Even though we're not living in the best of all possible worlds, recent events are all happening for the best. And I'll do my best to keep the streak alive. I'll take the lead for weekend activities, and Electra can play her Ravenhill game on Tuesday. She'll make her games win-win, as will I.

Zoe and Matt must have been watching because Matt opened the door before Alisha knocked. Zoe's cheerful words greeted her.

"You look great, and your eye patch is making a fashion statement as well showing that the Chameleon is also a Phoenix. You've risen from your fall."

"Both of you look great too, and I have to say the whole is greater than the sum of its parts." Matt picked up the hint.

"Let's eat while Zoe tells about her upcoming momtrepreneur role, for which I play the leading man." Matt talked as Zoe guided the group to the dining room.

"Jennifer called an hour ago. Russell fell down so they won't join us. She says he must have fallen into his walker because when she came home, he looked like a racoon stuck in a cage. Good thing she's completed more caregiver certification courses. She used a gait belt and lifting techniques to hoist him up and into his reclining chair. We'll wait until Zoe has dinner on the table before telling you more." Ten minutes later, Zoe twittered away as she handed out plates.

"I'm sorry to say Russell's slipped a lot, mentally as well as physically. He looks old enough to be Jennifer's father. Matt would know better than I what exercises she does, but she looks great. I guess working with Matt and caregiving for Russell keeps her mental and metabolic rates in tiptop shape." Matt's smile added to his words.

"And I'll help to make sure Zoe can juggle a baby, PR job, and working with Jennifer and me. Alisha segued to the next topic by asking Zoe,

"Didn't jesters juggle for their masters in some of Shakespeare's plays? Is that why you picked theater for the next social activity?" "Never thought of it, but I'll watch how they do it. Going to a theater series balances our bowling activity. And the pre-performance lectures are as good as going to a junior college seminar. You'll see. Now what's happening in your world? And how's Robin?"

"Robin's finally found herself. She brought a partner and several therapy dogs into her 'Sunshine Eldercare' business, so she's keeping fully engaged."

"Good for her, and what about you?"

Alisha gave an edited summary while Zoe filled in the rest of the chatter that lasted all the way to the lecture. Alisha commented to herself about the Shakespearean theatergoers.

They're older and more upscale than mainstream moviegoers. It takes years of living to feel what Shakespeare's characters are saying. And they could view classic performances or Shakespeare lectures on the Web, but people still prefer the immersive experience of live performance.

Aha, here comes our lecturer. He's a good-looking guy, could be a fine arts professor or a member of the theater company. Either way, I'll enjoy the show.

His opening remarks drew the audience into the magic of Shakespeare.

"Good evening, and thank you for supporting the performing arts, of which Shakespearean theater is arguably the best. Shakespeare's genius is timeless because his insights into the human condition are always timely, psychologically far ahead of his contemporaries.

"It's easier to hear rather than read Shakespeare because his rhyming scheme, primarily iambic pentameter, along with couplet phrasing and word choices are foreign to the contemporary eye but easier for the modern ear to understand.

"Attending my lecture will help you enjoy Twelfth Night that much more because there's so much that Shakespeare has layered into it. First performed in 1602, it's his final comedy. All his comedies have a thread of sadness running through them, and this one perhaps more than any of the others because he is about to turn his genius to tragedy.

"The name 'Twelfth Night' is chosen for the Holiday festival that climaxes in an eating and drinking revelry marking the end to the twelve days of Holiday celebration as well as the start of Carnival Season. Built into the play are subplots hinting at the end of youth, of certainty, of life, yet Shakespeare balances all this with much humor.

"The play's foundation is a love triangle among two men and a woman, but actually one of the men is a woman dressed like a man, a woman who must conceal her identity to survive in a foreign land. In Shakespeare's day, unlike ours, cross-dressing was something for jest, and lesbianism was not in the public discourse. The play humorously presents a battle of the sexes, which by today's standards would be politically incorrect but in Shakespeare's day was accepted. And even though tension and worry are sprinkled about, the play ends happily as two couples escape through marriage some of the frustration relationships may cause. Please note that marriage is a continuous theme in Shakespeare's comedies. Now that I've given an overview, let me take you in the time remaining to the next level..."

Both lecture and performance scored big with Zoe, as she explained on the drive home.

"That lecturer knew his stuff as well as the actors knew their lines. I'm so glad I've signed us up for the entire season. Maybe Jennifer and Russell can join us next time."

Matt asked if the ladies would like to have a drink at a social café, but Alisha declined the offer.

"Thanks, but no. I have a breakfast meeting tomorrow. But that reminds me, how is Carter?" Matt's answered filled an uncertain pause.

"Carter's put some distance between us. I think he may have a new romantic interest, but whenever I call him, he avoids telling me much. I guess he's found other tennis partners too. Goes to show how difficult it is to maintain long-term friendships. I hope the three of us will always stay close."

Alisha replayed some of Twelfth Night before falling asleep.

I can trace similarities between us and the play. Zoe and Matt are one couple, Jennifer and Russell another. Both are on the cusp of bigger changes, but while Zoe and Matt have happiness in store, poor Jennifer and Russell face a downward slope. And I match up with the heroine who has to pretend she's something else. But I'm happy to say the love triangle stays in the play. From what I see, I don't think anyone will come between Matt and Zoe, or Russell and Jennifer. And tomorrow, I shall see what Angus has to say about Carter.

"Jesus, Alisha, who punched you in the eye? Whoever did it made a big mistake." The words came through loud and clear as Angus's resonating voice welcomed her into his Georgetown home.

"I'm the one who made the mistake. I slipped doing a stunt, but I've picked myself up and am moving in the right direction."

"I'll take those treats you brought. Follow me to the kitchen. You know where to put your coat." Alisha hung it in the closet while Angus put butter, muffins, and yogurt on the table before pouring his coffee. Two twenty-ounce bottles of Coke were already set next to Alisha's plate. Angus continued after they were seated.

"I bought the Mexican Coke in glass bottles because it's almost the real thing. It's sweetened with sugar cane, not high-fructose corn syrup. And if you put in a shot of cocaine that it had originally, you'd have the first soft drink that hooked America. So, cheers to you and the Holidays too."

"And to you too. I apologize for not calling much during the last six months, but I've been almost as busy as you. The press is now calling you the public-spirited statesman-senator from Maryland and claim the rumors are true, you'll be the Democratic candidate for President. And aren't you glad that the 'Age of Social Media and Big Data' has compressed the campaigning time period? National elections don't disrupt for as long as they used to, although they still distort the truth if network security isn't constantly on duty ferreting out fake news."

"You're right on both counts. Are you planning to run for Congress again? You could win this time."

"I'm taking steps in different directions, but I'll continue serving as Texas NGA liaison."

"Well then, I recruit you to join my inner circle. And as you've done so in the past, you'll stay in the shadows as the power behind the throne. And I have your first assignment. Put together one of your patented white papers summarizing 'Surveillance Capitalism.' I know little more than the buzzwords tossed about in the media, but you have a knack for bullet-pointing to the meat of the matter."

"I know enough to get started. The media uses a catchy phrase, saying Surveillance Capitalism is beyond Orwell's 1984 Big Brother and is into the realm of 'Big Other.' I'll send you my white paper by New Year's Day. If you like it, you can keep me on your team. And let me guess. Carter's off the team. It appears he's switched sides." The scowl matched his reply.

"Our boy Carter must have struck a deal with Gardner. Insiders say Jared likes his economic policies, so he's moving up in the Guardian Party pecking order. Do you still chat with him?"

"Rarely, he's distanced himself from me as well as you. What gossip do you have about him?"

"Enough to piece together a picture that I compare to the popular retro sci-fi classic, Jurassic Park. In my picture, our 'Team of Rivals' matched the group pulled together to investigate the Dino park. And I led our team to keep Jared under control. Well, your boy Carter is playing the role of the skeptical geologist, but Carter's been hooked by Jared's line. And he's put only two people in his reconstructed brain trust. There's a female who plays the role of the movie's blood-sucking lawyer, and there's a fellow who plays the role of the ethically clever chaos theory scientist. I don't know much about either, but according to rumors, they're empty-suited mouthpieces rather than independent thinkers. Little wonder Jared is getting closer to the edge on sociopolitical issues at home and abroad. I'll need to repair damage if I win."

"What security issues pop up on your radar? From what I hear, T-Plague and Middle East Terrorism are no longer threats, and government Cybersecurity defenses are better than before. At least now the CIA and watchdog agencies are able to diagnose and fix infrastructure issues faster."

"So far I agree. But I'm privy to insider information supplied by our Intelligence Community. Though no incidents have occurred at home, CIA and NSA are gleaning from attacks in Australia, Canada, and Europe that there's some sort of rogue operation striking random targets as diverse as mines and banks. But there's no corroboration from the NCSD." Alisha's quizzical smile provoked more details.

"Sorry, I didn't mean to test your acronym I.Q. NCSD stands for National Cybersecurity Division. What do you think?"

"I would infer that whoever or whatever is responsible has gone dark. You won't catch them by snooping in Cyberspace. You'll need to use Cold War security assets, boots on the ground. Sorry, that's not my area of expertise. But if you keep me posted, perhaps I can help put the pieces together."

"I'll do that. And I'll invite you to all campaign team meetings. You can attend in-person or via videoconference. So, we'll talk again in January."

The Electra-Alisha duo had only one meeting left, the one that Electra would handle. Professor Ravenhill's surprised look matched his words.

"What happened to your left eye? Whatever the mishap, I hope it didn't affect your brain. I've always suspected you conceal a singularly sharp inner eye. I'm counting on you so we can get our names on another article." After Electra gave an edited summary of her accident, Professor Ravenhill outlined what he needed.

"So, here's the scoop. I'm supposed to review and add a couple of sections linking biotech to artificial intelligence and the Singularity. I know a little about A.I. and the Singularity, but I'm supposed to link all this with language, you know, linguistics. That's what I need you to do." Electra's internal dialogue ran ahead of Ravenhill's.

I've already connected linguistics to A.I. so I know how to reach for the Singularity. Ravenhill will be impressed. She started talking when Ravenhill stopped.

"I think what you're describing is at the cutting edge, but that's why they've asked you for help writing about it. If you'll give me until early January, I'll give up what might help."
"I knew you'd come through, just like you did on rare earths." "Are you still following rare earths?"

"Only when an associate mentions it. The last I heard there were some mining mishaps, but that doesn't affect R&D. We scientists leave those sorts of things to the grunt engineers." Electra decided to adjust Ravenhill's attitude.

"You're mistaken. If it weren't for engineers and practical people, your theories would be of no use other than to impress the tenured brotherhood." Ravenhill backtracked immediately.

"I didn't mean to offend you, and I do see your point. I often use the same argument to clip the wings of those in liberal arts and the soft sciences who think they know what numbers are. I apologize."
"No need to, I'm just being authentic. Well, I'll get out of your way and start thinking about the Singularity. Happy New Year to you…" Electra felt happy and safe as a clam at high tide when returning home because awaiting her were eight days of uninterrupted joy at a favorite location, her home workstation, a fortress of solitude where she thrived by collecting, analyzing, and drawing conclusions from Big Data. First up would be Professor Ravenhill's Singularity White Paper, followed by another for Angus' Surveillance Capitalism, and then final adjustments to next year's project plans. After a routine workout and a grazing-style dinner (the duo's preferred dining regimen), Electra sat poised to log on but paused to consider how fleeting good fortune can be.

No matter how well I plan, I can't will what I want, so when serendipity smiles, I must give thanks to an unknowing providence. But I have to plan for upcoming events that are indifferent to me and can be good or bad. Silly of me to think I can make the good times roll on. I recall a verse from Elinor Wylie's poem Nonsense Rhyme, reminding me to welcome whatever comes my way.

Reason's a rabbit in a hutch,

And ecstasy's a werewolf ghost

But, O beware the nothing much
And welcome madness and the most!

Indira can match this with a verse from her "Mystical Memory Garden" that I also recall.

Tomorrow's harvest depends you,
Its bounty whether short or long.
Remember today in all you do,
Blow a kiss to the future keep singing your song.

The same sentiment emerges from either, learn to make a game out of change and adversity. As I mature, my gamesmanship does this better than in my callow years. And if I'm clever enough, perhaps I can avoid bitter tears lurking in old age. My grandfather and Hud's father Holy knew the secret. I can only hope that Russell Conklin figures it out. But that's not my worry, at least not for tonight. I have eight days of total enjoyment facing me. Now I shall surf my way to the Singularity.

Searching first among her personal directories for any relevant work already completed, Electra came away with her white paper linking linguistics to artificial intelligence. Then, after searching the Web for what she considered the eight best articles, she extracted enough information to build a bullet point list that served as an initial draft of her Singularity White Paper.

Two hours later she searched the Web again to find the four best online professional seminars or university lectures, after which she spent three more hours adding more bullet points to the initial draft. And though it was 1 a.m., progress and enthusiasm powered her onward until Alisha interrupted.

"You should take a break before your obsessive-compulsive predisposition takes you past the point of diminishing returns. Why not shovel some snow? A combination of exercise and change of scenery will reenergize your mind as well as drain away muscle tension and fatigue caused by sitting in one place and thinking for too long."

Taking the advice, Electra was immediately rewarded because the forecasted snow showers lingered, the wind swirling their powdery essence into a sparkling display that danced in the glow of the streetlights. She stopped for a minute to absorb all its pristine beauty.

Now I remember why as a child I loved to help Grandfather shovel. Our DNA remembers the primal necessity of dealing with the elements. Her stream-of-consciousness musing suddenly brought a mini-epiphany.

Now I know why some cities are starting to use driverless garbage removal trucks. They are A.I.-programmable because of low speeds when running to and from designated dump sites on standard routes according to repetitive schedules. But not so for snow plows. Ditto for robo-warehouse order pickers and some types of factory jobs, but not for building rehab contractors. I see opportunities for man and Cyborg cooperation instead of conflict. It's time to return to my white paper so I can see how long it may take robots to muscle in on man's thinking jobs. And I'll remember to break before I reach diminishing returns.

A Coke and banana slices spread with peanut butter added all that was needed for Electra to complete the white paper two hours later. Even she was impressed.

This is one of my better papers. Professor Ravenhill will like its subtitle – Waiting for Godot – because the Singularity won't get here anytime soon. Like vampires, it'll show up only in Sci-Fi. And the reason? The human brain is not smart enough to break the general A.I. barrier because it can't exceed DNA-imposed asymptotic limits. And even if it could, it will never reach even the first-level Singularity because linguistics contains too many nested semantic sub-theories requiring Modal Programming Logic that today's programming languages can't handle. So, what's the bottom line? We'll never build a Terminator that can think and emote and move like a human because scientists aren't smart enough to build three A.I. personas – Cognitive, Emotional, Physical – and integrate them into an entity reaching third-level Singularity. Singularity researchers have to agree with this paper's conclusions. Those that don't are conjuring a world of fantasy.

Professor Ravenhill must read the paper carefully plus the Linguistics white paper I've attached to it. And when he does, he'll see my workaround teaser outline for reaching general A.I. But the details are for my eyes only.

So, what's next? I could work on my Surveillance Capitalism white paper, but I'll start it later. I've worked into the early hours of December 24th. I better take a break before Alisha scolds me again.

Although the rest of the day stayed cold and cloudy, the sky began to clear late afternoon, complementing Electra's efforts to remove items from her to-do list. In a span of only twelve hours, she had written two white papers that ranked among her best. Electra's final pass through her handiwork said so.

Angus will like my clear and concise summary showing how Orwell's 1984 foreshadows today's invisibly intrusive collection of personal data. And Surveillance Capitalism is not a new technology, but merely an extension of current economics using available technologies powered by rudimentary A.I. that increases profits for the large platform companies that collect personal data, storing it in the Cloud. No wonder Big Data is a goldmine. It stores what is euphemistically called the personal exhaust of market transactions that A.I.-empowered companies can repackage and analyze and sell to other companies that want to project or control consumer behavior. This latest form of capitalism offers the promise of more efficient business operations and marketing, but also the peril of concentrating too much power in too few aggressive developers. Longer-term implications are ominous. Critics claim it could make democracy obsolete if social purposing companies can't play a needed watchdog role. Supporters claim there'll be ample time for a great public debate if people pay attention. But will they? Watch out if platform companies distort facts into fake news. I'm sure Angus will pay attention. And now I'll pay attention to the calendar. It's Christmas Eve, time for Alisha to take control.

The Electra-Alisha duo had made no plans this year, not even for having a traditional baked beans and Swedish meatballs dinner or watching iconic Holiday film classics. Holiday traditions are important only when sharing among family and friends, and the duo had long since outgrown any need for solitary remembrance of Christmas past, but a sudden inspiration came to Alisha.

I've been to only one Midnight Christmas Eve service. I think I'll walk to a nearby church to enjoy whatever tradition it honors. And I won't dress up because casual attire is de rigueur these days.

She surfed the Web to check that a neighborhood church had what she wanted. Two hours later she trekked a mile along neighborhood sidewalks mostly clear of yesterday's six-inch snowfall. Alisha didn't need to rush, instead enjoying the soft crunching of her slow pace, commenting to herself that few people walk to do even local shopping. She, on the other hand, made a game of walking instead of driving to run errands because not only did it provide exercise but it also kept her conditioned to the elements. She kidded that the great Mongol warrior Genghis Khan always instructed his troops to stay in the countryside after conquering a village so they would stay strong. Good advice, especially in today's stress-filled, sedentary world.

The solitude of her two-and-from walk complemented a modern Christmas Eve sharing service where several families shook her hand and wished Merry Christmas. The entire episode relaxed her into falling asleep by 2 a.m., but an hour later, a familiar voice coaxed her awake.

"Electra, Electra. Please awaken and receive my singular Christmas present. My advice is a timely reminder for both you and your alter ego."

A calm, melodic voice speaking from a glowing white apparition at the foot of the bed drew Electra to a sitting position.

"Mother, you've returned. The lightning brain must know I need your help. Please tell me what I need to know."

"No, my precious daughter. The events you have survived during this most challenging year have catapulted you beyond the pale of even my insights. Your entire odyssey, from the lightning bolt at birth through the beating that blinded you, has been one of exceptional growth whose significance you take for granted because you are the process. My visit tonight is to bring into your consciousness a full awareness of what you have become and what may await. Please listen." Electra obeyed, not daring to say one word.

"Two philosophic sayings are appropriate. The first, 'You can see the Child in the Man,' announces that our best traits remain with us our entire lives and live on when we bequeath them to our children. And the second, 'You are not fully an adult until you are next in line,' implies you aren't fully formed until both parents have departed." Indira paused, smiling softly at Electra's rapt expression.

"My departure, and your father's too, happened so soon, so suddenly. You have stood alone, confronting the realities of the human condition and striving to be better, starting at an age when children are just beginning to walk. And I have been your practically perfect role model that you have now surpassed. I shall always remain the inner voice for you and your Alisha persona, but my dream-state visits will soon come to an end. I sense you are ready to redirect your steps onto new paths, so be aware that feelings of incipient doubt will accompany you. Embrace them, turn them to your advantage by exploring possibilities you might use if the currents of life sweep you to them. My precious daughter, I must depart but my love remains." Electra had one remaining question. "What would you say about the plans I've made for the coming year? Are they accurate?" Indira smiled whimsically as she gave a final answer before vanishing.

"Accuracy doesn't matter. Having options does. But I shall leave one question for you. Who is the one person you have forgotten to contact before the new year begins? Think it through, then make the call." Indira vanished at the blink of Electra's right eye.

She awoke mid-morning, fully refreshed and alert as sunlight streaming through a half-curtained window added to her Christmas morning joy. She suited up for a morning run, and soon her dancing footfall carried her safely over a familiar running trail as her mind cruised through Indira's visit.

I shall double-check all plans this week and decide who else to contact. I must have overlooked someone important. Who can it be? Between now and New Year's Eve, I'm certain it will come to me. Electra raced home, ready for Alisha to lead the way for the remainder of the Holiday.

During the days after Christmas, Alisha called Austin and Hollywood contacts while Electra fine-tuned next year's plan. There were a couple of power and communications outages, but they caused only a minor inconvenience because local systems came back online within four hours.

New Year's Eve ticked towards midnight as Electra powered down her home workstation. She was ready to watch the New Year's Eve countdown when the answer to Indira's question flashed into her brain.

I know who I must contact. I shall send an Email after I toast in the New Year. My New Year's greeting will be quite a wakeup call.

Jared Gardner numbly stared on New Year's Day at a computer screen in the Oval Office, reading for the third time a chilling Email. "Happy New Year Mr. President. Get ready for big changes.

By now you've probably figured out why Unger never came back. You thought he could track me down using boots on the ground. That didn't work. I survived and he and his accomplices are permanently out of action. As you shall soon be, metaphorically.

I will leak to the press all documents and communications I kept that confirm your treachery and illegal activities. I hope you glanced at what I attached to this Email before everything self-destructs. I have destroyed all copies stored everywhere in Cyberspace as well as 3-D Space except my originals. Call your lawyer and cancel plans to run for President again. You can run but you can't hide from the facts.

This is my final communication. I am going dark."

Jared's thoughts did the same. Finally, when a last gasp idea came to mind, he placed a call to his Chief of Staff.

"Corfu, get your ass to the Oval Office pronto. I've got a problem you need to handle."

"Yes, Mr. President. I'm on my way."

Dean Corfu came running.

Chapter 15
February 2128

"On Guard"
(Thread 3 Chapter 4)

Jared read one more time from his computer screen this week's favorite news bulletin that brought smiles to his two Oval Office guests.

AP News Feb. 16, 2128
(Top-Rated Accurate/Unbiased News Source per
Social Purposing Alliance)
VERDICT IN: GARDNER EXONERATED
By TruthSeeker 24 hours ago

After six weeks of in-depth analysis by a multi-party Congressional panel as well as from intense public forum debate, unreliable evidence and overwhelming support keep U.S. President Jared Gardner in office. The panel's spokesperson said the fantastic conspiracy claims leaked on New Year's Day regarding an alleged Chinese attack six years ago to decapitate the government's leadership are unsubstantiated, and may in fact be fake news fabricated to derail the President's reelection campaign. The same conclusion holds for information leaked that link President Gardner to sexual abuse, prostitute murders, racketeering, authorizing fake news, and obstruction of justice.

White House Chief of Staff Dean Corfu endorses the findings. "No one cares what happened six days ago, let alone six years. And if there were a shred of evidence to support what is now being considered fake news, why didn't any of it leak out before now? President Gardner managed to survive a cowardly T-Plague attack, refusing to rush to judgment, and standing tall against demands made by an unknown blackmailer while staying the course the people want. As you can judge from overwhelming public support, the intentions of whoever polluted the media with this fake news boomeranged because the results add momentum to President

Gardner's campaign train."

Other opinion leaders have similar sentiments, and even though the blackmailer's identity remains unknown, no one cares because the allegations leaked are dead issues. The panel agrees, recommending any additional leaks pertaining to this matter be ignored.

"Dean, you did it. You took my idea and ran with it. Great work. And now more people will fall in line."

"Yes, Mr. President, but the fellow sitting next to me deserves a lot of credit. As the leader of your 'Team of Rivals,' he supplied me with talking points the public liked. Carter, take a bow and speak up." Carter cracked a smile before talking.

"I've come to realize that Jared's policies are pointing the country in the right direction, just like my economics programs are taking us to a promised prosperity. And I've got two people on the team that'll flesh out the right kinds of sociopolitical pieces. Dean, it's up to you to wordsmith so Jared seems kind and gentle enough at home and abroad." Jared glanced at the monitor one more time.

"You two are my kind of guys. Get me the programs and the votes so we stick around another four years. You keep watching out for me, and I'll do likewise."

Jared wasn't the only one holding a news bulletin review meeting. Electra was meeting a day later in Angus' office.

"Jesus, who could have leaked the truth? Six years ago, only five knew, and Mariah is dead and Conklin's senile. That leaves only you, me, and Carter. And all of us destroyed anything linking us to what went down." Electra listened attentively to herself as well as Angus.

I made sure of that by cleaning up in Cyberspace what they overlooked. Only I kept all the documents.

"This is gonna blow headwinds into my campaign. What do you think?"

"I know I destroyed all my incriminating evidence, but I can't vouch for everyone else. Did you?"

"I thought I did, but maybe I missed some. You got any ideas?"

"It doesn't matter who leaked whatever evidence they had. Everyone's moved past the issue. And whoever's the blackmailer must have been smart enough to figure out that if Jared has enough smart people working for him, they could launch a social media campaign to discredit what was leaked. And it worked. People think it's all fake. Carter might have helped because he's smart and he's now firmly entrenched in Jared's camp." Removing his glasses, Angus rubbed his eyes before replying.

"Carter never went into much detail, but the last time I talked to him he mentioned reading Huxley's Brave New World Revisited. I won't ask if you've read it, because I'm sure you have, but let me give you the gist of what Carter said. Then you can correct me where I'm wrong."

"I'll listen, but don't do what I used to do." "Uh, what do you mean?"

"Don't give me an information overload." Angus grunted.

According to Carter, Huxley wrote it in the 1950's to show that his dark predictions for the future were marching ahead faster than when he wrote the original twenty years earlier. All of them except runaway population growth had legs. He was right about fake news, DNA tampering, mood-elevating drugs, and bloated government bureaucracies threatening democracy and controlling people. And when the T-Plague dummied down enough of the world's population, the threats became immanent. I think Carter believes he's smart enough to implement economic programs he likes by cleverly manipulating Jared. You and I both know that Carter likes economic efficiency and profits much more than human rights and ethics." "Your points are well-made and well-taken. We'll have to pay close attention to Carter from a distance." Angus's hearty laugh ended the meeting.

"I'll second exactly what you just said. I used that same oxymoron when I met Jared ten years ago. It seems like the cliché 'What goes around comes around' fits us today. And I can't help but notice you're wearing a concave fitted plastic eye goggle instead of a patch. Its smaller, and looks more comfortable than what you wore last time. Can you get different reflective coatings?"

"Yes, and they're made to order to guarantee the right fit as well as color. I have black, blue and green. The neoprene edging gives a comfortable seal while preventing any leakage. They also make a fashion statement. Do you like how it looks?"

"They're becoming, but I'd rather see your eye actually working. Any chance your optic nerve will heal itself?"

"That's a possibility. We'll have to wait and see..."

Truth be told, Electra didn't need to wait because she had regained partial sight just before a mid-January visit to Dr. Holbrook, who would soon measure the amount nerve regeneration. As she drove north along a stretch of I-95 through northern Jersey, she made a wry comparison.

Jersey's called the Garden State, but light haze blanketing an industrial sprawl is a stark contrast to the Pequot Reservation's combined pastoral and littoral landscape. America should give thanks to those environmentalists who can balance progress and preservation. And balance is necessary to maintain economic growth. Indian reservations offer a good example.

According to Doctor Holbrook, the Eastern Pequot Tribal Council has done more than most tribes to improve living standards. School and drug-counseling programs are better now for many Native American tribes than forty years ago, as are employment opportunities, but housing and income are still below expectations, which is unfortunate for the 20 percent of Native Americans who want to maintain their cultural heritage by living on tribal lands. If Doctor Holbrook likes my idea, she can help me convince the Council to buy into a plan that's good for the Tribe and for me.

Arriving promptly at 1 p.m., Electra was ushered into the examining room.

"Where did you get that fitted eye goggle? Not only does it look good, but it's better for your eye than a cloth patch."

"They're a special order. I'll tell you more after you tell me how my optic nerve is." An hour later she gave surprising news.

"According to my scans, your optic nerve is 85 percent restored. I won't give you another treatment, but keep using your Neuro-Knitter. The injection I gave you last time might have surpassed a regeneration barrier. I'll need to see you in four weeks."

"I didn't want to tell you before you did your testing, but I knew my vision had improved. And I've come up with a business opportunity as a thank-you. It can help you, your Tribe, and my R&D. May I tell you what I have in mind?"

"Go ahead."

"My plan has four prongs which we'll want to discuss with the Tribal Council, but not all at once. Number one, provide Neuro-Knitter restorative therapy for optic nerve and associated vision treatments. Number two, market designer eyecare products. Number three, allow my company to build an R&D lab on the reservation. Number four, and this we'll defer until your Council likes the results on the first three, add enhanced Cyber-Theaters to your gambling casino." "I don't think your first point is possible. Won't the government prohibit it?"

"The Federal Government can't because Indian reservations are not restricted by U.S. medical regulations. You don't have to jump through regulatory hoops. And your clinic will be the first to offer Neuro-Knitter optic nerve therapy. You can advertise, bringing in new customers who'll buy our designer eyecare products. You can hire some reservation people to run the store."

"What's gained by putting a lab on the reservation?"

"Time and money for my company, and jobs for your people. We'll hire and train Pequots." The doctor said nothing, so Electra pushed ahead.

"And it won't cost you anything. I'll give you the Neuro-Knitter and train you as soon as your Council gives the OK. So, that's my short-term plan. What questions do you have?"

"Can you address the Council when you come back?"

"Yes, and if their vision is as good as mine, they'll see it's a great opportunity. And I'll see you in four weeks…"

After spending the next week in Austin developing a detailed timeline and events schedule for relocating labs to the Indian reservation, Electra explained to Hud why the move made sense.

"By consolidating all labs and manufacturing into one domestic location, it'll save time by bringing all researchers closer and save money by eliminating a second facility. And it'll eliminate government scrutiny."

"If you can get that council to go along, I will, too. And I'll coordinate the project, but you gotta stay involved."

"Trust me on both counts."

Electra split the time following two weeks between assisting Tim and Kwame's device and software development, while working independently on cloning. And before returning to DC, she held an online meeting to brief Su and Kameyo about possible relocation.

While driving to Stonington, Electra was about to practice her Council presentation one more time, but Alisha ordered her to take the night off.

"Don't be so focused, so tightly wound. Remember the advice given by a world figure skating champion – never leave your best performance on the practice rink."

The advice paid off; Electra's relaxed delivery gave the Council enough time to digest what she presented; by 3 p.m. she and Dr. Holbrook had closed the deal. Electra would have Hud contact the Pequot Council leader – Chief Strongarm – early next week to set plans in motion.

The drive back to DC reminded Electra of a happy childhood soccer caravan leading to a playoff victory party that included cake and ice cream, so she rekindled it in spirit by detouring off I-95 onto Route 1 for a dessert specialty at the Princeton Diner: a six-inch thick slice of New York cheesecake topped with strawberries. Electra's grandfather had split a slice on a drive back from one magical New York City weekend museum tour when she was ten. The menu declared its cheesecake topped the caloric chart, weighing in at 950 calories and worth every ounce it might add.

I know that 3500 calories equals one pound, so I can do the math. Although one slice is .27 pounds, I'll round it to a quarter-pound weight gain. But that won't happen, today I expended more nervous energy than that.

Suitably fortified, Electra happily motored home, but happiness would have morphed into concern had she known about Max the Popper's upcoming presentation.

Maksim's team had inserted him via stealth VTOL jet at the first annual T-Cube meeting location. He had never led teams tasked to attack African locations because the Dark Continent had never shown up on any hit lists, but if it had, the terrain and temperature would have been situation normal. The Popper could take care of business anywhere.

Today's meeting, orchestrated by Darla Tinibu, would be the first opportunity for her and her T-Cube partners – Sergei Zaitsev and Chen Xu – to communicate since T-Cube creation. The meeting agenda would be as direct and blunt as its organizer. Darla had everyone seated at a Spartan conference room table in her Harare headquarters. After listening to Sergei and Chen, Darla would summarize and then let the Popper talk.

Sergei and Chen rattled on until Darla interrupted.

"We get the picture. Each of you is muddling through, striking assigned Cyberspace targets. Some of your Cyberweapons penetrate network defenses but most don't because the enemy has upgraded to better Cyber-ware. Keep doing what you're doing, because after Maksim speaks, I'll give him an additional target that should help. Maksim, let's hear what you've got to say." Unlike the others, the Popper spoke from an audio-visual podium, his commanding persona towering over his audience.

"My friends, let me first congratulate you for how well the dark infrastructure you have put in place functions. I have taken what I want and have built S-Cube into an invisible, unstoppable force that strikes according to a target list you gave me, wherever and whenever I want, using whatever means at my disposal. It is unnecessary for me to tell you anything else. However, I will show you a video sample of S-Cube in action." Maksim turned the lights off and the projector on.

Even Darla gaped because the action was more graphic than most action-adventure sci-fi movies. Wearing exotic exoskeleton suits, the strength and agility of Popper's troopers wielding weapons of superior power, blowing away targets while leaving no evidence, only rubble, blew away the audience. The Popper concluded his show fifteen minutes later.

"So you see, I have met your expectations. You can ask me questions now, some of which I might answer." Chen turned to Sergei who stared at Darla, who finally spoke.

"Where did you get tactical nukes?" Maksim's curt reply ended that line of questioning.

"No nukes. I employ thermo-barics, which pack nearly the same power but no radiation, a perfect combination for my short-range tactics – disrupt, overwhelm, destroy. Next question." Darla had another.

"They leave nothing but holes in the ground. But how do you avoid surveillance detection?" Maksim's longer answer displayed his pride. "I use my one-of-a-kind EM-Pulser. It sends out from a spherical radius that encloses my team a high-energy electromagnetic radiation pulse that interrupts all radar and communications. My targets are instantly deaf, dumb, and blind."

"How do your troops wield such power?" Once again, the Popper's pride showed.

"Perhaps you have heard of A.I.-intelligence joints, gaming suits, and their control platforms, as well as UWMs, an acronym for unattended weapons masters. They are in the commercial domain, but my sources are several generations ahead. There are also chip implants for brain-to-weapons feedback control and mood-altering drugs that force-multiply neural stimulation."

"So, what are you using?" Maksim maintained a code of silence, forcing Darla to back down.

"If there are no more questions, I shall return to base."

"Well, now we know why governments have said nothing. They have no evidence, not even a clue, so they keep their people in the dark. Before we go, let's add one more target to your hit list. And all of us remember, stay dark."

By the end of April, no additional optic nerve treatments were needed because vision in the left eye of the Electra-Alisha duo had been completely restored, but each had a different reason for wearing the eye goggle. While Electra wanted a "cover" that adversaries would mistake for weakness, Alisha wanted a fashion statement; the tinted goggle, like her lightning bolt earrings and serendipitous scars, added to her mystique.

Activities requiring two trips whirled ahead. Alisha would lead the first, another Hollywood filming adventure; this time there were no missteps.

Three weeks later, Kathi Lauret treated Alisha to a wrap-up dinner at home that Zaby and Abila had prepared. After clearing the dessert dishes, Abila dragged Zaby away to study, giving Alisha an opportunity recruit Kathi's help.

"Thanks for keeping my name private when you spoke at last December's fundraiser, but I have good reasons for not reporting the incident. I've come to terms with that episode in my life. In fact, I'd like to make a related public service advertisement the studio can place where it'll do the most good."

"What will it cover?"

"I'd rather show than tell. If you would you please schedule a shoot before I fly back to Austin, I promise to give a great performance."

"You always do. I'll call Vince now and we'll shoot tomorrow. What props will you need?"

"I'll wear my Supergirl costume. Please have a forest-at-sunrise backdrop. Play an upbeat intro tune like that retro favorite: Sunny, Yesterday my Life was filled with Rain, then dial it down and bring me into the foreground. I'll take it from there."

Early Thursday afternoon, Vince pointed to his crew after two practice runs.

"Are you ready?" When they nodded, he said, "Right. Let's make this the one." Then he pointed to Alisha.

"Hello. My name is Alisha Kittner, but I am better known as Supergirl. And I want to thank all of you for listening to my comments about issues America must still resolve. I also want to thank Cyber-Max Studios for all the support they have given me by scripting an episode spotlighting why Supergirl wears an eye goggle. Some of the reviewers like the fashion statement, but there's more to it than making Supergirl even more exceptional. Let me explain.

"I fell from a ledge last October doing a stunt, and the fall caused optic nerve damage that doctors said would leave me permanently blind in my left eye. And how ironic. Supergirl, who is supposedly invincible, is merely human after all. It is a sobering lesson for each of us. No matter who we are, we should always remember that we are but one step away from a mishap than can spiral out of control. "But serendipity smiled after my mishap. I sought unconventional medical treatment and found a remarkable doctor who removed darkness by repairing my eye better than what the medical experts thought possible. She is a Native American ophthalmologist running an eye clinic located on the Eastern Pequot Tribal Reservation in Connecticut. I have come to know the good doctor and her Tribal Council during my treatment. What a wonderful example of a Native American tribe rising from the ruins caused by European conquerors. But even after five hundred years, they are still fighting the good fight to preserve their culture, to reclaim what is rightfully theirs. "And America has helped Native Americans for much of the 21st century until a perfect storm hit our nation – Middle East Terrorism, T-Plague, and harsher government policies. Most of that storm has ended, and I challenge our better angels to help lift further our Native American tribes. I urge our government and our compassionate people to reach out to our Native Americans at home rather than to people in distant lands who often don't respect America's singular greatness. I stand before you not as Supergirl, but as a mere mortal whose vision was returned to the light by the grace of Doctor Betje Holbrook, a member of the Eastern Pequot Nation Tribe. I shall do my best to repay them, and I ask each of you to help restore part of a splendid civilization that thrived on the North American continent long before the beauty of fair Greece and the grandeur of old Rome emerged.

"Why not visit the Pequot Website, or other Native American tribes, to learn about their culture and donate to support them? Not only are you helping them now, but you are also helping preserve a cultural heritage as well as helping build a stronger future. Thank you for listening. And may each of you always see the truth and the beauty that abounds."

Alisha faded out as the camera panned in a glorious forest sunrise as the music built. There was a moment of silence before those watching applauded.

Vince said, "We've got your heartfelt call to action in the can. I think it'll grab the public. Kiddo, you're ready for other roles…"
Zaby hugged Alisha as Kathi said goodbye.

"I'll make sure the Studio releases the announcement as soon as possible to East Coast channels. And by the time you come back, Zaby will tell you what she learned by researching that famous quote."

Zaby wrinkled her nose. "Which one?"

"The one Supergirl used in her announcement, 'the glory that was Greece and the grandeur that was Rome.' Everyone should learn it." Zaby's pleading look provoked an answer from the source of the assignment.

"Actually, I quoted what Edgar Allen Poe wrote originally in his 1831 poem To Helen: 'the beauty of fair Greece, and the grandeur of old Rome.' Momma-K cited the revision written in 1845. The entire poem celebrates the nurturing power of woman, and of course the title alludes to Helen of Troy, who is considered the most beautiful woman who ever lived, according to the goddess Venus in the myth referred to as 'The Judgment of Paris,' for her face launched a thousand ships, such as the 'Nicean barks' of the poem, borrowed from the Coleridge poem Youth and Age." Zaby was about to interrupt, but Kathy put a hand over her mouth.

"Poe also refers to Helen as Psyche, a beautiful princess who became the lover of Cupid. Psyche represents the soul to ancient Greeks, and Poe is comparing Helen to the very soul of 'regions which are Holy Land,' meaning the soul of Greece, from which so much of our ideals of beauty, democracy, and learning sprang forth. In ancient Greek, the name Helen literally means 'sunlight bright as the dawn.' Her 'agate lamp' may refer to the moment when Psyche discovered the true identity of Cupid by shining a lamp on him at night. It also refers to the enlightened knowledge of the ancient world, which still influences Western culture today."
Zaby finally got to say what was on her mind.

"You talk too much sometimes, just like my teachers. But you're much more fun to listen to."

"I apologize, but I get that way when I'm passionate about my subject. I'll practice so the next time we talk, I won't use so many words in the same place."

Electra took over the next day, calling the same contact who had arranged the first trip to Japan. Trevor Jarvis, a freelance soldier of fortune who ran a movie-like "A-Team," would once again smuggle her in and out. The only difference this time would be the codename: Mohican. Afterwards, she sent Su her agenda for visiting. Four days later Electra entered the rebuilt Fukushima lab. Su and Kameyo had already prepared the conference room for their meeting. The trio ate a light lunch featuring sushi, tempura, and Kare Raisu (Japanese curried rice). Su and Kameyo sipped hot tea while Alisha did likewise to a Coke while summarizing the agenda. "Number one item is a discussion of your time and events schedule for moving the lab and manufacturing facility from here to a new location Hud's building. We're relocating to an East Coast Indian reservation to reduce costs, travel time, and any government interference. You should plan to be up and running by January. Does that seem reasonable?"

Su answered, "Yes. We can continue our research here until the end of November. I'll coordinate moving the manufacturing facility, Kameyo will do the same for the lab."

"Excellent. Number two item is a review of the current project status for the ones you control. You two are working on the next-generation T-Plague vaccines and an Alzheimer's vaccine patterned after those for T-Plague.

"And number three is my update on the cloning project, which I am controlling. I can report outstanding progress because Kameyo's assistance has helped.

"And number four is my explanation of a new project you'll control. Let's cover number one this afternoon, two and three tomorrow, and four the day after, when I depart. Any questions before we get started?" Kameyo asked just one.

"Last time when you visited, you used the codename Gemini. Why Mohican this time?" Su had already guessed the answer.

"You know that Electra likes word games, and though you are smarter than I, I know better than you how her mind works. She is alluding to Cooper's book, The Last of the Mohicans. But our move will make us the first Biotech researchers to work on an Indian reservation, so we become the first of the Mohicans, a tribe sharing much tradition with the Pequots."

"Right you are. You know me better than anyone does, so it's no wonder you and Kameyo are always at the top of the good list. And I'll help to keep you there…"

The trio checked off items one and two on schedule, but ground to a halt Thursday afternoon when talking about cloning. After two hours of Electra's numbingly detailed instruction, neither Su nor Kameyo understood what Electra wanted, but a grim-faced Kameyo raised a more serious concern.

"Even though I do not yet grasp your theory, I understand what you are attempting and will make every effort to follow. But I am becoming uncomfortable working on this project. I fear we are moving too fast and too soon, overstepping an ethical boundary that once crossed can never be pushed back. Su, please help me articulate to Electra."

"Very well. Kameyo and I have tiptoed until now around your unstated intentions. We agree with you that the Chinese are leading the DNA cloning race, and no matter what any international regulating committee decides, cloning R&D will continue. But perhaps you are now trying to play God, and not even your brilliance and good intentions are up to the challenge of cloning life." Su stopped, wearing an expression as blank as Kameyo's, waiting for

Electra. I didn't expect ethics to interfere so soon.

"I empathize with your feelings, so let's do this. I'll work alone and more cautiously until I have developed a less ambitious goal. And while I'm doing that, I have a new project for both of you to work on. We've done enough today and are getting tired, so I'll give you all the details tomorrow, but let me give you an outline now. An unreported strain of mutated T-Plague virus has now become a virulent, rapid-onset sexually transmitted disease. I want you to develop a pill that will either cure anyone infected, or, when used with vaginal sprays and condoms, will protect sexual partners. Before I leave tomorrow afternoon, I'll leave a sample you can culture. Your current vaccine solution paths should lead you to a safe and effective new product. Let's pick up tomorrow morning."

Electra used the fourteen-hour flight home to organize cloning activities going forward.

I no longer need Kameyo's help because I've already used her results to identify DNA segments and genes for heartbeat ignition and control, and for adjusting metabolic rates. And I know the ranges for parameters controlling musculoskeletal growth and brain development. Now I should be able to control basic pieces for longevity, muscular coordination, and intelligence of my clones. And I can eventually turn them into my R&D dream team. As I do more Dark-DNA experimentation, I'll learn more about what additional gene combinations I can modify for improving the good traits and removing the bad. The fetuses I'm growing are coming close to full-term in vitro gestation. I may give birth not long after Zoe.

Alisha, who had been listening from the shadows, had something to say to her alter-ego.

"Yes, you know what to do cognitively, but think about the correct Why-How-What priority. The best leaders envision every goal like a target whose bullseye is labeled 'Why,' its inner concentric circle 'How,' and outer concentric circle 'What.' And remember that every arrow you shoot at the target delivers important emotional consequences you must fully consider, so please listen to my emotional perspective.

"You think you can handle all the ethical dilemmas emerging when trying to play God as you create life, but what about the impact this will have on your creations? You are creating cognitive entities that think and feel, not some genetically modified vegetable. And what about your feelings towards what might be considered your children? Unconditional parental love is embedded in your genes. How do you plan to erect a two-way emotional barrier?"

"That's easy. I'll simply use my self-control to deny any emotional attachment."

"I know how thoroughly you think about your actions, and how confident you are about handling contingencies, but aren't you beginning to sound pridefully arrogant, the worst of the seven deadly sins? We both know that when push comes to shove, emotions always trump reason, so please handle carefully."

"I promise I will. And I'm counting on you to step in if I step out of line."

"And I will, because that's the reason the lightning brain created me. But before we sleep, answer one final question: Do you want a boy or a girl?"

"I know how to play this game. Robin accused me of acting like a psychiatrist when I was counseling her, so I'll answer your question with a question, how do you know I won't have twins?"

"OK, you win. You're supposed to be the smart one. But remember this, I'm considered the better half of what makes humans the singular creation in the Universe. As far as we know, humans are as good as it gets. And I know what you're about to say, so I'll say it to end this Socratic debate: perhaps. Now, let's rest and let the lightning brain work away."

Chapter 16
August 2128

"Love's Labour's Lost and Gained"
(Thread 1 Chapter 5)

"Thanks for picking me up. Attending a Shakespeare play should give me the boost I need because working on the campaign is so depressing. Angus is gonna lose."

Alisha didn't argue because the polls agreed, but she had invited Ruben to serve her purposes, not to improve his mood.

Ruben rounds us to three couples. None of the others know him, so that might tone down the Conklin's bickering, which'll make Zoe's Shakespeare outing better.

"You'll like my friends as well as the play, Love's Labour's Lost. My friend Zoe has become quite the Shakespeare aficionado. She's been going to a lecture series hosted by a professor who teaches performing arts. She'll summarize for us at dinner so we can skip the pre-performance intro. She and her husband Matt should already be at the restaurant. Russell and Jennifer Conklin might be a little late because Jennifer has to load and unload him. You'll see for yourself why she's become his caregiver. And she's his wife, not daughter. Please don't talk about marriage, health, or age, even if Russell brings any of them up. If he does, let Zoe and Matt talk. I plan to be a silent observer. By the way, Zoe's expecting their first child in September."

"Thanks for cluing me in so I don't make a gaffe. I've learned from politics you have to know as much as possible about your audience before talking. Anything else?"

"Matt and Jennifer run a holistic healthcare business where Zoe works part time. Russell had planned to be its business administrator after retiring from the NIH a couple of years ago, but he's spiraled downhill. Judge for yourself when you meet him."

"I've never been to La Tasca. Who chose it?"

"I've only heard about it from Zoe. I imagine she picked it because tonight's play is set in Spain. It's supposed to be a stylish Spanish tapas restaurant, and according to the parking lot, the food should be good. Ah, there's Matt's van…"

When they walked in, Alisha spotted Zoe waving from the head of an elegantly set table. Matt rose from the other end to greet the first couple, placing them on one side. Alisha was about to introduce Ruben when Zoe's motions signaled Jennifer's arrival, so she waited until Jennifer trundled Russell's walker to the other side and him into a chair. The flurry of activity momentarily distracted Zoe, so Matt played host.

"Good we're all here and glad Russ and Jennifer could join us this time. Alisha, why don't you introduce your guest, and I'll do honors for the rest?" Alisha did her part, then sat back and watched the action unfold. She didn't expect Russell's first question to be so quarrelsome.

"What sort of game of love are we playing after dinner? You know I don't move very fast."

"I told you we're going to a play that's about the game of love, not to a game of love-play. Zoe, help me out. Tell us about it." Zoe did so as soon as Matt placed the order for two pitchers of Sangria and a selection of tapas.

"Love's Labour's Lost is an early Shakespearean comedy and shares a common theme running through all of them, comparing and contrasting love in all its forms, like family, friendship, sex, and romantic love. It should end happily ever after, but along the way expect to see the differences between how men and women behave. And the humor lies in how courtship games usually lead to unintended consequences. In Shakespeare's day, being in love was considered a sickness affecting mind and body. But on the whole, he presents love and marriage in a positive light, simply warning lovers to appreciate rather than overanalyze. After we see it, we can talk about its title." Russell had heard enough.

"I don't want to. Can I go home now?"

Jennifer complained, "You sit at home too much doing nothing but thinking about the past. I want you to keep active by doing things. That's the only way to be happy when you get old."

"Don't you say that to me. We're supposed to be partners, but you never ask me how I feel or what I want."

"That's because you're always telling me how bad you feel. Since you retired, that's all you talk about, and you stopped asking about me." Jennifer stopped abruptly. Matt tried to cover an embarrassing silence by recruiting a volunteer.

"Jenn and Russ are exploring some fascinating issues that all couples face. And I know at least one person at the table who always has novel approaches for most topics. Alisha, would you like to enlighten us?"

"I've made a pledge not to meddle. Recall what happened at the bowling outing."

Zoe said, "This is different. Last time we didn't ask, but this time we'd like to hear your opinion. Just don't use too many words."

"OK, but I may be the target of Jennifer's ire because I understand both sides and empathize more with Russell. Many people think they'll take bold steps in new directions when they retire, but most don't know where to begin, so they frustrate themselves by reading self-help books or listening to retirement training lectures. I've read some and watched some, and their catchy phrases and pictures are engaging, but let's face it. Very few people have the ability or resources to start a vineyard, open an art gallery, or build an airplane. I'll mention two philosophers that take Russell's side, Cicero and de Montaigne. Retirement and old age can free us from anxieties caused by ambition and competition. So, let Russell be happy by revisiting those happy moments that live in his memory." No one spoke until Jennifer offered a defense.

"That's easy for you to say because you're an observer, not a participant. It's a lot different when you're the one dishing out the care. I deserve some fun, and that's what tonight will be." Alisha turned those words to everyone's advantage.

"Why not do this? I'll take Russell home after we eat. Ruben can take you to the play. That way, everyone has a good time. I'd like to hear Russell revisit some of his past. Let's swap keys..."

Alisha's actions salvaged the evening. By the time Jennifer came home, Russell talked more like the Russell of old, but Alisha's hugging him goodnight sparked his plaintive hope.

"I wish you could bring Christi when you come back. Bless you, and please visit more often." Jennifer walked Alisha to the front door before speaking.

"Thanks for being with him tonight. I needed to get away. Please don't think I'm being too selfish. Now go, Rubin's waiting."

Ruben did most of the talking on the drive to Alisha's.

"You saved the day and the play. Jennifer's really a warm and caring person. She's just getting tired of the same-old same-old Russell causes. She's so youthful in mind and body. I hope Russell didn't bore you too much."

"Not at all. And I'm glad you had a good time meeting my friends. They're good people."

Electra spent the next morning diving into the Web, coming up with enough geriatrics-related information to draw a variety of conclusions about Russell's condition. She summarized before a lunch break what she had uncovered.

Most people don't want to age gracefully; they don't want to age at all and will try whatever they can afford to keep young physically and mentally. But Russell isn't afraid of aging. He just wants to enjoy his last years. And his long-term memory is in good shape. Brain imaging studies show that memory and cognition are associative patterns of interconnected neurons localized in the hippocampus and prefrontal cortex. When he relives events, he's exercising his brain, and that stimulates neuron generation and strengthens existing connections. It's good for him to reminisce, but research also confirms that engaging in new activities is even better. If he can avoid serious accidents or illness and can stay centered in the present, his decline into senility should be a gently downward-sloping curve.

Jennifer is the one who makes me sad; she risks losing Russell if she doesn't share their memories. The Yeats poem When You are Old paints a poignant loss if she refuses to bend:

When you are old and grey and full of sleep,
And nodding by the fire, take down this book,
And slowly read, and dream of the soft look
Your eyes had once, and of their shadows deep;
How many loved your moments of glad grace,
And loved your beauty with love false or true,
But one man loved the pilgrim soul in you,
And loved the sorrows of your changing face;
And bending down beside the glowing bars,
Murmur, a little sadly, how Love fled
And paced upon the mountains overhead
And hid his face amid a crowd of stars.

But it's Jennifer's problem.

I'm not going to make it mine.

Before returning to Austin two days later, Electra met briefly with Angus to find out what help she might provide for his uphill election campaign battle. Neither saw anything new she could do. Neither were disheartened, just realistic. Angus would carry the fight to its conclusion, and no matter the outcome, he would seek her counsel going forward.

Electra had to return to Austin because cloning was reaching a climax as three in vitro fetuses were nearing full-term development and would need 24/7 neonatal care if they survived. They would also require Electra's careful preparation for confronting all ethical issues because the entire project would be classified in vitro therapeutic cloning, banned internationally but never scrutinized closely because no researcher had ever come close to a successful in vitro human birth.

Electra had studied all bioethical ramifications of birthing a motherless infant – designated in vitro gametogenesis (IVG) – and like any radically new technology it drew more criticism than praise. One damning quote from a highly regarded institution firmly anchored the public in the condemnation camp: "IVG may raise the specter of embryo farming on a scale currently unimagined, which might exacerbate concerns about the devaluation of human life." Electra had crossed the bioethical Rubicon years ago and could recall the words she had spoken only to herself. She repeated them again as she itemized what she would do.

Mere mortals have already released the cloning genie from the bottle. They can't match my cognitive or ethical abilities, so I'll work alone and share nothing. And it's silly to look for ethical nuances human nature would ignore anyway. I know when to say when, and I don't have to seek permission or ask forgiveness. I can make decisions, and I can live with the consequences.

But I must always remember my limits. Although I might have a god-like intelligence compared to mere mortals, I'll never understand ultimate reality. Some phenomena are inaccessible, even to me. So, am I making the right decision? I'll never know all the consequences for my actions, but I'll borrow the answer given by Indira's Buddhist monk. Perhaps always fits.

So, here's my bullet point explanation for skirting detection and controversy:

- Only Su and Kameyo will know about my cloning experiments. And I must lie that all the clones died. If any live, I'll say I had to adopt infants to learn firsthand the intricacies of raising children.
- If any of them live, I'll sequester them until they're big enough to bring out.
- I won't travel until yearend and will keep them with me at all times.
- I'll create online all birth certificates and supporting documentation that officially make them my adopted children.
- By the time we open the new lab on the Pequot Indian Reservation, they should be mature enough to blend in, no questions asked.

And that's it. There's nothing to consider further until I give birth to potential members of my dream team; now it's time to think about other projects.

The night before her flight to Austin, Electra's sweep through all Email directories came upon an unopened Ravenhill eMail that could throw her travel plan into a tizzy. He had another assignment for her that he had to explain in person immediately. She deleted it and then composed a scathing nastygram using a selection of her favorite four-letter words to make herself feel better. Then she did the right thing; she deleted the nastygram and agreed to be at his office tomorrow at 10 a.m.

Professor Ravenhill projected his usual gruff exterior when she entered his office.

"Kittner, I've got an assignment that won't get us published but will keep watchdogs at bay. I've just been appointed my department's representative on a newly-formed university-wide bioethics committee. I don't have the time or temperament to put up with bureaucratic make-work, but you're always a quick study, so please send me a white paper summarizing what I need to know. Depending on what the committee actually does, I'll find a way to get our names on another paper or two."

"Thank you for considering me. I've done background reading, and I appreciate the opportunity to learn more. I'll send it the week after Labor Day if that meets your approval."

"Yes-yes, so chop-chop and impress me like you always do."

After rescheduling her flight, Electra used the rest of the day to surf for what she would add to what she had written a year ago. But she soon realized she had stumbled into a byzantine labyrinth that would need more than a mythological Ariadne's thread to find a solution to Ravenhill's assignment. Luck was on her side. She surfed the Web to find large chunks of material she could use as is.

I'll call my write-up a Bioethics Committee Primer, and I'll copy-in these items: Ethics and Bioethics Definitions, Mission Statement Template, a List of Current High-Priority Bioethical Issues, and a List of Websites for additional information. And at the very end of the Primer, I'll give an assignment to the Committee. They can use this Primer to guide Committee development. And I'll include an Ethical Systems Cheat Sheet that will help Professor Ravenhill avoid useless debates.

I won't email this to Professor Ravenhill until the Friday after Labor Day so I can pretend how hard the assignment is. That way, I'll avoid the "Ratchet Principle." Time to reward myself with another Coca-Cola and more Oreos.

Upon returning to Austin, the Electra-Alisha duo cruised through a carefree Labor Day weekend, waiting until mid-week to chat in person with Hud about progress on the lab relocation project. He was happy to see her, and she was pleased with his summary. "According to Su and that Tribal Council Chairman, the move will be completed a week ahead of schedule, so you can use the week after Christmas to set up your experiments. Tim and Kwame report the same, but their move is much simpler. All they gotta do is upload files, move some devices and computers, and they're good to go. Either way, it shows you hired good people."

"We're lucky to have them, but they're lucky to have you for the guy at the top. And they won't miss a beat during the move to the reservation."

"Tarnation, it's gonna be lonely with all you people gone. I'll just have to keep busy developing some of those new business ideas you gave me. I've got separate groups of Permian Basin associates that are interested in solar panel farms and Martian farming."

"Excellent. But under no circumstances are you to tell anyone about moving the lab or our people. It's important we attract no attention. We have to stay below everyone's radar. I've given Tim and Kwame the same instructions."

"So, I shouldn't say anything to Sam and Woolly?"

"They know I travel to DC and Hollywood, so my extended absence is normal. And I'll come back at least once a month for meetings regarding my Texas NGA activities."

"You're always a step ahead, so I guess what you're doing is situation normal."

"I hope so. Well, I have work to do, so I'll run back to the lab. Take care."

"Uh, before you go, let me tell you what my Permian Basin contacts told me. A lot of voters wrote your name on the primary write-in slot. They're telling me you could win if you run again. Anything you want me to tell'em?"

"Please thank and tell them I'm keeping my options open. That's what every politician is supposed to do. I might run for office again, and if I do, I'll remember to spend more time meeting people in person, not in Cyberspace."

Electra's just-completed travel whirlwind had kept her from keeping tabs on Robin, so she made a belated effort to call her only remaining childhood friend before withdrawing into her lab to control the birth of the first members of her hoped-for dream team. Electra was pleased with what she inferred from the conversation.

An adult Robin has finally emerged, now fully engaged in the business she's building while controlling her mental issues. I'm glad she invited me to accompany her tomorrow on a client visit. I can meet her partner at Sunshine Eldercare's new office. And I might see bioethics in action. And like Robin said, she no longer needs Electra's counseling, so Alisha will be the visitor.

All Sunshine Eldercare employees came to attention as soon as Alisha entered. Located in a typical strip mall, the office had a pleasant greeting station that led to a carpeted open area housing two counseling offices bordering each side. Robin made the introductions.

"This is my partner, Hope Abrams, and her associate, Cooper. He's the only male employee, but so far he's been able to keep up with the ladies. In fact, he's been a therapy dog role model for Electra and Alisha." Alisha knew from the smile and firm handshake that Hope could be a steadying influence for Robin.

"I'm pleased to meet the legend. Robin has told me so many extraordinary stories."

"If they seem that way, it's only because Robin helped make them so. Just like you two and your big pups make what you're doing special. And I imagine you've molded Electra and Alisha into useful therapy dogs."

"It's been easier than what the training manuals say. Border collies might not be the first choice for therapy or caregiver dogs, but Electra and Alisha are smart, and Robin has instinctive dog-training skills. You'll see all that today." Hope paused for Robin to continue. "Alisha will join me and the girls at the Lamar Senior Activity Center. I stop there every two weeks to play the piano and lead a group sing while the collies pay attention to whoever needs it. I'm supposed to be there by 10:30, so we better leave now. Come on, we'll take my van."

As she followed Robin into the Center, Alisha had never seen such a large gathering of walkers and three-pronged canes, but most of their owners seemed healthy enough to navigate independently. Alisha observed from the sidelines as Robin and the collies greeted those who were ready for music. A sprightly woman standing behind a weather-beaten man in a wheelchair spoke to Alisha.

"Do you know Robin? We just love her piano playing and big puppies. And she's so easy to talk to. She takes the place of so many sons and daughters."

"Robin and I are friends dating all the way back to grade school. And she's a remarkable person." Alisha's comment sparked a comment from the man in the wheelchair.

"Darn right she is. I was down in the dumps a couple of weeks ago, so she came over and sat next to me, not giving advice but just listening. When I told her I sometimes think about killing myself, she showed me her wrists. Told me she knows how I feel. The more we talked, the more I felt like finding good reasons to keep going. We're so glad she visits. And we like her guitar-playing partner too. You tell her that."

Robin wrapped up the show by noon, declining Alisha's offer to treat her to lunch.

"I have to be back at the office for a 1:30 new client session. We'll have lunch next time."

"OK. Maybe then we'll have more time to talk. By the way, I've been studying bioethics, and your business puts you in touch with a number of important geriatrics issues. Hospice care, euthanasia, healthcare rationing, and quality of life come to mind. Do you ever compare what ethical systems say to what you actually do?"

"Now you're beginning to sound like Electra. But that's OK. I try to like you no matter what personality mood you're in. And my answer is no. I know enough about ethics to trust my instincts. When I'm talking to my patients, I listen and then let my empathy lead the way. And that's what my collies do too."

Alisha's afternoon run marked the end of today's obligations. Her mood elevated as she considered what she had observed during the day's visit.

I've just seen what can be the depressing end of the age spectrum. Robin's found a nice way to help people when getting near it. Good for her.

Now I'm ready to take care of business at the other end. I've cleared my calendar and to-do list of everything so Electra can deliver her dream team.

Matt's calendar never cleared because Jennifer piled enough client physical therapy sessions to keep him fully engaged, and for the past month Zoe's false labor episodes added to the load, forcing him to rush her to the clinic, making Zoe irritable and himself stressed.

Early in her pregnancy, the obstetrician advised hospital delivery because Zoe's tests indicated a risk of eclampsia (pregnancy-induced convulsions); a concerned Matt was always on duty.

As Matt trudged into the business office late Thursday afternoon to get tomorrow's schedule, an uncharacteristically fidgety Jennifer greeted him.

"You look as stressed as I feel. But the cause of your stress should end soon. The pressure will ease when Zoe delivers."

"I hope so, but I'll have to share the newborn load as well as Zoe's affection. But that's my job. And maybe I'm missing something, but what's been getting you down lately?" Jennifer placed pen and reading glasses on the desk before slowly walking close to Matt.

"An online investment scammer duped Russell again. I get so frustrated because he doesn't take my advice. Instead, he take-take-takes all my spare time and energy, draining me emotionally." Jennifer stopped to wipe away a tear about to trickle down her cheek. Matt put his arm around her shoulder.

"We all have emotional needs that need our partner's attention. Otherwise, what's the point of co-friendship or marriage?" Matt could feel Jennifer respond to his touch.

"Russell and I haven't slept together for over a year because he no longer can perform and I no longer want to pretend. Sometimes I feel like screaming." Matt felt an odd sensation tingle in those intimate places that had been reserved only for Zoe. Jennifer felt it too as soon as her eyes met his, and she softly kissed him on the lips. Matt drew her close, held her tight as his tongue gently explored an inviting opening.

Jennifer gasped one time only, then entwined her legs around his as her tongue responded, her arms embracing him fully. She whispered urgently just before her intoxicatingly honey-sweet lips sucked away all his inhibitions.

"No one has to know. No one will get hurt."

Matt could feel ecstasy rising towards a level reached one time only in the days before Zoe. The office was closed for business so it was safe for Jennifer's imagination to come out. Matt turned off his cell phone before Jennifer made the next move, knowing he wouldn't have to wait long for her to lead the way.

Matt felt relaxed and totally alive three hours later as he drove home. Feeling ready for tomorrow, he remembered to turn his cell phone on. It clanged immediately.

"Matt Fortier here. How can I help?" Matt recognized the agitated voice of an EMT at his former employer, the clinic Doc Kittner ran many years ago.

"Where are you? I've called six times but no answer. Zoe went into labor three hours ago, and this time it's for real. She's dilated but the baby hasn't moved very far down the canal. We gave her shot of oxytocin thirty minutes ago, but the contractions haven't been strong enough, and we can't give another because she'd be at risk for postpartum hemorrhage. We'll have to do a c-section if her condition worsens. She needs you, so get here quick."

Matt drove like a mad man pursued by demons, sprinting through the emergency room entrance after parking in a staff-only space. He changed into scrubs, then confronted the on duty EMT whom he knew well.

"Zoe's in labor and I know the drill, take me to her." "OK. It's good you've got experience. Come on…"

Good indeed, because Zoe's screams pierced his ears as well as his heart. Her head tossed from side to side, like a wounded animal whose wild eyes were searching in vain for an escape. Sweat covered her face as one of the nurses tried to calm her. Matt's medical training surged to the fore as he knelt at the head of the bed, grasping Zoe's hands.

"Baby, I'm here. We'll get all this pain out of the way in a jiff. Just follow my lead." Then he cupped her head in his hands and kissed her lips while telling her to relax and think about all the good things they had talked about during the last nine months.

"Baby, a nurse and me are going to stand on opposite sides behind you, supporting under your shoulders as we bend your legs upward. Then we'll want you to push. So, let's get ready and get to it."

Matt kept up a constant monologue, punctuated only by Zoe's screams that alternated with panting moans.

"Oh God Matt, it hurts, it hurts."

"Baby-doll, don't think about pain.

Think about the picture my words are painting…"

Matt paused only long enough to wipe her face with a cool, moist cloth. Zoe's loving look of gratitude tore at his insides but he fought to stay strong. Finally, after two exhausting hours of collective struggle, the ob-gyn shouted encouragement.

"I see the head. Come on Zoe, keep going." Matt saw what could help so he added his own instructions.

"Nurse, you and your partner each bend a leg. I'll give support under both shoulders." As soon as the nurses were positioned, Matt leaned forward and kissed Zoe one more time and whispered.

"Baby-doll, please push for all its worth. I'm right here for you." Suddenly, Matt felt Zoe shudder as a wave of contractions swept through, accompanied by one primal scream. And then, miraculously, her body relaxed after propelling a newborn into what at first must have seemed like a strange land. A slap welcomed the new arrival, who cried out in surprise. Five minutes later, an exhausted Zoe nestled her infant son on her bosom as tears of joyful relief from mother and father intermingled.

"Oh Matt, thanks for being here. I promise to be the best mother and wife, and I know you'll be everything a father and husband can be."

Matt buried his face in mother and child as he knelt down, bawling uncontrollably as he made a silent pledge to live up to Zoe's great expectations. Suddenly, he felt resolute joy burst forth.

"Baby-doll, thank you for giving us a son all our own."

Zoe beamed, hugging father and son, knowing full well that other labors of love had just begun.

Chapter 17
November 2128

"The Movable Feast"
(Thread 2 Chapter 8)

"It's good to hear you've regained your bounce after such a difficult delivery. And lucky for you Matt's such an attentive father, sharing the load. Sounds like he's studied all the latest techniques." Zoe was ready to tell Alisha more.

"He wanted a son and now we have Carlton. Matt knows all about holistic child rearing, which includes neuro and attachment parenting. He wants to add parenting and childcare services to our business, but we'll need to hire the right person. Jennifer and Matt are fully loaded, and I'm Carlton's primary omni-parent."

"Maybe you could omni-parent Carlton while handling that part of the business."

"That's actually a good idea. Matt's made us members of two parenting groups whose meetings we can attend in person or online, so I'm learning a lot and keeping fit too. Taking care of a baby takes a lot of energy because there's so much to do, but there's nothing I'd rather be doing. It's true, the bond between mother and infant takes caring to a whole new level. And Carlton's so easy because he's so healthy. He hardly ever cries."

"What does your pediatrician say?"

"His birth weight and length and growth rate are all at the 50th percentile, and he recommends formula feeding because of my particulars."

"If it's OK with you, I'll call Robin right now. She'll want to hear your good news. And I'll mention that she should contact the Conklins. Russell needs a cheery call to pick up his spirits after breaking his hip."

"While you're doing that, I'll tend to Carlton. I hear him calling now, so I better say bye to you and hi to him."

After disconnecting, Alisha thought now would be a good time to compare Zoe's delivery to Electra's, so she fired away.

"Your delivery was pain-free physically, even though you had triplets to contend with. But it was more painful emotionally, because two died after only two days, and try as you did, mother-child bonding trumped your attempt to stay emotionally detached. You've connected more intensely to Ariadne than you had intended." "I've always said that emotion trumps reason. A mother's love for a newborn is the strongest bond there is. And statistically, Ariadne had the best chance of surviving because she was the longest and heaviest and had the highest APGAR score. All that correlates with her growth pattern. She's gaining over two pounds and two inches each month, which is twice the average. I want to do additional neural scans for a preliminary assessment of cognitive development." "Grandfather said your neural pattern looked like a forest of lighted Christmas trees. And he and Jason provided nonstop neural stimulation by playing music or media broadcasts. Can you determine if her brain is actually comprehending?"

"Possibly, but I need to study it so I can correlate neural patterns and Brain Probe measurements until she begins talking. I started talking at nine months, half the time most infants require, and when I did, I talked in complete sentences."

"How will you feel if Ariadne doesn't meet your expectations?"

"I'll answer your question if you answer mine first. Why did I choose the name Ariadne?"

"Because in Greek mythology Theseus uses a ball of red thread given to him by Ariadne, a princess, so he can mark a path leading out of the Labyrinth after slaying the Minotaur. I guess you plan to use Ariadne like a petri dish. You'll test some of your theories that might you lead out of the labyrinth of consciousness theory."

"If you're supposed to be the one with all the empathy, you've given a very cold answer. But to answer your question, I'll accept Ariadne for what she is. That's what parents should do…"

Electra left a brief voice message for Robin, summarizing what Zoe had told her, then looked in on Ariadne.

"Hello, Baby-A. I hope you like all the neural stimulation I'm providing. You're luckier than I was at your age because I had to keep my brain a secret even from Grandfather, that's Doc Kittner, and my father, that's Jason. I played secret brain games with them, and you'll play secret cloning games with me. And I'll take you with me wherever I go. We'll leave soon for Hollywood, California. "You'll like California. It's warm and sunny.

"I wish I could compare your neural scans to mine when I was born, but I don't have any. But yours show much more activity than normal three-month-olds, and your growth rate is double the norm, so I have great expectations. And as you develop, we'll see if the rest of you matches what DNA editing predicts. And as soon as you start talking, I'll know even better what to expect.

"Your full name is Ariadne Indira Kittner, but people like to have nicknames, which are easier to remember and fun to use. Yours will be Baby-A until you grow out of it. Then, we'll find one that fits better.

"My full name is Electra Alisha Kittner, and I have a nickname – Kit – but I use it only when playing sports. You can call me Momma until you're old enough to help me pick another you like better. And you'll sometimes hear people calling me Electra, while at other times Alisha. Here's the reason why.

"Everyone has three personalities – or personas – we show to the external world, Cognitive, Emotional, and Physical. When I want to be serious, I'm in my cognitive state, which I call my Electra persona. And when I want to have fun, I'm in my emotional state, which I call my Alisha persona. It's not complicated, and I know it'll be easy for you to understand, especially once you start talking to me. And by the way, our physical persona is always present for our cognitive and emotional personas to call on.

"I'll bet you're hungry because you're growing so fast, so how about trying some baby food while having more formula?" Baby-A giggled while peering into her mother's eyes.

During the flight, the Electra-Alisha duo saw how much respect travelers and airlines give a mother-infant combination. Fellow passengers smiled and Ariadne flew free of charge.

Kathi gushed as soon as she saw Alisha's adopted daughter. "Goodness, you're working with an outstanding agency. You could almost be her birth mother."

"I gave the agency a bonus for finding Ariadne. And thanks for letting us stay with you. We'll be no bother, and I plan to keep Ariadne with me when doing shoots this week."

"That should be fine. And why don't you stay for Thanksgiving? We can celebrate the end of your shoot and the start of your mother-daughter relationship."

Filming wrapped up without a hitch; Kathi invited a small group to a Thanksgiving dinner party hosted in a private room at a popular restaurant. Alisha held Ariadne on her lap while talking with Lisa Perugino, the new Continuity Coach.

"I'm sure you're as talented as Ricky. Please tell me about your background."

"I've worked at the studio since graduating ten years ago. I fell in love with the Hollywood mystique when I was just a little girl, I majored in fine arts and took a certification class for 3-D face printing. That got me a job working in makeup and costume design, and from there to continuity coaching because I have a good background in art, history, and language."

"Would you show me how the studio does 3-D mask printing? I wear them for some of my Chameleon roles."

"I'd be happy to. And you might enjoy my showing you a current exhibit at the LA County Museum of Art. It shouldn't be too crowded tomorrow because most people will be doing Black Friday shopping. Bring Ariadne with you. Viewing works of art is supposed to stimulate infants as well as adults."

Black Friday shopping activity had finally risen to levels approaching those of the pre-T-Plague decades, adding to every shopping area's Holiday excitement. Kathi took Zaby to Echo Park in Central LA for its traditional multi-cultural Christmas festival, including lunch at the famous Stories Books and Café.

That left Lisa in sole possession of Alisha and Ariadne, and her prediction proved accurate. Traffic was light, making for easy parking close to the Wilshire Boulevard main entrance. Lecture attendance was lighter than normal, so Alisha sat in the first row, Ariadne on her lap.

The speaker, a late-twenties lady whose tailored dark-grey uniform, accented by a boldly-patterned red Goyard scarf (Alisha knew most famous designers' patterns), complemented the museum's sleek minimalist décor. As she began, the screen behind her displayed a larger-than-life-size image of Edvard Munch's most famous painting, The Scream of Nature, just below the exhibit's title: "The Persistence of Culture in Art." Her articulate voice drew the audience in.

"Good morning, and thank you for coming to our lecture. Many people prefer listening to lectures or viewing art exhibits online, but some are like you, and I applaud your choice, deciding that a museum's ambiance is the best way to experience the essence of art, and why, in its manifest forms, it possesses the power and the beauty to move us.

"So why, you may ask, did I choose this painting to tease your curiosity? Because it captures the sentiments of many people when viewing contemporary art in all genres of painting, literature, music, and film. Why is that iconic face screaming, and at what?

"The original and all copies are displayed in Oslo, Norway, the home city where expressionist and symbolist painter Edvard Munch lived and died. Of all the interpretations, I shall use the face to be humanity screaming at the alienation and anxiety Modernity causes. "My lecture will suggest that in all art forms there runs a common thread tracing what is contemporaneously important to all countries. And the face is also screaming because many people don't understand what the arts today are saying. Some critics accuse contemporary art of obscurantism, which is the practice of deliberately preventing the facts or full details from becoming known so artists and spokespersons can promote a social agenda, and of foisting on the public worthless objects labeled great art.

"I offer no value judgment because art and beauty are intensely personal, so you must decide for yourself. What I have done is assemble into an exhibit a selection of paintings in our collection selected from all genres and periods, matching each with music and literature and Hollywood film agreeing thematically. You'll see how emphasis transitions from the spiritual to the secular, from faith to reason, from optimism to pessimism, and so forth.

"And now, let me briefly summarize the periods and their importance…"

Electra held Ariadne close on the early Saturday morning flight back to Austin, insulated by enough space so her words remained a private conversation.

"Now I understand better why Grandfather was always smiling whenever I was with him. No matter the topic, I never tire talking to you, even when streaming out ideas regarding my R&D. And some of the ideas might stay in your brain. I'll set up your own computer next to mine and show you how to use it so you can practice. And

I'll take you with me when I run. That's definitely good for both of us."

"I hope you liked your first Thanksgiving, which I label my favorite secular movable feast. A movable feast is actually a celebration on the liturgical calendar that changes its date from year to year, but occurs on the same day of the week. The memoir A Movable Feast, written by Ernest Hemingway, was published in 1964 and popularized the use of the expression as an idiom. Please remember that secular refers to items not associated with religion, while liturgical refers to the outline of a public worship services. I'll teach you more words as you begin talking to me." Baby-A giggled as she playfully reached towards her mother.

While keeping Ariadne at her side, Electra split time the following week confirming that all move-to-reservation activities were proceeding as expected and developing additional cloning plans.

"I can clone and raise only one infant at a time because I must devote full attention to your development. I'm going to suspend additional cloning until you're older and I understand better which genes to link for enhancing traits.

"And I have to believe that Quantum Theory explains how the laws of probability affect embryo growth. That part of Quantum Physics is called the Uncertainty Principle. Your siblings died because chance differentiated their DNA from yours. I think your survival and accelerated growth is a metaphoric stroke of lightning. But only time will tell."

Time ticked off the days to Friday, which would hold the duo's last airplane flight of the year to DC, from where Electra would monitor as well as visit the new lab. She spent the weekend settling into what would become extended East Coast visits because she would spend more time in DC or on the reservation and less in Austin. She started calling friends Saturday morning because she planned to visit them while being in her home for the Holidays. Angus, first on her list, ordered she come for brunch Sunday morning. And this time, he would supply the muffins and yogurt.

The second call was equally brief, but this one turned grim as Jennifer's fatigued-filled voice relayed bad news.

"Russell's had a terrible setback. He contracted a MRSA infection during the hip replacement operation. Doctors had to put in a temporary hip impregnated with a long-acting sustained-release antibiotic. I have no time to do anything but care for him, so please don't visit until I see my way clear."

"I'm so sorry. I'll keep out of your way. Please give Russell my love."

Electra placed another call immediately, speaking after Zoe answered on the fourth ring.

"I just found out from Jennifer that Russell has a MRSA infection. Is it as bad as Jennifer sounds?

"Probably worse. According to Matt, he almost died. Even a full week's hospitalization followed by a week of rehab therapy didn't get him up on his feet. I feel sorry for Jennifer. She's running herself ragged."

"Isn't there an obvious solution? She should hire a caregiver to help out while she's working."

"She says she can't afford it because Russell lost so much money. Matt and I don't know how to help her, but something will turn up. As you always say, something always does."

"I'm staying in DC for the Holidays. How about I call you closer to Christmas so you and Matt can pick a time for me to meet Carlton?"

"We'd like that. Please call me when you're ready to pick a day." Electra placed a final call to Robin right after Zoe disconnected. "Sunshine Eldercare. How may I help you?"

"It's Electra. I just spoke with Jennifer Conklin and Zoe. Russell contracted a MRSA infection from his hip replacement operation and almost died. I don't think he's recovered much, so Jennifer told me not to visit until the outlook is clearer. What do you think?" Electra paused for Robin's reply, which came later rather sooner.

"She's probably right. I wouldn't bother them if I were you. We can talk more the next time we're together."

"Uh, OK. And remember, I'm spending the Holidays in DC."

"You already told me that. I'm sure you and Ariadne will enjoy a white Christmas. I gotta go, so take care."

After the call ended, Electra kept talking.

"Baby-A, you are learning a lot by listening to these calls. Lady Fortune sends much our way that we can't control. And always remember the Greek meanings of the term. Fortune can mean chance or luck, or what life sends, regardless of its value or cost."

Ariadne's smile faded until Electra kissed both cheeks after picking her up.

"And you're a wonderful example. You mean more to me than anyone else alive. And tomorrow, you'll get to meet another person who means a lot." Ariadne giggled again.

"Jesus, Electra, come on in. I didn't even know you were pregnant. And now you have a mini-version of yourself. Congratulations." Angus reached for the infant with the strong but gentle arms of an experienced grandfather as he steered Electra towards the kitchen. "What's the name, and how old is this big girl?"

"I adopted Ariadne three months ago. She was three months old then, but she's big for her age because her growth rate is significantly above the norm." Now seated at the kitchen table, Electra put the infant on her lap while Angus sat opposite.

"I like the name. Comes from Greek Mythology, and she looks like she came from you. Whatever, I hope she's smart like you so she can help you help me find a way out of a labyrinth of DC problems." Angus paused to put butter-spread muffins and a Coke in front of Electra, then retrieved a yogurt for himself. Electra spoke after taking a bite.

"You're in a good position to do that, because even though Jared won the election, you can watch him from your senate seat. The public likes both of you, but for different reasons. Your platforms have much in common, but he pushes hard from the right compared to your centrist diplomacy, and he might become more authoritarian because he's in his final term. Do you agree with what he's saying about the CIA's latest international security assessment?"

"I do. We no longer have to fear global T-Plague or Middle East Terrorism, but China and Russia are back in the spotlight. They've been thorns for nearly two centuries in the side of the UN, but each is taking a new approach for upending the world order. China's using A.I. and gene editing to dominate economically and spy everywhere. Russia's adapting hi-tech to weaponry and unmanned vehicles. And both continue attacking in Cyberspace, even though our improved Cybersecurity foils most of their mischief. That's why American exceptionalism needs to lead from the front. The EU is too ideology-bound and Japan too insular while India, Africa, and South America still struggle to join the ranks of first-world nations."

"What do you think next year holds for domestic politics?"

"Jared's got the political and academic progressives on the run because Mainstreet likes Jared's realpolitik toughness, but he needs to steer for a better balance between conservative and progressive liberalism. And he's gotta become less divisive. And I'll say the same for his boy Carter, who must be the brains behind Jared's economic programs. They're mostly about money. Only scraps are thrown at core social programs. But I'll give them credit for reducing deficits and blunting job losses caused by automation and A.I. And they replace inefficient government programs with corporate-led initiatives. But enough talk about macro issues. Tell me how you are..."

Electra departed two hours later, satisfied that Angus had enough political clout to shine a spotlight on Jared if or when he becomes a loose cannon, then devoted the rest of the day to Ariadne and the upcoming reservation trip, the details of which she explained to her constant companion.

"I need to use my Electra persona because lab and reservation projects are serious. And we'll pretend I adopted you so Su and Kameyo don't question me too much about cloning. We'll arrive Tuesday afternoon, meeting first with them so we can see the lab setup and confirm their project priority list. Then we'll do the same with Tim and Kwame. Friday morning, we'll have Doctor Holbrook convince the Tribal Council to take the next step for building more business on the reservation. And we drive home Friday. So, you stay close and learn a lot. And pay attention to how I tell the truth. I never lie, but I sometimes stretch the facts to meet my ends. As long as I stay inbounds and work towards the good, that's what good negotiators are supposed to do. And this will be your first car trip, so I'll give you drive-by descriptions of what we pass through." Baby-A applauded.

Su didn't wait for an introduction to start talking when Electra entered the lab.

"Who is this? I thought you suspended cloning experiments." "This is Ariadne, my adopted daughter, now six months old." Kameyo said, "She's big for her age and looks like you."

"And she's smart too. I decided to adopt so I can practice child-rearing before I do more cloning R&D. Come on, please give me a tour before we talk about the projects."

Su set everyone at a conference table forty-five minutes later, waiting for Electra to convene the meeting.

"I'm impressed. The lab is already operational, and manufacturing will ramp up in January. And please talk with Doctor Holbrook so we can hire from the reservation as many people as possible." Su let Kameyo reply.

"That is our intention. And our project priority list is unchanged from what you gave us. But now that we are in our new lab, we can fill in more details. Su and I have prepared agendas that will take until tomorrow afternoon to cover. May we start now?"

"Please do…"

Electra ended the session ninety minutes later.

"I like what you have, but I will add an additional project. I'm sure you know about ongoing research to find five genes that control intelligence, strength, longevity, personality, and appearance. Great opportunity awaits any society that can edit or repair them if it can avoid ominous eugenic implications. I want you to develop a starting point research plan by searching the literature to find the frontier. And I won't ask you to launch actual research until I can assist, but please map out an initial solution path."

Kameyo nodded slowly.

"You are asking for a map to Genetic Engineering's Holy Grail. I will speak with my network of academic researchers for their suggestions. We might need to collaborate if the scope becomes too big, but I shall do my best."

Electra had only praise for her biotech researchers as she concluded the mid-Thursday afternoon meeting.

"If Tim and Kwame are as thorough as you two, I might leave early. I think I'll check them out now after I get a snack for myself and Ariadne. She needs energy to grow, and I need it to keep up with you. Please keep doing what you're doing."

Kwame pounced on Electra as soon as she entered their lab.

"Your timing is spot on. You can help us finalize plans for attending early February's Las Vegas Cyberspace Expo. Tim and I are cashing in our prize voucher to enter the National Go Speed Team Tournament and you can be the third member." Tim changed topics. "Hey, who's the kid?"

"Ariadne, my adopted daughter. You'll have to teach both of us how to play. When can you do that?" Kwame answered before Tim.

"If we can teach you now, we promise to give you a dynamite presentation tomorrow. Tim will explain the rules as you watch us play a game. And you have until the end of January to practice. Deal?"

"Deal. Su and Kameyo nearly wore me out. I'd rather watch you play than watch you present." Tim seated everyone at a table while Kwame set up the game, then waited for Tim to begin.

"Think of Go as a two-player board game battle played on a square grid made of nine, thirteen, or nineteen parallel lines. Kwame and I practice on a nineteen-square grid because that's what pros use. One player uses white markers called stones; the other black. The goal is for players to surround as much board area as possible with their stones. Each grid intersection enclosed is worth one point. One point is also earned when capturing opponent's stones by immediately surrounding a group of one or more same-colored stones with those of the other color. All captured stones are removed from the board. Got it so far?" Electra signaled yes, so Tim said more.

"The weaker player, using black stones and given seven-and-a-half points immediately, starts the game by placing one stone on any line intersection, including edges and corners. White follows and play alternates. The game ends when all board space is surrounded, or a player resigns, or, if there's a limit, time expires. There's a lot of jargon and agreed-to particulars that are set before the game begins, but focus on the rules I recited, those are the biggies. Now, watch us play." An hour later, Kwame gave his summary.

"You can see why it's the most popular board game in the world. And it's the oldest game still played according to original rules, attracting over a hundred million players worldwide. Major tournament winners become celebrities. And think about this, Go is the simplest and also the most complex game ever invented. The number of potential scenarios is greater than the number of atoms in the known Universe. And even though Go-playing A.I. algorithms usually beat world champions, occasionally one of them wins, giving hope that free will may exist after all. So now that you know all this, won't you join our team?"

"Perhaps, but only if your presentation makes Ariadne smile..."

Next-day's presentation thoroughly covered what Electra wanted so there was nothing left to discuss except a final warning.

"You summarized nicely who's leading what and what we'll do short-term. Tim handles Neuro-Knitter and Cyber-Theater, Kwame does the same for GUI interfaces and network security toolkit, and develop extensions. Your accomplishments put us ahead of the competition. What we now have will attract too much attention if it were ever to leak out, so please be discreet when swapping stories, and that includes before, during, and after the Go tournament. It's OK to be victors of the tournament, but not victims of our excellence, so please be good boys and watch what you say."

Kwame teased by asking, "Ariadne seemed to follow game action yesterday. Why don't you ask her if she's ready to play?"

Holding her with both arms, Electra sat her on the table and then said,

"Baby-A, are you ready to play a game of Go?" Her head nodded vigorously, so doubting Tim asked a follow-up question.

"I don't believe she understands what you're saying. Ask her who she'll play with."

"Fair enough. Baby-A, please tell me who you want to play with." Her eyes darted to those at the table before giggling and waving at Electra. Tim was unconvinced.

"No way. I won't believe any of this until she talks, and that won't happen until she's at least a year old." Kwame poked Tim.

"Hey, give the kid a break. I didn't communicate much until learning Visual Basic computer programming, but I knew more than I let on." Electra decided it was time to adjourn.

"Baby-A, please say something to Tim and Kwame."

She looked at Electra before pointing at Tim and saying in a giggly voice,

"Goo bah, Goo bah."

"I second her emotion. Goodbye."

Electra didn't need to practice for tomorrow's Indian reservation meeting, so she spent the evening helping Ariadne play on the computer.

"You are almost four months old. So much is going on inside your brain, and at least half of what you'll become comes not from genes but from environmental interactions. So just keep thinking and doing and interacting, and talk to me when ready. And I'll keep talking to you."

Dr. Holbrook was ready and waiting at the eye clinic when Electra surprised her.

"You didn't tell me you adopted a little girl. What's her name?" "Ariadne. She's six months old and very well-behaved, so she'll be no bother at the Tribal Council Meeting. Are you set?"

"Yes. I already summarized your idea, and the Council wants to hear you explain more details. So, I'll introduce you and then you carry on. We'll hold the meeting at our recreational center. There'll be the eight-member Tribal Council, our two ambassadors, and one medicine man. Are you going to use slides or videos?"

"I'll speak for about twenty minutes using some PowerPoint slides. Then you can lead the discussion."

"You're well organized. We should get you set up now, so I'll drive..."

Electra had the first slide showing on the screen by the time council members trooped in, accompanied by their invited guests. Dr. Holbrook mingled among them, mentioning the public service advertisement; Electra knew she was facing a friendly audience when she started talking.

"Good morning to members of the Tribal Council and their guests. My name is Electra Kittner, here today to explain business opportunities for your people living on the Reservation. I believe Doctor Holbrook has already explained how I came to know about your proud tribal nation, so I'll simply thank her again for restoring partial sight in my left eye. And I think you have seen me in the public service advertisement, so I won't go over that, but I would like to explain business opportunities that extend its message. And as stated on my first slide, you are working to maintain and expand what the Reservation offers your people."

Business Opportunities for Eastern Pequot Tribal Nation
- A Proud Nation and Rich Heritage
- Working to maintain Cultural Diversity
- Working to expand Reservation Economy
- Electra clicked to the next slide.
- Current Reservation Businesses
- Dr. Holbrook's Native American Eye Clinic

- Foxwoods II Gambling Casino and Resort Complex

- Worldstar Biological R&D Lab and Manufacturing (nearing completion)
- "There were two businesses on the Reservation when I first came here. And after I got to know Doctor Holbrook and the Reservation better, you decided to let me build a lab on the reservation. Now I have two new business opportunities. The next slide describes the first." Electra paused to pique audience interest before continuing.
- Organic Growth Business Opportunities Greenfield Opportunity: Optic Nerve Treatment Center
- Offer Optic Nerve Treatment via Dr. Holbrook
- Use Beyond-State-of-the-Art Medical Device
- Offer Designer Eye Care Products
- Develop Untapped Market
- Expand to other locations
- Employ Reservation people
- Has Zero Cost AND Unlimited Profit Potential

"Organic growth means building on the current business. Greenfield opportunity means a new market unconstrained by current business practices. I won't read the slide to you because Doctor Holbrook will lead a discussion after my presentation explaining all the details, but let me highlight what I consider most important. You'll have an opportunity to offer regenerative optic nerve therapy that can be done nowhere else, and it will cost you nothing because my company will donate the equipment. And because you are a sovereign nation, intrusive U.S. governmental regulations imposed by its bureaucratic agencies, like the FDA and NIH, won't apply. You have a business model that can't be copied. Now let me describe another opportunity."

Second Opportunity Extend Foxwoods II Resort Complex

- Add Cyber-Theater to Sensual Pleasures Café
- Add Seasonal Outdoor Recreation tapping into Indian Heritage
- Add DIY Indian Crafts Center
- Add Indian Performing Arts Center and Gift Shop

"You have a great opportunity to leverage your current Foxwoods II Resort Complex by extending into businesses that are highly differentiated, which means it will be difficult for a competitor to take business away once you build the market. And you can run one advertising and promo campaign to build awareness, interest, desire, and action to a largely untapped market, especially in today's sociopolitical and right-leaning climate that respects diversity and cultural heritage." Electra proceeded immediately to her final slide.

You Make the Call

Next Steps

1. Decide which Opportunities to pursue.
2. Make Dr. Holbrook Project Leader for Optic Nerve Treatment Center.
3. Assign another Project Leader for Foxwoods II Expansion.
4. Hire me to be your Project Consultant.

"I've talked long enough, so I've put on this slide your next steps, which we'll cover after a short break. But let's get item four out of the way right now. You might ask me why don't I donate my consulting services for no charge? Here's the short answer; everyone places a zero value on what's given to them free. So, you should pay something so you'll remember that what you're getting has value. And I'll close using a line immortalized in The Godfather classic film. This is an offer you can't refuse..."

Electra drove home late that afternoon, basking in the setting sun's warm glow now magnified by the Tribal Council's decision. Electra glanced in the rearview mirror.

"I hope you paid attention today, Baby-A, because if you did, you learned a lot about the art of negotiation." Though no words spilled out, Electra saw a happily wriggling child nestled in a safety seat. "Just keep doing what you're doing, and soon you'll tell me all about what's going on in that exceptional brain of yours. And I hope you'll like word games as much as I do. After all, if you'll pardon my pun, I can say you're a chip off my DNA block."

Chapter 18
December 2128

"Arrivals & Departures"
(Thread 1 Chapter 6)

Only two activities remained on the Electra-Alisha calendar for December. Electra would be the omni-parent, leaving for Alisha the social director's role. Alisha reported what to expect.

"I've adjusted our usual Holiday schedule because this will be our first parent-child Christmas. We'll take Ariadne to a Christmas Eve service and have Christmas Day dinner at Zoe and Matt's. And we'll ring in the New Year at home, devoting full attention to our daughter. No matter how much or little Ariadne remembers, early childhood experiences deliver a major developmental impact."

"Yes indeed, and I think she'll remember much because I can tell she's getting smarter each day. Tomorrow I'll take another brain scan to confirm her paranormal intelligence. And I've conducted enough research to begin using my Brain Probe so I can mold Ariadne into what I want her to be." Alisha sounded a cautionary note.

"Please remember to follow the Golden Rule of Parenting: Treat your child as you would like to be treated if you were in the same position. And pay attention to its six corollaries." Alisha recited all of them before saying more:

1. Learn to trust your gut feeling.
2. Don't let children overpower you.
3. Do away with stereotypes.
4. Take a closer look at yourself so you let children become their dreams, not yours.
5. Treat children like grown-ups, being strict when necessary.
6. Teach children to be good human beings.

"I'm sure you understand all this, but please pay special attention to number four. You want Ariadne to become the first member of your dream team, but if her abilities and interests take her in a different direction, you must let her go her own way. Otherwise, you risk frustrating her and disappointing yourself."

"I'd add one more, don't underestimate emotional bonding. The parent-child connection is the strongest humans will ever experience, and it force-multiplies what you just listed. And at the rate she's growing, I'll need to follow all these rules sooner rather than later."

"And you'll need to replace the Baby-A nickname. What do you have in mind?"

"Several. I could use Ari, but that's more for boys. I thought of Aria, but three syllables are one too many, so I'll choose Airee, which is a girl's name for a balanced and harmonious personality." "Excellent choice. Well now, you're on duty until you complete Airee's additional testing. Then I'll take charge of our social calendar. And I guarantee we'll have a jolly time."

Electra arrived at her GWU lab early the next morning, bringing Airee for brain scans that gave promising results. She thought Airee would like to know, so she spoke while holding her close.

"The number and activity of neural control centers continue growing, and I'm going to stimulate two regions of your cerebral cortex – Broca's and Wernicke's areas – that are responsible for speech. Then I'll compare before-and-after neural patterns to determine if that worked. My intention is to have you speaking soon. And then you can tell me if you like your new nickname, which will be Airee. We can go home now and stay there until January because I can give you Brain Probe treatments there. And that's the best place to be, especially for the Holidays."

Robin wouldn't agree that being in Austin for the Holidays this year would be the best place, for she had just reached another epiphany that would take her in new directions. She told no one but mailed instructions to Hud and Hope before loading her van and departing in the middle of the night, setting a course that would eventually take her home again for the very first time. Every mile she drove left doubt further behind, strengthening her resolve and lessening her multi-dimensional mental illness.

As she did last year, Alisha hiked to the same church, but this time carried Airee to an early evening children's Christmas Eve service. Milder temperatures and snow decorating only the grass made the walk pleasant for commenting on outdoor displays that Airee might find particularly interesting.

The Christmas Pageant captivated mother and daughter alike, but for different reasons. For Airee, it was building memories that would be with her forever; for Alisha, it was bringing back memories of her grandfather's loving, omni-parental role and showcasing the breadth and depth of parental love.

Now I feel all the emotion that powers parents to sacrifice for their children. I'll have to ask Zoe and Matt tomorrow if caring for Carlton affects them the same way.

Zoe answered when Alisha arrived promptly at four; Matt stood at her side beaming proudly, holding his son as Zoe did all the talking. "Where did you find that lovely baby? Come in and tell us after we introduce both of you to our Carlton."

Parents chatted happily while newborns crawled together. Both seemed healthy and happy, but as Alisha had expected, Airee was bigger, stronger, and more active, so she stretched the truth about Airee's birth date. After dinner, the children rested together while Zoe described her joys of parenting.

"Matt and I read lots of books on parenting, but the best advice I found said we should treat each kid as one-of-a-kind. And I'm so fortunate that Matt knows how to share the load."

Matt said, "I hear him calling. I'll be right back." Alisha asked as soon as he was gone.

"Has becoming a mother affected the way you deal with emotions?"

"It's made Carlton my number one priority. Sometimes, I have to remind myself to make enough room for Matt, but he understands. We couldn't be happier."

Twenty-four hours earlier, Jennifer would not have agreed. She was home alone taking care of Russell's declining health, but in spite of her best efforts to lift his sagging spirits, he saw only darkness ahead, complaining bitterly.

"My life started falling apart when Christi died. She should be here now and take care of me. She was a good daughter. And she always knew –" Jennifer's frustration boiled over as she interrupted.

"Our daughter was headstrong and self-centered, and if it weren't for Electra and Robin she would have gotten into more trouble. You don't remember how she hated school, how she dreamed of becoming a rock star. You should have been a better father, being here more and showing more interest in your family. But no, you devoted yourself to a botched career. You let her chase a dream her talent would never let her reach. I'm the one who kept the family together. Stop quivering your lips." Tears running down both cheeks accompanied Russell's halting words.

"I, uh, I'm sorry. You make me feel so bad." He could say no more; he put his head down and wept as Jennifer hugged his head to her breast.

"I'm sorry too. I don't mean what I said. You were a wonderful father. I'll try to—" An insistent doorbell interrupted.

"Who could be coming here on Christmas Eve? Well, whoever it is, let's greet them at the door and wear smiley faces." Jennifer wheeled Russell into the entryway before peeking through the viewer. "Oh my God," is all she said before flinging open the door.

At first Russell didn't recognize the young woman standing before them, two dogs sitting alertly on either side. But as she spoke, her voice brought back a cascade of memories.

"It's me, Robin. I've come home to take care Mr. Conklin." Then she stepped into the hallway. Jennifer hugged Robin while the big pups greeted Russell. There were no words from Jennifer, but she would have much to say on Christmas day.

Alisha had just recited a Tiny Tim line from Dickens A Christmas Carol when her cell phone chimed. It was Jennifer, inviting her to come over New Year's Eve so she and the Fortiers could help Russell welcome in the New Year. Alisha accepted, then explained to Airee after the call.

"I've told you about our good friends, Jennifer and Russell Conklin. Well, Jennifer's invited us and the Fortiers for a New Year's Eve get-together. She's even arranged for Matt to drive all of us. She sounds much happier, and she says she has a surprise for us. We like good surprises, don't we? I'm sure Jennifer will have something good. Now, let me continue our reading."

Robin played New Year's Eve hostess, escorting a speechless group of guests into the Conklin's family room for Jennifer to hug each as Russell greeted everyone using the right name. Although Robin was in charge, it was Jennifer's place to explain a fortunate turn of events; Robin served champagne as Jennifer announced a change for the better.

"Robin's come home to be Russell's caregiver. And we'll add caregiver services to the business. Robin, please tell which ones you'll handle."

"I'm sure clever Electra already knows it will include eldercare using my therapy dogs. We'll also include childcare, but with all these changes, we need to rename the business. Clever Electra is good with words, so let's have her come up with a new one." Electra spoke to herself first.

Robin's patronizing me, but I understand why. She's finally broken away, knows what she wants, and wants everyone to know. I'm happy for her. Living with the Conklins and working with Matt and Zoe will give her the stability she needs.

"That's a great way to reposition the business. Why not choose CFS Holistic Unicare. Uni suggests united or a unity, which is the essence of anything holistic, and last name initials are a prefix. And on Website or letterhead, explain it's an acronym for Capitol Finest Services." Matt seconded the recommendation, leading to a unanimous decision pending further review.

Parents roused infants to watch their first ball drop; laughter and singing added to the cheer. Alisha held Airee close so only she could hear.

"Well, my little darling, all of us are set for new directions in the New Year. What would you like to say about that? Ariadne's tiny voice spoke what Alisha would always remember.

"Goo bess Momma."

Only Airee saw Alisha brush away a single tear from her right eye before kissing her.

"It's time Matt take us home so you can rest because we have lots to talk about tomorrow and all the days after that, as long as we're together."

Chapter 19
February 2129

"Skirmishing with the Enemy"
(Thread 3 Chapter 5)

Electra borrowed a page from the child development book her grandfather had used during her early years. Doc Kittner tested her physical and mental development at least monthly because the lightning bolt that had struck at birth made her exceptional, but in ways he didn't know until their presence emerged via neural patterns. Electra expected the same for Ariadne because of the alterations she had made to her DNA, changes she hoped would improve the rate and results of physical and neural development.

During two January visits to the reservation lab, Electra had completed a battery of tests, concluding positive results for Ariadne's accelerating growth rates. She detected no physiological abnormalities, and as hoped for, data analysis from scanning and Brain Probe testing showed more centers of neural activity, placing her daughter over four standard deviations above the norm. But it didn't come close to Electra's extraordinary brain. On the drive back to DC, she summarized to herself what the findings meant.

Airee's plenty smart. And if her personality blossoms like I hope, I can mold her into the charter member of my dream team. She's the first of my clones to survive. I must do all I can to ensure she thrives.

Alisha decided to point out some additional observations to her alter ego.

"Relocating to the Pequot reservation was the right move. We can get to and from faster, and we avoid the hassles of flying. And if I may, please let me congratulate your bio-tech accomplishments since the move.

"You've helped Su and Kameyo reformulate the pill that treats your T-Plague STD, and you've explained how they can improve existing T-Plague vaccines. They can use those very same solution path modifications for their Alzheimer's vaccine. And meeting face-to-face with Tim and Kwame lets you explain faster and delegate more." "Right you are for both hardware and software. They'll take my Big Data Analysis app to the next level, which is already several steps ahead of what the best counterintelligence snoopers can do. Only I can compute multi-level probabilistic correlations between seemingly random events and causes by running my app on each event separately or together, like statisticians do when running analysis of variance tests. And the guys will release my next-generation Network Security Suite and its array of offensive weapons as soon as I give them my latest module updates."

"What about the Brain Probe?"

"Just like cloning and DNA editing, I keep the best pieces for myself, but I can give Tim a wearable cap and embeddable chips he can install in a Cyber-Theater line extension."

"While you've been doing all this, have you realized that becoming a parent has further softened your hard edges. You're so patient with Ariadne. I'm pleased that as you help her grow, she's helping you."

"That's why I keep her by my side. And I'm taking her when we leave this coming Monday, the thirteenth, for the Las Vegas Cyberspace Expo. We have three days to prepare and pack.

"I hope our luck is better than the departure date. Tell me, what are we doing there?"

"I'll attend seminars that discuss the latest A.I. impact on employment and platform company tactics. And I'll be on Tim and Kwame's Speed Go Tournament team. And while I'm doing that, you can think about your next Hollywood shoot and what our close friends are up to. What do you say to all that?"

"I'll use some of your commando lingo, Roger that."

An unexpected call interrupted Ariadne and Electra's Saturday evening play session. Tim's agitated voice came crackling through. "The Speed Go Tournament rules have just changed. Teams can use any standalone Go apps they've written as long as they fit on a handheld device, but Internet connections must be disabled. Have you written any?"

"You fellows are the Go-pros, not me. We'll have to use whatever you have."

"That's bad news. Ours are pretty basic. How good are your Go-playing skills? Have you been practicing?"

"I've had better things to do, but I'll do you a favor. Airee and I will play between now and the start of the tournament."

"Who's Airee? Oh, I remember. That's your daughter. How's teaching her gonna help?"

"By now, you should know the answer. The best way to learn any subject is by teaching it to others. If you've been paying attention, that's what I've been doing for you and Kwame, and also for Su and Kameyo."

"OK, but the tournament starts Friday. Do you want me to send you a copy of my app?"

"No. I guess you've forgotten Euclid's famous quote when the ruler Ptolemy asked for a shortcut to learning geometry: 'There is no royal road to geometry.' So, I'll have to break an intellectual sweat sans app."

"Huh? I don't understand what you just said. You're—" Electra interrupted.

"Yes, I'm playing with you, like I always do when I can find a clever way to make a point. You've got until Friday to figure out what I just said."

"OK. Good luck to both of us. See you in Vegas."

Electra let Tim and Kwame walk the exhibits on Tuesday and mingle with attendees while she simply meandered while toting Ariadne. She stopped for snacks – Coca Cola and Oreos for herself, cooked fruits for Airee.

"I'm so proud of you. You are talking better and better. And soon you'll be walking, because you're getting so big and so strong."

"Yes, Momma. I good girl, just like you." Electra gave her a hug before trekking on.

Electra's Wednesday seminar covered current A.I. research and its impact on the job market. Because speakers and audience came from hi-tech, most attendees nodded knowingly at the optimistic picture being painted.

Electra sat in the back, taking mental notes as the facilitator marched through four introductory slides that would segue to comments from a panel of experts:

> A.I. Reality Today Bringing You A Better Future
> • Consider A.I. the Industrial Revolution on Steroids
> • Every new technology is a Short-Term Disruption and a Longer-

Term Deliverance
- Short-Term Job "Right-Sizing" leads to unparalleled Longer-Term Job Growth
- Booming Economy promotes stability at Home and Abroad
- Listen to Hi-Tech Experts, not the Know-Nothing Critics A Sampling of Benefits
- More Meaningful and Economically Rewarding Careers
- A.I. Robotics handle Mundane/Dangerous Jobs (Examples: Trash Removal Factory Work Toxic Spill Cleanup...)
- Cheaper ProductsSustainable Economy Environmental Protection
- More Virtual Reality Entertainment Choices
- Robo-Assistants for Education and Elderly
- Embedded Chips to monitor/assist People

Why It's Working Now
- Of the three factors needed (Computational Power Data Intelligence) A.I. Algorithms didn't have a critical level of Intelligence. But that's no longer the case.
- Deep Learning led to Deep Facing and Deep Voicing
- A.I. Software now codes its own Updates
- Linguistic Programming Apps interpret and reply to Users
- Image Recognition and Prediction apps are better than what humans can do
- Affective Programming simulates Human Emotion
- We're on the way to General A.I. and Beyond!

What to Expect Soon
- Non-Human Intelligence exceeds Human Intelligence
- Trans-Humanism improvements
- Nano-computer Chips "Everywhere"
- Fully A.I.-Mechanized Future

"IT'LL BE THE BEST OF ALL POSSIBLE WORLDS!"

Electra listened carefully during the subsequent Q&A session, deciding to withhold comments. She spent the rest of the day attending to Ariadne while practicing the game of Go.

Thursday's Platform seminar followed a similar format, but this time the facilitator needed only one slide before his panelists took over:

Platform Markets and Companies Where It's At and Where It's Going.

Platform Definitions:
- Platform refers to Cyberspace-based markets and companies that reduce transaction costs and empower networking.

Why Platform Companies do "Good":
- Facilitate Big Data generation
- Empower Social Media
- Spread democracy to the People
- Spread the "Truth"
- Eliminate control by an "Elite"
- Convert the separation of Buyers and Sellers into Producer-Consumer
- Empower each person to become an "Entrepreneur" How they do It:
- Become a "Virtual Company" by harnessing A.I. and the Internet
- Monetize data collection to create jobs and data
- Transform the Market Economy into a Sharing/Caring Collaborative Economy
- Promote Surveillance Capitalism What they do:
- Package data and create tools to turn data into information, projections, and recommendations
- Self-regulate via approved "Social Purposing Agencies"

This time, Electra jotted down her combined takeaway from both seminars.

Litany of Risks
1. Humans not smart enough to reach "The Singularity."
2. Hi-Tech rushing in where it hasn't "earned the right."
3. Public fears what Hi-Tech is featuring.
4. Job replacement only for those "smart or interested enough."
5. No Moral Compass.
6. Human Dignity Devaluation.
7. Virtual Reality Addiction.
8. Fake News indistinguishable from Truth.

9. Power concentrated in "The Few."

10. Prediction morphs into "Mind Control."

11. Expanding Government-A.I. Platform Complex.

At the very bottom she underlined a one-line summary: "The whole is more ominous than the sum of its parts." Then she tucked Ariadne into the baby carrier and left before the exit clogged, speaking only to herself as she left the convention center.

The arrogance on display is frightening. These people are too smug. I better find a way to follow their intentions, but that's for another day. Today, Airee and I will finish our Go training.

Tim led his team to its assigned table, then summarized tournament rules.

"This is a single-elimination tournament for teams of three. We can use our Go Game hand calculator if we want to because the judges approved our app. If we don't lose, we'll play three one-hour matches this morning, and three this afternoon, whittling the number of survivors to sixteen. Each team must play an average of at least six stones per minute. Otherwise, both teams are eliminated." Kwame explained what would happen on Saturday. "Tomorrow gets real interesting and draws a big crowd. The morning competition will hold two 90-minute rounds that'll take the field down to the final four. And there'll be two two-hour rounds in the afternoon that will decide first, second, and third-place winners. Any questions?"

Electra asked the obvious. "Who judges?"

"Each team polices the other, and they can report any infraction to any official contest judge patrolling the room. I hope you've learned enough to help. And you can't sit and think too long. We gotta move quick."

Tim and Kwame played fast and furiously from the get-go, rarely using the calculator while talking, Tim placing stones. Electra watched intently, talking only to Ariadne as the team won the morning rounds. Tim returned to the table carrying three box lunches.

"Sorry, Electra. You'll have to share yours with Ariadne." Kwame smiled as he needled her good-naturedly.

"We didn't hear a peep from you this morning. You must be saving yourself for the afternoon rounds. The competition's gonna get tougher, so speak up if you can help." Electra smiled, letting Ariadne talk first.

"Momma knows. Momma go."

"From what I've read about elite Go players, they can see the board position in their heads and intuitively pattern-match game position to the stone they'll play. I hope to give moves to you this afternoon."

Electra's brain came alive midway through the second game as she talked to Ariadne while telling Tim where to place stones. His team handily won, and Electra's pace accelerated during the third match. But as time wound down, one of the opponents suddenly got up and left, returning a minute later with a judge who, pointing to Tim, stopped the game.

"You've violated the rules. Your team is disqualified."

"What do you mean? We're not even using our Go Game calculator, and we're playing way more than six stones a minute."

"You have four persons on your team. The child counts."

"What do you mean? She can't even walk or talk much, let alone think. You think she understands Go?"

The judge blustered, "Rules are rules, and I'm surprised that any team you defeated earlier didn't protest. Was the child present this morning?" Tim was about to yell, but Electra cut him off.

"Tim, shut up. The judge is right. I should have known better. I apologize to all." The judge softened his tone.

"You're the first person I've ever seen playing a tournament while holding a toddler. We do hold age-group tournaments. If your child can learn to play, why not enter one of them?" Electra nodded but said nothing else.

Electra treated her crestfallen teammates to dinner that night, trying to buck up spirits by quoting from the famous Doctor Pangloss.

"Look at the outcome this way. All has turned out for the best because you had fun playing, I honed my Go skills, and we didn't attract a lot of attention by getting to the next round. And I'll give each of you one thousand dollars you can use for gambling tomorrow." Tim looked at Kwame before replying.

"That's not a bad consolation prize. What are you gonna do?"

"I'll take Ariadne on a helicopter tour of the Grand Canyon. She's old enough to enjoy a four-hour tour. And if she needs more excitement when we get back, we'll challenge you to a game of Go.

And she'll throw stones at you if you start cheating."

Though Carter currently understood only slightly more about the economics of Cyberspace than he did about Go tournaments, his purposeful stride towards his morning meeting with President Gardner matched his confidence because he knew he was smarter than all others in Jared's close circle of advisors. The President didn't like to read, preferring instead to have those he trusted explain recommended programs, and that weakness played into Carter's strength. He had already outlined an approach that would be a win for himself as well as for the President, and he believed that Jared's instincts would seize the opportunities. Jared rose to greet him when he entered the Oval Office, setting him on a chair next to the sofa Jared reserved for himself.

"Carter, my boy, help yourself to whatever you want to snack on. The programs you're putting together meet my expectations, so keep doing what you're doing. And while you're munching, I'll explain further. Pour me some coffee and get me a donut while you do the same." Jared continued a couple of minutes later.

"I don't know about Cyberspace, but my instincts tell me there's money to be made. What ideas do you have?"

"I see two possibilities. One dives into the Deep-Dark Web, finding legitimate companies that collude with criminals. I can't get there, but if you can put me in touch with a CIA Web snooper, I can piece something together that skirts most ethical issues and stays in bounds according to our rules. And the other leverages all the top security data the Government has. Surveillance Capital companies would kill to get it. Let me explain…"

Darla knew more about Cyberspace than Carter ever would, and she knew targets to contact for accelerating her plans, but she didn't want to reach out directly until she had vetted them.

The name Tim Godfrey popped up once again on her radar after a thirty-second news flash mentioned his team's Go contest disqualification. He had been her primary target several years ago when attempting to pirate network security software, but when her agents never reported back, she picked softer targets.

When she heard about Tim's bad luck at the Go Tournament, she snooped on the Web to find his current whereabouts but came up empty. That puzzled her, so she added his name – and his partner

Kwame Chyral – to a hit list she would pursue at a later date.

Maksim Popovitch posed a different challenge. She knew the general outline of his activities and liked the damage being done to competitors' rare earths mines or to gold reserves held at European Central Bank locations. She also surmised that seemingly random attacks worldwide on countries' infrastructures were signs of S-Cube terrorism. But her T-Cube Triumvirate saw Maksim only once a year and that made her angry. Darla always wanted to be in control, but S-Cube was beyond her reach. She would have to find a way to reel him in before he stepped too far out of bounds.

Hans Klammer never worried about reeling anything in or out unless ordered to do so; only then would he apprehend offenders, using the speed and efficiency Germans are noted for. Because he had followed orders for his entire twenty-year career serving Germany's Strategic Surveillance Command (KSA: Kommando Strategische Aufklärung), he considered his current sinecure assignment – Chief Guard at the Schacht Konrad underground toxic waste storage site near Salzgitter (a hundred thousand population hinterlands town 250 kilometers west of Berlin) – a reward for faithful service. No one ever visited the securely sealed barrels that never budged an inch. The hardest part of his twelve-hour shift was picking two of his guards twice a day to hike two hundred meters from the guard building to the mine entrance, make a cursory inspection of inventory, and then return. He and his three guards spent the rest of the day talking politics or watching whatever interested them on media or Internet. And they played two news-related games daily. Whoever made the wittiest remark about morning reports covering Washington or afternoon reports covering the European Union would win a beer when the four stopped nightly at a local hofbrauhaus.

Hans had sent Gerhardt and Fritz on a late afternoon patrol ten minutes ago when Helmut complained about the broadcast reception. "Was ist los mit da electric juice? We got no more lights or sound." Hans frowned while using his two-way radio, but that didn't work either. He was about to curse when suddenly two unmarked military choppers swooped low, disgorging rope-sliding teams of unrecognizable commandos. One rushed to the mine entrance; the other dashed to the guard center. The spectacle froze Hans and Helmut: exotic exoskeleton-clad soldiers running as fast as sprinters, carrying weapons and munitions whose intentions were obviously lethal. The guards were overpowered before they could reach for weapons. The commando leader at the guard house asked his prisoners one question only.

"How many?" Unable to speak, Hans held up four fingers. The leader radioed the other team.

"Got two here. Find two more and bring them to the guard building after wiring explosives. Over."

"Roger that, over," crackled the reply. Twenty minutes later, two teams merged into one as it bound the guards and finished wiring explosives. The commando leader motioned all men back to the choppers, speaking briefly to his prisoners.

"Comrades, battle cannot be left to politicians. It is for us, the warriors, to decide. I salute your devotion to your generals, but they are on the wrong side. And so are you. But do not worry. You shall die instantly in the fires and be buried in the debris. Auf wiedersehn."

Ten minutes later, Maksim kept his promise as two thermobaric fireballs blasted toxic waste and rubble skyward, lighting a dusk-filled sky and mimicking awesome mushroom clouds. Maksim gloated as he spoke via radio to his teams.

"Well done, S-Cube Warriors. When returning to base, we shall enjoy watching the videos our choppers recorded. And then, we shall listen to broadcasts from our clueless adversaries who can't explain what blasted holes in their bold ambitions. And they never will."

Chapter 20
May 2129

"Tending the Garden
(Thread 2 Chapter 9)

Alisha had answered a Friday evening call because she was expecting one from Hollywood, but instead it came from Angus. She disconnected after a brief chat, then talked to Electra.

"Why is Angus so worried? Should you prepare an agenda like you usually do?"

"He didn't say too much, but he will when I meet with him. And no, I won't prepare an agenda because I'm losing interest in what I know he'll cover. Frankly, I prefer tending our three-flower garden than chasing after what no longer matters much to us. We have Ariadne, R&D, and Hollywood to keep us occupied."

"You've become a remarkable parent. I imagine her latest test results confirm you have a green thumb for taking care of her." "She's smart, growing fast, and has a lovely little disposition to match. And not that it matters too much, but she's cuter than most kids her age."

"Now you sound like a typical mom. All parents say their kids are better. And grandparents exaggerate even more."

"I'm not exaggerating, soon she'll be mature enough to need less supervision, and then I can grow another set of clones. But I've gotta be careful. I've detected minor abnormalities in several physiological parameters that I'll have to track closely. I might need to change my cloning protocols."

"Have you been tracking how I'm doing in Hollywood?"

"It's all good, but I've noticed that your vanity sometimes shows. If it weren't for your acting career, you wouldn't train so hard to stay fit." Alisha giggled before replying.

"That's my job, to keep us looking good. Just like yours is to keep our brain in tip-top shape. And I'm sure it's ready for breakfast with Angus."

"Here's another job you're doing well, teaching me about networking. You're particularly skilled navigating the human network, which helps us greatly in politics. And today's Cybernetworks have changed the equations for power distribution among institutions and nations. Someday, when I have the time to research further, I'll connect the two networks in one of my white papers."

"I like our division of labor. You can think and I can do. Just heed my warning, don't think for too long without coming up for air."

Airee liked riding in the passenger seat rather than in a baby carrier. Electra liked that for Airee too, because she could treat her like the mini-adult she was quickly becoming.

"You met Angus once before. Do you remember him?" "Yes, Momma. He like nice big bear."

"Yes, he is. You have a wonderful memory; I'm so proud of you. He'll be pleased you remember him. And do you remember the game we are playing? We never tell anyone you are my special daughter. Instead, we say you are adopted if they ask. And we don't want to show anyone how smart you are just yet, so let me do all the talking."

"Yes, Momma. I like play games with you."

"Me too, you too. And today will be our first visit where you can walk next to me. Just make sure you hold my hand and don't let go." "I will, Momma. I walk fast. I think fast. Just like you." Electra was almost sorry they had arrived because talking with Airee was fast becoming the joy of her life.

Angus opened the door as soon as they approached, booming out in his baritone voice while lifting Airee.

"Why hello, Airee. Do you remember me?" "Yes. You Big Bear."

"Why, that's the best name I've ever been called. Let's go to the kitchen and see what Big Bear has for you to eat…"

Angus had as much fun at breakfast as Airee, and when finished, Electra gave her a computer tablet to play with while she and Angus got down to business.

"Now I understand why you haven't done as much policy analysis for me as you used to. Your daughter is much more fun for you to think about. But I've got a list of problems I'd like you to look at. I've divided them into three groups. By the way, I've euphemistically labeled them challenges, like you always do. Take a look at what I've got." Electra studied his handwritten one-pager for several minutes before replying.

Challenges
International Issues:
- European Union Relationship
- Changing World Order
- Rogue Terrorism (?)
- Emerging Rare Earths Cartel (?) Domestic Issues:
- Political Polarization
- Public's "Harsh Measures" Mentality
- Public's fear of Hi-Tech Future Economic Issues:
- Strong but Polarized Economy
- Disappearing Jobs
- Concentration of Power

"I'm sure you realize Jared didn't cause them. Like you, he's trying to find a political solution. And you can't solve them simultaneously. Pick one from each category."

"Which ones?"

"I'll pick three I thought about before Airee came into my life. Focus on European relationships, domestic polarization, and job loss. They make a nice package and have short-term solutions."

"I can buy that, but how should I look at the European Union? Got any ideas?"

"You need to read Fukuyama's books. I told you about them years ago. Did you read them?"

"If I did, I don't remember. Maybe you can write up one of your patented white papers."

"No, but I'll give you a crash course right now if you'll give me a pen and pad of paper." Angus was happy to oblige. He entertained Airee while Electra scribbled; ten minutes later, Electra gave him her first diagram.

Emerging World Order (European Union Perspective)

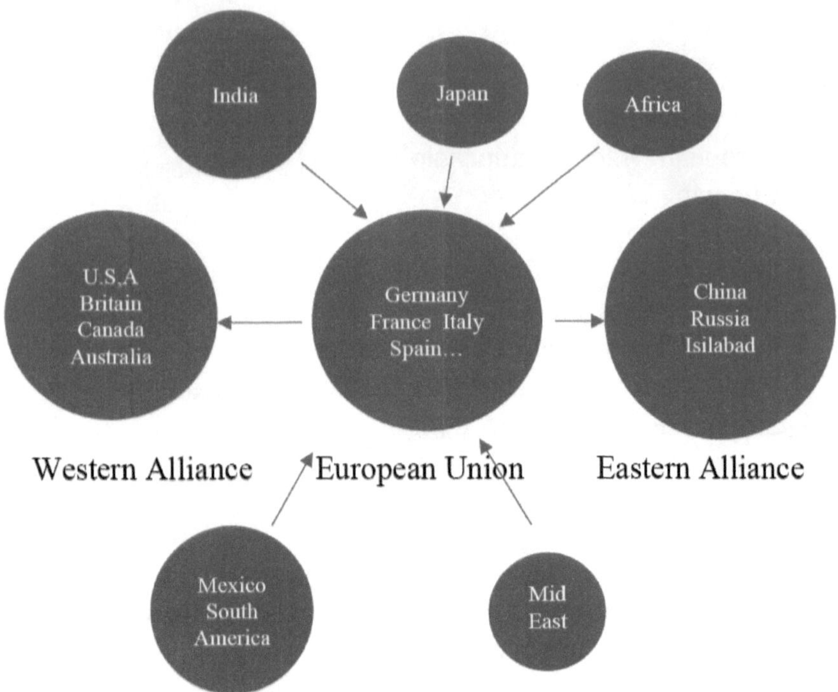

"Start with the World Order from the EU's point of view. Different-sized circles represent the labeled nations. Arrows pointing toward the EU indicate those countries the EU wants to draw into their sphere of influence. Those pointing out are those that want to draw the EU into theirs. How I've grouped nations should be obvious." OK so far?" Angus nodded.

"Good. Now, pay close attention to the next." Electra slid the next diagram in front of her diligent pupil.

Western Europe's Historical Trajectory
Greece
Rome
Christianity/Catholic Church
Constantine
Alaric
Justinian
Clovis

Charlemagne

Spanish Kings   French Kings   German Kings   British Kings

Aristocracy   Church   Peasants

Norman Conquest
Magna Carta
Renaissance

Martin Luther Reformation/Restoration
Peace of Westphalia

Enlightenment

American Revolution

French Revolution
Napoleon

Revolution of 1848
Bismarck
Marx/Lenin
Socialism   Democracy   Totalitarianism

Russian Revolution
Stalin/Hitler/Mussolini/Mao
20th Century World Wars
Cold War
United Nations
China Great Leap Forward
Post-Modern Peace / Soviet Union Collapse
Democracy   Paternalistic Socialism   Authoritarian/Directed Capitalism
European Union
End of Middle East Terrorism   End of N. Korea
Rise of Generic Terrorism

"You need to understand Western Europe's historical trajectory if you want to know the why and what and how. If you don't remember some of the names or events, your homework is to find out. And don't put too fine a point on the people I've picked. You can let academic historians parse my framework further, but it won't improve your understanding. Do you see the trend?" Angus nodded grudgingly.

"I think I do. It explains how the EU grew from Europe's feudal system roots."

"And that takes us to my final diagram. Here's my list of European Union puzzles that you, as our leading statesman-senator, have to get Washington to negotiate. I shouldn't have to explain them to you."

America-EU Conundrum (Solution is Work-In-Progress)
- American Exceptionalism vs America #1
- American Insensitivity to European Ideology and Roots
- Cultural Sensitivity
- Belief in the Enlightenment
- Strategic Autonomy
- Different Economic Intentions / Work Ethic
- Free Trade vs Fair Trade
- Nationalism vs International/Liberal Community
- Environmental/Climate/Hi-Tech Concerns
- Ideological vs Pragmatic Politics

Angus nodded; Electra wrapped up the discussion.

"I think you know all the pieces I've put together, but seeing them laid out like I've done should give a clearer picture."

"I guess so, but I'll have to go over it again. Then I'll show it to my people. And if I give you credit for all this, will you come back?"

"Not at this time. Keep your people at attention by telling them all this is yours."

"All right, but please, let's keep in touch." As Electra stood to collect her tablet and daughter, Angus asked his final questions.

"There are two challenges on my list that puzzle me. Are you aware of any rumors about random rogue terrorism or an emerging rare earths cartel?"

"I haven't been looking for them, but I should think the CIA and its related snooping agencies could find them for you."

"Well if you start looking, please let me know what you find. You used to be my go-to person for finding stuff. And if Airee keeps growing as fast as she is, you can recruit her to help."

Electra enjoyed the drive home even more than the drive to. "Did you like visiting Big Bear?"

"Yes, Momma, but I call him Angus next time. I be like you."

"Very good. You're talking like a little grownup. I bet you like the alphabet game videos we play."

"I do, Momma, but go make bigger words. And bigger numbers too."

"After your nap, how about we play some number games?"

"I like. And show wideo of little kids. Two kinds. One like me, one like Carlton."

"Please pronounce v like a 'v,' not a 'w.' I'll show you a 'VIDEO' of little children playing. That reminds me. You can play with him soon."

"OK Momma, but he not smart like me."

"Ariadne, you're the smartest little girl I know, but never brag and always be kind to others. I'm thankful you're so special, and you should be too."

"I am, Momma." Electra continued talking as she pulled into the garage.

"Here we are, home safe and sound. And my top job is keeping you that way."

"Yes, Momma. Me too you too." Electra pulled Airee close before lifting her out.

All the remaining days of May merged seamlessly as Electra tutored her gifted daughter. Airee's reading ability grew in tandem with her Internet viewing, allowing mother and daughter to work side-by-side. When told about the upcoming Memorial Day weekend adventure to Six Flags America, Airee promptly asked to view its Website; Electra taught her more about the basics of search commands while finding it.

"Momma, please me let ride rollercoaster. I want go fast. Tram too. It go over Hurricane Harbor. I like splash."

"That will take a lot of energy, so let's make sure all of us get a good night's sleep. All adults too, because we have to keep up with you. And do you remember who's taking us?"

"Yes. Doggy Lady. I like her. She got strong hands. Make tunes." "You can call her that, but please remember that adults call her Robin. She'll come get us after picking up Carlton and Zoe. And she's bringing another special person. Do you remember Russell Conklin? You met him once, and you'll have a jolly time playing with him too. And remember, our friends will be playing my Alisha game. That's what they call me when I want to have fun. But you just call me Momma and I'll always come running."

Robin loaded Russell first, securely belting him into the passenger seat before folding his wheelchair, placing it next to a baby stroller before saying goodbye to Jennifer and Matt while Zoe and Carlton claimed the van's second row. Zoe twittered happily.

"Thank you for being our designated driver. After you pick up Alisha and Airee, we're on our way." Robin nodded, waiting for Matt to speak for those who would stay behind.

"Jenn and I will work out next week's schedule while all of you are having fun. And we're in luck. The weather's perfect for a theme park outing. It's bound to be crowded, but that adds to the Memorial weekend excitement. And the park is only twenty miles east of DC, so it'll be an easy drive. Drive safe."

Matt's predictions proved correct, as did the division of labor. Robin and Alisha took turns pushing Russell's wheelchair. Zoe handled Carlton's stroller while holding Airee's hand as she and the toddlers talked. Zoe was fully engaged, so Alisha chatted with Robin while Russell tried his best to understand.

"If Matt and Jennifer have to work Sundays to plan next week's schedule, I guess that means CFS Holistic Unicare is doing well." Robin merely nodded, expecting Alisha to ask away. "Do you plan to add another caregiver dog?"

"We don't need to. I bring Russell to help on all my calls, and that helps him too. Doesn't he look better?"

"I'd say he's holding his own, but that's a victory for him. And you deserve all the credit." Though she said nothing, this time Robin smiled.

Two hours and four rides later, Robin declared a timeout for snacks after parking Russell's wheelchair at a shady table. Zoe unpacked cooked fruit for the children while Robin tended to Russell and Alisha came back with food and drink for the adults. Everyone listened politely to Russell's confusing words, but there was no mistaking the love in his eyes when Robin helped him unwrap his sandwich. There was a pleasant pause as the group ate, punctuated only by Alisha's announcing the afternoon itinerary.

"Zoe and I will trade places. I'll take Airee and Carlton on the Great Chase kids' rollercoaster, and after that we can walk to Hurricane Harbor so I can take them on the aerial tram ride. And after that, I think we should head for home." Zoe agreed.

"That's just the right amount of play for one day. And why don't we bring pizza home for dinner. We can reward Matt and Jennifer for all the work they're getting done. I hope they're not overdoing it." Jennifer languidly kissed Matt a second time before unfolding their intertwined limbs.

"Come join me in the shower so we can wash each other's back. Matt propped himself on one elbow before answering.

"I love your touch. And as you keep telling me, no one will ever know or get hurt if we keep watching each other's back. But please keep reminding me so I don't feel so guilty." Jennifer stroked his cheek slowly.

"There's no reason to feel guilty. You give Zoe everything she wants, a wonderful father for her son, a secure home life, and a job she likes. And you give me what I need, someone I like who helps me scratch my sexual itch. And that's what I give you. And forget about Russell. The man I married is no more, and Robin likes taking care of its replacement. Everyone wins, so don't go on any more guilt trips."

"You always know what to say to fix up my feelings. I hope I do the same for you."

"You do, and I'll fix lunch after we shower. Then we can get enough work done to impress our Six Flags adventurers."

The aerial tram ride, scheduled to last twenty minutes, looked even more impressive up-close than in its video. Open cars hung a hundred feet high, suspended by a hook from the ride's motorized cable, allowing the car to swing as it traveled a route that made several 180-degree turns. Robin and Russell waved goodbye as Zoe took pictures of Alisha buckling the kids into their seats. Then the three observers sat at a nearby bench, waiting for the riders to return. Zoe asked Russell if he remembered taking kids to amusement parks when he was an active father. He looked at Robin before stuttering a reply.

"Tuh-tell her about thuh, uh… "Three Queens." Robin dutifully described enough to keep Russell happy. Zoe was about to add more to the story but a sudden park disturbance erupted. People started running pell-mell, accompanied by screams and the sounds of rides crashing. Zoe stared mutely at the aerial tram cable that was now speeding cars dangerously. She was about to scream, but Robin yelled first.

"Stay with Russell, I'll find Electra and the kids."

Electra came to the fore as soon as she felt a sudden jolt caused by the car's acceleration. Airee and Carlton shouted gleefully because they thought it was part of the ride, but Electra knew otherwise. From her lofty perch, she saw a rollercoaster plunge off its tracks and gondolas of a Ferris wheel sway precariously. She spotted danger ahead as her car raced towards a 180-degree turn. She said nothing, simply hugging onto Airee and Carlton like a rock climber scaling Yosemite's el Capitan; centrifugal force hurled them outward and upward, and then gravity took over, arcing them on a downward trajectory when the hook connector broke. The tumbling car splashed into the murky water upside-down, sinking immediately.

Opening only her goggled eye, Electra could barely see shadowy outlines. She groped to free herself, then struggled to release the kids. Only one buckle snapped open before her lungs cried out for air; she kicked to the surface, dragging one child. She exploded through, gasping for air; so did Carlton. She towed him by the hair towards shore twenty yards away. Three people who spotted her churning for survival rushed to pull her and Carlton to safety. Electra screamed as she coughed out water.

"My daughter's trapped."

Then she stripped off shoes, slacks, and blouse before diving in and knifing back to the spot where she had surfaced.She took a giant gulp of air, then plunged towards the bottom but ran out of oxygen before locating her sunken treasure.

Fighting water and panic, she recharged her air supply and dived again, this time finding the car but was unable to loosen the belt, forcing her to surface before her lungs exploded. She took an enormous breath then kicked down to the car, this time not to be denied. Her fear-strengthened fingers finally ripped Airee free.

But her fear turned to panic when she surfaced; Airee, limp as a rubber doll, wasn't breathing. She used a turn-and-tow to thrash towards shore where six people had now gathered. Still trembling from the adrenaline rush, Electra was about to push away the person trying to breathe life back into Airee but stopped abruptly when coming face to face with Robin, who said matter-of-factly, "This is my job. I can do it better than you."

Wrapped in a blanket and sobbing unabashedly fifteen minutes later, Electra hugged Airee and Robin as Zoe held Carlton and Russell looked on. Airee's cheery words brought smiles to everyone.

"Don't cry, Momma. Doggy Lady help us." "Yes, Airee, she sure did…"

Now safely home that evening, Electra listened to the news while Airee slept at her side. A late-breaking story captured the top spot on every channel.

"The CIA has not yet confirmed rumors that amusement park disasters hitting at least a dozen locations across the country are acts of Cyberterrorism. Eyewitnesses claim there were no boots-on-the-ground causes for the melee that killed five people, including two children, and injured scores more. A spokesperson for the Oval Office says whoever is to blame will be treated harshly…"

Electra agreed.

Chapter 21
September 2129

"The Time of Their Lives"
(Thread 1 Chapter 7)

The amusement park misadventure proved to be but a glitch in the otherwise magical procession of months that serendipity rolled out for the duo and their special daughter. Ariadne blossomed like a flower kissed by sunlight and nurtured by the right balance between learning and playing. Electra made preparations to grow additional clones and wrote more A.I. software while Alisha finished filming by mid-July Superman's next season. There was little time left to pursue much else, but Electra carved out a late-August weekend to visit the Indian reservation because Dr. Holbrook needed help. In return, Dr. Holbrook would find an activity for Ariadne while Electra and the doctor meet with the Tribal Council Chief. Dr. Holbrook explained Friday evening what she needed. Ariadne paid almost as much attention as her mother.

"I haven't told you about the Inter-Regional Tribal Council. It's a voluntary Native American political organization comprised of Tribal Chiefs from across America. At their June meeting, our Chief talked about the success we're having with your Cyber-Theater and Optic Nerve Knitter. Several tribes are interested, so he'd like you to help him coordinate similar projects at the best locations. We'll meet with him tomorrow morning at his office in the recreational center. And while we're doing that, your daughter can attend a Saturday morning kids' tribal culture play session." Airee spoke right up when Electra asked for her opinion.

"I like. I want to play with kids like I see on TV." Dr. Holbrook knew it would be a good experience.

"You'll have fun and learn a lot. Some of the children are older than you, but you're just as big and talk very well. You must be very smart."

"Thank you. Momma always teaching me, and we play too." Electra patted Airee's head.

"Well now, let's get a good night's sleep so you're ready for fun tomorrow. And I'll do the same…"

Morning activities started well for both mother and daughter. One of the older girls inducted Airee into the tribe when Dr. Holbrook introduced her, and as Electra's meeting unfolded, she found an opportunity to make Chief Strongarm's proposal even better.

"Your plan is good but too broad. You can grow into it if you launch it in stages. And I'm too busy to handle it alone, but if you want me to handle an expanded role, give me the title 'Adjunct Ambassador' and assign two of your people who'll report to me dotted-line, Doctor Holbrook for managing eye care clinic franchising, and whomever you choose for managing Cyber-Theater franchising." The Chief liked the idea.

"Franchising is viable. We collect our fees and the tribes that buy tend to the details. But can you train the franchisees?"

"Not a problem. Do you have first-franchise tribes in mind?"

"Yes, the Seminole Nation in Florida, and the Navajo Nation in Arizona. I will give you names and phone numbers of your contacts as soon as I confirm they are still interested. Do you travel west often?"

"To Hollywood. And once I make a couple of visits, much of the follow-up can be done by Internet. If you contact the Navajo Nation soon, I can visit them during my September trip.

"I will do so immediately. By the time your weekend stay with us ends, you shall have what you need."
Airee bubbled joyfully on the Sunday afternoon drive home.

"Oh Momma, my blood brothers and sisters play nice. Maybe you can find more playmates for me at home too. Please ask Carlton's mommy."

"I will, and please tell me his parent's names and what they do."
"Zoe and Matt. They and Doggy Lady Robin have a hole business."
"You are so smart. They have a holistic healthcare business that makes people feel good. But not as good as you make me feel."
Airee positively glowed.

"Oh Momma, me too you too…"

Alisha placed a call Monday evening to Kathi, who picked up on the fourth chime.

"I'm so glad you called. I can't give you the details yet because the Studio hasn't made a final decision, but plan to get here September 15 and stay with me for a week. Will you bring Airee?"

"Yes, and she's looking forward to playing with Zaby. You'll be surprised how fast she's growing. Is there anything you need me to prepare?"

"No, just bring yourself and your little girl. Bye-bye." The duo switched to its Electra role for the next call. "Hello, this is Jo Maipetal. Who's calling, please?"

"My name is Electra Kittner. Chief Strongarm of the Pequot Nation gave me your name. Is now a good time to talk?"

"It is. He told me about his plan and your visit. Please tell me when you would like to come. I'll make all necessary arrangements..." Kathi hugged Airee first. Zaby did likewise when the guests entered, then whisked Airee away into a child's world, leaving the adults in one much more serious.

"How was the flight and limo ride?"

"No delays. It seems that transportation security can keep ahead of any Cyber-Terrorist attacks. I hope the bad guys get caught or give up soon. How are you and the Studio?"

"Why don't you freshen up and then come to the kitchen? Then I'll tell you the latest."

Alisha listened calmly to Kathi's summary of Studio current events, saving her comments until Kathi had finished.

"Your bosses are making the right decision. Every series has a shelf life, and the Superman series has exceeded my expectations. The same for Mission Impossible which still has one more movie. What does Tyger want in it?"

"He'll explain details tomorrow at an all-hands meeting, but your character, the Chameleon, meets an uncertain end that leaves plenty of avenues for a spin-off. There may be a role for you in it, but you'll have to audition if it materializes. Please don't be offended if he asks you to do that."

"Of course not. I don't want to join the overpopulated ranks of people who stay afloat on the waves generated by reputation rather than ability. And I'll decide if I want to extend my acting career after I hear what he has to offer. Thanks for letting me know. I'll be ready."

Vince and Tyger led the kickoff session. Their positive attitudes turned what might have become a grim briefing into one that saluted everyone's contributions. Vince reminded cast and crew that Superman had maintained a loyal fan base, which is a major accomplishment in an entertainment world where audiences demand novelty, and Tyger pointed out that all but extras or day players could earn residuals if reruns go into syndication. He then marched through storyboards and scene summaries for what would be covered during the next ten days, and ended by inviting all to an onsite Studio party next week Friday.

Ariadne alternated between coming to rehearsals or playing with Zaby, and Kathi let the girls choose each day at breakfast between dinner at home or at a kid-favorite fast food restaurant. The girls surprised Kathi by choosing eating in more often than eating out because dinner at home gave them longer-lasting parental attention. Kathi talked about this and more after their daughters had gone to bed the evening before the party.

"I'm always surprised how much Zaby knows about all the latest kid-fads. I guess it shows the impact of advertising on the Internet. Companies use Big Data to target consumers of all ages and get them to buy. Ariadne's precocious development poses a challenge for you. She'll wear you out if you don't get a nanny."

"I'm surprised you say that. Both of us made a conscious decision to raise a child. It might be different for an unplanned pregnancy or family obligation, but I've discovered that the more time I share with Ariadne, the better I feel."

"You have more energy. That's why I hired Abila."

"And my attitude towards sex has changed too. Has yours?" "I've never thought about it. What are you getting at?"

"You and I know the difference between sex and love. Love is deeper than sex, and the only love that rivals a parent's love for a child is a child's love for the parent. Now that I have Ariadne, I think my unconditional love has replaced some of my sex drive."

"It might come back as she gets older and needs less from you. And as for myself, I'm happy to date casually. I never wanted the baggage a co-friend can bring, but even if I had a partner, I'd still want a nanny. And I don't have to feel guilty when I go out because Abila is here. And I never bring anyone home. I keep my sexual activity out of Zaby's way. She'll learn about dating and sex soon enough. And that reminds me, are you going to the party tomorrow?"

"I thought I'd put in a cameo appearance. How about you?"

"Why don't both of us dress up? I think we've earned a night of adult fun. Let's go shopping tomorrow for new outfits. The kids will like that too."

Alisha agreed, so next morning's shopping expedition was fun for adults and children alike. Airee's fashion statement said it all. "Momma, you look like movie star."

Zaby said, "Well, she is, but she usually looks like Supergirl." Kathi's comment ended the judging.

"I think your mother would look good in an old bathrobe. Come on, let's buy our dresses and go to McDonalds."

Abila had the girls in tow by the time the party-goers departed. They agreed to mingle separately, and Alisha decided to act the part her dress suggested after spotting several interesting fellows. An hour later, she motioned to Kathi she was going out for dinner. Kathi smiled, blowing her a kiss for good luck.

Alisha's escort, a tony looking early-thirties day player who had good night moves too, selected a quiet Italian restaurant whose warm ambiance encouraged intimacy. Alisha liked the way he continued talking while pouring the wine, rolling the bottle to avoid spilling even a drop. The conversation continued to flow, but when Alisha spotted the waiter approaching to take dinner orders, a different picture replaced the intimate adult evening she was contemplating.

"I've enjoyed meeting you and I thank you for the wine, but I'm not in the mood tonight, so I'll ask our waiter to call me a cab."

"I'm disappointed you won't have dinner, but I do understand. Let me drive you home..."

Alisha kissed him on the cheek when Kathi greeted her at the door. Then the ladies talked in the kitchen before calling it an evening.

"I got home first because I didn't meet anyone who caught my fancy, but you did. What happened?" Just then, Zaby and Airee, awakened by adult voices, came looking for their mothers.

"He's very nice, but I told him home is the best place for me." Airee's innocent joy showed when she pleaded for Alisha to read to her before going back to bed, but Alisha had something even better.

"Why don't we have even more fun? You can sleep with me, and I'll read until the Sandman visits. Do you remember who he is?"

"Oh yes, Momma. He sprinkles magic sand in my eyes that brings me nice dreams. Does he do that to you?" Alisha hugged Airee before answering.

"He doesn't need to, because you do that even better…"

Alisha had arranged one more studio visit before flying Monday to Albuquerque. Lisa Perugino would show her and Ariadne the art of Hollywood makeup and 3-D face printing. In return, Alisha would treat Lisa and her co-friend Steve to a mid-afternoon lunch. Steve did the driving in addition to joining the face printing demonstration. "It's so simple even an adult can do it. All I do is push buttons to scan in a picture of the face I want to make, then I punch in the dimensions of the head that will wear it. Once that's done, I push one more button and the machine sprays layers on an adjustable model head and presto, I get the finished product. The hardest part usually is reading the instruction manual because most of the machines are made in China."

"Would you do me a favor? Would you let me practice making a couple of masks I could wear? I even brought pictures to load into your infernal Chinese machine."

"Sure. We'll let Steve judge the finished product." Alisha modeled one of the masks so Lisa could show how to apply special makeup. An hour later, Steve agreed that Alisha's new look might fool even the best facial recognition software that scans for disguises.

As promised, Alisha treated to lunch at a restaurant of Lisa's choice. She chose an open-air café inside Bluff Creek Dog Park to keep her black Lab Phoenix and Airee busy meeting other canines and pet people. Lisa commented while watching Airee play.

"Stevie and I are definitely pet people. We like most of our friends' kids, but pets are so much easier to understand, and they give unconditional love. When your daughter gets older, be prepared when she asks for a dog. My friends say pets are much safer for their daughters than hormone-motivated fellows. You have lots to look forward to." Alisha smiled while giving her favorite one-word answer, "Perhaps."

Electra came to the fore on the early Monday morning two-hour flight, helping Airee search online for information about their destination. By the time they landed, mother and daughter knew basic facts about New Mexico's most populous city.

Tracing its roots to a Viceroy of Spain's New World colonies, Albuquerque's one-million population ranks 32nd in the nation, and its 5000-plus foot elevation places it near the top for major U.S. cities.

Its modern core contrasts with the Old Town Albuquerque district, founded in 1706.

Airee liked the Internet video but wanted to see more. "Can we walk before we fly away?"

"Why yes, and maybe Johana Maipetal could tell us what to see. We're supposed to meet her at Hotel Albuquerque, which is near many sightseeing destinations."

Johana's greeting when Alisha knocked on her hotel room door was as cold as ice pellets blown by a blizzard, prompting Electra's whimsical warning. I don't think I want to ask her where to go.

Jo wasted no time on small talk, instead getting right to the reason for the meeting.

"I'm meeting with you strictly to humor my tribe's Chief. He and Chief Strongarm are National Tribal Council friends, and Strongarm says you have good ideas. I've talked many times to 'de eyoni' like you. You are nothing but an outsider who thinks you know what's best for my people. Go ahead and talk, but not until I give you some background." Jo launched into her history lesson.

"If you know anything at all about Native North American tribes, you'll know we are classified geographically into five regions: Northeast, Southeast, Great Plains, Southwest, and Northwest Coast. Even your little girl can figure out which one we're in. And archaeological digs confirm that the Navajo have been here for over ten thousand years, part of a continental network of tribes living in harmony with the land and trading among themselves.

"We Navajo, like our closest trading partners – the Pueblo and Hopi – learned to survive in a barren environment, dry riverbed lands pockmarked by foreboding canyons and scrub vegetation, supporting only herding and minimal farming, mostly maize. Yet we clung to the land until soldiers drove us out after your Civil War, starving us on a 450 mile walk after burning our villages and slaughtering women and children." Airee's innocent outburst suspended Jo's diatribe. "Momma told me. We sorry. Your DNA comes from Asia. Does your mommy live there? That's on other side of Earth near China. Momma says Chinese people drink tea because antioxidants. I learned on Internet. Momma says don't trust Internet. Do you?" Finally, a crack appeared in Jo's frosty demeanor.

"Your little girl is very smart. I can't compete with what she just said, so why don't you tell me what might be good for my people?" Electra sat Ariadne on the chair next to her before talking.

"I don't pretend I know better than you what your people need, but Chief Strongarm likes what I suggested. I do know that East Coast tribes have a richer environment than yours. They developed 'Three Sisters' farming by interplanting corn, beans, and squash. And they domesticated more animals than your people. And I know that today, many reservation people suffer from alcohol or drug addiction, substandard housing, and limited job opportunities. Government programs have done some good, but it's much better if your people and leaders take the initiative.

"I'm ready to go, but before I do, here's what I think might work. You can't compete against Las Vegas brick-and-mortar casinos, but you can use something called a Cyber-Theater to build virtual reality casinos that are new and exciting. Have breathtaking aerial tours of all the natural wonders on your lands. You can turn some of your hotels into combo-casinos and tourist education centers. And I'll offer two other suggestions; put solar panel or Martian farms on your barren lands.

"That's all I want to say. I'll ask at the front desk about sightseeing that my daughter will enjoy. Have your Chief call Chief Strongarm if you think any of what I said might help. And I wish you good luck." Electra towed Airee away before Johana could recover.

Now that work was over, Alisha came back, switching tickets to a later flight, then asking at the front desk for sightseeing suggestions. The young lady knew what Ariadne would like.

"You're in luck because the best sights are nearby. You can have a quick lunch at the Central Grill and Coffeehouse before going to the Albuquerque Museum of Art and History. And if your little girl wants to see more, take her to the Albuquerque Aquarium. And leave your luggage here. You can pick it up when come back to catch a ride to the airport. I'll have one of our staff take your bags and get you a cab."

The itinerary worked to perfection. Alisha let Airee romp just enough so she would sleep most of the way home. Soon after the plane reached cruising altitude, Electra praised Alisha's planning. "Ariadne will always remember this trip because you took the time to take her places we may never visit again. We're giving her the time of her life, and she's giving the same to us." Alisha connected Electra's comment to a favorite song from long ago.

"Since I'm the artistic one, I probably listen to retro music more than you do. A song titled Time of Your Life, released by the studio band Green Day on its American Idiot album, helped it win a Grammy. Its lyrical refrain echoes what you just said about life's adventure: 'It's something unpredictable but in the end is right, I hope you had the time of your life.' I hope serendipity gives us much more time for sharing all we can with Ariadne."

Electra agreed.

Chapter 22
December 2129

"Angels in Flight"
(Thread 1 Chapter 8)

Even the irrepressibly optimistic Electra-Alisha duo, if asked to judge autumn according to the filled glass metaphor, would have to say it was two-thirds empty, not one-third full, because when using the Benjamin Franklin close, there were three items in the plus column:

1. Electra had made excellent progress modifying the Brain Probe for special applications. She had even set up in her basement a small lab containing scanners and test equipment so she could work surreptitiously.
2. Electra had earned Johana Maipetal's respect because Chief Strongarm reported that Navajo and Pequot reservation projects were moving ahead.
3. Alisha would audition early next year for a role in whatever
4. Mission Impossible spin-off materializes.
5. But there were six in the minus:
6. All cloned embryos or fetuses died before reaching full term. Electra was beginning to fear even she couldn't cope with the combinatorial complexity of so many interacting causal genes impacting so many second order characteristics.
7. Though Electra told Angus she didn't have enough time to help, he kept asking her to snoop for suspects who might be constructing a rare earths cartel or causing random acts of terrorism.
8. Electra didn't have time to investigate platform companies that might exceed ethical red lines if they conspired with the government or A.I. developers.
9. Chief Strongarm wanted her to play a bigger tribal role, but she didn't have time for that either. The best she could do was promise to visit the Seminole Tribe sometime next year.
10. Alisha had little success reducing Robin's growing anger that she directed at Jennifer and Matt. (Whenever she asked Robin

why she was angry, Robin would shout: "Mind your own business.")

11. And the most serious item concerned Ariadne's health. Electra took her twice for a medical exam: once for nausea and another for dizziness. Finding nothing wrong, a doctor diagnosed the symptoms as merely growing pains but as a precaution wrote a referral for a brain scan that Electra discarded because she was already doing them using her Brain Probe.

The list of challenges was longer than the Christmas shopping list and with Christmas Eve only ten days away, the duo had people to see before taking their traditional planning for the new year Holiday break. Angus occupied top spot.

Electra brought Ariadne with her, and when she told Angus in her precious little words how big his office building is, his deep-voiced chuckle brought smiles to mother and daughter.

"Well that's because a big bear like me needs room to roam, and the Senate office building complex gives me plenty of space. I'm sure your Momma will take you on a big tour soon." Electra chatted for five minutes more before zeroing in on politics.

"I've already told you I don't have time to snoop, but I do have another reading assignment that will help you understand better how to deal with domestic and international issues. You have neither the time nor temperament to grind through the series, so have one of your staffers write a summary. I'll give you an overview right now; I think you already practice a lot of its teachings." Angus nodded, so Electra soldiered on.

"The five-book Incerto series, written over a hundred years ago by Nassim Nicholas Taleb, has become recognized as an incisive investigation of luck, uncertainty, probability, opacity, human error, risk, disorder, and decision-making in a sociopolitical world we don't understand. His conclusions apply to economics as well, but let's leave economics for another discussion. There are five books in the series, published in this order: Fooled by Randomness, The Black Swan, The Bed of Procrustes, Antifragile, and Skin in the Game. When first released, reviewers' opinions ranged from brilliant to baloney, but the smart ones realized that Taleb deliberately uses an often annoying and imprecise meandering style to force readers to think. And it works. His series should be considered a quasi-probabilistic sociopolitical philosophy firmly grounded in Enlightenment thinking and updated to include the best contributions from Modernity. And the reviewers in his camp agree with his criticism of the then-rampant collaborations among the Progressive Left, the Academic Intelligentsia, and the Self-Serving Media. He labeled all of them IYIers. Have your people check it out." Angus's impatience began to show as he started drumming his pen. "OK, I will, but what's your overview?" Electra rubbed Airee's hair before answering.

"It's impossible to summarize in a couple of sentences, but at the risk of being too simplistic, here's my list of takeaways for you to jot down. Are you ready?" Angus fumbled for paper while grumbling.

"I think I liked you better when you were less busy. Go ahead." "The entire series traces the impact of errors people make when applying chance to circumstances. They look for causality when there is none, and they underestimate the probability of Black Swan events. These are catastrophes people think will never happen, but when they do people are clueless because they don't understand fat-tailed probability distributions, and then they look for one-size-fits-all superficial solutions that don't fit. Instead of building bullet-proof but rigid plans, they should try to build antifragile systems that adapt when Black Swans land. And most importantly, they should never trust anyone who doesn't have skin in the game, which is Taleb's term for game-players who have nothing at stake and incur none of the risks. Nor should people trust thinkers who aren't also doers. There's much more, such as moral hazards caused by too much concentration of power, but ask your staffers to tell you about that." Angus tapped his fingers on the desk before asking.

"Did politicians back then follow some of his recommendations?" "Sometimes. A hundred years ago during the birth of Social Media, the public demanded more ethics and openness from government, and our political system gradually improved. But I've already told you about the perfect storm that washed away a lot of the progress, which statesmen like you are trying to restore. Give me a minute to write a checklist you can use when engaging the other side in a debate." Electra scribbled a list she slid across the desk two minutes later:

How to Keep Both Sides Honest
1. Know definitions.
2. Spare fear-mongering (Threats don't equal evidence).
3. Don't plead for a special exemption.
4. Stop pretending Big Government Statism doesn't exist.
5. Don't use government policy to justify government policy.
6. Don't shift the burden of proof (You can't prove a negative).

Angus shifted in his chair.

"This is some of the good stuff you used to talk about when you helped in the past. Maybe next time we can talk about how all this might apply to economics or to cartel and terrorist tracking." Electra gathered Airee as she prepared to leave.

"You'll always be a great negotiator. You keep asking because the worst I can say is no. We'll have to see what unfolds…"

Electra stopped for lunch at a McDonalds because Airee wanted to add a McDonald's Christmas Happy Meal toy to her collection. After opening the box, she chirped excitedly.

"Look, Momma, it's a little angel. Could I dress up like one on Christmas Eve when we visit Carlton? I want to fly like an angel." "We'll have to go shopping for a halo and wings, and I know just where to place it on our to-do list. It goes at the top, so we'll get them after lunch and you can wear the halo home. Now slow down and don't gobble. We have plenty of time to shop and then visit the Doggy Lady's office."

Electra knew that only Jennifer would be there because Matt and Robin would be visiting clients and Zoe would be working from home. Jennifer needed a private discussion to see if Electra could help keep a personal problem from snowballing out of control.

She told Airee the golden halo looked cute, then gave her a laptop she could play with while the women talked.

Electra sat opposite in a consulting room as Jennifer straightened her shoulders before talking pointedly.

"Has Robin told you why she's angry with me?"

"No, and I don't want to pry. She gets prickly if I ask her too many questions. You can tell me what you think, but I'm not going to pry into your affairs either."

"Robin's been mad ever since she discovered Matt and I are having sex, and she's threatening to tell Zoe and Russell if we don't stop cheating. She hasn't confronted Matt – just me – and she won't accept my explanation."

"So, what is it?"

"Matt and I aren't in love, but we need sexual satisfaction our partners aren't giving us. I love Russell, and I'm thankful Robin handles caregiving duties, but my hormones are still active. Matt loves Zoe but she gives Carlton top billing, so there's not much romance left for Matt. Look, we're not cheating. I help him and he helps me. Besides, neither of us wants to use fantasy clubs or escort services. And he showed me his marriage contract that contains a clause that lets him satisfy a sexual whim all males have as long as he doesn't stray into deviant sex. So, what do you think?"

"What I think doesn't matter. It's what you, Russell, Zoe, and Matt think. I guess Robin is standing in for Russell. Personally, I don't think you're hurting Russell." Jennifer leaned forward.

"You're Robin's best friend. Could you do Matt and me a favor by explaining this to her?"

"You're all adults. There are lots of movies covering similar themes. Why don't you watch some and see what Hollywood does? I don't want to get in the middle because I risk alienating Robin further. The three of you need to agree. If you can't, then bring Zoe into the mix." Jennifer immediately shifted topics.

"Did you and Robin ever talk about her pregnancy? If I brought that up, maybe she'd realize everyone has sexual issues."

"I didn't ask and she didn't tell. You can go there at your own peril, but I'm not." Just then, Airee came into the room.

"Momma, where don't you go? I won't either." Electra scooped her onto her lap before answering.

"We won't go where we can't help. But let's go home so we can help each other. What would you like to do?"

"I'm tired and my head hurts. I want a nap. And tonight, would you read me the Jesus story again? I want to hear the angels sing." Jennifer smiled wearily. "You've had a busy day, little angel. No wonder your head is tired. You and your Momma better fly home so you can rest your pretty little head and make more Christmas preparations."

Chen Xu made only one Christmas preparation: he programmed his Cyberspace weapons control software to launch a random pattern of attacks that would coincide with America's Christmas Eve bad weather forecast for the East Coast. Although his success rate had been declining steadily, he reasoned that those monitoring Cyberspace might be getting overconfident and let their guard down on Christmas Eve. And even if his Christmas presents didn't get through, he'd be off the grid when they launched.

Electra's Christmas preparations were much cheerier. They centered on what every parent wants to give their children: magical memories that will live forever no matter how young when created or how old when recalled. She shared all the fun with Ariadne, letting her help when setting up Doc Kittner's artificial tree and deciding where to place his special ornaments, a game Electra played as a child only with him. Airee clapped gleefully when they placed the most special ornament, the Blue Bell, at the top of the tree, the only place it was meant to be.

Of course, they baked Christmas cookies and went to a children's Christmas concert. Electra had other surprises ready but four days before Christmas she cancelled all activities that required leaving the house because Ariadne had a headache and low-grade fever. While she recovered, Electra made a final pre-Christmas video call so she could talk with Hud and his two Holiday visitors, Su and Kameyo. Electra dispatched the small talk first.

"Ariadne and I are invited to Matt and Zoe's for Christmas Eve. I don't know if Zoe will dress Carlton in anything special, but Airee will wear a little halo and angel's wings if she feels good enough to go. She might have a slight case of the Flu." What will you be doing?" "Hud's taking us to Sam Ryder's for Christmas Eve, and then he'll deep fry a turkey on Christmas Day. Kameyo and I will take care of the rest."

Electra switched to business, asking Hud to summarize his activity first.

"My Permian Basin partners will have another solar panel farm online by the middle of next year. And they've picked up a contract to help a Navajo Indian Tribe. Depending on what happens, we might set up a Martian Farm. Just goes to show how the new technology can generate blue collar jobs that require the human touch. Good for us." Electra asked for Su's summary, but she deferred to Kameyo.

"We can report satisfactory progress, but we could make more faster if you would visit more often. So, please consider this for next year." Hud chimed in before Electra ended the call.

"According to the news, the Northeast has had a cold snap and a bit of snow. And tarnation if that didn't bring some electrical power glitches to boot. Did any of that affect DC?"

"No, and they were supposedly caused by frozen power lines and grid overload. The government hasn't mentioned any Cyberspace or infrastructure terrorism in months. I think the network security software they bought from you works. What does Tim say?"

"He'd agree, but he always says it's impossible to prevent all attacks from getting through. And I think we should be worried until we know who might be stirring up trouble. But like you always say, we shouldn't worry about what's outside our control. We're gonna have a Merry Christmas here, and we hope you and your little angel do too."

December 24th brought the start of a white Christmas snowfall that was forecast to intensify during the day as higher winds and lower temps blew in. Ariadne's headaches and fever had gone away, but ever-watchful Electra took her to the basement lab for a quick Brain Probe check-up. Airee giggled as Electra dialed the controls that varied input intensity and frequency. Both of them could view her real-time brain image on a nearby monitor.

"I can feel tickles in my brain. Does my brain look pretty?"

"Yes, darling. It looks like you're getting smarter and smarter. And I think you're outgrowing any nasty neural spikes. I'll call Zoe to tell her we'll visit at three. That will give you and Carlton time to play before dinner and the Christmas Pageant. You'll have even more fun than last Christmas Eve."

Zoe's voice sounded perkier than usual.

"I'll tell Carlton his favorite playmate will be here at three. Matt's been following the news and doesn't think the weather will be an issue, but there are reports of localized power outages. Ours went out briefly last night and again early this morning. Were you hit?" "No. And it's good the outages were brief. That shows the grid is able to reboot, which means any other interruptions will be manageable. We'll see you soon."

Though the storm intensified more than expected, Electra arrived as planned; Zoe checked to confirm that the Christmas Pageant would be held, but Matt thought otherwise when the power went out.

"If the lights don't come back on in thirty minutes, we're not going. I don't want us driving in the dark." The power came on soon enough not to spoil the fun that had been planned. Ariadne and Carlton played while the adults talked, and after an early dinner the group departed in separate vehicles for the Pageant. Though the twinkle of Holiday lights barely penetrated the swirling snow, driving conditions remained tolerable.

The church was standing room only because most parents braved the conditions, but halfway into the program the lights flickered out and were still dark 30 minutes later. As the congregation jostled towards the exit, Airee fell, bumping her head on a pew. Electra quickly picked her up.

"Did you hurt your head? Let me rub it." "I got dizzy, Momma. I sorry."

Midway on the drive home, streetlights flared back to life.

"It's good you got to see half the Pageant. And when we get home, we can watch some Christmas movies." Electra waited for Airee's usually happy reply, but nothing came. She swerved to the curb as soon as she saw her daughter in trouble.

Ariadne shrieked, "Momma, it's coming for me!" before losing consciousness. Her head jerked from side to side and eyes rolled as her stiffened body thrashed. Electra knew instantly that Airee was in the grip of a grand mal epileptic seizure caused by too much electrical activity in the brain.

She raced home, skidding to a stop in front of the house, then clutched Airee in her arms as she ran to the front door, nearly slipping on a snow-hidden patch of ice. Once inside, she placed Airee on the sofa after removing her coat. Still unconscious, Ariadne's breathing became erratic as the thrashing intensified. Airee in her arms, Electra rushed down the basement stairs, but she lost balance as the lights flickered out. She tumbled awkwardly but shielded Airee from too harsh a landing. Five seconds later the power surged on again.

Electra propped her daughter in a chair next to the Brain Probe, then locked its cap in place. What appeared on the monitor was an electrical storm raging in Airee's brain.

I've got to neutralize currents before they destroy too many neurons. Electra dialed the controls.

Thank you, Jesus. The storm's subsiding. Airee's breathing became regular as her convulsions stopped and she regained consciousness. And then disaster struck.

An enormous power surge blasted through the local grid, sending a mega-current into the Probe and Airee's brain. The Probe exploded, igniting cap and hair.

Ariadne shrieked, "Momma it hurts, make it stop."

Electra screamed, "I will, I will," while ripping off the cap and smothering the flames before cradling Airee's head in her hands.

Airee stuttered, "I - I love you, Momma," before her eyes slowly blinked shut. Electra folded her in supporting arms, shaking to awaken what looked like a sleeping child, but it was too late. Ariadne's vital signs disappeared as the last vestiges of neural activity vanished. Her body went limp; only a tiny smile remained on a now impassive face as her essence submerged into an uncharted infinity of indifferent stars.

Electra sat, mechanically rocking her daughter.

"Don't leave me this way... Don't leave me this way..." After ten minutes, not even the lightning brain could think of anything that would bring Airee back.

Sobbing uncontrollably, Electra hugged her daughter as she stumbled up the stairs and then into her bedroom, gently placing Airee on the bed before removing all clothes, first from mother and then daughter. She drew back the blanket and sheet, then collapsed onto the bed, drawing covers over her head and Airee to her breast for a final night's rest. Neither numberless tears nor angels in flight could lessen the grief that would visit tonight.

Alisha became uncharacteristically silent the next day, leaving all the grim necessities in the experienced hands of Electra, who at the age of only thirty-three had become inured to grief's impact. She felt less stress than when burying her father or grandfather, or when losing Adom or Mrs. T because a child's history is simpler. There would be no wake or religious ceremony; it took only three days to schedule a cremation and collect ashes. Nor did Electra call even close friends because she preferred to grieve alone so she could focus her thoughts while privately marching through the four stages of loss

–anger, grief, remembrance, and renewal. And she gave herself an assignment that she had been postponing until an accumulation of events matured her further.

Ariadne's death had aged Electra, cognitively and emotionally, giving her somber insights that she could use to keep busy, to keep from tumbling into a deeper depression.

Electra disappeared into her fortress of solitude and didn't emerge until late New Year's Eve. And when she did, she brought with her a document titled Ariadne's Lagniappe, one she would add to her philosophical writings. She summarized it to herself one more time before tucking it away.

I created my daughter from my own DNA. She is not some manifestation of a remotely anthropomorphic God. Yet even I am conflicted when confronted by this brutal fact, Humans are nothing more than an emergent ensemble of complex bio-electrochemical reactions that shall never be unraveled. A more poetic metaphor would compare life to a candle in the wind. Where does the flame go when the candle is extinguished? Smart as I am, and exceptional though I be, the answer exceeds asymptotic limits that will always be a barrier for me. The mind-brain conundrum is but one of many dualities that will forever be problematic, but collectively they outline a One World Universe from which everything we experience emerges. And that includes cognition and emotion.

Humans emerge from carbon-based substrate evolution. If A.I. ever reaches the Singularity, its counterparts will emerge from silicon-based processes. Will human and A.I. cognition have enough intelligence to communicate? The answer lies beyond my limits, which are determined by the laws of probability and quantum physics. But Man's destiny is to push towards what he cannot reach. Some good always comes from the effort.

And that is just like the good coming from my extended philosophy, whose name I have changed from Neurosci-Extended Deconstructed Emergent Post-Pragmatism to Quantum+NeuroSci-Extended Deconstructed Emergent Post-Kantian/Pragma/Phenomenological Synthesis. That's too much of a mouthful, so I'll abbreviate it QNS-Edep-K/P/P Synthesis. I got it simply by adding the best of Boethius, Hegel, Husserl, and Heidegger while emphasizing an objective rather than subjective turn. I doubt anyone will ask, but if they do, I can explain my worldview.

The powers of my cognitive and emotional personas have increased dramatically during the past two years. I understand better and empathize more deeply than ever before. And they will guide what I choose for future goals. If I had known when I embarked on cloning what I know now, would I have continued? Probably not, because I am responsible for Ariadne's death. The DNA modifications I made must have led to that fatal seizure, and I forgot to build a surge protector into my Brain Probe. I must accept the consequences, which shall always color my future.

Writing this document has been a catharsis, cognitively and emotionally, but has been draining. I'm exhausted. What a singular New Year's Eve this has been. I'll watch the Times Square Ball Drop and then pack it in.

Electra always considered that event a testimony to America's audacious optimism. Through best and worst of times since 1907, thousands of people have braved all obstacles for a traditional sharing of hope. Watching the celebration took her thoughts away, helping her prepare for bed. Twenty minutes later, she fell into an indifferent sleep.

"Electra, my daughter, the exceptional one. Awaken now and listen, my visits are finally done. I shall explain what you have now become." Indira's familiar voice roused Electra to a sitting position as she beheld a shimmering apparition. She was about to speak, but Indira, placing an index finger to her expressionless lips, commanded silence.

"You have now become what you have been reaching for since my first visit sixteen years ago, an authentic, self-actualized person standing atop your hierarchy of needs, no longer needing anyone, able to stand alone. Ariadne's death places you beyond the pale. The hardest grief to bear is the death of a child because it's a tragedy that inverts life's natural progression. You have learned all that Alisha or I can offer. The lightning brain has already subsumed her as it will me when I depart. You have become your own inner voice, having integrated fully your cognitive and emotional personas.

"There is no need for you to seek counsel from anyone or ask questions. Listen only to yourself. Tuck us three – Ariadne, Alisha, and me – into pleasant corners of your memory, but visit sparingly. Focus instead on being. And I leave you with my poem To Be that speaks to your becoming. Follow its verses."

Electra heard the verses echo as Indira's pristine image softly faded.

"Become your body when exertion is due,
Become your emotions when feelings break through.
Become all your senses when feeling the pain,
Become in the moment again and again.
Become the problem when puzzles arise,
Become the solution when light meets your eyes.
Become the other when helping the child,
Become what you will when dreaming runs wild.
No matter the future no outcome yet told,
So live in the present and revel in bold.
Forget all your doubts so you set yourself free,
Unleash your potential be all you can be."

By the time they ended, Electra was about to enter an undisturbed sleep, knowing full well whose company to keep when she awakens. It would be herself, ready to assume control. And she would know what to do.

Chapter 23
February 2130

"On the Firing Line"
(Thread 3 Chapter 6)

Electra used the first two weeks of January to recalibrate expectations as she adjusted to new realities. She added a new hobby to fill some of the void left by Ariadne's death and revised some of her independent study documents. As she had already done for philosophy and R&D, she updated two others, working first on her Statist Manifesto, which covered political organization. She talked to herself as she added more details.

Of all the quotes I've ever collected concerning how to control leaders, Madison's is the best. If men were angels, control wouldn't be needed, or if angels were in control, there'd be no need to worry. But we saw a hundred years ago that even Catholic Church leaders can't be trusted, so society has to do a better job reining in runaway power.

And that's what America did in the 21st century, putting in place people and safeguards to control what is still the most powerful nation-state the world has ever known, the U.S.A. But we are in danger of regressing.

People who can handle the truth know that governments use legitimized violence to achieve results for the greater good. This principle has held since the dawn of civilization, but implementing it has become more complex as social entropy increases with the number and size of nation-states. And threats of nuclear annihilation conspire with economic processes to fuel bloated bureaucracies that serve themselves instead of the people.

There will never be an endgame state of perfection for any organization. We must constantly monitor all power-hungry organizations, be they nation-states, religions, corporations, or special interest groups. I shall remember this no matter what future roles I choose to play.

Electra was about to shift subjects when an odd thought occurred. I can think of one civilization that doesn't need state control, Star

Trek's Borgs, because all of them are linked to a collective Hive Mind. If the Singularity arrives, is there a possibility it will usher in another enemy of humanity's imperfect state? Yes, but I think the probability is essentially zero. I think Nassim Taleb would agree that this Black Swan's tail is thin indeed.

Electra took a lunch break followed by a workout, then spent a couple of hours before dinner reviewing a second document, her personal manifesto, noting to herself what changes to make.

The context of my life has come full circle. I started my odyssey battling a three-part Perfect Storm containing Middle East Terrorism, T-Plague, and a harsh government. My Perfect Storm has mutated to a whirlwind of Possible Rogue Terrorism and Platform Companies colluding with the Government, an emerging Biotech and A.I. Plague on society, and an ever-present risk of Out-of-Control Statism. And unless I prefer to wither and die, I better continue doing something. And I better maintain a nucleus of close friends and personal goals. What else?

I sense my sex drive has sublimated. And Ariadne's death has reminded me to treat commitment and unconditional love carefully. What can I say about this? How about declaring the following for sex and love; been there, done that, and now moving on.

I'll have to find new interests to tickle my fancy and new targets to put on my firing line.

Kathi Lauret's call from Hollywood came the last week of January, coinciding perfectly as Electra began setting up targets. She answered on the third chime.

"Hello Kathi and a belated Happy New Year. I recognized your caller ID. How are you?"

"I'm still employed but not as happily as six months ago. There's been a shakeup at the top that's still rippling through the Studio. That's why I'm calling, but you sound different. How are you and Ariadne?"

"We're doing fine."

"Good. Listen, the reason for my call is to warn you that the shakeup will affect you too. Vince and Tyger are gone, replaced by a new director – Vito Buono – who has the ear of the man at the top. They want a sensational and darker spin-off series you might not like. It won't feature Chameleon. Instead, it will create a new female that's the opposite of the hero in the retro Death Wish series. When bad things happen to her, she doesn't take revenge but instead leverages bad to her advantage. He's calling it Angel of Evil. He's not certain you're right for the part but he might let you audition. You'll have to meet with him first to convince him. Are you interested?"

"I might be, depending on what he offers."

"I thought you'd say that, so I'll arrange for you to meet him third week of February. Stay with me and bring Ariadne."

"Please set up the meeting, but I'll stay at a hotel and won't bring Ariadne. Would you please make limo and reservations like before?"

"Will do. I'll Email them to you. Anything else?"

"Would you please include a list of producers I could contact if I don't like Vito? There might be other opportunities, and a recommendation from you would be a big plus. I'm looking for other things to do."

"I can do that. And let's plan to have dinner sometime during your visit. See you in a week."

There was no shakeup at the top for Carter. Jared Gardner's mid-term State of the Union address would confirm his tight grip on the nation's rudder, and it would highlight one of Carter's new economic programs that would add revenues to the Government's bottom line. Carter knew Jared would like all of them and would find a way to add some of the revenue to his bottom line and that of his top economic advisor, a position Carter enjoyed occupying.

As he stepped smartly from the car, Carter reviewed an additional program that he had labeled "Cash in on the Crooks." It would have the CIA use whatever methods it wished to catch rich domestic or international crime lords, then manipulate the facts to give them reduced sentences if they forked over illegal gains Jared could use secretly to fund his foundation. Carter had others in mind, but he'd withhold the details for another time when he could use them to extract favors.

Electra used the week before her Hollywood trip to begin snooping on targets of interest: Platform companies and their suppliers of surveillance data software or A.I. control algorithms. Chaining together Big Data search criteria, she used her extended linguistic-SQL coding app to build a prioritized list from which she chose the top candidate: a venture capital company. She would learn more if she could infiltrate an upcoming meeting, but she needed an invitation; fabricating one would be difficult for anyone but Electra. She thought of a dearly departed friend as she outlined her plan of attack.

Alice Bickerwith taught me to use the British adjective easy-peasy for what I can do no muss, no fuss. And thanks to my Network Infiltration and Security Toolkit, I'll build a bogus software company and play the presidential role, giving myself fake I.Ds. Then I'll plant fake data that will dupe all the Platform or Surveillance Capital companies. And then I'll plant a fake invitation so I'm on the guest list. Hmm, what name should I use? Suddenly, an inspiration came her way.

I've often used random number generator apps when doing simulations. Now I'll use a random name generator app. Five minutes later, Electra had her fake name, Viola Nadira.

Perfect. And I have a couple of days to practice my venture capital act.

I've done enough today. Time to reward myself. I think I'll practice some of my new hobbies. And tomorrow I'll prepare for my Hollywood trip. I'll surf the Web for info on Mr. Buono so I know how to handle him.

Having studied Vito's online profile, Electra stepped confidently at 1 p.m. into his office, which matched his mid-fifties suave European exterior. She sat on a designer chair next to a deep-cushioned sofa while he described in flawless Italian-accented English what he wanted. Electra listened carefully while he enthused about the opportunity. After fifteen minutes of monologue, Vito asked his only question.

"Ah, but there is much more to say, so I invite you to dinner tonight. Will you join me at the Polo Lounge?"

"That's very generous of you. I've never been there, but it and its Beverly Hills Hilton location make a statement. I shall dress for the occasion. What time shall I arrive?"

"I shall expect you at eight. And until then, ciao bella…"

Electra asked the driver to leave her at the Avante Garde boutique so she could make her own statement that evening, one fitting for Vito, whose name, when expressed in English, spoke of the good life. The fashion consultant found a low-cut red dress and black stilettos that would leave a remarkable impression whether or not Electra talked or walked over her dinner partner. Returning to her hotel, she had just enough time to exercise before showering, then prepared for what she expected to be a titillating evening.

Vito's preparations were as thorough as Electra's. When she arrived fashionably late, a gracious host welcomed her, explaining that Mr. Buono awaited at his regular booth. He guided her through a sea of elegant tables to one of the curvaceous booths rimmed with plants that accented the elegant decor and indirect lighting, then said "Buon appetito" as Vito rose to greet her, warmly holding her hands before sliding her in on his right.

"Salve, bella Electra. You are a feast for my eyes. And I trust you find our restaurant suitable, no?"

"It looks as good as its reputation." Vito beamed.

"And you shall find its menu exceeds your expectations. We shall order from the Charter Member selections." A minute later, a tuxedo-jacketed waiter appeared for drink orders.

"I shall have my regular, Johnnie Walker Black with a splash. And you, my dear?"

"I would like Glenlivet 12 on the rocks, small cubes please." The waiter glided away as Vito began leading a charming discussion, first describing his European and Hollywood directing careers before pausing to light a cigar.

"I trust cigar smoke will not offend you, no? I find Cohibas meet my expectations." Electra removed from her purse a white-tipped mini-cigar.

"Why not at all. I shall join you. I smoke Black Tiger minis when having a drink." Vito had a spectacular view of more than her inverted-cross tattoo when she leaned forward. He was momentarily at loss for words, so Electra filled the void with a perfectly-formed smoke ring that drifted insouciantly away from the table.

"Aha, the lady knows her cigars. May I ask why you prefer Black Tiger?"

"You may. I am part Oriental Indian. Black Tigers are made in India by Fenn Thompson, the tobacconist who supplied Winston Churchill. I particularly like their lightly-flavored minis." Vito was making comparisons between Cuban and American tobaccos when the waiter reappeared with drinks and gave the menu to Vito.

"I could order for us, but why don't you take a look and do the honors?"

The waiter said, "Perhaps madam would prefer a pause to study our selections." Electra glanced through it before replying.

"No, that won't be necessary. Why don't I order a selection of smaller portions we can share?" The waiter glanced at Vito, who nodded, so she proceeded.

"We'll have an artichoke heart salad to start, then the terrine of lamb with pink shallots in a curry sauce, followed by a combination sea scallops and medallions of beef in a bearnaise sauce served with stir-fried green beans and red peppers." She returned the menu to the waiter, who said,

Very good, madam. And may I say, those are all excellent selections."

"You may, thank you. Also, we'll have a bottle of Chateau Margaux vintage 2123. I believe the village earned premier cru that year."

"The lady knows her wines. An excellent choice for your dinner. I shall return with your salad."

After the waiter left Vito said, "I am intrigued. There's a mystique to the tattoo and eye patch. Perhaps you will reveal more if I choose you."

Vito led the conversation through all the courses, detouring briefly into politics.

"I love Hollywood. It speaks to me and vice versa. But I do not like the words spoken in Washington. Do you agree?"

"Don't mistake style for substance. Our President at times can be blunt, but a lot of what he says makes sense, especially economically. Europe is still mired in paternalistic Big Government that stifles innovation and turns jobs into entitlements. The net effect is low growth that worsens inequality. Compare northern to southern Europe and you'll see."

Vito decided to move to a safer subject, so he described how his series needed a sophisticated, assertive lead who could handle contemporary adult topics. He continued moving closer to his offer as the waiter arrived for dessert orders. Once again, Vito deferred to his guest.

"I shall order two that we can share. One piece of triple-fudge flourless cake, and a two-scoops serving of vanilla ice cream topped with hot caramel sauce. And two coffee's, please."

Vito moved even closer after the desserts arrived. Electra smiled serenely, enjoying alternate bites of ice cream and cake, but Vito's right hand was busy under the table, stroking higher and higher between her thighs. When it moved into the danger zone, she decided to change the playing field.

"You aren't enjoying the sweet delights that are on the table. Wouldn't you like to try the cake?"

"No, I shall leave that for you. But why don't we return to my office to discuss more about my offer?"

Electra adroitly shoved the remaining cake into Vito's wide-eyed face, then gingerly wiped her fingertips.

"It's not your offer, but mine that's important. You've been all eyes and mouth and hands this evening, so call me if you wish to hear what I want, but I don't expect you will. Arrivederci."

Electra left the table, never glancing back, then called for her limo. She was too wired to sleep, so she swam endless laps in the hotel pool while making plans for tomorrow. By the time she climbed out, she felt better about tonight and was ready for the next day.
Electra called Kathi from the airport late the following morning.

"I apologize for not calling sooner, but I've changed my plans. I'm not the right lead for where Vito wants to go, so I'm flying home. Thanks for all—" Kathi interrupted.

"You shouldn't have turned off your cell phone. Vito says you've got what he's looking for. He kept it a secret from me too, but last night was your audition. He positively loved how you handled yourself. You might want to stay another day or two, so please call him immediately if you want the role."

"I'll do that right now. And now that I know how Vito handles himself and vice-versa, I think he and I will become quite a team."

Chapter 24
April 2130

"Rings Around the Enemies"
(Thread 3 Chapter 7)

"Welcome to the meeting, Ms. Nadira. I hope you enjoy the day. Please give me your cell phone, POV camera, and any networked devices in your possession." Viola smiled blandly at the registration desk clerk.

"All I have is my cell phone. Why are you taking it?"

"We want to keep the presentation and follow-up discussion uninterrupted and confidential. According to your registration form, you are the president of a company called B-Ware. What does it do?"

"We develop A.I.-based predictive apps. My company's tagline is 'the Future of Brain Software.' You should visit our Website to learn more."

"I'm sure we've already done that because you're on the invited list. Here's your information packet. Move along, now."

Viola recognized no one but chatted pleasantly as she mingled among attendees waiting outside a conference room in a hotel near the Javits Convention Center, no doubt chosen because the meeting attendees would blend invisibly into Manhattan's bustling throng. She stepped aside when the doors opened at nine forty-five, waiting until ten to take a last row seat when the speaker, displaying one slide, began talking.

The Syntagra Opportunity "Bringing It All Together"

- Unites cutting edge technologies used in: Big Data Platform Companies Surveillance Capitalism Artificial Intelligence
- Investors can collaborate via Syntagra, skirting detection and legal issues.
- Syntagra software given at cost to investors.
- Investors share Syntagra profits proportionately.
- Limited Time Offer

- Must buy in and transfer $250,000 down payment before leaving conference room.
- If you do, additional information will be forthcoming.

"Good morning to you smart visionaries. I represent a start-up company called Syntagra, whose plan is just like yours, capitalize on the short-term opportunities that global markets and state-of-the-art computer technologies offer. Please pay attention to the only slide I will present. As it says, Syntagra is bringing it all together.

"All of you work for companies that either develop or use the technologies spelled out in my first bullet point. Think how much more you could do, or how much more money you could make, if you could work together. But you can't because of government regulations. But you can skirt all issues if you invest in Syntagra. "Because Syntagra is a privately held offshore company, investors collaborate below the radar via Syntagra, not via their individual companies. And investors can get rich in three ways; they get all Syntagra software at cost, they get a proportionate share of Syntagra profits, and they can collaborate to maximize their company's market share.

"That's all to my presentation. Now, here's what I want the audience to do. Divide into groups matching the first bullet point's classification, select a leader, and be prepared to participate in a discussion that starts at eleven. We adjourn at 3 p.m. This is a one-time only opportunity. If you want to buy in, you must do so before you leave, transferring $250,000 immediately. If you invest, you can take your industry, your company, and yourself to the next level. Are there any questions before you break into groups?" There were none.

"OK, have at it."

"Viola sat with the A.I. group for the first hour, then circulated among the others for the remainder of the day, often impressed by the devious intentions that emerged. She was one of many to invest, but her method of payment was unique. She hacked into a corporate account of an unsuspecting person, transferring via Blockchain the amount needed. Viola left unnoticed after submitting all requisite forms.

Electra didn't remove her mask until she was miles away, driving south on I-95 towards DC, enjoying the self-contained solitude of her Mustang as she planned the next move.

She called Angus the following evening. His gruff greeting always delighted her because it differed so from the thoughtful person underneath.

"Hello Angus, it's Electra. How are you?"

"Good, and it's good to hear your voice. You sound different. Are you ready to work for me again?"

"Yes, and I did some snooping. Here's a name for your CIA contact to investigate, Syntagra. It's an off-shore start-up developing A.I.-related software tools for Big Data and Platform companies. And as I've already told you, these tools can cause sociopolitical problems when the wrong people start using them. The next time we meet, we can compare what the CIA tells you to what I've found out."

"I'll talk to my guy tomorrow. And wherever we meet, you can always bring Ariadne."

"That won't be necessary. She no longer needs my close supervision. Please call me when you're ready."

Electra carved out additional time the following week at her GWU lab to insert her latest Linguistic Analyzer app into her still experimental Strong (aka generalized) Neural Net. Unlike her set of Weak (aka narrow) Neural Net apps in which each member could "think" about one subject only, the Strong Net would be her stepping stone to the Singularity. Previous tests had been encouraging because each time she launched its latest version for an extended run against Big Data, its intelligence grew. This time she would point it to parallel process all her hidden directories as well as Big Data.

As she drove home that Friday, she decided to reward herself by visiting a popular sensual pleasures café where she could practice some of her new hobbies.

Keeping busy by engaging in the new helps me stay centered in the now. My authentic self says I can handle both cerebral and emotional issues no matter where. Thinking and doing are now my raisons d'etre.

Chen Xu rewarded himself every Sunday by taking an early morning drive around Beijing in his black Ferrari, a prized possession that only the privileged could afford, a class he belonged to because he was thriving in 22nd century Beijing, the most populous capital in the world, sprawling and flat, containing 22.5 million people and covering 6500 square miles. And he knew the city's history too, which stretches back three millennia, but today the city is known more for its modern architecture than for its ancient sites like the grand Forbidden City complex, which was the imperial palace during the Ming and Qing dynasties. Nearby, the massive Tiananmen Square pedestrian plaza is the site of Mao Zedong's mausoleum and the National Museum of China, displaying a trove of cultural treasures.

Today he would watch a ceremony at the National Flag Pole located at the center of the Square: twice daily (sunrise and sunset) China's national flag is hoisted or lowered by soldiers. The routine, which takes only three minutes, is watched by hundreds of visitors every day.

Unlike driving in the hinterlands, where China's infrastructure remains a work in progress, Beijing's transportation system is a 22nd century marvel. Highways containing double-digit numbers of lanes accommodate rush hour traffic that is monitored by the world's most sophisticated surveillance system, able to spot traffic problems immediately. The Beijing Municipal Public Security Bureau (still tightly controlled by the Peoples Republic of China Army – aka PLA) dispatches a military SWAT team if any situation appears threatening.

The drive began pleasantly enough as a cloudless approaching sunrise and light traffic gave Chen an opportunity to assess current events. Recent infrastructure attacks he had launched against American targets had all been intercepted, so he wanted to compare his results with those of his T-Cube partners at their upcoming annual meeting. But as he approached the center of Beijing, his Ferrari began acting oddly, veering sharply onto the second highway ring around Beijing and racing away, out of his control. Though he was clutching the steering wheel and pounding the pedals, something else had a grip on the car. It steered across lanes, into and out of approaching traffic, speeding the black streak off and then on entrance ramps.

Chen spotted a convoy of chase vehicles. His Ferrari slowed to let them catch up, and then proceeded to swerve wildly, causing a chain reaction pile-up of pursuers. Whatever had control sped towards the first ring and repeated its performance.

SWAT vehicles appeared in front and back, but the Ferrari was faster and more agile; it dived off the ring and raced directly into and around Tiananmen Square as if the treasonous "Gang of Four" were in pursuit. What had started as his usual Sunday drive had become a demolition derby in which he was a feckless passenger. His last view was that of the National Flag Pole dead ahead.

Electra noted with pleasure the performance of her augmented VR GUI attached to her Network Infiltration Driving app. It gave the same thrill as if she were racing the Ferrari, but none of the pain. That was left for Chen. Electra crossed another target off her list.

Darla still had no clue how $250,000 had vanished from a Cybergard slush fund that only she controlled, but the successful launch of Syntagra – another creation in her expanding Pan-Africa Network Systems corporate portfolio – kept a portion of her anger bottled up. She tapped into it when preparing the agenda for an upcoming T-Cube meeting, satisfied the topics would meet her needs and confident that Chen, Sergei, and Maksim would report results that would meet her expectations, even though her Cyberattacks launched against regional U.S. banks were becoming ineffective. Maybe her partners could explain why. But her agenda would not include Blockchain hacking and other hidden Syntagra intentions. Those were for Darla's benefit only.

Maksim – aka Max the Popper – never bottled his anger because he practiced what Aristotle had preached in ancient Greece:

"Anybody can become angry; that is easy. But to be angry at the right person and to the right degree and at the right time and for the right purpose and in the right way — that is not within everybody's power and is not easy."

Maksim knew much about military power as well as the power of philosophy, but none of his superiors knew that Maksim wanted to be a Russian reincarnation of Pericles, the "First Citizen of Athens," that most influential Greek statesman, orator, and general during the Golden Age of Athens. Max idolized what Peter and Catherine the Greats had set in motion: a march towards a czarist version of the

Enlightenment that was halted by the Communist Revolution. If Max were the "First Citizen of Post-Modern Russia," he would lead Russia to the greatness he envisioned, greatness that needed his fortitude and formidable military power.

The Popper used all the power at his disposal to prepare for the next S-Cube attack.

His plan was a model of military simplicity: keep your forces hidden until ready to strike and then mass troops to overwhelm the enemy. He inserted into London a team of three packing enough uniforms, weapons, explosives, and dollars to accomplish the first objective: convert a large truck into a combination mobile hideout and bomb. The team would then contact him via encrypted Deep-Dark Web communications channels, awaiting further instructions.

Four days later, the team leader called Max at midnight London time. The Popper did most of the talking.

"Well done, my S-Cube Warriors. I and a team of two of your comrades will rendezvous in forty-eight hours at the coordinates I shall give you now. We shall then have twenty hours to reach our final destination. That will be plenty of time for perfect practice." Max's stealth VTOL jet transport inserted himself and his team at the designated time and location, a grassy field next to a deserted highway leading towards Folkestone. Flashing headlights signaled the truck's location; five minutes later the six-Warrior team huddled briefly for the Popper's commands.

"I shall drive us to our staging area. Then we shall eat before I give you final instructions. And then we practice for perfection. Are there any questions?" Five heads nodded no in unison. The Popper smiled as he congratulated his men.

"You are my S-Cube Warriors. You are invincible. Let us go."

The Popper summarized for the last time at 7 p.m. what they were about to do.

"It is good we S-Cube Warriors are strong in brain as well as body, because our attack tonight will turn the enemy's hi-tech sophistication against itself. The small number of guards, tunnel personnel, and train operators who are still needed have become fat, dumb, and lazy, relying too much on computers instead of themselves, but that plays into our hands. We shall be the last truck loaded onto the Euro Shuttle Train departing at eight for the destination terminal in Calais, France. The five of you hidden in the back will activate our EM-Pulser before leaping out to terminate all that greet us. Then we rush to the front of the train, terminating any guards or operators we encounter, and commandeer the engine. Then we drive the train 60 kilometers into the tunnel before decoupling the engine. Ten kilometers later we rendezvous with our extraction jet. Once airborne, I shall detonate our thermobaric bombs. The French won't even be able to say "Au revoir" because we strike invisibly as we continue running rings around our enemies. So, if there are no questions, let us suit up, gear up, and go."

Next day's news around the globe spluttered stories like the one that stunned Darla.

"British and French officials are at a loss to explain why a late evening Euro Shuttle Train blew up while still under the English Channel. Even more of a mystery is how the engine decoupled from the train. It escaped the blast, coming to a stop only when it crashed at full speed into the Calais terminal. All tunnel traffic is suspended until wreckage is cleared. Rescue workers have not yet reached the train, but given the enormity of the blast, the odds of finding survivors are slim indeed. And now to traffic, weather, and sports..." Sobering news, even for dark-hearted Darla. Though it would not cause her to revise the agenda, it did raise warning flags that required careful discussion at the upcoming T-Cube meeting. By the time she deplaned in Harare, she thought she knew how to handle everyone.

Darla's anger showed at dinner the next evening because an important person had not yet arrived. Sergei's cursory chatter hadn't silenced her drumming fingers, but he bravely pushed on.

"Chen is merely a half-hour late, and given how far he has to trav—" Darla's glare froze his next word.

"Chen is never this late. He would have broken our code of silence if something had happened. He didn't contact me. Did he call you?"

"No, and I don't have a contingency contact. Do you?"

"Yes, but Chen often operates on his own. But no worries; I'll follow up after we meet with Maksim tomorrow. And our worst-case scenario isn't that bad. You and I will be proxies for China."

Darla forced herself to be pleasant because she needed Sergei's support. If she wasn't careful, she might be dethroned at tomorrow's meeting because there would be two Russians versus one African.

The meeting began as soon as Maksim landed; he joined Darla and Sergei fifteen minutes later in the same conference room used last year. Darla asked a leading question as soon as the Popper sat down.

"Did the Euro Tunnel train disaster surprise you?" Sergei looked at Max. Only a crease at the corner of his mouth belied his stoic answer.

"Bad things happen all the time, especially to those who are unprepared. But to comrades like us, we embrace whatever opportunities come. There will be others." Max said nothing else, forcing Darla to fill the silence before pointing a question at Sergei. "I have to report that most of my Cyberattacks are being intercepted. Only rarely am I able to penetrate regional U.S. banking networks. What about your money center attacks?"

"I must say the same. Evidently, the CIA is sharing its improved network security software with its allies. I think your President still calls them the 'Coalition of the Smart.' Having heard enough, the Popper took control of the meeting.

"Your results compared to mine show once again that physical power trumps brain power once we strip away the thin veneer of civilization. I think we should adjust our roles. Chen isn't here, but three of us can vote. I nominate myself to be the leader of T-Cube." Max said nothing else, instead placing his SIG Sauer on the table. After the unanimous vote, Max let Darla lead them through her agenda, after which he concluded the meeting.

"Starting immediately, communications go one-way, from me to you. And you can keep doing what you are doing. See what you can do about your Cyberattacks being intercepted. And find out what happened to Chen if you wish. Neither concern me, but I am pleased your rare earths cartel is gaining traction. And I shall continue my random attacks where they will do the most good.Are there any questions?"

Darla kept her mouth shut but would mutter angrily on the flight home because she would have to think rings around the Popper, her newest enemy. For one of the few times in her life, Darla felt outgunned, and that made her even angrier.

Chapter 25
August 2130

"The Hustle"
(Thread 1 Chapter 9)

Electra hustled to fill more of the void left by Ariadne's death by doing more for Angus and R&D projects and taking additional racecar driving lessons. (She had raced go-karts when in high school and could handle motorcycles like a pro.) And every evening before falling asleep she would review her to-do list so she would keep busy the next day. After a late August pre-breakfast exercise session, she would accompany Robin on a visit to elderly clients needing her holistic touch.

When Electra closed the van's passenger door, Robin's intrusive question surprised her.

"Why aren't you letting Ariadne play with Carlton?"

"I already explained why to Zoe. I've taught her how to surf the Internet. She's busy working on her own when I'm not with her." "That sounds pretty grim, but I guess you know what you're doing. And here's another question, guess who's pregnant again?"

"Unless this is a trick question, I have four candidates. And I won't include either of your dogs. So, it could be Zoe or you, or perhaps Carter's latest significant other. Or it could be Jennifer. And from the way you asked me, I'll pick Jennifer."

"You know, sometimes I really do hate you. You're so damn smart and always skate through whatever problems pop into view."

"You shouldn't say that. I have my share of scars and I still wear an eye patch."

"Oh, come on. Your scars look like beauty marks or sexy tattoos and your physique is to-die for. And you must have changed your exercise routine. You're not as gaunt as you were. You've filled out your hard edges in all the right places. What are you doing differently?"

"I've cut back on my training intensity, and for cardio I'm using an elliptical trainer instead of distance runs. It saves time because I watch Internet videos while exercising, and it saves wear and tear on my joints because it's low impact. And I've reduced sugar and caffeine intake by eating smaller portions five times a day. I feel better physically and emotionally."

"I think you're exaggerating again. You told me the same story about feeling better when you adopted Ariadne. But you're not a real mother, like I almost was. She can't mean that much to you or vice-versa." Glancing at Electra, Robin gloated when she spied Electra's involuntary wince, knowing that her cutting remark had scored a direct hit. Having done enough damage, she now directed her criticism towards Jennifer.

"Well, you guessed it. Jennifer's pregnant and Matt's the father. Remember, when we were in high school, how we used to obsess over how fit and youthful she looked. We believed it was a combination of genes and makeup tricks she learned from modeling, but all along she was secretly taking drugs and getting gene therapy to push back the aging process. She even did calorie restricted nutrition and got young blood transfusions until Russell couldn't afford it. Well, it worked because it kept her menstrual cycle running. Her due date is sometime in December."

"Did she and Matt tell Zoe and Russell?"

"Here's another example of your always being right. You told me not to interfere because the four of them had to work things out. Well they did, and it turns out neither Russell nor Zoe is upset." Electra nodded but said nothing, so Robin filled an uncomfortable silence.

"I didn't mean it when I said I hate you. We're still friends, aren't we?"

"We'll always be friends, but when we have a friends' face-off I have to tell you how I feel. Your hostility towards me strains our relationship. We've grown apart and I don't enjoy your company as much as I used to."

"Well, aren't you going to tell me what to do?"

"No. You're thirty-three years old. I've given you all the help I want to. And I've corrected my annoying habit of dumping too much information on people."

"Come on, at least give me a clue what you think I should do."

"I will since you asked, but pull over so we can look at each other." Robin found a place to stop; Electra continued.

"I'll make this brief. Read The Second Sex, written by the greatest modern female philosopher, Simone de Beauvoir. It'll help you become an authentic person. I'm going to walk home from here. I've been with you long enough today."

"Wait. This is the first time you've ever told me to read a female philosopher. Why?"

"You'll find out when you read the book, but I'll give you a head start. Until about two-hundred years ago, men treated women like inferior objects, controlling what they could do and keeping them out of male-dominated positions of power, prestige, and authority. De Beauvoir paved the way for most of the progress made by the Feminist Movement. She's often called the greatest Post-Modern female thinker and Feminist philosopher. So, read it." Electra reached to open the passenger door but Robin's words stopped her.

"Please tell me a little bit more about her."

"She was born 1908 in Paris, the older daughter of a wealthy bourgeois banking family. Her brilliance emerged early. She earned multiple degrees at several universities, graduating second from the Sorbonne at the age of only twenty-one. Only Jean-Paul Sarte finished ahead of her, and only because she helped him. Many fellow male classmates who became leading lights studied with them, and they said she was the smartest. Although she and Sarte never married, they lived an unconventional lifestyle together for fifty years until he died in 1980, six years before she did."

"Some of the books you tell me to read put me to sleep. Is this one better?"

"Decide for yourself, but you should find her writing very clear. You'll like how she uses female physiology – aka the menstrual cycle – to explain why men and women differ. But she methodically shows there's no reason for women to be second to men. Male-dominated cultures throughout the ages have deliberately objectified women as the 'Other' so men could control them legally and economically. Women have every right to become free subjects, and she defines freedom as the ability to choose what's right in spite of ambiguity and uncertainty. That's part of her definition of authenticity, to which she adds acting as an individual, not as a member of a group, and always carefully questioning your choices because there are usually no obvious pointers. By the way, she was bisexual. She provided for a number of young women, actually adopting in 1980 one she first met when the woman was seventeen and she fifty-seven. You fill in the rest." Electra closed the door before Robin could stutter goodbye.

The sunlight shining on surroundings that Electra had never hiked through until today helped settle her emotions enough so she could think about this morning's face-off.

Keeping friendships fresh follows the same recipe for keeping love alive, and it should be easier because sex-related complexities should be absent. I've kept up my part; I've been open and honest and sharing and caring, accepting Robin for what she is. But our friendship is becoming toxic, and her feelings towards Jennifer have poisoned that relationship too. I feel better that I told her how I feel. And some good is coming from it; I get a chance to think about other women philosophers.

Only five are universally recognized, Hypatia of Alexandria, Mary Wollenstonecraft, Hannah Arendt, Ayn Rand, and Simone de Beauvoir. All illustrate how context and commitment fuel the drive towards authenticity; they willed what they became. And unlike their male counterparts who were propped up by clubby networks, they achieved greatness standing alone and owning themselves. There could have been others if women had not been classified second class, and although Modernity has torn down the barriers in most cultures, work at the margins must still be done. But today, men and women can stand as one to make it so and, unlike other aspects of society, I doubt the pendulum of progress will ever reverse.

Perhaps someday, historians will resurrect other great women philosophers, as they did for the first great poetess, Sapho of Lesbos, whom Plato called the tenth Muse.

The walk and talk to myself has brought me home and calmed me down. I'll do what's on my to-do list after I have a peanut butter snack.

When placing a call to Chief Strongarm that afternoon, she got his voice mail, so she left a message that she had to postpone her post-Labor Day trip for visiting Florida's Seminole Indian Tribe. And she called Zoe that evening.

"Matt and I've been wondering about you. How's your day been?" "Interesting, and I just finished an elliptical trainer workout to cap it off."

"Do you have the pro model that has built-in routines and avatars projected on a video display? That's the kind Matt recommends to his clients so they don't get bored and give up."

"No, I chose the basic model because I plan my own workouts and watch videos on the Internet while pumping away. That works for me. And I imagine you're working hard balancing Carlton and your careers."

"Carlton is never hard work;he's my joy. Please think about letting Ariadne play with him again. But that's not why I'm glad you called. I'd like to invite you to something new. Matt is taking Carlton on a Labor Day weekend Zoo outing orchestrated by Jennifer. It'll include all three plus Russell and Robin, who's doing the driving. And while they're talking to the animals, I'm going to be talking to a financial advisor. I don't know much about money, but I'm sure you do, so why don't you come over for brunch on Saturday? It'll be just the two of us, or three if you bring Ariadne. You can teach me about investing before we meet the advisor. I'll even make pancakes. And I'll be sure to have plenty of butter and syrup."

"I accept, but I'll come alone. See you soon."

Electra rehearsed while exercising Friday evening what investment advice she would give, afterwards neatly writing an investment cheat sheet for Zoe, and before falling asleep she surmised what Zoe must be thinking.

Of all my female friends, Zoe's the most authentic. She's constructing her own narrative instead of following what society puts together for her. She knows how Matt fits in her life and accepts how he gives Jennifer what she needs and vice-versa. And the zoo outing will be a good childcare exercise. Matt will have to be with Jennifer a lot more after she delivers. And I'm happy that Zoe is doing investing. That'll make her even more independent, no matter what direction she wants to go. But wherever that is, I'm sure she'll bring Carlton with her.

Zoe had stacks of pancakes ready when Electra arrived at eleven. She said that only Robin criticized Jennifer's pregnancy but her sniping didn't impact working relationships, and that Matt had explained to Carlton he would soon have a baby brother because noninvasive prenatal testing had confirmed the sex. After helping clear the kitchen table, Electra steered the conversation towards investing.

"I've written up an investing cheat sheet to help you avoid some of the pitfalls when talking to a financial advisor. Take a look at it." Electra waited for Zoe to reply.

Investing Cheat Sheet

- Purpose of investing: Maximize return for a given level of risk. There are two kinds of risk.
- **Systematic Risk** is the risk inherent to the entire market or market segment. Systematic Risk also known as "undiversifiable risk," "volatility," or "market risk." It affects the overall market, not just a particular stock or industry. This type of risk is both unpredictable and impossible to completely avoid.
- Unsystematic risk is unique to a specific company or industry. Also known as "nonsystematic risk," "specific risk," "diversifiable risk" or "residual risk."
- Modern Portfolio Theory: MPT is a statistical theory of investing that builds a portfolio of stocks which reduces risk via diversification.
- Capital Asset Pricing Model: CAPM uses regression analysis (OLS) to develop, for each Stock, a linear equation expressing the Stock's return: Return = Alpha + Beta X Market Return.
- Alpha: Alpha is the Active Return of a Stock. It measures the risk-adjusted excess return relative to the overall Market.
- Beta: Beta measures the Systematic Risk of the stock relative to the overall Market. Beta = covariance of the Stock's return with the overall Market divided by the variance of the Market. It is equal to the correlation coefficient of the Stock with the Market X the ratio of the Stock's Standard Deviation divided by the Market's Standard Deviation.
- Note: Alpha is usually close to zero. Beta usually greater than zero. If it is greater than 1, the stock is more volatile than the Market. If it is less than 1, the stock is less volatile than the Market.
- A portfolio of stocks also has an Alpha and a Beta. The more stocks you add to the portfolio, the smaller its Beta, but Beta can never be less than Systematic Risk. Rule of thumb: A portfolio containing 25 stocks has all the Nonsystematic Risk diversified away.

LET COMPUTER SOFTWARE CALCULATE ALPHAS AND BETAS.
How to build a Portfolio:
1. Determine how much money you want to invest.
2. Determine how much risk (i.e. Beta) you are willing to accept.
3. Let a Financial Advisor build a stock portfolio for you OR
4. Let a Robo-Advisor build a portfolio for you OR
5. Pick an Exchange Traded Fund (An ETF is mutual fund that trades like a stock) that matches your Beta and buy it online.

If you buy it online, you avoid paying high commissions.
Caveats:
1. You can't beat the market.
2. Even the current MPT formulas and Robo-Advisor algorithms can't adjust for human emotion. Behavioral Finance and Behavioral Economics teach that the Rational Economic Man (aka Homo economicus) does not exist. They replace him with the Irrational Economic Man, whose behavior cannot be modeled by mathematical equations. Read Kahneman's classic book Thinking, Fast and Slow.
3. Financial Advisors and Robo-Advisors will rebalance your portfolio without telling you. Doing so MIGHT generate commissions and capital losses. Quiz before trusting your Advisor.
4. YOU must make your own investment decisions.

"This is so thorough. I knew I could count on you. I'll make sure to ask good questions when we meet the advisor. I want to talk to a real person, not some computer program, so I don't make mistakes like Russell's. He must have pushed wrong buttons or gave too much personal information. And you can sit and listen. If I get into trouble, please speak up."

"I will, but take a look at my last caveat. You have to make your own decisions so you don't hold others accountable. There are too many stories about friendships being ruined by accidentally giving bad advice. I've said enough, so let's go when you say."

Electra parked at 2:30 in front of a conventional strip mall office that contained a front reception area and four glass-paneled offices further back. A greeter checked off Zoe's name, then escorted the pair to an awaiting advisor named Warren, a professionally-dressed young man who, though his greeting sounded mature, looked barely old enough to shave. He launched into his memorized script as soon as everyone sat.

Electra listened patiently as he dished out investing platitudes, using several to deflect Zoe's questions. After fifteen minutes, Electra nonchalantly lighted a mini-cigar and blew from a knees-crossed position a perfectly formed smoke ring that redirected Warren's monologue.

"I'm sorry, but smoking isn't allowed."

"I'm simply keeping you company. You're blowing smoke too. Look, I'll give you some free advice. Investors today expect you to work for them. Maybe you can invite Zoe back when you know how to talk to her." Electra said nothing further but Zoe did.

"Meeting with you has been very helpful, but we have other places to go so our meeting is over. Please call me when you're ready to let me talk."

As they drove away, Zoe asked about one of Electra's newest hobbies.

"You look so sophisticated, what with your eye goggle and mini-cigar. I've never tried one. Would you let me light up?"

"Sure, I like smoking a mini when having a drink. It's better than an E-cigarette, but don't inhale deeply. Let the smoke fill your mouth so you get the flavor, then exhale."
Zoe liked what she tasted and wanted more.

"I've got an idea. Why don't we stop at a fantasy club so I can compare the taste before and after a drink? Does it go with wine?"
"It goes better with hard liquor, so you should switch from pinot griggio or syrah. Which club do you have in mind?"

"Let's go to the place Carter picked for Matt's Guy Party. It satisfied all the guys, and we can decide how good it is for the better sex. And we don't have to rush home. Matt can practice all domestic duties until I get there."

Both of them liked what they saw when they entered. The spacious lounge had a comfortable number of men and women, paired and single. Electra picked an elevated circular table surrounded by four swivel chairs. Zoe glanced around, then commented after a bow-tied waiter took Electra's drink orders: a Glenlivet 12 for Zoe and a Johnnie Walker Black with a splash for herself.

"It's good we reward ourselves by coming to places like this and trying new things. I like the looks of the crowd and the game rooms. Let's shoot pool after we sample the drinks and light up. How did you know what to order?"

"Some of my Hollywood associates know their liquor." Electra was about to say more but stopped because the waiter brought their drinks.

Zoe spoke after tasting hers.

"This scotch has an earthy flavor. Let me try another mini so I can compare before and after." Electra obliged, doing the same. Zoe said more after several puffs and sips.

"I must not have a discriminating palate. I can't tell the difference. Can you?"

"Sometimes, but I always find the combination enjoyable when drinking socially. It really brings me into the moment. And that's what I hear about pool. It's very relaxing because it forces you to focus on cuing and striking the balls. Do you know how to play?" "No, but maybe we can ask for instructions." Just then, one of the nattily-dressed middle-aged fellows at a nearby table came over.

"My friend and I play pool, and you'll enjoy the game much more if you know the rules. I'm Jake and that's my business partner Joe. We volunteer to teach you the basics of 8-ball. It's the most popular pocket billiards game. May I ask you for your name?"

"I'm Zoe and this is my friend Electra. You're not going to hustle us, are you?" Jake laughed before answering.

"Everyone who comes to a fantasy club wants to be the hustler or hustlee, but we're harmless. We're here just to talk and have a good time. Hey Joe, why don't you describe the rules?" He ambled forward while talking.

"I'd be honored. And we'll have team competition, men against the ladies. And we'll give ourselves a big handicap. But, let's get to the table first so it'll all make more sense." Joe continued five minutes later.

"Billiards is a game that uses physics and geometry. When you look at the table, visualize it as two squares joined together. And notice the diamond marks along the rails. Experienced players use them to line up shots and measure angles. 8-ball is played with a rack of 15 balls. Those numbered 1 to 7 are solid-colored, those 9 to 15 are striped. The solid-black 8 is placed in the center of the rack. After the break, each team picks either solids or stripes and alternates shooting. A person shoots until he fails to sink his team's ball. And a team must sink all its balls before going after the 8. To be good at pool, you have to know how to apply spin to the cue ball so you can control its location. And after the break, good players study the entire location of all balls so they can plot a strategy for running the table." Jake interrupted before Joe could say more.

"There are a lot more rules, but let's not get too fancy. These are enough to get us started, and we'll tell you more about shot-making as we go." Joe explained the handicap when Zoe asked.

"Here's what we'll do. Any ball you or Electra sinks will count, and when it's your turn, we'll let you shoot until you sink one of your balls. We, on the other hand, have to call our shots and get penalized for scratching. That's when the cue ball goes in. And your scratches won't count. By the way, the game is divided into innings, which pair up each team's alternating shots. Why don't you watch Joe and me play one game? Then we'll start a friendly competition. We'll buy all the drinks when we play a five-game contest, each counting for one point. And the losers have to buy the winners dinner at the club, but we'll cap the dollar amount at $100. Fair enough?"

The ladies agreed. Electra had one suggestion after the men completed a demonstration game.

"You have custom pool cues. Can we shoot with yours?" Jake grinned when he answered.

"We normally don't share, but we'll make an exception for you. Let us break to spread out the balls. Then you ladies can take over." Playing beat even Electra's always high expectations. Jake and Joe were pleasant conversationalists as well as excellent pool instructors. Zoe's cueing improved with each game, and she managed several times to sink balls on consecutive shots. Electra held her own, and even though the men won the first four games, everyone liked the bantering being traded, regardless of the score. Joe made a generous offer as the fifth game was about to begin.

"Attention, players. The fifth and final game counts for four points. If the ladies win, we have a tie and the men buy dinner. And we'll let the ladies break. Is game on?" Zoe said yes and told Electra to break.

BAM. Electra opened the table like a pro, dropping the 1-ball in a side pocket and spacing the others across the table while putting the cue ball in the center, right where experts try to place it. Then she studied the table to determine the best shooting sequence. Jake and Joe watched in amazement while Electra commented as she lined up shots.

"I've got a straight shot at the 2, and I'll draw the cue ball for another." BANG. The 2-ball rocketed into a corner pocket.

Her next shot at the 6 had a similar result, the cue ball coming to rest several ball-diameters from the rail, midway between a corner and side pocket. Electra called her next shot.

"I'll kick the seven off one rail so I pot it in the corner, but I'll shoot it soft so I don't bounce it off the pocket sides." Electra's smooth stroke dropped the ball and positioned the cue ball for her next shot. "I'll one-rail bank the 4 into a side pocket, but I'll shoot soft and apply side English and follow so I'm positioned for the next." Electra tapped the cue ball just hard enough for it to roll into position after dropping the 4. Zoe's gleeful clapping drew several new spectators.

She chirped, "Only two solids to go. You go girl." By this time the men were applauding too.

Jake said, "You can walk the 5 down the rail, leaving a soft kiss to drop the 3. If you sink them both, we'll let you combo the 8 with a stripe." Electra waited for Jake's final ruling before proceeding to the 8.

"Gads, we've just been hustled by the prettiest pro I've ever seen. Go ahead and combo the 8. Electra smiled demurely.

"No, I'll jump the cue ball over the 10 to get it." Then she elevated the cue and using a fingers-only bridge popped the ball up and over and into the 8, which dropped securely into a corner pocket. Joe had to ask after the hurrahs.

"Tell us the truth. how long have you been playing?"

"At least an hour a day since February. When I'm shooting pool, I think about nothing else. And when I'm finished, I feel relaxed and reenergized."

As they walked to the club restaurant, Electra made an offer the fellows couldn't refuse.

"I've had more fun today than I expected, so I insist on buying dinner. But you have to pick up the dessert tab."

Zoe asked, "What do you fellows do when you're not hustling women?"

Joe answered, "We're financial advisors, and believe it or not, we make money the old-fashioned way. Many investors don't trust robo-advisors, so Jake and I take the time to find out what clients want before giving advice. If you ever need some, or know someone who does, we'd be happy to help."

As Zoe reached into her bag before volunteering, Electra kidded to herself that Jake and Joe would be kept busy answering a slew of questions.

Economists say there's no such thing as a free lunch. Well at least for tonight, Zoe will make sure the fellows have to earn their dinners.

Chapter 26
November 2130

"Doubling Up"
(Thread 3 Chapter 8)

Angus didn't expect his current staff to match what he had when Electra ruled invisibly behind his throne, but it was plenty good and marginally better than a year ago now that Electra had rejoined, although more as an observer than a participant. She had called him yesterday, promising to attend this week's meeting and she didn't disappoint. She had arrived ten minutes early, chatted briefly, and was now sitting in his senatorial office, Angus at the head of a small conference table and his staffers dutifully spaced around it. Pointing to one of his people, he wasted no time getting into details.

"Tell me the latest about Syntagra."

"There's nothing new to report because information is scanty. We already knew that it's headquartered offshore, somewhere in Africa, and our CIA contact has uncovered nothing new that would suggest collusion with platform companies. He doesn't think much more will turn up." Angus grunted before asking for more.

"What about Isilabad?"

"Not a peep. Either it's gone dark or has been dropped from whatever partnership it was part of. But let's not kid ourselves. Its festering animosity towards the West is in remission for reasons unknown. Good for the Administration and the UN for the time being. We shouldn't expect a shooting war, just more of the usual political posturing." Angus pointed to the next staffer while praising the fellow who had just finished talking.

"You've done good with what you've got to work with. Just keep doing your best. OK, let's hear the latest socioeconomic assessment."

"We gotta give Gardner's administration some credit. It's created a lot of infrastructure rebuild jobs while introducing new revenue-generating programs. And the public doesn't care if some of them are heavy-handed. In fact, the public continues to be mean-spirited because a lot of people are scared of computers taking away their jobs or biotech creating smarter people to replace them. Gardner's in a tough place because the country can't turn its back on the future that biotechnology and computers are creating. Maybe he can hatch a plan for balancing people-job creation against automation and A.I. job loss. China's pushing hard to dominate in those areas. And though not a threat yet, India might do the same."

"What about Russia or Africa?"

"We better watch out for Russia's weaponry.It sells almost as much to the rest of the world as we do, and it continues to meddle in world financial markets. Africa, on the other hand, poses no military or hi-tech threat because it's still reaching for First World status. And it's possible they could be a major player in rare earths markets. Some of its supplies are tightening." Angus nodded, then pointed to the last staffer at the table, a no-nonsense young black woman who covered international politics.

"Post-Modern European nations recognize they need America to fulfill its exceptional role, and let's give Gardner credit for being less combative. He's getting along better with the UN now that Isilabad is quiet, and he openly welcomes competition from China or Russia because he champions survival of the fittest, which plays into his America First policies. And Gardner's trying to balance what economists label immigration policy's biggest conundrum, letting in the right people the country needs to fill hi-tech jobs while keeping out those that drain our social support system or flood the low-tech job market." She took a deep breath before moving on.

"I'll answer before you ask me about rogue terrorists. Our covert ops contacts have nothing but unsubstantiated rumors. There's neither pattern nor footprints leading to who might be sponsoring them or where they're hiding, if in fact they exist. That's the best I can do." Angus sat up straight, preparing to end the meeting. "You've done well. All of you have. Keep finding facts, not fiction, and use your brains to draw supportable conclusions. OK, go get busy." All rose to leave except Electra, who waited for what had become his patented post-meeting question for her.

"What can you add?"

"Not much. You've trained your people well, especially that black staffer, Jovita Winsalla. She's concise and seems competent."

"She's got the right attitude. If some of my political maneuvers come to fruition, I might ask you to mentor her. Would you be willing to help?"

"I might, but I can't promise. Call me when there's something tangible to talk about. And I'll call you if I uncover something on an upcoming trip. I've inveigled an invitation to a Syntagra-related meeting."

"You've always had a knack for sitting yourself at the table, or close enough to read the notes. Mind telling me where you're going?"

"There's no need for you to know, but I'll tell you since you asked. The meeting's in Chicago. Have you been there?"

"No, I'm sorry to say. Any city not orbiting around Washington is outside my solar system. Bring back a souvenir for Ariadne."

"I'm sure you brought back souvenirs when your daughter was little, and knowing how good a diplomat you are, I imagine you brought back something for your wife as well. Did your associates do the same?"

"All the men did, but my female counterparts brought back something only for the kids. All their husbands wanted was their wives to take charge of the kids when they got home. But I'm sure you already knew that working men and women handle family life differently."

"The difference is narrower today than thirty years ago."

"Well whatever the difference, I don't need a souvenir. All I want is for you to get back safe. Any information will be a bonus."

Jared didn't want a souvenir; he wanted his economic advisor to bring back a signed contract from a major platform company and a promise from a high-ranking Syntagra executive for future clandestine payments. These would profit a Jared-controlled service company and a Jared Action Committee Fund. In return, the company would receive tax breaks and favorable legal rulings whenever needed, and Syntagra would join a growing government-dictated Military-Surveillance Complex. Carter Quavah would arrive in ten minutes for a private Oval Office meeting to confirm the details. Corfu brought Carter to Jared, who rose to greet him, pointing to a chair after his chief of staff left.

"Carter, my boy, we're ready for you to put into play two more of your programs. Our people have greased the skids so you and your lawyer can slide into and out of a Syntagra closed-door meeting starting Wednesday in Chicago. And tell me again why the programs are bulletproof."

"Our lawyer confirms that independent review isn't needed because the contract covers non-governmental entities. Our target company, which is the first of several, is charging a fair price for legitimate services. And only an idiot thinks PAC contributions have no strings attached. All you need to do is put enough people between you and Syntagra so you can say you don't know what information or favors are being traded. But no one's ever going to catch on if we keep posting enough fake news about the benefits of platform company surveillance." Jared smiled as he redirected the conversation.

"Have you been to Chicago? Ever since it elected a female minority mayor, it's been a model for enlightened local government. But reputations live a long time. The city is still known more for all its crooked politicians than its skyline."

"Only to O'Hare Airport. But our lawyer has, so I'll ask her to brief me. Where's the meeting?"

"At the Gleacher Center. You've got two rooms at the Fairmont, one for you and one for Buffy Gunstein." Jared rose to end the meeting, giving parting advice as he led Carter to the door.

"By the way, there'll be invisible security at the meeting. Our people tell me Syntagra plays for keeps, and I don't have to tell you surveillance capitalism and the platform economy are major league. I know you can handle yourself, but remember this, if you want to run with the big dogs, you gotta learn to pee in the tall grass. Make sure you and your lawyer keep your eyes and ears open."

That evening at Buffy's upscale condominium, Carter paused between a light dinner and an anticipated heavy bedroom session to talk about the trip.

"No one needs to teach you about cooking. Your chicken piccata is a pleasure to my palate. I'll consider dinner a repayment for what I've already taught you about platform companies tapping into Big Data. Now we'll force-multipy their impact by sharing government surveillance data with the major players linked to Syntagra. It's definitely a win-win, and your job is to make sure any audit trail steers clear of Jared." Buffy rose to clear the kitchen table.

"You know we think alike, so I've already got that taken care of. Come on, help me load the dishes before I take care of you in the bedroom. And if you're good tonight, I'll tell you all about Michigan Avenue's Magnificent Mile. I've shopped there before, and you can buy me something nice at one of its boutiques. Jared's paying you enough so you don't have to bury it in your expense account." Carter had no time that evening to talk about shopping.

Electra put on her Viola disguise before driving to Dulles airport early Monday morning for the first flight to Chicago, packing only a shoulder bag because she planned to stay no more than a day, hoping to avoid the bulk of pre-Thanksgiving travel congestion. Her flight would land at nine, which gave her three hours to reconnoiter before the meeting. She used the two-hour flight to review her plan. I can snoop for links if I keep a low profile. I'll listen to the talks, sit in on sidebar discussions, and schmooze appropriately. And I know how to get from O'Hare Airport to and from the Gleacher Center, which is University of Chicago's Downtown business grad school campus, supposedly a world-class corporate meeting center. Should be a great meeting venue. All I have to do is take the Blue Line to the Jackson stop, then cross under to the Red Line and take it north to the Grand Avenue stop, then hike a couple of blocks. Compared to the Big Apple's subway system, Chicago transit system – aka the CTA – is easy to navigate. And I've got my cell phone for backup. And if there's a reason to stay an extra day, I'll extend my Chicago Marriott reservation.

Arriving on time, Viola was one of many corporate road warriors trudging resolutely through O'Hare's network of terminals, following signs and riding walkways to subway departure. As the train sped towards the downtown area (aka the Loop), she was disappointed by its noise level and rough ride when compared to transit systems in newer cities, but she knew that older places like Chicago, even when their infrastructures are modernized, can't match the glistening cities that have sprung up in China, the Far East, and some of the Arabian States.

The elevated sections of the route sliced through Chicago's storied Northwest Side, a once-gritty mix of ethnic neighborhoods that have benefitted from fifty years of urban gentrification. The cold overcast and barren trees belied Chicago's "City in a Garden" motto.

The prettiest Chicago virtual tours I've seen must have been recorded in spring and summer months. I'll have to come back then to enjoy its architecturally stunning waterfront skyline.

The trek to the Gleacher Center crossed Michigan Avenue, giving her a dramatic contrast to what she had just seen. Sullen clouds accompanied by a biting wind couldn't dull the view of immaculately maintained buildings, but light street and foot traffic surprised her.

Chicago's the third largest city in the nation, but when compared to the largest cities in the world, it looks deserted. And I'm not complaining. Virtual tours of international mega-cities have the ambiance of crowds rushing from the Superbowl. No thanks.

Viola timed her arrival so she would blend in with other meeting registrants. When she picked up her packet at the check-in table, she asked one of the officials why there was less screening this time than before.

"Oh, don't you worry. Our security is just as tight, but it doesn't need to be as visible because everyone attending has already bought into Syntagra. You'll be plenty safe. And this time, you can keep your electronic devices. Enjoy the meeting."

Electra sat in the back of the auditorium, reviewing the two-day agenda before the welcoming speaker talked.

There are a couple of breakout discussions I should attend tomorrow, so I'll confirm my Marriott reservation. And this evening's mix and mingle cocktail hour will give me a chance to eavesdrop. I might see someone or hear something I'd never learn about anywhere else.

As the afternoon speakers droned on, Viola paid more attention to the audience than to what was being said. She scored when playing her own game – identify the security people – because doing so fine-tuned her early warning system. And she jolted to attention just before the meeting adjourned.

Carter Quavah is here. I better mingle near him and listen to what he has to say.

Watching Carter obliquely, Viola filed into an adjoining club room already set for drinks and hors d'oeuvres. She smiled to herself when his eyes scanned briefly in her direction but kept moving while talking to an attractive lady who was obviously his business partner. She looks about his age and his type too, attractive features and brownish hair, smart, fit, and trim; she's presentable anywhere. She looks predatory too. I'll have to move closer to get a better view.

She did but heard nothing substantial, other than their intention to begin contract negotiations with at least one of the premier platform companies. Viola continued to circulate but nothing caught her attention, so she decided to depart for the Marriott, but a sudden revelation hit when she picked up her coat.

Carter always keeps his laptop close-by. I saw it tonight. If I can swap and copy and return, I can snoop into his plans. Now I know what I'll shop for on the Mag Mile."

She sat in a now-empty reception area, using her cell phone to find a nearby electronics store, picking Cyber City located in the Hancock Center because she could window shop part of the Mag Mile. Tiny Italian lights twinkled gaily in trees and on storefronts already decorated for the upcoming holidays, adding to the vibrance of a surprisingly large crowd of shoppers.

Viola bought everything she needed: two laptops and requisite carrying bags plus cables and controllers for transferring all operating system software and directories. She also bought a handle and wheel-equipped carrier that could hold her laptops and shoulder bag. She put everything in it and wheeled away before buying a couple of bananas at an organic food kiosk en route to the Marriott. Then she bought from a vending machine two bottles of Coke before locking herself in for the night. After carefully removing her disguise, she downloaded from her home computer network all network security apps she needed to transfer, hack, and decrypt everything on Carter's computer. Then she set the alarm for 5 a.m., falling asleep immediately because she hadn't slept in 24 hours.

After waking fifteen minutes before the alarm, she went to the front desk to obtain a complimentary swimsuit that she wore first in the fitness center and then in the pool. By 8:45 she was one of many in the meeting room waiting for breakout session announcements. Spotting Carter, she sat close enough to listen so she would know which he would choose, and a half-hour later she was sitting just behind him.

Luck was with her that morning because Carter's behavior pattern hadn't changed. He placed his laptop underneath his chair; forty-five minutes later the facilitator called a fifteen-minute break, which gave Viola all the cover needed to swap computers. She placed her jacket over the back of her chair and, after ducking into the check room to retrieve her second laptop, went to one of several Wi-Fi rooms and proceeded to transfer everything from Carter's computer. The few people who noticed her returning ten minutes late soon forgot because others straggled in after her. After re-swapping, she congratulated herself while listening to the speaker.

Mission accomplished. Now I can forget about Carter and pay attention to what others are saying. And I can leave after lunch because by then I'll have heard enough.

But plans changed abruptly when people filed into the buffet room. Viola spotted a late arrival, Darla Tinibu.

There's a connection between Darla and Syntagra. I can walk away with a double play if I can download her laptop too. And lucky me. My laptop is identical to hers. This is going to get interesting.

Viola shadowed Darla until the second afternoon break but found no opportunity to duplicate the morning swap, so she prepared an alternative meant to trip up Darla. As people filed out for a snack, Viola orchestrated a collision that tripped the person in front of Darla. Darla fell clumsily, swearing at the oaf she landed atop as her laptop and cell phone clattered loose. Pretending to be startled by the commotion, Viola stumbled over the pair on the floor and dropped her laptop too. In the ensuing commotion, she picked up Darla's laptop and phone, then faded into the background. Then she retrieved all her belongings and left, putting her warning system on high alert.

It was good she did, because Darla yelled to the security person picking her up that the person who had tripped over her had taken the wrong laptop and cell phone. No one knew who it was, but the security guard radioed for a partner to scan the surveillance monitors. Five minutes later they identified the person – a woman – and plugged into Chicago's police surveillance network to track her, coordinating "soft pursuit" via local law enforcement.

Though the wheeled carrier slowed her down, Viola blended in with the afternoon subway commuting crowd. She watched for security guards, detecting none on the train. She spotted none at the Jackson stop where she would transfer to the Blue Line. Rush hour trains to O'Hare come every five minutes, so she boarded one before a CTA guard who had spotted her could catch up. But Viola saw him board several cars away.

The chase is on. Time to take evasive action.

Viola got off at the third stop, a bustling transfer point among several subway lines, but the CTA guard did too and pushed through the crowd to catch her as she stepped onto an escalator.

"Oh, Miss, please come with me. There's a complaint you took someone's belongings by mistake."

Viola acted surprised when she turned to face him. But instead of speaking, she kicked him in the groin, then kneed him in the chin as he fell forward. The blow tumbled him backward, causing a chain reaction that tumbled people into a clump. Viola disappeared into a crowd heading towards a down escalator and resumed her flight to O'Hare.

She encountered no problems until reaching the O'Hare terminal where she spotted two more security guards, so she headed to baggage claim. She paused at a carousel to plan her next move, acting instinctively as another set of guards closed in. She ran to the conveyor belt opening that recycles luggage not picked up, jammed her carrier into it, and then dived through. She covered her tracks by jamming enough luggage to stop the belt, then dragged her carrier to another conveyor where she climbed through the opening.

She ripped off her Viola mask after ducking into the nearest bathroom, stashing it in one of the laptop cases, then exited carrying only two laptops, inconspicuous among a stream of ladies. She had already divided the contents of her shoulder bag between the laptop cases.

I'm nearly in the clear. All I have to do is check in for my flight and keep alert while waiting in the frequent flyer lounge.

Electra used the time to confirm both laptops had survived the escape. When her flight was airborne three hours later, she could finally stand down, satisfied that today's excitement had exceeded her expectations. She made only one more wry comment before letting her brain freewheel.

I forgot to buy Angus a souvenir. Well, I'll do that when I deplane. He'll think I bought a Chicago Bears cap at O'Hare. Or maybe I'll get a Cubs hat. Or maybe a Bulls or Blackhawks cap. Or maybe one of each. No, I don't want to exceed his expectations. At least for souvenirs.

Chapter 27
December 2130

"Unexpected Exchanges"
(Thread 1 Chapter 10)

"Roger that, Trooper-One. You are ten clicks away and five-by-five in the pipe. Am tracking your armored personnel carrier leading two supply vehicles and one infantry fighting vehicle riding tail shotgun. And you have one eye in the sky. Over."

"Roger that. Nothing in our scopes. Desert weather conditions making mission SOP. ETA in—" the transmission stopped abruptly and all radio gear went dead in Comm Base Echo's communications center. The lead tech scratched his head before barking to his backup,

"Run a failsafe test. If hardware gets a green bar, reload the software. Do it now."

Max the Popper already knew the results before leading his attack sortie into battle. He had activated the EM-Pulser, disrupting all communications and was poised to issue orders from his lead APC. "Warriors, our target is deaf and blind one kilo away. My team will use our drone to take out theirs and then blast the tail IFV with thermobaric missiles. Second team, take out lead APC and terminate any troops that try to flee. Then we insert into the convoy and proceed to the communications base. We go now and make it so." The drivers in the supply and troop exchange vehicles gaped at the scene now unfolding before leaping out to defend themselves. Two unidentified military vehicles streaking across the terrain had just pincered into their convoy, destroying front and rearguard APC and IFV before disgorging exotically-clad troopers who raced to terminate any survivors. Ten minutes later, Max gathered his troops. "Well done, my warriors. Now we lead the convoy to our next victory."

"Equipment's working again. I'm tracking the convoy, but they aren't answering. Whatever took us offline must have done the same to them. Tell our guards to expect convoy in ten minutes."

Late afternoon desert heat and a glaring sun had sapped the guards' attention, and they looked forward to swapping places with personnel the convoy was bringing. They still practiced incursion defense daily, but their zeal had diminished because there had been few attacks in over two years on any of the UN communications bases dotting the desert landscape. The guards waved the vehicles into the compound, not knowing that the consequences would soon test their last acts of valor.

The Popper's troops stormed out, blasting anyone or thing in their way. All personnel on the base rallied to fight, but an incredibly fast-moving force using flash-bang action disoriented the defenders, ending the battle in fifteen minutes.

Max addressed the five survivors after his troops herded them into in the compound yard.

"I salute you, who are about to die, for fighting bravely. And I give you a choice. You can die with honor, battling one-on-one against my soldiers, or you can wait until we destroy your base. And we will let anyone who wins live to die another day. Choose your weapon if you wish to try." All survivors stepped forward, facing Max eye-to-eye. The shortest volunteered first; he would not be the last.

Forty-five minutes later, the Popper addressed his troops before they would drive to a remote extraction location.

"Our enemy fought well. They are well-trained, but we train better. They have adequate weapons, but ours are superior. You have seen once again the firepower our turret-mounted automated Mega-Gattling Gun can unleash. And I shall detonate our thermo-barics once we are safely away, burying everything in a pile of rubble. Let us go…"

The UN quashed rumors surrounding what appeared to be another addition to a list of unexplained disasters that conspiracy advocates would try to connect to a phantom terrorist group. Angus had heard about the attack only through his CIA backchannel contacts, but he didn't mention it to his people because they wouldn't have a clue how to investigate until tangible evidence materialized. So far, there were no tracks leading anywhere from the ruins.

Angus called Electra sooner than she had expected, offering to cook his signature Sunday breakfast in exchange for what she had brought back from Chicago.After disconnecting, Electra hurried to her workstation to print out a document she had downloaded from Carter's laptop, deciding how much to share with Angus.

Carter is venturing into areas beyond his reach. His so-called great game takes him into an economic and military minefield. I don't know if he's given Jared what I'm looking at, but I'll give Angus a summary that I'll talk him through. Then he can let his people dig deeper. An hour later, Electra printed out a page she would use at Sunday's breakfast.

I have a couple of days to practice what I'll say, so it's time for a break. I think I'll let my subconscious rehearse while I practice shooting pool.

The Great Econo-Military Game
(The Quavah "Great Game" for the New World Order)

Major Player Alignment:
- United States India
- China Russia

Significant Minor Players aligned with United States/India:
- Canada Mexico England Australia Western Europe Japan Israel Taiwan
- Significant Minor Players aligned with China/Russia:
- Pakistan South America Middle East Isilabad Micronesia/Far East South Korea

Still in Play:
- Africa
- U.S/India Alignment might maintain long-term dominance:
- Russia continues Imploding
- China overburdened by Aging Population

But the Future is unknown. China/Russia can cause serious problems.
- Authoritarian/Directed Capitalism has short-term advantage
- "Pivot to Far East" could increase wages in Authoritarian-States and decrease Democracy's lure
- Rationale for the Alignments:
- U.S. and India "think alike." U.S. supplies Technology/Weapons India supplies Brain Power/Boots on the Ground

- China and Russia share flawed Ideological Roots but push Authoritarian/Directed Capitalism. Russia supplies Weapons and Financial Mkt ControlChina supplies Targeted Technology (Biotech A.I.-Robotics) and Econ. Power

Issues for Consideration:
- Nuclear WMDs assure "Word War III" a Pyrrhic Victory (Wars will be limited in scope and duration and won by superior technology)
- China continues maneuvering to secure Sea Lanes and Energy Supplies
- Russia clings to hope for regaining parity on World Stage
- Pakistan plays U.S. versus China for Military/Economic Gain
- India/Pakistan hostility rooted in Religion/imperialism
- Isilabad/Middle East Conundrum remains

What the U.S. Must Do:
- Remain the only "Exceptional Superpower"
- Dominate Outer Space and Cyberspace and Advanced Weaponry
- Keep Capitalism as effective as Authoritarian/Directed Capitalism
- Strike "America First" Alliances with "Favored Nations"
- Work around the UN
- Be "Tough Enough"
- Keep People Employed
- Use Big Data and Surveillance to maintain control
- Control Biotech and A.I.

Electra reviewed her document one more time as she drove to the upscale Georgetown neighborhood where Angus lived, hoping he would like it as much as she would like breakfast. Angus explained his recipe as he served in the kitchen.

"Challah French Toast is heavy any way you look at it. Heavy on taste, heavy on cream, eggs, butter, and cinnamon. Heavy on calories too, but Nikita's visiting our daughter in Pittsburgh so I won't tell her if you won't. And after breakfast, you can tell me what you learned in Chicago." Electra reached into her bag.

"Will do, but first I want to give you a souvenir. This Chicago Bears cap has an adjustable strap so it'll fit you no matter how big your head has to get to absorb all the info I have for you." Angus modeled it before taking another bite.

"It fits. I'm ready. So, what else did you pick up in Chicago?"

"Your boy Carter attended the Syntagra meeting. Or should I say Jared's boy. I'm not going to snoop any further on this, but have your staff investigate further." Angus leaned in for the details. "Carter's the point person for a Big Data contract between some of Syntagra's partners and something he and Jared have conjured. Of course, he wouldn't tell me any details, so have your staff talk with your contacts. And don't mention to anyone that I saw Carter. And if by chance you run into him, don't say I saw him. We don't want him thinking that I'm spying."

"I won't. What you've found out is news I can use if Jared strays too far. You did well."

"But there's more, and it has ominous implications. I asked Carter if he likes working for Jared. You know what he used to say. Well, his story has changed. He likes what Jared is pushing for, and he told me about a grand plan he's hatching. I listened carefully as he rushed through the highlights, and I've written down for you all I could remember. Let me explain what I have." Electra continued after giving Angus her summary page.

"Carter's beginning to connect economic programs to possible military adventurism, dividing the international order into two camps, the United States and India versus China and Russia. And he's already placed the other nations in one or the other. Only one continent is still in play, Africa.

He thinks that the other camp might leverage authoritarian capitalism to eclipse democracies, so his recommendations are meant to keep America at the top of the pecking order. It's a worthy goal but needs a diplomatic touch that Jared doesn't have. Maybe his successor will, but don't count on it. Look through this and ask me questions before I leave." After rumbling to another room to get his reading glasses, Angus did so while skimming the page.

"I guess he calls it 'the Great Game' because he's comparing the current situation to the 19th century confrontation over Afghanistan and Central Asia between England and Russia. Do you think he's on the right track?"

"In places. I think jobs and economic growth are keys to growing the middle class and shrinking income inequality. But he better balance too much surveillance and too many hi-tech hindrances against the public's demand for privacy and China's aggressive patent piracy for DNA and A.I. dominance. And I agree that the Middle East will continue to be a conundrum. There's a lot here for you and your staff to digest, but now you know what might be heading your way. So, there you have it. And I have errands to run, so I'll be on my way." As they walked to the front door, Angus had one more question.

"Uh, before you leave, let me push my luck. Did you pick up anything about a rogue terrorist group? I don't think you heard about a UN communications base that exploded. No survivors, no clues. Did Carter mention anything?"

"No, and I don't plan to snoop about that for you, but I'll let you know if I stumble across something. And if I do, I'll trade it for another breakfast. Happy Holidays."

Electra placed her first Holiday call that evening to Su and Kameyo, learning the pair would spend Christmas this year like last, visiting Hud in Austin. He planned to give them tours of Solar Panel and Martian Farm operations his partners had built. Su ended the call by assuring that all drug development projects were on target per their last conference call. Afterwards, Electra added Chief Strongarm to her call list before calling Professor Ravenhill.

Ravenhill's gruff voice changed to a more pleasant tone when Electra announced herself.

"Yes, yes, Kittner. Merry Christmas to you. How is that clever brain of yours?" Electra gave an edited summary that took about a minute, then asked about him.

"I've been getting my name in an article or two. Did I ever thank you for the Bioethics Primer you sent me? It was a big help. And I'm glad you called. What do you know about Quantum Information Science?"

"Some of the basics. Why do you ask?"

"The Information Sciences department asked me to write a blurb for a QIS book one of their professors is writing. I don't have time to read it, but maybe you could. I'm supposed to put a biotech spin on what I write. If you give me a good enough summary, maybe I can get both our names mentioned."

"Just use yours, not mine. Email me the book's galley proof so I can build a bullet point summary that you can wordsmith into as much as the editor wants. Consider it my Christmas present to you. Would it be OK if I send it the first week in January?"

"Yes, yes. I'll Email it first thing tomorrow from my office. I knew I could count on you. You're always at the top of my list."

Electra spent the next two days reading what Professor Ravenhill sent, connecting it immediately to her knowledge of Quantum Physics and Quantum Biology.

QIS is merely the application of Quantum Physics for defining entropy at the most granular level— the atomic level – because entropy is Nature's process for encapsulating information. The author has categorized QIS into three components, computing, sensing, and communicating. All three are used at a cellular level, and only Quantum Biology can explain how organisms work. Hydrogen ion transport supports enzyme synthesis, drug receptor communications, and even photosynthesis.

And I better point out that when entropy increases, information decreases. This may seem counterintuitive because although the entropy in the Universe is always increasing, so is information humans have. But this illustrates the distinction between internal versus external processes. An organism can decrease its entropy because its cellular exhaust increases the entropy somewhere else.

I'll title my bullet-point list Consequences of Quantum Information Science. And I won't send him my summary until January. And I'll tell him it was harder to summarize than I thought. That'll make him even more beholden to me.

Electra reviewed her bullet-point document before having a dinner snack, convincing herself to walk through the neighborhood after eating so she could view Christmas lights.

I sometimes get stuck in my own rut, so I'll do something different. It's good, mentally and physically, because whenever I change my routine, I always feel more alert. But why is that so? Maybe, if I think too long or exercise too long, I deplete localized neurotransmitters. Maybe I'll study that someday.

Electra let her brain think about random thoughts as she wandered about the neighborhood, the bracing air and twinkling lights stimulating her senses and bringing to mind a melancholy folk Christmas carol, I Wonder as I Wander, its lyrics and melody nearly bringing her to tears. The emotional outburst left as quickly as it came, leaving her surprisingly refreshed and reminding her again that unprovoked events can cause unpredictable feelings.

I've just had what the great early 20th century novelist Marcel Proust called a Proustian moment, which has left me happy just to be alive.

Electra called Chief Strongarm early Monday morning to set a firm date for her Florida trip. His kindly baritone voice reminded her of a cheerful, slower-paced Angus.

"And Holiday greetings to you. The winter solstice arrives this Thursday and we shall begin our winter festivities by gathering for our traditional storytelling. How is your little girl? She might enjoy the singing and dancing too. If you have time, please join us."

"I appreciate your kindness but I'm unable to break away. Maybe next year. And I'm calling to confirm a mid-January visit to the Seminole Tribe, assuming you want to extend my programs."

"I do. Pequot and Navajo projects are doing well. You visit the Seminoles and decide what could be done and I will coordinate your recommendations. And we shall build on that triad because you have a strong head and heart to match. Let me give you once again a contact name and number. I shall tell her to expect a call from you this week…"Electra added it to her call list.

Electra paced herself for the remainder of the week by interspersing calls as she filled in details for next year. She reminded Tim and Kwame that she would join them early February at the Las Vegas Cyberspace Expo, and when she called Hollywood, Kathi told her to block out two weeks in February for shooting part of Vito's next Angel of Evil movie. As Friday afternoon dwindled down, so did the names on her list of people to call. Only one remained, the most problematic. Electra thought carefully about what to say to Robin.

The last time I called her she was as angry as ever at Jennifer and Matt. I'll ask if she read The Second Sex and what it has to say about becoming authentic. That might settle her down if she still sounds hostile. Call planning didn't help. Robin seized the conversation as soon as Electra said hello.

"So, guess what? Jennifer delivered a big surprise last Friday, a Down Syndrome baby boy. From what Zoe told me, she's devastated. Serves her right. And she and the baby haven't come home yet because she's still in post-partum counseling."

"Have you visited her?"

"Are you kidding? No one but Matt has seen her or the baby. It's good our client calendar is light until January because he's been going to the counseling sessions too. Zoe and I've been carrying the load at the office." Electra tried to soften the conversation but Robin kept talking over her.

"Zoe says prenatal screening missed the genetic markers, but the obstetrician noticed a big problem and ordered a blood test that confirmed Down Syndrome. Raising a Down Syndrome kid is going to sap the life out of Jennifer and a lot of money out of Matt's savings. I feel sorry for Zoe. Matt's probably going to dump some of the childcare onto her, and Carlton's going to suffer. The only one who won't be bothered is Russell because I've taken him completely off Jennifer's hands. He's been staying at my apartment for the past month." Robin had to stop for air, so Electra finally had a chance to talk.

"How do Russell and your two dogs all fit?"

"Very well. My apartment is like a sleeping and staging area. I take all of them every day to the office and on my client calls. The more I keep Russell involved, the better for him and me."

"I guess you've trained him as well as you've trained Electra and Alisha. So, what do you think will happen next?"

"Zoe's the only one who's planning anything definite. She asked Matt to bring Jennifer and the baby for an early Christmas Eve dinner. She asked me to bring Russell, and why don't I bring you too? You're good at easing tension. Have you made plans for Christmas Eve?"

"Nothing definite. I'll come."

"Good. I'll pick you up Sunday at three. Will you bring Ariadne?"

"Not unless she feels better. She might have a mild case of the Flu, and I don't want to get Carlton or Jennifer's baby infected. What's his name?"

"I didn't ask. We'll find out Sunday. See you then."

Electra spent Saturday researching Down Syndrome, and in her typical fashion summarized while exercising on the elliptical trainer.

Down Syndrome is also known as trisomy 21, which is a genetic disorder caused by the presence of all or part of a third copy of chromosome 21. It's typically associated with physical growth delays, mild to moderate intellectual disability, and characteristic facial features.

And Robin's right. Jennifer and Matt will have a lot to do because early intervention can make a big difference. Each Down Syndrome child is different; treatment will depend on the individual and will be needed throughout all stages of life.

But there are support services available today to help the parents share the load. And it's up to three people to divide it, Jennifer, Matt, and Zoe. My opinion doesn't count.

Electra dashed through a light snowfall to Robin's van, careful not to slip on a couple of ice patches left from a previous storm. She hugged Russell, then sat in the passenger seat next to Robin, who apologized for how she had sounded on the last phone call.

"Thanks for coming. I'm sorry I got so carried away when you called. I used to be a nicer person. We're still friends, aren't we?"

"We'll always be friends, and you never need to say you're sorry if you stay authentic. You've already lived through a lot of challenges and are doing well – most of the time. Robin flashed a tiny smile as she started driving before talking further.

"You've become such a genuine person. How have you managed to do it?"

"I constantly remind myself to be kind, to be authentic. And I always tell myself to keep learning and to stay engaged in new opportunities. Even problems are opportunities if I put myself in the right state of mind."

"Tell me again the title of the book I should read."

"The Second Sex. Read it to remind yourself you're a first-class person when you want to be. I'm certain Russell agrees." Russell beamed while nodding his head.

Zoe did her best to lift people's moods to match her Christmas decorations, but only Carlton rose to the occasion. He danced among the guests, unaware of the uncertain looks on everyone except Russell. Hearing muffled cries coming from another room, Electra played out what she thought would be a safe opening.

"You look good, Jennifer. But then you always do." Matt filled the pause.

"Yes, she's coping quite well, and she'll feel even—" Jennifer's angry words spilled over Matt's.

"Let's stop pretending. I feel terrible and until the kid is placed somewhere, I won't feel any better. Let someone else pick a name. I should have had an abortion, but no, I didn't because Matt wanted another son and Zoe wouldn't deliver. I'm too old to be an active mother, even if the kid didn't have that extra chromosome. And Matt doesn't have extra time..."

While Electra and others listened to Jennifer's rant, Robin slipped away to find the infant, spotting him wrapped in a blanket, slowly turning his head from side to side as his arms reached for a missing person. Robin leaned closer. One long look is all it took for her emotions to start pouring out. She swept the baby off the bed, holding him close, cooing and calming him the way only mothers can. As soon as his cries turned to giggles, Robin marched into the living room, stopping the conversation.

"I'll start taking care of Gabriel right now. You don't want what you delivered, but I do. I'll be his mother and Electra will be his godmother. So, let's exchange Christmas presents. Mine is Gabriel and yours is Russell. Come on, Electra, let's go. You hold Gabriel while I drive." Electra snatched her coat and Robin's before hustling out the front door, grabbing Robin's arm as soon as she caught up.

"Put your coat on and let me drive." Electra held Gabriel for a couple of seconds, then Robin took him back and sat in the passenger seat. Moments later, Electra drove away.

"So, where to?"

"We'll go to my apartment and rearrange it to make room for Gabriel. It might be a little snug, but as soon as Matt and Jennifer clear out Russell's stuff, we'll be just fine. And I'll make a list of what Gabriel needs. Will you help me go shopping tomorrow?"

"Sure. I'll hold Gabriel while you pick things out." Neither spoke for several minutes until Robin broke the silence.

"I feel so wired, so connected to what I'm doing. For the first time I'm beginning to see the authentic me. I feel like standing naked before the world and screaming I know what I am and I know what I want to do."

"I think—" Robin interrupted.

"Shut up and let me finish. You know I'm crazy, but you taught me how to deal with my craziness. Gabriel and I will help each other. You'll see. And do you know who made me pregnant? I did. No one knows I was Matt's entertainment at his Guy Party. Matt's the father of the child I almost had. Gabriel makes up for my miscarriage. OK, I've finished. Now you can say something. What are you thinking?"

"I think everyone should be happy except Matt because he wants another son. Why do you think Zoe doesn't want to get pregnant again?"

"You should know the answer to that. She thought delivering Carlton was going to kill her, and she never wants to go through childbirth again. I know how much it hurts and I'm never going to get pregnant a second time. Maybe someday, a woman can give birth without carrying her own fetus or using a surrogate mother. It's barbaric to pay someone to absorb all that agony. Maybe you're smart enough to figure a way around all that pain." Electra wanted to break into the monologue, but Robin had more to say.

"I feel bad I said you aren't a real mother. I hurt your feelings and I'm sorry I did. You are so good to Ariadne. I hope I can be as good a mother as you. I'm counting on you to make sure I am." Robin had run out of words, so it was now Electra's turn.

"Since you appointed me godmother, I will. And that means I can give you advice, so don't yell at me when I do. By the way, I love the name you picked. The angel Gabriel announced the birth of Jesus, and your Gabriel proclaims the authentic you. Let's get you and Gabriel home…"

Electra offered to pitch in if Robin needed any help, but after they completed Christmas Day shopping, Robin never called nor did Zoe, so Electra used the quiet time to add another page to her worldview philosophy document. She titled the page Electra's Universal Conjecture, reading it one more time before saving the file.

I'll always be a work in progress, cognitively and emotionally, because no matter what serendipity brings it always gives me new insights. I see more clearly how an infinite Universe points to an emergent One World Unity. And this time, I can picture an uncountable infinity of infinite numbers, but I can't articulate what I see. I fear it's beyond the reach of language, an asymptotic limit Wittgenstein succumbed to. But there must be additional infinite numbers beyond the limit of what I can see. Have I just invented Hyper-Infinite numbers, akin to Hyper-Reals? Maybe so, but I've reached a level of complexity that's beyond my grasp. I'll have to let the Singularity figure it out. My thoughts are getting disjointed; I'd better drop the subject to avoid depressing myself further. I know what I'll do, I'll call Zoe. She's the most upbeat person I know.

Zoe picked up right away.

"Thanks for calling. I haven't heard from Robin, but I'll see her at work next week. And I can report that Matt's been a great help to Jennifer. Russell has settled in nicely."

"Robin will be pleased to hear that. And how are you and Carlton?"

"Doing fine. I'm happy for Matt to split time between Jennifer and Carlton."

"But what about you? Do you see enough of him?"

"It's not the quantity of time, but the quality that counts. Robin's done all of us a big favor. But what about you? How are you and Ariadne? Did she get over the Flu?"

"She's OK, but we'll have to see what next year holds. It's bound to bring even more surprises. Let's hope most of them are pleasant..."

Chapter 28
February 2131

"Las Vegas Chase"
(Thread 3 Chapter 9)

"So, what do you know about the Seminoles?" Electra knew as soon as Dyani Hache asked her first question that all the planning she had done for her trip would pay big dividends. Smiling politely, she waited for Dyani to sit at the head of a small conference room table, using the time to center herself.

Her appearance and style match her Reservations Program Director title. She looks fit, dresses well, and gets right to the point. I know what to say, and I'll make sure I keep smiling, speak slowly, and engage her with dialogue, not disengage with monologue.

"You are a proud, progressive, and unconquered people, the only Indian tribe that never signed a peace treaty with the United States. The government finally learned, after losing the third Seminole War, your people can't be defeated. American war historians occasionally compare the Florida Everglades to Vietnam."

"You have the facts straight. American soldiers didn't know how to slip through seven-foot saw grass that can cut like a knife, and they couldn't handle the heat and swamps like my tribal ancestors." Electra added additional tidbits.

"Not even Andrew Jackson, often called America's Napoleon, could defeat your great warrior-leader Osceola. I believe that the Seminoles, who are related to the Creek Indians, are the only people ever to settle in the Everglades. And they accepted black slaves who escaped into Florida. Didn't they eventually form the Black Seminoles?"

"Correct. Slaves and Seminoles sought refuge in the Everglades. Do you know much about the Everglades?"

"It's a national park on Florida's southern tip, covering over a million acres of wetlands. It's often compared to a grassy, slow-moving river made up of mangroves, sawgrass marshes, and pine flatwoods. And it's home to hundreds of animal species. Both Britain and Spain wanted it because it's strategically located for maritime commerce. That's why the Seminoles not only traded from there but had to fight to keep them out."

"So, what happened to my people? By the way, the word Seminoles means renegade or runaway."

"After the third Seminole War, which ended in 1858, the American people were on the Seminole's side, but as sociologists like to say, demographics is destiny. As the expanding population and economy usurped more land, your leaders knew they had to resettle most of the tribe. I read that only three hundred Seminoles stayed; the rest went to Oklahoma Indian territory. But those that remained founded the Florida Seminole Nation. And only after World War II did it decide to integrate into the mainstream U.S. economy."

"I'm impressed. You've done your homework. You know we're proactive and make our own decisions because we've always been free. Today, we have six reservations on which we run resort hotels, casinos, and golf courses. We even have a bureau of tourism. You and I are meeting in our Seminole Hardrock Resort and Casino. And our Tribal Council, of which I'm a member, controls our own business empire. Every Council member is highly qualified. I have an MBA from the University of Miami."

"Then it's no wonder the Seminoles are the most successful Native American Indian tribe. But your economic and social success has diluted your tribal heritage. Every ethnic group eventually is assimilated. From what Chief Strongarm told me, your Tribal Council wants to do what the Pequot and Navajo councils are doing. And that's why I'm here. I would like to describe economic programs that would extend the businesses you already run. May I tell you more?" "Go ahead. Chief Strongarm says I can trust you." Forty-five minutes later, Dyani summarized what she thought.

"You have clever ideas. Adding virtual reality Cyber-Theaters will be a profitable extension to our casinos. And Florida's overflowing geriatric population is a fertile target for eye clinics. You're sure that Chief Strongarm can help me coordinate these projects?"

"Yes, and I serve as his consultant. I can assist when needed." "Good. I have a staff that can handle virtual theme park development and adventure partnering with Disney and NASA, and our museum staff can build educational virtual tours, making us a destination that complements cruise lines. What's your name for it?" "I branded it the 'Surf and Turf Tour – for Body and Mind. Cruise the Seven Seas and the Seminole Reservations.' Have your people wordsmith it to make it better."

"I'll have to get the Council to buy in to what you're proposing. I'll present your programs at the next Council meeting. Now, let me buy you lunch. And this afternoon, if you're a golfer, let's play on one of our courses."

"Golfing is on my to-do list. Perhaps you can give me some pointers. But what about the stories that alligators lurk in water holes? Are they true?"

"Yes, but if you hit your ball into the water, I'll give you another one, and I'll even waive the penalty stroke."

Dyani was a gracious hostess as well as a 7-handicap golfer. She gave Electra a discount on club rental and the golf wear she bought as well as a complimentary room that evening. She even drove her to the Miami airport the following morning, serving as golf commentator and tour guide.

"You must have athletic DNA. For someone who's just learning, your swing has few hitches, and your club face makes good contact with the ball. Does the goggle hamper you? All sports requiring eye-hand coordination need binocular vision."

"I see pretty well. Doctor Holbrook's treatments have repaired much of the damage to my optic nerve, and the goggle screens out disorienting bursts of light. And I can certainly see why Miami is called the capital of Latin America. It's a marvelous blend of U.S. and Latin American culture. Have you lived here long?"

"My entire life. It's a great city, named after the Mayaimi tribe that lived near Lake Mayaimi. Archeologists claim indigenous tribes linked to Mayans and Aztecs inhabited the area by themselves for thousands of years until Spaniards came. It's the only major American city created by a woman, a wealthy citrus grower who owned most of its land. Miami was recently voted America's cleanest big city. Its Metro population of 7 million ranks seventh in the nation, and it ranks 7th in the world according to purchasing power. It also has the largest concentration of international banks, and it's the cruise ship capital too."

"And judging from what I saw when landing, the city has

an impressive waterfront skyline. I'll have to do more sightseeing next time I visit." Dyani pulled into a departing passengers drop-off spot. "When you do, fly into Fort Lauderdale. It's closer, smaller, and easier for me to pick you up. Plan to stay an extra day. We can golf, and I'll take you to see the nightlife."

"I'll be ready for both, and next time I'll pick up the tab. Thanks for your hospitality."

Chief Strongarm had nothing but praise when Electra called the following day.

"You acquitted yourself nicely. Dyani agrees that you have a strong head as well as heart, and she thinks she'll get her Council to approve what she wants. And that will put in place three tribes pushing ahead on your programs. I might ask you to join us at a National Tribal Council meeting, but let us wait for the year to unfold."

"There's more we can do if your National Council is as smart as you. I think you have wisdom as well as patience."

"Your spirit is many-sided and holds many surprises. I marvel at how all the contacts you have provided fit so well. The Navajos like Hudson Haller's wisdom and trust manner, and as soon as I tell Tim Godfrey to drop all the computer lingo, he is easy for me to work with. Doctor Holbrook tells me the instructions you have given her are adequate, and all of this lets me manage from afar. But I might need you to help me more if the depth or breadth of our scope increases. Will you be able to do that?"

"You'll be pleasantly surprised. I always under-promise and over-deliver. You'll see."

Electra saw her way clear for the next two days to focus on business closer to home. When she met with Robin and Zoe to talk about their healthcare business, Robin's animated gestures highlighted her desire to extend services offered.

"I've already got eldercare certification, and I can add to it by getting Down Syndrome caregiver training and certification. We can bring children here or I can work one-on-one. Either way, Zoe can assist, and we can include Russell, Carlton, and Gabriel. And that frees up Matt and Jennifer to do what they do best." Zoe looked at Electra before Robin blurted while blushing.

"That didn't come out the way I intended. You fill in the right words..."

Electra started the weekend by preparing for the Las Vegas Cyberspace Expo, using her security software to examine Darla's laptop and cell phone, taking a break several hours later to collect her findings.

My snooping software meets even my expectations. I've found all of Darla's hidden data. I've traced two Email trails that lead to disturbing possibilities. She's definitely using her Syntagra-Cybergard connection to help her platform company partners. I'll have to hack into the Expo Website so I can shadow her in Las Vegas if she's registered. It's time for me to create a new name and fake I.D.s for another face mask. Then I'll plug my new identity into all my reservations.

After running a random name generator several times, she picked the name Suzanne Lorena (a mid-40's Web developer), then ordered online appropriate clothes and travel items to complete her disguise. She finished her preparations by sending an Email to Tim, saying she couldn't join him in Las Vegas but would call each day at 6 a.m.

That afternoon, after driving to the mall to pick up her order, she ended the day in her usual way, exercising before having a light dinner. Robin called as she was finishing.

"I hope your Saturday has been as good as mine. I've been practicing some of the Down Syndrome certification activities I found on the Internet. Maybe I'm imagining it, but the more care I give Gabriel, the less noticeable his Down Syndrome symptoms seem to be. What do you think?"

"You're right. Nature and Nurture contribute just about the same, so keep doing what you're doing."

"So, what are you doing tonight?" "I'm going to practice pool."

"Where are you going? Are you taking Ariadne with you?"

"I don't have to go anywhere. I've put a pool table in the dining room."

"What did you do with all the furniture?"

"I gave it to the Salvation Army. It's better I have my own because I can practice at home rather than at a pool hall. And I'm sure you can guess who'd tell me how cost-effective that is."

"That would be Carter. Do you talk with him anymore?" "We've parted ways. Does Matt ever talk with him?"

"Only when Matt calls. Carter's a different person now. I guess it's good you and he didn't become co-friends. It was a long time ago, but you never told me why."

"Ten years, to be precise. Why are you asking me so many questions?"

"You're my best friend, and I just want to know. You're a different person now than a couple of years ago, but you still keep your fences up. You never let anyone get too close. What do you do about sex? Are you seeing anyone in Hollywood?"

"Look, you're my best friend, but even best friends shouldn't tell everything. I'm pretty happy right now, and you should be too."

"You can fool other people, but you can't fool me. You hide it pretty well, but I know you deal with bouts of depression."

"Robin, you're my dearest friend, but please don't go where you don't belong. We'll talk when I get back."

"You didn't tell me you're going on another trip. Where to?" "To the West Coast."

"Please call me when you get back. And please be careful. I still need you."

Suzanne Lorena was careful not be noticed by anyone while waiting for Tim and Kwame's afternoon flight to land. Knowing what to say to get their attention, she would follow them to the Las Vegas Convention Center so she could casually introduce herself while they registered for the Expo.

Electra's disguise and introduction worked to perfection. After registering, the trio headed to check in at the Tuscany Suites and agreed to meet for breakfast before walking to the Expo's kickoff meeting. Later that evening, Suzanne waited for another flight, reviewing what she would do when another person landed.

Thanks to my snooping software, I know Darla's itinerary as well as she does. And I'll shadow her to eavesdrop.

By the time Darla and her two associates completed registration at the Expo and the Treasure Island Hotel, she knew how to handle Darla.

Her laptop and cell phone models are the same as the ones she had in Chicago. Now I'll try to swap laptops again at the first chance I get.

Suzanne primed the breakfast conversation with a question that would hook her new best friends.

"By any chance, are you Go players?" Kwame babbled happily until Tim interrupted.

"We'll continue this discussion later. It's time to hike to the Expo." Suzanne segued to another topic as they walked.

"It might be better if you fellows attend different meetings. You'll cover twice as much, and if you do, I'll be with one of you at all of mine. And that way, it'll be easier for us to compare notes." Suzanne's schedule matched Darla's. As expected, Darla planned to attend as many A.I. workshops as were offered. Suzanne positioned herself close enough to spy on her quarry, discreetly swapping, copying, and returning the laptop. Unlike the episode in Chicago, this time there was no commotion. That afternoon, Suzanne and the guys chatted as they followed Darla to a mix and mingle refreshment hour. Much to Suzanne's surprise, Darla chatted with Tim, ignoring the other two. Darla's ability to charm others when it suited her purpose worked. Tim gushed about what he and Kwame were doing. "And we would have won that Go tournament if that damn judge hadn't been so persnickety. Next time, Kwame and I won't need anyone else. In fact, we've used our latest A.I. app programming to load our laptops with beyond cutting-edge software."

Kwame blurted, "We've got code and GUIs that others would kill to get. Maybe someday we'll sell an older release, but not until the boss gives us the OK."

Electra cringed behind the disguise.

Watch out. You've broken my cardinal rule; you're talking too much about what we're doing. Fifteen minutes later, Darla offered to swap business cards, but Tim declined.

"Even in a Cyberworld, business cards come in handy. Sorry, but our boss doesn't let us give them out. But I'll give you my cell number. Call me if you'd like to talk more about software."

Darla bustled away and Suzanne excused herself after setting a time to meet for breakfast tomorrow. It was good the mask hid her anger.

I'm going to walk the Strip to calm down. I'll have to read those two the riot act when they get back to business.

Suzanne strolled to a nearby casino, stopping to eat at one of its snack bars, then immersed herself in the lights and swirl of the gambling crowd. She casually played slots for an hour, then picked up a Coca Cola before viewing the light show on Freemont Avenue, overarched by world's largest video screen, 90 feet high and stretching 1500 by 90. Her mood had elevated by the time she hiked towards the hotel, drifting into pleasant thoughts about previous visits to Las Vegas.

Suddenly, her warning system jolted her back to the immediate. Am I being followed? Whatever triggered the alert never materialized, but Suzanne remained vigilant all the way back to the hotel, feeling another jolt just before she entered, but spotted no one.

Suzanne and the guys stuck to their schedule the next day, as did Darla. By the end of the last seminar, the Electra behind the mask concluded she had learned enough about the latest A.I. software as well as Darla.

I hacked into Darla's computer last night, tracing an Email trail that talked about an upcoming trip to Africa. I'll have to hack deeper, but now it's time to plan for tomorrow.

Kwame's breakfast talk added to what he had told Darla last night. "Everything I've heard at all the workshops confirms no one is close to what we have. People are still working on what we've already built into our apps two years ago."

Tim added, "But I've got some ideas for add-ons. We'll tell the boss when we get back. We've got a flight tomorrow morning. How about you?"

"I don't remember if I'm staying an extra day. I'll have to check my ticket."

Tim poked Kwame before saying, "Let's make one more pass through the buffet and then get to our workshop." Suzanne finished her oatmeal while the guys hunted for more muffins. She spoke first after they sat down.

"You fellows and your boss must be pretty smart. Are you smart gamblers too?" Kwame answered right away.

"You bet we are. We're pros at blackjack and Texas Hold'em."

"I don't know much about gambling, but maybe I can learn if watch you."

"That'll make for a fun evening. Bet on us tonight. Come knock on our door at six. Then we'll go and knock 'em dead at the tables." Suzanne skipped the afternoon session so she could prepare for the evening. She went to a casino to withdraw $5,000, then strolled to the hotel, enjoying sights along the way.

The Strip bustles 24/7, and it's a selfie heaven for tourists, just like Times Square and Hollywood. She stopped to glance at a window display, satisfied with her reflection.

Lisa taught me well. My disguise looks as good as it did on day one. She said I could even wear the mask in water, but I'm not swimming on this trip. I'll exercise in the fitness center, then get set for gambling.

Tim led the group out of the hotel at 6:30, explaining what he and Kwame had planned.

"All Expo stuff is out of the way, so it's time to play. And our boss gave each of us $1,000 gambling money. All we have to do is return the loan, or what's left of it if we lose more than we win. Kwame wants us to start at MGM Grand. If our luck holds, we'll stay. If not, we'll go to Caesars. And we'll walk back to the hotel no later than 1 a.m. And we stay together. Kwame takes the lead for blackjack, then I'll do it for Hold'em. This'll be a night to remember."

Suzanne stood behind the pair. Kwame hit a win streak midway through their allotted blackjack time, so they walked away early, decompressing at a bar before finding a Hold'em table. Losing slightly more than he won, Tim folded after an hour.

"Let's try our luck at Caesars. Kwame can lead the way…"

Kwame walked them through its eight-pool complex, dramatically lighted and lined with Roman columns. Tim promised to lead them through its premier Forum Shop mall later if they walked away from the tables with more chips than they brought.

Kwame's winning streak held long enough for him to declare that he'd won enough for one night.

"I'm getting too wound up, so let's have a snack and then watch Tim play Hold'em."

Tim's luck improved the longer he played. The trio cashed in his chips and walked out winners, browsing the mall on the way out. Even the hidden Electra was impressed.

"If you can't find what you're looking for in Vegas, it's probably not worth having. And if you don't find it here, try the next hotel mall. You can walk a marathon doing so but I've done enough for one night." Tim took the hint.

"We'll grab a cab. You'll be in bed by one." The trio continued chatting all the way to the hotel, parting company at the fellow's room because it was on a lower floor. Suzanne congratulated them one more time for how lucky they had been, then scooted to the stairway.

Darla's thugs finally reported what she had been waiting to hear. After shadowing Tim and Kwame for six hours, they could finally take action.

Darla snarled, "It's about time. You're behind schedule, so follow Plan B. And call me when you've got what I want."

Following at a distance, the leader gave instructions to his partner. "Lucky for us the targets are sharing a room. We can stay together. And remember the drill. We change into hotel uniforms. When I knock on the door, I'll say the female ordered them a snack to celebrate winning. Then we roll in the cart, work 'em over, and roll out with their laptops. And don't shoot unless they give us trouble." Tim and Kwame sat in the afterglow of the evening's excitement, counting their winnings. Kwame reported first.

"I came away with about $600. How'd you do?"

"You beat me by $50. You know, we better get gambling out of our system before the Government forces casinos to use expert systems to track winnings. I read an article that said casino computers someday soon will use smart gambling chips to compare total chip value when a gambler cashes out to the total value of chips bought." Kwame thought that might have unintended side effects.

"That'll drive more gambling into the Dark Web because Uncle Sam can't track what goes on there. But that's not our problem. Hey, let's pack tonight so we can get up and out in a jiff."
They had almost finished when there was a knock at the door. "Room service."

"Tim stared through the peek hole before asking, "What cha got?" "Champagne, fruit, and a selection of sweets, courtesy of the lady you were with tonight." Tim unlatched the door, watching hungrily as two uniformed staffers wheeled in a cart. Suddenly, one pulled a silencer-equipped gun after the other closed the door.

"No one'll get hurt if you do what we want. We're here to collect your laptops. Show us where they are." Tim's eyes darted to Kwame's before both glanced mutely at the desk.

"Thank you, gents. I see them too. And we'll take your winnings as our reward. Now lie on the floor." Tim followed orders, but Kwame froze. The thug calling the shots motioned to his partner, who removed rope from the cart. He proceeded to gag Tim, binding arms and legs, then moved to a still-standing Kwame.

"You uh, you don't need to tie me up. I uh, I'll give you the laptops." He reached for one, then used it to smash his adversary over the head before tackling him. They crashed to the carpet, a tangle of arms and legs, tipping over a chair and spilling everything off the desk.

Tim made his move, rolling into the legs of the gun-toting thug who was gaping at the struggle. He fell backwards on top of Tim, tipping the cart and scattering fruit and tarts. Tim squirmed loose and though his hands were bound in front, used them to grab the hair of his opponent and smash the bad guy's head into the carpet, then lunged for the gun, but the thug recovered enough to pull Tim backward before rolling on top.

Meanwhile, Kwame had gained the upper hand until his attacker pinned him under a chair, which he used for leverage to spring to his feet and start kicking. Kwame rolled into a ball to deflect the blows, but the thug began using the chair as a club. Three blows later, Kwame was out of action, so the bad guy charged to help his partner, who was now pinned to the floor with Tim astride.

Tim saw the other thug coming and stretched for the gun, but in so doing his chin became a prime target, receiving a direct kick that tumbled him away from the gun. He tried to scramble back but the standing bad guy grabbed the gun and fired two shots that sounded like snakes hissing. Tim lay motionless on his back. The second thug struggled to his feet, about to spit out angry words, but the ringing phone stopped him. Instead, he grabbed the money, his partner seized the laptops, and the pair streaked for the stairs, leaving the door open in their wake.

Suzanne let the phone ring a dozen times before disconnecting. *How odd. I'm sure they didn't go out. Maybe Tim's in the shower and Kwame's getting ice. I better walk down to find out about breakfast plans.*

She didn't connect the sound of footsteps dashing down the stairs until she saw the wreckage in the room: furniture tipped and Kwame kneeling next to a moaning Tim.

Kwame bleated, "We were robbed. Two guys took our winnings and laptops." Suzanne knelt next to Tim.

"It's a shoulder wound, but the bullet went through cleanly. Why'd they pick you out?"

Kwame said, "They wanted our laptops, but that doesn't make sense. Just about everyone travels with some sort of computer." The hidden Electra took command. She pulled herself and Kwame up, then snapped orders.

"There's nothing I can do to help. You're not hurt much, but Tim needs an ambulance, so call the front desk. I'll go there to make sure your call gets through."

She watched Kwame stumble to the phone before racing to her room. Once there, a calming clarity centered her focus; all the pieces fell into place while she gathered what she needed.

Darla Tinibu sent them. She'll hack into the laptops if I don't stop her.

Electra jammed her laptop into its carrying bag along with a stack of $100 bills, then calmed her breathing during the elevator ride to the lobby. Flashing lights of an ambulance said she didn't need to say anything, so she walked out of the hotel, unnoticed before powering up her laptop. Five minutes later, Electra's flying fingers displayed what she needed.

I can chase down the laptops because my security software can track the micro tracking chips I embedded. Good thing the laptops are traveling together.

She was about to run for a cab, but changed direction when she spotted a young couple on a tattered motorbike, reaching it before they zoomed away.

"I need your bike. Is this enough to buy it?" Electra shoved a fistful of bills into the girl's hands. She and her friend stared at the stack for a couple of seconds before the guy spoke.

"Geez, this is enough for a new bike. Are you—" Electra interrupted him mid-sentence.

"I'm sure, and yes, I know how to ride. Just look at my laptop and help me plot a course to catch up with the dots." Three minutes later she had directions. The girl pointed while talking.

"Your friends are heading north on I-15 towards North Las Vegas. Go straight until you reach Nevada 159, then take a right. You'll hit I-15 in a couple of miles, then take it north. Too bad you don't have a rider to navigate while you drive." The guy yelled before Electra could reply.

"Hey, I've got a laptop holder in the saddle bag. Let me mount if for you." Electra zoomed away five minutes later.

Darla's thugs didn't need to break a land speed record for Plan B. When they called from the car, she directed them to a chopper pad used by a local helicopter tour company.

"Do you know how to get there?" "Yeah, we've been there before."

"Give the laptops to my associates, and they'll give you the rest of your payment. And don't get stopped for speeding."

"We won't. Adios."

Darla smiled gleefully after the call ended. Soon her men would bring her the laptops she coveted. Soon she would depart for Cybergard Headquarters where her software engineers would extract A.I. and GUI apps, pirating what they needed to make Darla's apps better than the competition's. Darla felt so good she almost decided to tell her men not to terminate the thugs.

The first leg of Electra's chase ended badly after only three stoplights when she broadsided a speeding car. She came away unscathed but her bike was now out of action. She dragged it to the curb where several late-night tourists offered assistance, pointing directions to the nearest cabstand several blocks away. Minutes later, she breathlessly explained her predicament to one of the drivers. "My friends left without me; I'm tracking their cell phones on my laptop. They're on I-15 heading to North Las Vegas, can you follow them to the party?"

"Sure. Sit next to me and help navigate."

"I'll give you double the fare if you get me there as fast as you can."

"Sorry, no can do. I'll lose my license if I get two more tickets. But I'll do the best I can."

"Electra's directions put the cab on the right path but the gap lengthened until the dots veered off I-15, coming to a dead stop several miles west of I-15.

"We'll be there in about fifteen minutes. And if your friends like to party like some of my other rides, that's just right if you want to be fashionably late. Why don't you text them to say you'll be arriving soon?" Electra smiled faintly while nodding. The driver talked more as they approached the stationary dots.

"Your friends picked a funny place for a party. Nothing much here but storage and car rental offices and a couple of chopper tours. What do you—" his words trailed off as one of the dots on the screen unexpectedly sped away. Electra spotted trouble when he pulled into the parking lot of Grand View Helicopter Tours, obviously closed until morning. There were only two vehicles, one with headlights blazing as two men jumped out. The other held indistinct silhouettes of two passengers slumped in the front seat.

Darla's security guard issued a brief report.

"AOK. Chopper just lifted off carrying the undamaged laptop. We'll take the broken one to our tech guy and – uh-oh, we've got a visitor. I'll call back."

"Drive on! Those aren't my friends. Head back to where you picked me up."

Electra's cab dodged out of the parking lot and sped towards I-15. She glanced back, relieved to see no headlights coming. The cabbie slammed on the breaks before squawking.

"What are you mixed up in? Get out of the cab."

"Use your head. You're in their gunsights too if they come after me. Keep going, and I'll track them on my laptop."

As the cab squealed away, Electra asked, "Ever been chased before?"

"I stay on the right side." Electra said nothing else, instead watching her tablet screen while entering commands as the cab swerved onto a gravel road, headlights off. A minute later she reported bad news.

"They're coming. I hope you know the roads better than they do." The cabbie did his best, braking and turning, but the pursuit car kept closing the distance. Electra fingered in additional commands as the glaring headlights approached.

The cabbie saw the crash in his rearview mirror before hearing it.

"Jesus, the driver just lost control. We're in the clear now." "Don't slow down. Get me back to where you picked me up."

The cabbie followed orders, saying nothing. Neither did his passenger, who was still working on her tablet.

Darla ended the call to her man aboard the chopper because she could hear the whir and see its approaching lights. It gracefully swooped down, discharging one person who jogged towards her vehicle, but he never reached it. The item he was carrying blew up, sending him sprawling.

The cabbie gratefully pocketed three crisp $100 bills, offering to take Electra to her hotel, but she declined the offer, preferring to collect her thoughts on foot.

I have the Deep-Dark Web to thank for keeping my laptops out of Darla's clutches. The plastics explosives I bought for boobytrapping them worked as advertised.

Whatever pieces remain become a humpty-dumpty puzzle for Darla.

Sunrise was an hour away, giving Electra four hours to pack and get to the airport for her noon flight to LAX. Planning to ditch her Suzanne disguise when safely in the LA terminal, she made a note to visit Lisa so she could print additional masks.

I have a fresh list of calls to make when I get to my LA hotel, but I'll plan for that later.

Electra puttered in her room until leaving for the airport, then daydreamed on the one-hour flight. By the time she registered at the hotel, she had outlined her plan for the next two weeks.

She made calls from her room, relieved to learn that Tim and Kwame were back in action and happy to hear that other activities remained on target. Then she unpacked, exercised in the fitness center, and swam a mile in the pool. As she came out of the shower, she decided to take the night off.

I've had enough excitement. I think I'll call room service for a light dinner, then surf the Web. Tonight, I'll take a virtual tour of the place where I can see the Holy See. I've studied Catholicism, but I don't know much about its world headquarters, so after dinner, Vatican City, here I come.

Following her customarily thorough approach when studying any new topic, Electra first learned enough history to put any reference into a proper context. Several videos gave her all she needed.

The Vatican's history as the seat of the Catholic Church began with the emperor Constantine's 4th century AD construction of a basilica over St. Peter's grave in Rome. The area developed into a popular pilgrimage site and commercial district, although it was abandoned following the move of the papal court to France in 1309. After the Church returned in 1377, famous landmarks such the Apostolic

Palace, the Sistine Chapel, and the new St. Peter's Basilica were erected within the city limits. Vatican City was established in its current form as a sovereign nation with the signing of the Lateran Pacts in 1929.

The Vatican remains the home of the Pope and the Roman Curia, and it's the spiritual center for some 1.2 billion followers of the Catholic Church. The world's smallest independent nation-state, it covers 109 acres within a 2-mile border, and possesses another 160 acres of holdings in remote locations. Along with the centuries-old buildings and gardens, the Vatican maintains its own banking and telephone systems, post office, pharmacy, newspaper, and radio and television stations. Its 600 citizens include the members of the Swiss Guard, a security detail charged with protecting the pope since 1506.

But what particularly captured Electra's interest was Vatican art. She surfed until midnight, completely immersed in the creative genius of artists through the ages who gave visual life to Christianity's compelling mythology.

Not even I am immune to its emotional tug. The Vatican has a staff of key-keepers who each morning at 5:30, starting at the Atrium of the Four Gates, walk four-and-a-half miles down corridors lined with 300 doors and decorated with priceless paintings stretching to the birth of Christianity. But even the immortality they depict would crumble to dust without an army of restoration workers. How fortunate we are to have all this information available via the Internet. I hope network security protects it as well as the Swiss Guard protects the Pope. How different a world for religions today, which like all social institutions, must either adapt to what people want or get out of the way.

And the same applies to me. I better stay out of Darla's way until I know what's on her mind. How nice that my apps are better than hers. I should always be able to chase down what she's up to.
Electra slept soundly that night.

Chapter 29
May 2131

"Number Games"
(Thread 3 Chapter 10)

Electra had decided immediately after Ariadne's death that all additional Brain Probe development needed to be thoroughly tested initially on one volunteer – herself – so she had recruited Dr. Holbrook to insert high on her left arm an unobtrusive UMPP (universal multi-parallel port) that would interface properly equipped devices directly into her brain. Now she could not only measure the effects of stimuli but also feel them. She always kept currents low enough to avoid neural damage, but experimented at levels high enough to reveal the enormity of her invention. By the end of April, she could articulate to herself, but never to anyone else, what she had accomplished.

I can dial in pleasure or pain, plant ideas, and control behavior. I can alter moods or memory, empower learning, and bring back past experiences. And I can kill or turn a brain into a vegetable if I dial the current high enough. And if I'm careful, I can add some of these features to Tim's Cyber-Theater and Dr. Holbrook's Optic Nerve Knitter. But not until I have A.I. software that's smart enough to control it.

Electra had no dream team to assist her, but because she was an assistant professor at GWU, Professor Ravenhill assigned her some of the best grad students to staff her projects. She parceled out enough work for them to march towards their PhDs while helping build A.I. components she could integrate into her apps, but none of the students recognized her intentions.

During a mid-May performance test, Electra recorded accelerated growth in her Linguistic Analyzer's processing power, proof that the new components worked as intended, and they worked even better when she made code modifications that only she could understand. What surprised her was the slower growth in memory storage than in processing power.

My Analyzer may have crossed a threshold into exponential learning. I'll let it run in the background. I don't know how long it will take until it can solve some of the harder problems I'm configuring, but it's definitely getting smarter. And as long as the exponent remains greater than one, my Analyzer's I.Q. will grow. Who knows, but maybe someday I can ask it questions to get answers for Angus. And that reminds me, I better call him because he hasn't heard from me recently.

Angus boomed a hearty hello as soon as he recognized Electra's voice.

"You missed our last couple of meetings, but you're making up for it now. Guess who invited me to play golf at his club? Our boy, Carter. What do you suppose he's after?"

"I can think of a number of items, but why don't you ask him? Be diplomatic and don't rehash what we've already covered. And don't tell him I occasionally attend your meetings. The less he knows, the better."

"It's too bad you don't play golf. If you did, we'd have a foursome and you could ask questions too. He's bringing that lawyer, Buffy Gunstein, who's on the team Jared helped him build. There's a rumor she and Carter might team up evenings also. I met her once. She's pretty good looking and looks pretty fit. And her personality matches what Carter's becoming. He always liked numbers more than people, but now he's even more willing to trade ethics for economics."
"How do you know I don't play golf?" "Uh, I don't. Do you?"

"I played on a recent Florida trip and practiced a couple of times since then. Why not tell Carter you've invited me? If you'll do most of the talking, I'll do most of the listening. When are we playing?"

"Sunday before Memorial Day. Do you have clubs? If you don't you can use my wife's. They're almost new. I tried teaching her a couple of years ago, but she's a bad student."

"How do you know you aren't a bad teacher? Why don't we do this? You can give me some instructions at the practice tee before we play. Then we'll know what kind of teacher you are."

"Fair enough, and why don't you watch some online golf videos between now and Sunday? That'll make my teaching easier, and we'll have better luck hustling Carter when I make him a bet. Be here Sunday at ten. You bring muffins and yogurt, and I'll supply the rest."

Electra followed his suggestion. She watched enough videos to imprint swing mechanics and instructions, repeating them one more time.

Use an interlocking grip and flow my swing. Position the ball forward of mid center, right shoulder slightly dipped before the backswing, then on the upswing, keeping hips stationary, move away shoulders, arms, hands, and club as one unit. Midway through the backswing, hinge my wrists and fold my right arm. At the top of the upswing, keep my feet planted, rolling left foot and bending left knee but keeping the right foot and knee straight, and coiling my torso. Smoothly start the downswing, shifting lower body slightly forward, uncoiling the torso and rotating arms and shoulders downward. Unhinge the wrists as I accelerate the clubhead into the ball, never taking my eyes off it. After impact, release the body so it continues to flow until it's fully released, wrists cocked again. Once fully released and stationary, look at the flight of the ball.

That's too much to recall before every swing. The only way to avoid paralysis by analysis it to practice enough so muscle memory locks in the details. I've watched and thought enough. I'm going to practice at a driving range.

Electra met Angus promptly at ten, handing breakfast to her wide-eyed partner.

"You certainly dress the part. Do you have black gloves to match your top?"

"I do, and because it's the Memorial Day weekend, I can wear a white golf miniskirt too."

"I told Carter to meet us at the practice tee. Clubs are already packed, so let's go. We can eat in the car."

As he drove, Angus talked briefly about the questions he'd ask, then pointed some at Electra as he pulled into the parking lot.

"Have you been to the club before?"

"About ten years ago, Carter and I played tennis here a couple of times."

"Didn't Carter throw a surprise Co-Friend Commitment party for the two of you?"

"I couldn't stay too long." Electra's cool smile told him to change subjects.

"Is he a good tennis player?"

"Very, and most tennis players are good golfers because they have great eye-hand coordination. He's a bad bowler, but he might be a better golfer. You and Carter can decide team scoring to make us competitive."

"I'll have a better idea after I see you swing. Let's get to the practice tee for your first lesson. Golf lesson, that is."

As she expected, Angus hit the ball well and gave good instructions.

"That's it… You've got good form… Stay within your swing… Don't try to kill the ball." Forty-five minutes later, Angus ended the lesson when he spotted Carter.

"Here they come. You're doing better than most beginners. And don't worry if you start slicing or hooking. I'll give you pointers as we play."

A confident Carter made the introductions.

"Buffy, you already know Angus, and this is my good friend Electra Kittner. Electra, this is Buffy Gunstein." Buffy's handshake was as strong as her voice.

"Good to meet you. Carter tells me you'd be a real stud if you were a guy."

"Uh, that's not exactly what I said. Anyway, it's good to see you. You sure look like a golfer, but I didn't know you injured your eye."

"You look good too. Different, but good. And the goggle protects the eye I injured in a fall."

Buffy said, "It's sexy. Makes a nice fashion statement too. Carter says you sometimes have acting roles in Hollywood." Angus had heard enough.

"Electra can play many roles, and today it's a wanna-be golfer. Come on, let's get started."

As tee time approached, Carter and Angus picked a popular team scoring method to even the competition: Bingo Bango Bongo. Carter summarized the rules.

"We'll play best-ball position. Each team hits from it. First team on the green gets a point, team closest to the pin another, and first in the hole another. And a team gets three bonus points for each hole it wins all the points. It's an easy game to score, and because Electra's good with numbers, how about we let her keep tab?" She agreed; Carter continued.

"Buffy plays often, so we'll handicap my team by having her hit from the men's tee. Electra can hit from the women's. And we'll declare winners for front and back nine separately. Front-nine winners get free drinks, back-niners get free dinner."

Electra played two games in one: golfing and listening to Carter. Angus gradually led to the right questions as everyone walked together towards next shots.

"Jared seems to be sitting in the public's sweet spot. How do you and he like the balancing act among federal government, private enterprise, and local control?"

"Just like you, we want less federal and more local, and we want more economic growth to keep people working. And I don't mind giving some breaks to business if they keep generating jobs. It's all relative."

"I guess so, as long as you know when to say when."

"And that's why Buffy's on my team. Lawyers know how far to go, and she understands the ethics of pragmatism."

"You bet I do. Those who scream the loudest are usually the ones who can't contribute very much. Carter and I like results. And we like to win…"

Scoring rules kept the competition closer than skill would have predicted, but the results for the first nine holes declared the Carter-Buffy team the winner. Angus bought drinks at an outdoor snack bar while Carter complimented the ladies.

"Buffy hits long and plays a strong short game. And for only her second round, Electra hits the ball nice and straight."

"That's because Angus is a good teacher. And he's been giving me more pointers as we play. I'll improve on the back nine." Angus used Electra's comment to segue to another question.

"Jared's quality of life should improve when he finally leaves office because he won't have the press sniping at him. He'll be out of politics and can pick and choose what he wants to do, as can you. Got any ideas?"

"My experience working for Jared should land me a nice promotion if I go back to the Fed. Or I could use my contacts to become an economic policy consultant, but I might want to work for Jared. He plans to establish a quasi-not-for-profit foundation to promote domestic and international projects he likes. Buffy can be part of that too. What about you? Do you plan to run for president again?" "It's too soon to know, but like all good politicians, I'm keeping my options open. And just like my open stance, it can help me hit what I'm aiming for." Buffy was ready for the back nine.

"If Carter and I win again, dinner's on you. I hope Electra brought some money."

"I always come prepared. I've finished practicing on the front nine. Now I put my game face on."

Electra let her length and accuracy build gradually, but Angus didn't play as well. By the time they reached the par five 18th, Carter's team had a seven-point lead so he threw Angus a new challenge.

"Match over unless lightning strikes, so let's modify the rules. If you go for broke and sweep the 18th, we'll call it even. But if you don't, you have to buy drinks and dinner. How about it?"

"I don't hear any thunder rumbling, but since we're in for a penny, we might as well be in for a pound. Electra, you hit first."

Lightning struck in the form of free-swinging Electra, who thundered a drive that reached the green. Carter's team needed three to reach it but Electra's ball was still closer to the hole. He and Buffy would putt first from forty feet. Neither made it. Electra told Angus to putt next.

"It's a tie if you sink it. Do it." And when he did, Buffy added another challenge.

"Let's see what Electra can do. If she can sink the same putt, I'll buy drinks and Carter will buy dinner and dessert."

Electra calmly lined it up, then drained a center-cut putt that echoed smartly off the back of the cup.

Angus whooped, "Jesus, a double eagle is rare, even for the pros." Carter congratulated her too, but Buffy said it best.

"Electra appears to be a quick-study combo stud and hustler, all wrapped in an attractive package. Carter, you should have known that."

"I guess I forgot, but Electra has always been full of surprises. Seeing another is worth a dessert."

Dinner conversation flowed as smoothly as her winning drive. Electra casually lighted a mini-cigar when the waiter brought drinks, surprising Carter again

"You look like you're from a James Bond movie. In fact, you look even—" Buffy cut him off.

"I've never had the nads to try one. Could I have one of yours?" "Of course. It's lightly flavored. Don't draw the smoke into your lungs. Let it sit in your mouth before puffing it out through your lips. Watch me." Electra used her lighter to get Buffy started after blowing a well-formed smoke ring.

The ladies smoked and listened; Angus pointed the questions back to business.

"You're the econ go-to-guy. Do you see any problems brewing in rare earths markets? I understand some of those needed for Quantum Computer chips are in tight supply."

"It could become a problem, and that's why I keep pushing domestic programs that give incentives to companies for creating infrastructure and manufacturing jobs. All this talk about environmental protection and green marketing is like an Electra smoke ring. When push comes to shove, people want jobs. And the same applies to the new breed of Washington's bald-faced social and anti-capital zombies who've fed at the public trough for so long they wouldn't know what to do if their meddling ever disrupted America's growth engine. They huff and puff on social media about forcing more corporate responsibility and regulations when the facts show just the opposite. Corporate ethics and efforts to benefit society are better than ever. So, don't be concerned, we're watching these developments." Electra listened attentively as Carter said more.

"And we're also monitoring China's attempts to leapfrog America's genetic engineering and A.I. expertise. They're world's best Cyber-hackers and pirates. Rumors persist that the Chinese are growing clones via in vitro gestation to increase their population, even though the international community has banned the technology. If it works, maybe they'll trade the technology for some of Russia's smart weapons. Russia's trying to supplant our number one ranking in weapons sales and international finance, and it's still trying to meddle in other countries' affairs via fake news. Just goes to show that old rivals at home and abroad never die, they just morph into more dangerous sorts." Angus waited for Carter to add more.

"One of my staffers quoted a recent computer industry article that several Chinese companies might have new algorithms that'll crack

RSA encryption. No one believes it, but it does cause anxiety among those not in the know. Good that all at our table aren't in that camp." Carter paused to sip his beer, giving Angus space to ask his question.

"I have contacts at CIA who tell me about a possible rogue terrorist group. Do you know anything other than rumors?"

"The attacks I've heard about appear to be random, but if new ones hit closer to home or threaten national security, all NSA will go on high alert. I sure hope we don't get to that because international economies and relations have been slowly improving." Carter glanced at Electra before saying more.

"You're much more reserved than a couple of years ago. What gives?" Electra paused between puffs and sips of scotch.

"I'm simply following your advice. I've learned not to give information overloads. And now that I'm a little older, I prefer to end the night earlier rather than later. I think it's time for Angus to take me home..."

Although Electra's fitness level placed her off the charts, playing a new sport always causes sore muscles, so the warm shower let her body unwind while her brain replayed some of the day.

I might not agree with a lot of what Buffy said, but I like her. She's authentic. So is Angus, but I can't say the same about Carter. Not only has he changed, but he's become opaque and untrustworthy. I've changed too, but I'm true to myself and to others. People can believe what I say. And that reminds me, I better talk to Robin.
Fifteen minutes later, Electra made the call.

"I'm so glad to hear your voice. It's been over a week since we spoke."

"Well, I'm calling now, and I hope you and Gabriel are AOK."

"He's doing fine. We played some therapy games today and I took him for a walk in the park. He's sleeping now. What did you do?"

"I played golf. I find—" Robin didn't let Electra finish.

"I didn't know you play golf? When did you learn? Who did you play with? Did you bring Ariadne with you? That's too--"

"Hey, slow down. Stop asking so many questions."

"Why didn't you leave her with me? She could have played with Gabriel." Electra listened to herself as Robin continued her scolding.

Friends are starting to wonder why they haven't seen Ariadne. I better give Robin the story I've invented.

"Look, I didn't want to trouble you with my concerns, but Ariadne's birth mother wanted her back because she can now take care of her."

"But you told me you adopted her. Parents who give up their kids can't get them back once the adoption papers are signed."

"That's how it works here, but foreign countries have different adoption rules. You're the first person I've told. Please don't tell anyone else."

"I won't. And now I know why you've sort of withdrawn into your shell. Don't do that. You need your friends more than ever. Let me help."

"You already are. Talking tonight has been good for me. I promise to call you sooner rather than later."

"Talking with you is good for me too. Good night, and sleep tight. And if I were tucking Gabriel in, I'd add 'don't let the bedbugs bite'..." Darla hadn't had a good night's sleep since arriving in Harare two days ago for the third annual S-Cube meeting, nor would she feel better tomorrow. She didn't like being disrespected by Max, and Sergei didn't do much to defend her. The Popper had surprised her when he brought two of his men with him, demanding she supply them with a wide-tired open jeep. She consoled herself that at least his men dressed like normal people rather than exoskeletal-clad warriors. At tomorrow's afternoon session, the Popper would conclude the meeting by giving marching orders to everyone.

Darla's bad nights had begun immediately after the Cyberspace Expo, when stolen laptops had blown up before she could pirate their GUI's and A.I. software she needed for her suite of Cyber- software that she planned to sell to target platform companies. Without the pirated software, her developers had struggled to make even marginal improvements that she would have to demo to customers. Only the growing success of the rare earths cartel kept Darla's dream of an African Silicon Valley from becoming a nightmare.

The Popper's interminable droning stretched the afternoon wrap-up session into the early evening. Sitting across the table, Darla had her laptop propped open as she recorded the Popper's orders but stopped when her cell phone interrupted.

"I need a potty break to take this call. I'll be back in five minutes." After she left, the Popper had something to say for Sergei's ears only.

"We shall do much better without her. Next year we shall meet in Russia, and Darla will not be invited. She will be engaged elsewhere."

"Indeed. Our opponents have learned to defend against her intrusion software. We may need to seek other partners to replace her and Chen. I shall consider options for our rare earths cartel, and I shall continue probing for weaknesses in other financial networks." "I'll leave Cyberspace to you, but 3-D space is for me and my super soldiers." The Russians continued speaking confidentially while waiting for Darla. Fifteen minutes later, an impatient Max ordered his men to track her down, giving them a choice: terminate before or after a final meeting with him. After they left, Sergei staked a claim. "Darla will have no further need of her laptop so I shall take it with me." The Popper nodded yes, but couldn't care less. He was already talking via cell phone to his men as they hunted her down.

Darla played only once the call that had gone to voice mail while she was still on the first, but that was enough. The clipped words from an unknown source froze her momentarily: "You are in their sights. Leave now." She had no idea how much of a lead she had over her pursuers, but fear galvanized her because she knew Max's men were fleet afoot. It diminished as soon as she jumped into her awaiting jeep, pointing and issuing orders as the vehicle raced into the twilight.

"Max's men are after me. They've probably put a tracker on the jeep, but there's no time to search for it, so you drive and you watch our rear." Darla snapped more commands once they were several blocks away.

"You know the way, so let's weave through the game preserve before going to the airport. And you in the back, keep alert for pursuers." No words broke the tension until the lookout yelled.

"I see headlights, and they're coming fast." The driver accelerated as he veered onto unpaved roads that led into the game preserve. Darla had planned ahead by planting a tracker on the other jeep. Both careened on a grass path that snaked back and forth and up and down. The distance between the jeeps shrank to less than twenty yards. As her jeep swerved out of a downward-arcing right turn, Darla typed one more command and tapped the enter key. Three seconds later, the pursuit jeep exploded. Darla's driver slammed on the brakes before she yelled more commands.

"Back up. Let's see if anyone's still moving." They got close enough to see the flaming wreckage, then carefully walked closer. Darla led, carrying a flashlight while her men carried rifles. Muffled screams and two pair of legs pinned beneath the overturned jeep greeted them. Darla said nothing until the roar of a distant lion jolted her to action.

"Let's go. We'll let nature clean up."

Darla gave final instructions just before exiting the jeep at the airport.

"Tell our Russian visitors if you drive them to the airport tomorrow that I had to leave early. And tell them nothing about the chase. It's their turn to sweat."

Maksim's extraction chopper circled the last known coordinates of his men but found only a burnt vehicle. A searchlight painted a widening spiral starting at the crash site, but the impenetrable darkness sucked up all the glow; only reflected light from a pack of eyes glaring at the chopper came back. The Popper knew a ground search would be too dangerous. He didn't want any of his soldiers to be quarry for beasts whose night vision could beat that of his men. Twenty minutes later the chopper returned to a course that would take it to safety.

Electra had been surreptitiously attending the S-Cube meeting for the past two days, courtesy of the communications software she had embedded in Darla's swapped-in computer and cell phone, learning enough to fill in some of the missing data that had eluded her. And the second she heard Max's plan for Darla, she placed an anonymous call. Though unanswered, it achieved what she wanted because she subsequently traced Darla's successful escape. She powered down her workstation ninety minutes later, happy to have the meeting over and Darla still in action.

It's better to have Darla live so I can toy with her another day. The devil I know is better than the devil I don't. And if Sergei keeps his word, I can track him via the laptop to learn more about the formidable Popper. I need to follow his trail, wherever it leads, and I'll need reinforcements if I ever meet him in 3-D space. But not in Cyberspace. That's a playing field where I can call the tune as soon as I have his number.

Like all commanders who lead men into battle, Max understood the finality of death and stoically mourned the loss, which he used to motivate his next attack. Three weeks later, he addressed his team as they were about to engage the enemy.

"My warriors, do not fear the African darkness. Tonight, it is our friend because the two mines we attack are located where no animals other than men want to roam. We have practiced where to place charges on the automated smelters. I shall detonate them as soon as our chopper clears the blast radius. Then we proceed to our second target. You should encounter few workers, but if you do, terminate with extreme prejudice. The blast will immolate any bodies and leave the experts vainly searching through rubble for explanations. Any questions?" There were none.

Stories surfaced a week later about explosions that destroyed all smelting operations at two African rare earths mines, completely shutting down production. The causes appeared to be identical: software glitches in computers controlling automated equipment. All mines around the globe that use Pan-African software and mining equipment had been instructed to suspend operations until further notice. Africa's Big-6 conglomerate might be hit the hardest, further tightening supply and raising prices.

Not even the Popper could resist gloating for a moment because he had more than evened the score against Darla. Revenge offers a sweet reward to the victor, and he knew that the score would always be in his favor whenever toying with her. There would be future games against opponents not yet chosen. They too would finish second as long as he planned and his super soldiers executed.

Max put his gloating away as he prepared for the start of another day.

Chapter 30
October 2131

"Playing with the Big Boys"
(Thread 2 Chapter 10)

Electra hadn't traveled far from DC since March because she had been able to coordinate via the Internet her far-flung activities, but now she needed to combine Austin and Hollywood visits into a mid-October trip. She paused for a moment after making airline reservations before returning to software R&D.

Good that I'm a terrific multi-tasker because I'm always juggling a constantly shifting array of activities. Serendipity always seems ready to replace those that are winding down with new adventures to take their place. Serendipity – one of my favorite words – is appropriate since it means the occurrence and development of events by chance in a happy or beneficial way. But what's the genesis of the word? I always remind my post-docs to know the background of words they use, so I better check it out. Five minutes later she knew.

Horace Walpole, 18th century English author of the first Gothic novel – The Castle of Otranto – coined the word from the classical Persian name of Sri Lanka. He came upon it while reading The Three Princes of Serendip, a Middle East fairy tale about the three sons of a king who forces them to travel so they may become wise. During their journey, chance leads them into predicaments that always result in happy outcomes. I hope to continue following their footsteps.

Electra's Austin stopover would be for lunch with Hud and Woolly, and then she would fly that evening to Hollywood, where Vito Buono would take her to dinner the following day. Hud was waiting when she exited from baggage claim.

"First time I've seen you sporting an eye goggle. Makes you look even more sophisticated. I hope you won't mind if we go to a new Tex-Mex place."

"I haven't had good Tex-Mex since my last trip here, and that's been too long. How've you been?"

"Doing fine. I'll tell you all the personal stuff while driving, then we'll start talking business over a beer for me and a Coca Cola for you. By the time Woolly arrives, we'll be ready for another order of quesadillas."

Electra listened carefully to Hud's recap of Pequot lab activity.

"Su and Kameyo make quite a team. Their vaccine line extensions keep us ahead of generics. And Tim and Kwame are quite a team too, even though I don't understand what they mean by UMPP. Do you?"

"It stands for universal multi-parallel port, and I'll tell you more about what Tim and Kwame are developing the next time we talk. And when we do, I might have another opportunity for you. How are your Permian Basin businesses doing?"

"The Solar Panel and Martian Farming joint ventures in West Texas are in the black. And me and my Permian Basin associates are operating two more Panel Farms on the Navajo reservation. Sure makes good use out of barren land."

"There might be an opportunity for you just below the surface. What do you know about rare earths?" Hud leaned in before answering.

"Not much. What can you tell me?"

"They have electromagnetic properties that are important for computer and communications uses. And prices have risen because of growing demand compounded by supply disruptions. It's possible that Russia, China, and Africa are building a rare earths cartel similar to what OPEC did in the 1970's. The U.S. industry has languished for years. Our rare earths deposits have been overlooked. Most domestic mines are shut, and that's an opportunity." Electra paused for a sip of Coke before continuing.

"Most of the deposits and mines are located on Indian reservation land owned by the Navajos in Arizona and New Mexico, and the Shoshone and Nez Perce in Idaho and Montana. The mining and processing technologies are well known. You could reopen and install new equipment to start producing in less than a year. And according to some of the geo-prospecting results, reservation deposits are rich in those rare earths most in demand." Hud's quizzical expression told Electra a question was about to come.

"All that sounds good, but we can't just gallop onto the reservation and start digging. What are we supposed to do?"

"Please remember that I'm the one who made Navajo Solar Panel Farm contacts for you. I might be able to do the same for rare earths mining. I'll know more by Christmas. Additional contacts might be my Christmas present to you. I see Woolly heading our way, so let's let him pick a new subject. And don't mention what we've been talking about."

Hud stood to shake hands, then Woolly shook Electra's after the men sat down. Never at a loss for words, Woolly spoke right up. "You look good as ever, maybe better. Hud told me about your accident. I hope your vision has improved."

"It has, and thanks for asking. How are Texas politics?"

"We Texans can still tolerate Washington. Gardner seems to be pointing us in the right direction, but Texas will put up a fuss if he doesn't. And your NGA liaison work helps our governor. Have you reconsidered running again for Congress? There's a seat in District 10 that'd fit you nicely."

"I don't know. I have a full slate, and that got me into trouble the last time. Voters thought I spread myself too thin."

"They might think differently this time. I don't need an answer today. The election's a year away, so be smart and consider it. By the way, District 10 runs diagonally from Houston to Austin. You should like the geography better than where you ran before. And if you decide to run, I'll handle your campaign."

Pleasant talk about present and future plans filled the remainder of the time to the airport. Electra hiked to the departure gate for her on-time flight, ready to enjoy an uninterrupted trip, but midway to LA an Email from Vito popped into her laptop:

"Palace coup at studio. I'm on A-list. New plans. Opportunity for you. I explain at 6:30 hotel breakfast. Ciao."

No need to role play for what I had expected tomorrow. I'll wait until I know what my new part might be. Let's see where serendipity leads.

Electra awoke at her regular Eastern Time Zone hour, which put her three hours ahead of LA's Pacific Time Zone clock, giving her ample time to exercise and swim laps before meeting Vito. She arrived five minutes early, walking into the restaurant just after Vito.

"Buon giorno, bella Electra. You look as fresh as sunrise." "Buona mattina, Vito. I'm always pleased to see you."

"Come, let us be seated. Then I tell you the news." Vito guided her to a booth before suggesting they order the buffet. He escorted her through the lightly populated line where she selected oat meal and a bran muffin while the waitress brought orange juice. Vito cheerfully bragged about California oranges while sampling his ham and cheese omelette before turning to business.

"So, my instincts proved true. Early this week I rejected the final script offerings given to me for our next Angel of Evil movie, and the president of the studio agreed. It's no secret Cyber-Max has underperformed, so la Presidenza used the moment to reorganize. A number of heads rolled, making room for me to move up into a dual unit manager and director role. You can't sign a contract for the next movie until we have a script I like, but I can offer you a position as a unit manager assistant working for me at day rates. And I will slot you into assignments that can give you skills for actual studio jobs. Many actors and actresses want to move into behind-the-camera roles when they no longer fit in front of the lens, but only those who have the right experience are chosen. Might you be interested?"

"I might, but tell me, did Kathi Lauret make the A-list?" Saying nothing, Vito shook his head no.

"Hmm, OK. Well, please tell me what my options are." Vito placed two sheets of paper on the table before explaining further.

Movie Production Basics for Bella Electra

Must have a Screenplay (movie Blueprint):
- 3 Acts: Beginning (25%), Middle (50%) End (25%)
- Acts divided into Screens: 1 Screen per Page. 90 – 100 pgs. 1 minute per page
- Each page contains: Slug Line Action Dialogue
- Four Generic Plots: Win Stop Escape Return
- Depicts four Emotions: Mad Sad Glad Scared
- Show don't Tell Action
- Numerous Characters supporting "Heroes" Journey
- Must paint: Settings Characters Theme Tone

Then do Pre-Production:
- Casting
- Select Film Crew
- Confirm the "Look"
- Select Location
- Develop Shooting Schedule
- Prepare each day's Call Sheet

Then Shoot and Edit

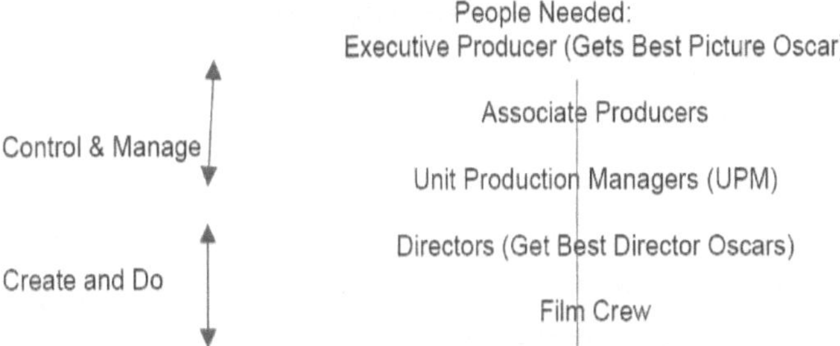

When filming, the scene is visually divided horizontally and vertically by "Rule of Thirds" when looking through the Camera Lens.

Film Crew

The Director is in charge of Actors and Film Crew. He brings his vision of screenplay to life. Actors bring their interpretation of characters to life. (Actors want clear, actionable directions.)
Director in charge of:
- Actors Designers Editors Composers
- Action Cinematography Sound

Cinematography (Video) Crew	Sound (Audio) Crew	Artistic Crew
Camera Operator Lightning and Rigging (Gaffer and Best Boy)	Mixer Mic. Operator	Costume & Makeup Hair & Background Design Special Effects Stunts

Clapper shouts "Lights Camera Action"
Keeps track on Slate: Act/Scene/Take
Film Set has: On-Set for ActionOff-Set for Base Camp
Base Camp: Actors' Trailers Medical/EMTFood Catering

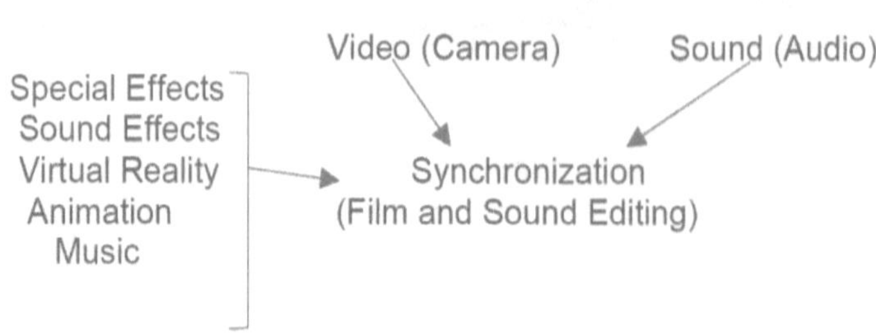

"I sang your praises to la Presidenza, and he will allow me to hire you, but he must interview you first." Vito stopped talking when Electra drew back, then hurriedly continued.

"No no, it is not like my audition. He wants you to convince him you are not just another pretty face. That is why I give you a summary of movie production and people who handle it. Let me talk you through what I give you." Vito pointed to the first sheet.

"Of course, we must have script before we start. Once we do, we do our pre-production planning, and then we do shooting and editing. And notice where I sit in the pecking order. Because I wear UPM and director hats, I control and I create." Vito shuffled to the second sheet.

"And here we see how director works with his actors and crew. Crew is divided into video, audio, and artistic pieces. And within each are many specialized roles. There is much hi-tech equipment used when filming and editing. La Presidenza doesn't expect you to know many details, but you must know what I have just shown you. It is a lot, but let's go to my office and I will go over it again before your 10 a.m. interview. I have not deterred you, no?"

"No, you're precious. But what's the name of la Presidenza?"
"Jespersen Abramson. Close friends call him Jess or Jessie. He is all business when it comes to movies, but he likes fast cars and big cigars, and golfing too when there's no more work to do." Vito and Electra rose to go.

Sitting across the desk from Jess, Electra observed this late-fifties, immaculately groomed Hollywood mogul as he dispatched orders over the phone.

His physique fits the description Vito gave me: reasonably fit, graying hair, and dimensions that fit in anywhere. Diplomatic too, judging from how he's handling the call.

"… We're giving you a generous parachute, and we'll give you a great recommendation when you use us for a reference. Call me anytime.Goodbye." Jess paused for only a moment before training his eyes on Electra.

"Hello, Ms. Kittner. Vito's already told me why he wants to hire you. Now you have one hour to convince me you have what's needed to grow into a studio career. Not only must you be smart, thorough, good at planning, and ready to learn new technology, but you must be diplomatic and empathetic to boot, able to lead a team. The floor is yours."

I've done all this, but just give an overview. And draw him into a dialogue. It's time to act a new role.

Jess ended the interview forty-five minutes later.

"You certainly are an exceptional lady. Let me talk again with Vito so I know all of us are following the same script. I'd take you to lunch but I have a 1 p.m. tee time for a nine-hole shotgun start at a male-female team PGA golf outing. By the way, it's a Producers Guild of America fundraiser. My partner backed out and I'm scrambling for a replacement. By any chance, do you play golf?"

"I do, but I didn't bring my clubs or outfit. Maybe I –" Jess completed what Electra was thinking.

"Let's take you to wardrobe. My people will make you look like a golf pro. Then all I ask is for you to try your best."

"I always do. Perhaps I'll meet your expectations…" Vito's cheerful voice greeted Electra early next morning.

"Felicitazioni, congratulations, bella Electra. La Presidenza agrees with me. You got what it takes. And he says that if you can play the Hollywood game like you play golf, you can play with the big boys. But one step at a time. I shall call you end of November to arrange when you like to start and tend to all the detail. Do you have any questions?"

"No questions for the time being. And I'll do my best so we can keep quoting the last line of Casablanca. Ciao."

Electra decided to place two calls before rescheduling her flight back to DC. Kathi, answering on the third ring, recognized the voice. "Congratulations. I hear you golf as well as you act. Are you going to accept Vito's offer?"

"Yes, but he intimated you're not on the A-list. Are you still working at the Studio?"

"I've been demoted, but that happens often in Hollywood, and it may be only temporary. And who knows? I might be working for you someday."

"If so, it's only because you paved the way. But please tell me if my instincts are working well. I trust Vito, and though I just met Jess, I think I can trust him too."

"Yes on both counts, but always remember that Jess is a hard-driving businessman underneath that polished exterior. He always goes all-in, and you're playing with the big boys when you're working for him. I have to go, but please call when you know dates for your next visit. I can help you get started behind the camera." Electra forced herself to delay making the second call until after breakfast because she felt herself reverting to an obsessive-compulsive tendency. She let her thoughts freewheel for thirty minutes, then dialed her half-sister Cassandra. No one picked up and the voice messaging service announced a different name. On a whim, Electra called Brandon Marshall, whose somber voice immediately dampened her high-flying spirits.

"Who are you? ... Electra Kittner? Do I know you?"

"I met you and your daughter Cassandra about three years ago. I'm her half-sister." Brandon's reply came after a lengthy pause.

"Oh yes, now I remember. Three years between calls is an awful long time. What do you want?"

"How's Cassandra, and how you are?" Electra waited even longer for the next reply.

"She killed herself two years ago after six months of intensive counseling." Brandon said nothing else; Electra had to fill the dead space.

"I'm so sorry. I know she had issues, but I thought she was beginning to deal with them better." This time, Brandon spoke quickly.

"You can't say that. You never really knew what she was going through, nor did you know what she did to my life and second wife. You're just saying words to make yourself feel better, but there aren't any. So, let's just be honest and stop talking. And I'll help by hanging up."

Brandon's chastening words left Electra feeling hollow.

He's right. My words are a feeble attempt to dodge any self- inflicted barbs. I'm trying to rationalize my inaction. No one can criticize me for not helping Cassandra. I'm not the main character in Nathaniel West's Miss Lonelyhearts. But I'm disturbed just the same. I better table any further self-criticism until later. It's time to reschedule my flight, go for a swim, and then go home.

Keeping busy until boarding the plane kept Electra from brooding needlessly, and once airborne she reclined her seat, making it easier to gaze mindlessly at the landscape below while letting her consciousness retreat into its fortress. As the cabin's white noise began working its soothing magic, she sensed an idea forming and though it didn't crystallize, her mood brightened.
Not to worry. I'll come up with something good.

By the time the plane prepared for landing, Electra could sense another plan forming.

Now I know what to do and who will help me put my plan in action just as soon as I build a Brain Probe line extension. Doctor Holbrook, Chief Strongarm, get ready.

Chapter 31
December 2131

"Christmas Treasure"
(Thread 1 Chapter 11)

Electra's obsessive work ethic, which she had relentlessly trained on A.I. software development since returning from Hollywood, yielded unintended synergies because she could plug several new Linguistic Analyzer apps directly into existing devices. A whimsical sense of humor added to her satisfaction.

This month, the Royal Swedish Academy of Sciences awards Nobel Prizes, and I shall be the first winner in my newly-created category, Serendipitous Software. I've dummied down from my master A.I. algorithms a set of apps giving everything needed for an improved Cyber-Theater, a better Optic Nerve Knitter, and a Brain Probe line extension I'll name the Mood Adjustment Device, or MAD, for a slick acronym. And I've also developed a new software suite I've labeled the SNIFFER package that's ready for sale to targeted platform companies. My newly-created disguise, a drab-looking Polish lady named Katrina Blanka, is ready to promote it via my newly-created virtual company, CAT Software. And if I can figure out how my Linguistic Analyzer is getting smarter, I'll award myself another prize next year.

Although the year was drawing to a close, Electra refused to worry about missing deadlines because she had arbitrarily set them. During the past two years, she had struck a better balance between wants and needs.

I no longer sweat the small stuff. And few things are big enough to pose actual risks to me or those I care about. Silly to stress myself if it takes away from the joy of living in the now. If all I live for is a succession of prizes, I'll die having never taken pleasure in the moment. I would like to complete a series of trips before the end of the year, but whether I do or I don't won't really matter, so I'll play it by ear.

Electra's first trip took her to the Pequot Reservation, where she met with Chief Strongarm the second week in December.

"So, please tell me about new opportunities."

"I have a device that Doctor Holbrook can use to extend the kinds of medical services reservation clinics can offer. It can be used to treat people suffering from addiction or certain kinds of psychological disorders, like depression or PTSD. You have an opportunity to roll it out, first here and then Florida, and then extend to other tribes. I can train Doctor Holbrook and assist Dyani market the program."

"Have you tested it?"

"I wouldn't be talking about it if it weren't safe and effective. And because reservations are separate nations, we have no FDA meddling to contend with. This program has long-term potential." Chief Strongarm briefly glanced away, then returned to the conversation.

"What is your second opportunity?"

"Some of the Western Indian reservations are sitting on valuable rare earths reserves. For the time being, take my word that rare earths are in short supply and at least three tribes – the Navajo, Shoshone, and Nez Perc – have inactive mines that Hud Haller can reopen in less than a year. Step back and look at the big picture. You and your National Tribal Council are on the cusp of empowering Native American tribes as never before if you act on my recommendations." Saying nothing for the longest time, the Chief took a deep breath before replying.

"Yes, I am beginning to see what you see. We can forge an actual country-in-a-country. But I will need you to play an active role as our plan unfolds. I shall arrange a meeting, first with the NCAI executive director, and then with the National Tribal Council, of which I am a member. Are you willing to commit your time and energy?"

"That's why I'm here, and I have other ideas too, but why don't I tell Doctor Holbrook and Hud to contact their counterparts just as soon as you tell me who they are. And you don't have to tell me what NCAI stands for; I already know it's an acronym for the National Congress of American Indians." The Chief's smile matched the warmth of his voice.

"I never need to tell you much. You have a wise spirit as well as a strong heart. Let us proceed."

Electra's next stop was the reservation lab where she held what became a brief meeting because Tim and Kwame understood immediately how to add the improved software to the Cyber-Theater. After loading it into their latest prototype, Kwame grasped the possibilities even faster than Tim.

"These A.I. apps are incredible. We're taking interactive theater to the next level by recursively feeding the viewer's output signals into an interactive plot selector routine. And for people who have embedded UMPP ports, the emotional jolts should spine-tingling." Electra cautioned the pair as she rose to leave.

"Remember to keep the intensity dialed lower rather than higher. You can dial it up on subsequent releases as an added feature. Talk to Hud about updating the units already in use. And please keep what we're doing confidential."

Electra deliberately slowed her pace by taking a Coke from the fridge before strolling into Su and Kameyo's work area. Looking up from the bench, Kameyo smiled politely, waiting for Su to speak. "You're here early. I hope that means Tim and Kwame did well." "They always do, just like the two of you. Shall we start our meeting now, or should I come back in a half hour?"

"We might as well start now. If you came back in six months, our story would still be the same." Su led the trio into a small conference room, then gave everyone at the table a one-page handout before Kameyo explained their predicament.

Genetic Evolution Research Black Hole

Overarching Biological Goal: Pass DNA's Heritable Traits to Next Generation

Pathways: Individual Selection   Sexual Selection   Kin Selection

Assumptions:
- DNA is Instruction Code for making Proteins and Enzymes.
- Genes control production.
- Genes embedded in DNA.

DNA Structure:

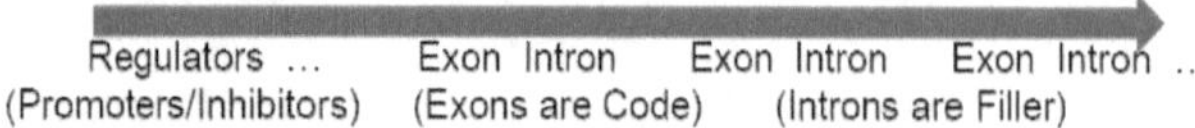

Production Mechanism:
1. Regulators determine which Exons are activated.
2. Enzymes cut out Introns and splice activated Exons during DNA-to-RNA Transcription.
3. Cells manufacture Proteins and Enzymes.

Disciplinary Linkage:

Evol. Biology ⟶ Evol. Genetics ⟶ Evol. Neurosci. ⟶ Evol. Med ⟶ Evol. Psych. ⟶ Evol. Psychiatry
⟶ Evol. Behavior

At each Disciplinary Link, Evolution "solves" Optimization Problem (constrained Energy and Entropy Laws)

Complicating Issues:
- Multiple Gene Interaction
- Inherited and Environmental Interaction (Intra and Extra-cellular Interaction)
- Micro-mutations at Molecular Genetics Level cause Macro changes in Organism
- Retro-viruses and Feedback Loops
- Punctuated Evolution implies significant changes occur within small number of generations
- Evolution caused by Nature, Nurture, and Chance

Overwhelming amount of: Analytic Granularity   Combinatorial Complexity
Can't find a way out...

"The handout doesn't apply to our shorter-term projects. As already reported, we are making adequate progress on T-Plague and Alzheimer's vaccines. The handout describes the black hole I fell into when I began searching for the Holy Grail of genetic evolution. There are too many gene interactions that defy molecular process decomposition. And DNA itself is controlled by an array of regulators that decide which Exons – the actual instructions transcribed into RNA – are used in protein-enzyme synthesis. And when I include the number of intra and intercellular factors, I am overwhelmed by the number of scenarios. No one in my professional network has had much success designing studies that hold enough factors constant so that we can test for significance." Kameyo's sigh showed in her dejected conclusion.

"You are much smarter than anyone I know, but I fear that not even you can find a way out." Su added more.

"When Kameyo first began telling me about the challenges she was encountering, I read some of the seminal books written a hundred years ago when disciplinary linkages listed in the handout were first conjectured. I also watched some of the Sapolsky videos that even today are compelling. It is indeed possible there is a Grand Unified Theory of Evolution that controls all physical, physiological, and social processes. I even skimmed a book – Darwin's Cathedral – that uses science-based functionalism to model religion like an adaptive organism that self-organizes all the pieces for group survival. Although none of its speculations can be proved, the book is thought provoking. But I too am stumped." Having nothing left to say, Su stared blankly at the table, waiting for someone else to speak. Electra's folded arms mirrored her doubt.

"Maybe I'm not smart enough either. I haven't studied all the topics listed in your handout, but you mention two that I've often thought about: analytic granularity and combinatorial complexity. I call them the asymptotic limits to the brain's cognitive capacity. High energy physics ran into them a hundred years ago, but biotech hasn't yet because it's much younger. We can still make breakthroughs, but I don't know how. Sorry, but I have nothing else to say. Why don't you take a break until January?"

"We haven't made any plans yet. Do you have a suggestion?"

"Why not stay with me instead of visiting Hud? Do you remember Robin and Zoe?"

"Didn't I meet them once?"

"You did, and now you can see them again, their families too. It's a rather complicated story, so they can explain when you visit. I'm sure Kameyo will like them too. I'll be traveling to the West Coast, but I plan to be home for Christmas. I'll give you a key so you can let yourselves in if I'm not back, and I'll also give you Robin's and Zoe's cell numbers. Think about it, and let me know…"

Electra had plenty of time while driving home to mull over what Su and Kameyo had covered.

Su talked about Evolutionary Religion. Well, why not have Evolutionary Politics or Evolutionary Economics? And the handout offers other intriguing possibilities. What if I extend the disciplinary linkage by using evolutionary principles to study Science, or Evolution itself? Then we come full circle, tumbling into a regressive nightmare. Unless lightning strikes again, I might never be smart enough to build a dream team by cloning myself. Creating from cloned eggs and editing for genetic improvements is like the smoke from a pipe dream, but at least I tried. I better put these thoughts away and think about something else. I know what I'll do, I'll call Robin.

"You haven't called me for a couple of weeks. Is everything OK? You sound tired."

"I'm driving back from some meetings, that's why. But I had a good day. I hope you can say the same."

"I did, and so did Gabriel. Bringing him on client visits is good for everyone. The more people he interacts with, the better."

"I invited Su and Kameyo to stay with me for the Holidays, so he'll have two more people to play with."

"I'll tell Zoe to expect two more for dinner on Christmas Eve. They can help brighten Jennifer's spirits. Do you know she's put Russell in an eldercare home?"

"What happened?"

"Russell fell when he had a mini-stroke three weeks ago. He needs 24/7 care, which is more than Jennifer or I can give unless we stop working, and Russell doesn't want that. I feel bad for both of them, but Jennifer's doing what she thinks is best."

"And so are you. I'll call you when I get back from my next trip. And I gave your number to Su. She might call you too."

Electra alternated working from home or her GWU lab while preparing for her next trip, a meeting in San Franciso to showcase software that Omni-Buy, a major platform company, might purchase to replace their current vendor's. She began by selecting a mask and printing I.D.s for Katrina, then used her snooping software to delineate Omni-Buy's place in the Platform Economy.

Omni-Buy's a global player for matching consumers and products, fully backward-integrated into manufacturing and warehousing. And like all the powerhouse platform companies, it's headquartered near Silicon Valley to partner with Big Data and Social Forecasting software companies. Katrina's story and software will convert Omni-Buy from a target into my unwitting partner.

Electra awoke early the Monday of her flight, exercising first then meticulously applying makeup after putting on her disguise. What she saw in the mirror would fool anyone.

Not even my close friends would recognize me.

Her cell phone chimed just after she put the makeup in her suitcase. It was an unexpected call from Robin.

"You didn't tell me you're leaving today. Can I give you a ride?" "Thanks, but no thanks. I don't want to cut into your client visits." "It's no bother. I'd like to—"

"I don't need your help getting to the airport. I'm OK."

"I just wish you'd tell me more about what you're doing." "I'll tell you when I get back. You take care, and I will too."

Katrina checked in Tuesday morning at Omni-Buy's security desk. "Yes, Ms. Blanka, you're on the visitor list. Let me escort you to the conference room. Our tech person will help you set up for your demo."

Twenty minutes later, Katrina had all software ready to run five minutes before a five-person Omni-Buy software integration team entered. The team leader made the necessary introductions as he started the meeting.

"Katrina Blanka represents CAT Software, a software company located in Warsaw, Poland that claims to have software for mining Big Data and forecasting target customer buying intentions that's better than our current vendor, Cybergard. She's here today to tell us why we should switch, and if we like her story, she'll install her software on our network so we can see how it performs. Katrina, the floor is yours."

Katrina spoke while sitting at the opposite end of the table, facing a screen that displayed her laptop's image.

"Good morning, and thank you for inviting me. Before I launch my software for you to test, I wish to provide adequate information about me and my company. I am a Technical Sales Consultant for Cognition-App Tech Software – better known in Europe as CAT Software. Our tagline is 'Prowling for Profit.' You have not heard of us because we deliberately maintain a low profile to protect ourselves and our clients. You have already signed a confidentiality agreement that binds both companies never to divulge our business relationship. And let me ask your first question, 'Why is a Polish company good at developing the kind of software you want?' Do you know why?" Katrina glanced around the table.

So far, so good. I have their attention but no answers. My bland appearance contrasts with my clipped European accent. Now I'll spin my story.

"Poland, named after the West Slavic Polanie tribe, has a rich heritage in arts and sciences. Do you know that we invented RPN – Reverse Polish notation, a most efficient algorithmic coding system – that reduces memory usage and execution time? And Benoit Mandelbrot, a pioneer in Chaos Theory, is a countryman.CAT developers have extended cutting edge A.I. coding into Big Data mining and forecasting apps that I am confident you will find superior to what you are currently using. What I will do is load my apps into your system for you to test. Please watch the screen as I load it. And would one of you please assist me?" Twenty minutes later, Katrina redirected the ongoing conversation.

"What I have loaded is a proprietary software suite available only to your company. I invite you to examine the code, but I do not think you will be able to decompile it. And that is not important because when you license our software, you automatically get our support. The screen now shows the GUI you use when selecting target customers. And let me bring up the GUI you use when forecasting." Katrina continued a minute later.

"You can use the same GUI to do back-casting as well, and that will allow you to compare what my software forecasts to what actually occurred. What I want you to do for the remainder of the day is to run my software. I will return tomorrow morning either to unload it or have you sign our contract. And as a bonus, I will include our proprietary security software at no extra cost if you buy. Are there any questions?" A smart-looking lady spoke first.

"We need to know more about your company. Are you publicly traded? How many clients do you have, and where are they located?"

"We are privately held. You do not need to know how many clients use our software, but it should be obvious where they may be located. Cyberspace is global. Are there other questions?"

A geeky fellow asked, "What coding techniques and languages do you use? How long has your software been on the market?"

"Techniques and languages are proprietary, and it does not matter how long our software has been on the market. What matters is how effectively it works for you." The team leader decided he had heard enough.

"I think we're ready to do our testing. Katrina, thank you for getting us started. We'll reconvene tomorrow morning, same time, same place."

Though she had never been to San Francisco, the damp overcast discouraged sightseeing, so Electra worked in her hotel room for the rest of the day, alternating between projects and Web-surfing. She even watched an online video that supplied a brief history and breathtaking views of the "City by the Bay."

Now I understand why this area is called Ecotopia. Its two cities – San Francisco and Oakland – and network of communities hold a seven million, multi-ethnic, and sophisticated population that's hatching the future of Cyberspace.

Native Americans had populated the region for thousands of years, but their luck ran out when Spanish missionaries arrived in the 1760's. Then discovery of gold in the 1840's sparked the first of many booms. The area rebuilt after the great earthquake and fire of 1906, then rocketed to prominence as the world wars, alternate lifestyle trends, and a succession of hi-tech revolutions fueled growth. And now, we have the Cyber-Rush that's digging out the gold buried in Big Data.

The video's drone camera captured views of iconic landmarks, such as Golden Gate Bridge, Alcatraz, China Town, and Golden Gate Park that would be hard to match on foot or tour bus.

It's easier to see twisty Lombard Street from the air than from behind the wheel. And next time I'll tour online some of the museums. Cyberspace is never closed, and the price of admission can't be beat.

Electra didn't think the results of next day's meeting could be beat either. Omni-Buy signed the contract, no additional questions asked. After hiking back to her hotel, she packed her bags and was about to catch a cab after checking out when the concierge warned her. "There've been network failures at a host of air traffic control centers, causing extensive flight cancellations. What's your destination?"

"I'm flying to LA, but I never bothered to check. Do you have any recommendations?"

"I would suggest you rent a car and drive the 385 miles. It should take a little over seven hours, but if you have extra time, why not take the scenic route? It's an extra 100 miles and four hours but it gives a panoramic view. And here are the easiest directions; take the Pacific Coast Highway, which is Route 1, from Pacifica all the way to San Luis Obispo; then take Route 101 all the way to LA. The rental agency's paper map will do just fine. And you're in luck. There's an agency office in the city that won't be swamped like all the airport counters. And do yourself a favor when you return the car. If you plan to travel east, check weather as well as network status. Storms are forecast to sweep from the Midwest to the East Coast, just in time for the Holiday travel crush. Let me hail a cab for you." Electra tipped him five dollars.

"I've taken enough of your time. I'll manage from here. You've been a great help." Electra exited, then immediately entered another hotel lobby, using its restroom to ditch her Katrina disguise in preparation for the next leg of her trip.

She used the drive for a welcome change in mental as well as physical scenery as she rolled along the cliff-hugging road whose breathtaking vistas exceeded expectations even though the weather hadn't cleared. Just before sunset, she found a bed and breakfast whose restaurant featured little-known local vineyards. They too exceeded her expectations. She called Kathi Lauret before going to bed to explain the change in her travel plans.

"I apologize for not calling sooner, but today has had its share of surprises. I'm driving instead of flying because of airport snafus. I'm staying at a lovely B&B just off Route 1 and will go to Vito's office after dropping off the car late tomorrow morning. May I stay with you tomorrow evening?"

"Please do. Vito showed me what he's scheduled for you. I think he'll want you to stay longer because he'd like to use the week after Christmas to ease you into Hollywood's frenetic pace. And I'd love to have you stay with Zaby and me."

"I'll confirm Vito's plan tomorrow, and if it's still a go, I accept your offer. Thank you."

"You're welcome. Would you like me to let Vito know your whereabouts?"

"Would you, please? That'll be one less call to make. I'll see you tomorrow."

Electra role-played before making her final call of the evening to Robin, whose forthright concern touched her.

"Airport congestion stories are all over the news. Did you get to LA OK?"

"I rented a car and am still en route. I'm staying at a B&B overlooking the Pacific. I'll know more tomorrow, but I might need to stay longer to begin learning my new roles immediately, and that would be better than sitting in an airport if network outages and weather screw up travel."

"I understand. Don't try to fly back if staying is better for you. Su and Kameyo arrive tomorrow, and I'll be happy to help them enjoy the Christmas Holiday, even if you're not here. We'll miss you but we can celebrate later. Whatever you decide, just be safe. Love ya…"

When Robin helped Su and Kameyo settle in, Su's godmothering instincts reemerged as soon as she met Gabriel, more than covering for Kameyo's discomfort. And Robin played the role of a dutiful hostess, made easier by the visitors' easygoing manners. Though the weather turned for the worse, she drove them early Christmas Eve to Matt and Zoe's. Zoe recognized Su immediately.

"I remember you. And how much nicer this Christmas Eve is than when we first met. Matt, put their coats away while I take them to the living room to meet Jennifer and Carlton." Once there, Jennifer rose slowly but Carlton eagerly took Gabriel and a reluctant Kameyo in tow, giving an opportunity for everyone else to get acquainted. Zoe carefully touched on a sensitive subject.

"Matt thought about bringing Russell, but we decided he'll be more comfortable staying put. He'd get confused by the new faces, and getting his wheelchair in and out is a hassle in winter." Jennifer grimaced.

"I've done all I can on my own, but he's too much of a load for me. I've developed a chronic sore back hauling him around. And he's getting excellent care. Robin and I take turns visiting."

Robin added, "On his good days, Russell's pretty sharp. But I empathize with Jennifer. He can try your patience asking the same questions over and over."

Jennifer huffed, "He often calls Robin 'Christi.' By now you'd think he'd get the names straight. And all he can do is talk about the past." Su tried to fill an uncomfortable pause in the conversation. "Neuroscience studies have identified different memory locations in the amygdala and hippocampus. How fortunate that Russell's long-term memory is still intact. I'm sure you and Robin do your best making him comfortable."

Matt stepped in to rescue Su by describing his business – CFS Holistic Unicare. He stopped when Zoe called everyone to dinner. "We'll attend the Children's Christmas Eve service, then come back for dessert and gift-giving. Matt, please retrieve Carlton and his people."

Parent-child talk filled the dinner table chatter. Jennifer's cell phone chimed, but she let the call go to voice mail. However, she answered the second. Her expression froze the conversation as if a blizzard had broken out in the dining room.

"Oh my God, no… How did you bring him back? … CPR didn't work?… The defibrillator did?… I'll be there as soon as I can." She repeated to everyone as soon as she disconnected.

"Russell went into cardiac arrest, but they revived him. I'll go to him now." Robin issued orders before Jennifer could get up.

"I'll go. You stay, and everyone, go to the Pageant. And if I don't get back in time, Matt can drop Su and Kameyo at Electra's. Zoe, take care of Gabriel."

Robin arrived at Russell's side forty-five minutes later. The staff had him resting as comfortably as possible and was happy to have Robin assist.

"I can understand him better than you, so let me talk to him in private." When the staff closed the door, Robin reached with both hands for Russell's cheeks, calling to him by his nickname.

"Mr. C, do you recognize me?"

He panted, "Cu – Christi. Huh – help go. Nuh way tuh lih – live. Want uh – digty." Robin knew precisely what Russell wanted, but to give him that meant she would have to relive a personal nightmare that had released Hud's father from his. But when her eyes met Russell's, she saw what needed to be done. She kissed him on the forehead, then spoke calmly.

"Father dear, I hear you. I'll get what I need and come back to you soon." Russell could no longer speak, but he didn't need to. Loving tears welled from his smiling eyes.

Robin dashed out, yelling to the staff, "I'll be right back. You've got my cell number. Call me if he goes into cardiac arrest. And check your records, he's DNR."

Robin skidded on the roads, coming to a sliding stop at her apartment thirty minutes later before rushing in to retrieve a bottle and needles.

I used this five years ago. Why did I save the pentobarbital? I don't know but I'm glad I did.

She was about to run out when her cell phone chimed.

"Robin, this is Pleasant Valley Eldercare. Mr. Conklin just passed away..." Robin numbly listened to the voice before talking.

"We've already paid for all you need to do. Have the body cremated and follow the remaining instructions. I'll stop by tomorrow to clean out his room." Robin walked slowly towards her van after ending the call, glancing at the heavens that were sparkling now that the clouds had drifted away. She imagined Russell's face emerging from a crowd of stars and it gave her hope because those who die live on by gracing the lives of those who treasure all they had offered.

If Electra were here, she could add to my sentiments, but mine'll do just fine. And Russell would give me the same advice Holy gave me, keep busy living.

Robin gave silent prayer after slumping behind the steering wheel. Thanks to the Almighty for sparing me a repeat nightmare. I'm ready to rejoin Christmas present.

Then she straightened her shoulders and drove away, anxiety lifting as she reached a freshly plowed street. The rest of her road ahead would be clearer too; those dearly departed had already told her what to do.

Chapter 32
March 2132

"Double-Crossers"
(Thread 3 Chapter 11)

Darla could see her grand plan for an African Silicon Valley behemoth starting to melt away, like a snowman standing in early spring's bright sunlight. Big-6's share of the rare earths market continued shrinking because explosions had closed a number of its mines, while others were operating at reduced output levels. Compounding the problem, other countries refused to purchase automated mining equipment from her company – Pan-Africa Network Systems – for fear it was the cause of the explosions. The net result: less cash coming in from either direct sales or payoffs from the Big-6 Diggers Conglomerate.

And her problems went deeper than that. Cybergard sales continued sliding as more platform companies switched to better Big Data mining software and regional U.S. banks upgraded network security software purchased somewhere else. She hadn't a clue who her competitors were, and her cyberweapons couldn't penetrate to uncover weaknesses or new enemies, so that left only one person for Darla to blame: Max the Popper.

After being routed out of T-Cube, she knew Max would try to destroy more African mines and instruct Sergei to do the same for her A.I.-related businesses. Only retaliation would calm her anger, but she had few options because no one knew Max's location. Finally, two came to mind for double-crossing her erstwhile partner: plant clues about T-Cube that government security agents could stumble over, or reconnect with China and Isilabad. In either case she could use a proverb that had often been quoted by her former Isilabad conspirator: "The enemy of my enemy is my friend." And though she didn't know who had replaced Ziarmal and Chen, her network security hackers would find out. Darla hustled from her office to assemble a small team that would make it so.

Darla would never know that Electra had stolen some of her

biggest customers, and they in turn would never know how she was using her software's trap doors and hidden apps to spy on them. She had recently followed Email trails and hidden directories through a maze connecting platform companies to Syntagra, and from there to contracts, collusion, and questionable donations coordinated by Carter Quavah, which by obvious implication ensnared Jared Gardner.

I have big plans for what I've learned and I'll share some of the info, but only after I've used it; then I'll turn more of it into more clues for Angus.

Electra was keeping busy on a mid-March Friday at her GWU campus lab, using her snooping software to root out other Syntagra trails connecting Darla to Pan-Africa, giving her a detailed picture of Darla's schemes.

She's clever indeed, synergizing rare earths mining and platform company software for her benefit. She's my visible enemy in those games, and Popper is a still-invisible adversary in another game, rogue terrorist attacks. I can't track him, nor do I ever want to confront him. That's for the CIA and its array of weaponry, not for me.

She was about to lock up for the day when Professor Ravenhill came to visit. He stopped at the doorway before entering, an act of courtesy he had begun exercising late last year.

"Kittner, got a minute? I could use your help."

"Hello, Professor. For you, I always do. Please come in." Ravenhill parked himself in a chair across the desk, getting right to the point. "I've been invited to represent our Biotech Department at a Chaos Theory seminar and panel discussion. There'll be speakers from biogenetics, physics, chemistry, and engineering systems to name a few, maybe even some from the soft sciences. You have this knack for interdisciplinary analysis, so I want to know what suggestions you can give me." Electra began scribbling notes and diagrams as she talked.

"We'll start with the unifying concept. Chaos Theory is a mathematical treatment of dynamical systems that are highly sensitive to initial conditions. Even for deterministic processes, ergodic trajectories are difficult to forecast. Those in the hard sciences tend to be the easier ones to deconstruct because they don't have to account for irrational behavior." Professor Ravenhill's waving hands brought the mini-lecture to a halt.

"Stop playing your word games. Make your explanation simpler."

"Sorry. Here's a good example, the quintessential butterfly effect on weather. A butterfly flapping its wings in China might trigger a blizzard in the Alps two weeks later. Theoretically, if you know the temperature, pressure, humidity, and velocity at all points in the atmosphere, you can predict future weather. But second and third order interactions, compounded by the overwhelming number of data points, exceed even the smartest Quantum Computer's ability to calculate."

"What about chemical or engineering systems"?

"The same applies, and the difficulties escalate once you talk about biological behavior. There are too many subtle linkages among genes and enzymatic reactions to conclusively trace their impact. And I'll give you an example taken from a sex study you can use to silence anyone in the audience who doubts your expertise. Do you remember what an ethologist studies?"

"Uh, human behavior and how it evolves, I think."

"You're correct. Well, an ethologist published a refereed article that statistically confirms exotic dancers get dramatically larger tips if they're wearing the right amount of the right perfume. And some of his other research findings are just as quirky. He concluded, by measuring activation in brain regions associated with pleasure, that the anticipation of sex yields for some study participants more intense sensations than the actual climax. He also claims the female orgasm may be a spandrel, the term a molecular geneticist uses to label superfluous inherited traits. I doubt most women would agree, but no one in the audience will challenge you if you use my bullet points to explain these observations. I'll write down several more from behavioral genetics you can use." Ten minutes later, she handed two pages to Professor Ravenhill, who issued a grade several minutes after that.

"I don't follow any of this. How'd you come up with it? You better send me an edited version."

"It comes from the research I've done, but the more I do, the more I realize how little I'm able to accomplish, even if you were to double the number of post docs assigned to me. Sometime, please invite me to give a talk on asymptotic limits that determine how much humans are able to comprehend."

"That's a deal. And don't get discouraged or be so hard on yourself. You're the best. And I'd say that even if you weren't my go-to person when I need answers. Go home and enjoy the weekend." Electra followed the advice, considering as she drove home what the weekend might hold.

Robin wants to take Gabriel to a kid's reading tomorrow morning at the library. I might go, or I might knock out what Professor Ravenhill wants. I'll have to see what fits best.

As Electra was about to pull into the driveway, she saw what might become a problem. She stopped to observe a squad car idling in front of her house. Nothing else upset the view until an officer exploded out the front door, pursued by Robin wielding a pool cue like a baseball bat. She broke it over his head just before being tackled by a second policeman. Electra leaped from the car.

"I'll kill her! I'll—" Electra tried intervening as the cop shoved Robin's face into the grass as he handcuffed her arms behind her back.

"Officer, this is my house. What's the problem?" The first officer came to Electra's side.

"It's a domestic matter. Go inside and talk to the social services counselor." Electra ran into the living room, finding Gabriel in the clutches of Jennifer, the social worker standing in front. Electra calmed herself before talking.

"Hello Jennifer. What's going on?" Jennifer let the social worker explain.

"Mrs. Conklin wants to take her son home. Ms. Setdarova has been nice enough to look after him while Mrs. Conklin was caring for her husband. Now that he is deceased, Mrs. Conklin's made all necessary arrangements to take care of Gabriel." The conversation stopped while the two officers dragged Robin in. Electra spoke first. "I don't think she's a danger to anyone. Why don't you remove the handcuffs?"

"She assaulted an officer. We have to book her."

"Please, why don't all of us sit down and handle the situation like sensible adults?"Robin and Electra were the only ones remaining forty-five minutes later.

"Why did you tell Jennifer to meet you at my house?"

"I thought I'd have an advantage here. But I didn't know she'd bring a social worker and the police."

"If their POV cameras were rolling, the cops have hard evidence you threatened her."

"If I do kill Jennifer, you'll be my lawyer. Thanks for convincing them not to press charges. What do I owe you?"

"A new pool cue. Are you calm enough to talk about what you want to do?"

"No. Jennifer hit me without warning, I'm too upset to think straight."

"Let's go shoot pool for a couple hours at the place I bought my cue. I'll teach you how to use it the right way, but if you ever get in another fight, do what you just did. It's a lethal weapon in your hands. And then we'll go to a sensual pleasures café…"

Four hours and several marijuana-spiked drinks later, Robin was in a better mood.

"Jennifer's double-crossing me. And please, don't try to explain what she might be thinking. Maybe she and Matt are scheming behind my back, I think I'll quit, and until I sort through everything, I'll plant a vegetable garden in your backyard to give me something to do. Would that be OK with you?"

"Sure, but have you ever done that before?"

"I'm sure I can figure it out. Raising veggies has to be easier than raising kids. And you can give me advice whenever you like." Robin pouted for a minute before speaking again.

"I'm still numb, but I gotta have a child to take care of. It keeps me centered. I don't want to go through the ordeal of pregnancy; maybe I should adopt." Electra nodded, but said nothing until Robin prodded her.

"I know you. The wheels are always turning. I'm sorry I used to yell at you for giving me advice. But I'm past that. Tell me what you're thinking." Both leaned forward as Electra unfolded a new plan.

"You told me about what you did when plugging yourself into Matt's guy party. Do you still have Matt's sample at the Austin Fertility Clinic?"

"Yep. I've kept paying the annual storage fee."

"How would you like me to fertilize a couple of your eggs using Matt's donation to grow your own child?"

"You can do this? I thought it's against the law." Electra shifted uncomfortably before answering.

"Only in some countries. China is actually doing it, and other countries are trying. I won't be breaking any laws because I'll do it at an Indian reservation lab. I can't promise results, and if you give the OK, you have to live with the results and tell no one."

"How do you get my eggs?"

"We'll take you to a fertility clinic for an egg removal procedure. It's safe and speedy. Give them to me, then get the Austin clinic to send your Matt sample to my reservation lab. I'll fertilize three eggs, and for all the fetuses that grow to full-term, I'll prepare birth certificates and adoption papers so only you and I know the truth. If more than one egg keeps growing, you decide if you want to abort it."

Robin gaped before asking, "How did you learn all these tricks?" Electra deadpanned, "I'm ruthless and devious. And I have killer instincts." Electra's smile disguised the truth that no one living knew. I better stop talking. I don't ever want anyone getting too close to what I can do.

Robin smiled too.

"I know you're kidding, but I have one requirement, you're the godmother."

"Deal. Now, let's get you home."

A month later, Electra had three eggs incubating in NLVs at her lab. She had suspended further software development or Internet snooping while doing so, but headline news prompted her to call Angus, who was happy to hear her voice.

"You dropped out of sight since we last talked. Good to finally hear from you. What do you make of what's being reported?"

"That's why I'm calling. I can't believe what the media is saying. Do you think the Guardian Party is secretly conducting rogue terrorism to keep the world guessing, or to strengthen Jared's role on the world stage?"

"It's all baloney unless the press is better than the CIA at tracking clues, and I know from my CIA contacts that the clues are leading to Russia, but that info won't go public until it's confirmed. Unlike the media, our government isn't yet in the business of planting fake news. I think it's another colossal media failure caused by blue-chip pundits chasing their tails or wrong trails, either to hype the news or discredit Gardner because he's a shoo-in to get reelected." Electra interrupted so Angus could calm down.

"I'm happy to hear that. And you might be happy to hear that one of my contacts told me about possible platform company collusion coordinated by Syntagra. Your CIA contacts might like to know."

"Uh, they might. Got anything more specific?"

"Have them look into possible links between Omni-Buy and political contributions. I'm sure they can ferret out facts."

"Good suggestion. And I'll keep sending you invites to my staff meetings. I'd rather be talking to you in person. But even if all you can do is send Emails or phone calls, let's keep in touch."

"Either way, by now you should know you're always at the top of my A-list."

"I won't ask what the 'A' stands for, but I'll assume it's good." Electra's joking reply ended the call.

"Usually it is, but never get too comfortable, like the guy falling down the elevator shaft who says so far so good until he hits the bottom."

Sitting alone in the Oval Office, Jared gawked in disbelief as he read an Email that had just come into one of his hidden accounts: "The CIA will soon trace Omni-Buy contributions to you, and I know more than they do. Get ready for a change in uniform if you don't desist."

As it self-destructed, Jared muttered harsh words before calling someone who could help.

"Buffy, it's Jared. Get your ass to the Oval Office pronto."

Max the Popper's jovial mood surprised Sergei because the soldier's tone usually echoed nothing but disciplined military commands.

"Yes, I too am pleased how Darla's double-crossing news leaks are working. If the media wants to blame the Guardian Party, all the better. And I am planning another attack that will cause even more confusion."

"Can you tell me where and when?"

"I could, but of course I won't. Just keep watching the news and following my orders. And have patience, for one day you shall see more proof of our superiority. That is all I wish to say. Dasvidaniya." The Popper terminated the call before Sergei could say goodbye in any language.

Chapter 33
September 2132

"Running on Empty"
(Thread 3 Chapter 12)

"Mamma Mia, how you write this? I have you reviewing movie screenplays and you find time to write this documentary? How can you do so many different things?" Vito's expression mixed admiration and surprise as he studied the script while Electra sat across from him in his studio office. She waited patiently while he read enough to offer a verdict.

"It is good. It is different. And even though Cyber-Max not big in documentaries, maybe you lead a new trend. Tell me, how you come up with it?"

"I've always admired Native American Indians. Their culture has many characteristics that Americans have finally learned to embrace. Holistic medicine and sustainability are two of many that come to mind. And as a nation, we've always reached out to those people who need help, often in proportion to the distance from our shores. I think it's time for us to do more for those who were here before we came."

"You got an outline we can use to pitch your script?"

"Let me walk you through it." Electra handed him a copy, pausing for a moment before continuing.

"Here's the title, The Invisible Americans – A Micro-Nation Rising Again to Greatness. And here's the documentary's theme – American Indian tribes had thriving continental civilizations long before Columbus discovered America. Each tribe had distinctive customs attuned to its land and religion. And they cooperated, not as a unified nation but more like a forerunner of the UN. Early settlers thought Indians were primitive because they had no science or technology like the Europeans, but archaeological and anthropological studies have shown they are the equals of other great civilizations from Antiquity. It was their misfortune that European expansion exterminated them." Vito interrupted.

"Sad but true. But the public doesn't want a sad story. You got a happy ending?"

"Follow the outline. After an intro and a summary of prehistoric roots, we compare Native American civilizations to those that flourished in other parts of the world. Then we trace, from the time Columbus discovered America, how Indians at first cooperated with explorers and settlers, and then had to fight to preserve what belonged to them. We'll portray the battles and ultimate defeat realistically, and then trace the aftermath. And then, we'll show how today's Native American tribes are like the Phoenix, rising from the ashes. Phoenix segues nicely to numerous Native American birds of myth and legend."

"But I don't see the Phoenix. How are they rising?"

"You, like most Americans, don't see it because no one has promoted what's a work in progress. I've been working with some of the tribes and their National Tribal Council, an affiliation inside the NCAI, which is a buffer when dealing with the Bureau of Indian Affairs." Vito's skepticism began to lift.

"So, you got tribal contacts in Washington?"

"Not only that, but reservation contacts as well. Onsite filming will be a snap, and I can be the narrator. And think about this; we can produce a series of appealing documentaries patterned after this one. We can highlight ongoing activities, or promote new ones, that keep America great."

"I think we got something that can make money and do some good too. I'll find a time for you and me to pitch it to La Presidenza next time you come back. And since you're leaving tomorrow, come, let me buy you dinner in cafeteria."

Vito continued the happy dialogue after selecting a booth.

"I would take you to fancy restaurant, but I must go back for a surprise videoconference meeting at eight."

"I'm happy with the food here. If there were a Hollywood studio culinary competition, Cyber-Max chefs would earn five-stars. And dining with you makes the entire package ne plus ultra."

"I like how you play with words. No wonder you write good. And this time, I know. 'Ne plus ultra' comes from Latin, no? And means no more beyond. Yes?"

"I expected you to know that. After all, the Italian language comes from colloquial Latin."

As the conversation continued, Vito led it in a surprising direction after the waitress took their orders.

"Why don't you sit in on videoconference? You will learn more about studio politics and negotiations, very valuable if you want to move ahead. And you are my prize unit manager assistant. But tell me, do you want to keep juggling a Hollywood career with all your others?"

"I would like to because computer technology force-multiplies my planning and multi-tasking skills. For me, juggling careers is stimulating and synergistic instead of scary and uncertain."

"Maybe so. Just keep surprising me with what you're doing and soon I have you doing more."

Dinner conversation moved along nicely all the way back to Vito's office, just in time for another surprise. When he logged in for the teleconference, the monitor displayed an LA TV station news anchor delivering an emergency bulletin as the conference moderator supplied an alarmed voiceover.

"The Big Lift is under attack. One of its pumping stations has been blown up. Listen to the bulletin. I'll cut in after we've heard enough."

"… More details are now streaming in, but it has just been confirmed that a sundown catastrophe that destroyed the Colorado River Aqueduct's most remote pumping station is not an act of Nature but instead an act of terrorism. Caltech's Seismic Center reports no earthquake activity. Cell phone videos coming in from hikers clearly show plumes that could only come from manmade explosions. I'm cutting away to a Southern Cal Metropolitan Water District briefing for the latest."

Seconds later, the monitor displayed a split-screen, one of which contained a harried spokesperson rattling information.

"… and the Aqueduct is called the Big Lift because it pumps half the water Los Angeles uses, lifting it 2000 feet over mountains on a 250-mile journey starting in Nevada, flowing over four dams, through thirty tunnels, and out five pumping stations. The loss of any pumping station essentially turns off the tap. We can't give you a repair time or cost estimate until our engineers inspect the damage, but from the videos we've received, Los Angeles is facing a crisis."

The spokesman stopped for a question, then answered.

"No, we had no warnings from the pumping station, but all electronic communications went dark just before the catastrophe. We have to investigate further--" Vito's moderator cut back in. "Meeting adjourned. We'll reschedule after the dust settles."

Electra had to battle traffic and airport congestion the next day because of a rapidly growing exodus swollen by hyped and fake news. By the time she landed in DC, several conspiracy theories had taken flight; she called Angus the following evening.

"I'm glad you're not in LA. Four months is a long time to have water taps running on empty. You can't live on nothing but bottled water. But I agree with you. I can't imagine Gardner used a covert operations strike to punish LA just because a majority of its voters don't like him. The CIA suspects a link to international terrorism, and they're starting to piece together evidence. If your contacts ever uncover more, let me know…"

Although LA's water shortage placed her Hollywood activities on hold, Electra had more than enough work on her home turf. She alternated weekly stints at her GWU lab for improving software and Brain Probe with those at her reservation lab for cloning and related DNA work. Robin insisted she view fetal development, forcing Electra to bring her along in mid-November for her first visit to the Pequot reservation. Electra warned the de facto expectant mother when entering.

"What you'll see here is not like your high school biology lab." A hint of chemical aromas brought out uncertain feelings.

"I feel like I've just entered foreign territory. Holy Shit, are those my eggs growing?"

"That's right, each fetus is developing in its own Neuro-Life Vessel. I started with three, but one self-aborted earlier. The remaining two are healthy and growing at a slightly accelerated rate, probably because NLV embryonic fluid environment is optimal."

Robin peered speculatively at the emergent life forms floating inside the glass vessels.

"Hard to believe all of us started this way. It's sort of disturbing, takes away most of the mystery. I never felt the same way about hot dogs after we learned in grade school how they're made."

"Not for me. Watching life emerge is awe-inspiring. But as I said when we started, these are your prenatal babies and we can abort them before they reach full term, but after that you must live with the consequences. Do you want to abort?"

"Don't talk like that. How can you be so cold? I want both. And I'm glad I came. I'm old enough and finally strong enough mentally to handle the truth. You know that."

"I do, but remember, we tell no one, not even Su and Kameyo, who we'll visit next. I didn't tell them I was coming, so we won't stay long."

Robin wanted to know more as the pair walked to another building. "Who watches my embryos when you're not here?"

"The NLVs' smart software. And I can monitor remotely, which is another example of how empowering A.I. can be. And no one can enter my lab without my authorization, thanks to IOT." Electra added more when she saw Robin's puzzled look.

"IOT stands for Internet of Things. As long as the power stays on and firewalls work, life is good. And we don't have to knock to get into Su's lab. I have the entry code."

The visit was cordial but brief because Su and Kameyo reported that projects were advancing per their last status report.

As they left the building, Robin asked, "They sure are a great team, but according to Kameyo they could make faster progress if you assisted. Why don't you?"

"I have my own project list. There's only so much I can do. We have one more stop before we go. We'll say hello to Tim and Kwame."

That visit was identical to the previous, quick and easy.

As they drove away, Robin said, "Until today, I never saw you play an R&D role. Your teams really look to you for guidance. You're a different person when you take charge. We all can play different roles, but when you do you bring a whole new personality and set of skills."

"That may be true, but I have limits too. There's only so much I can do unless my teams get smarter and can handle more of the load."

"You do a good job hiding your superiority, but I know you better than they do. I think that's the reason I sometimes resented you. But today I've seen firsthand why those who have a lot are expected to do a lot. There has to be a Biblical quote for this. Go ahead, tell me what it is."

"It comes from Luke 12:48. 'For unto whomsoever much is given, of him shall be much required.' And I'm all for it, but sometimes I feel my brain is close to running on empty. I'm unable to overcome major roadblocks in my biotech and software projects. And it frustrates me because I hate disappointing myself or my teams."

"Well, you're not disappointing me. When do you think my eggs will be ready to hatch?"

"In less than a month. We'll come back before Christmas. And until then, just keep doing what you're doing. I will too…"

Though Electra worked full-time the following week at her GWU lab trying to deconstruct why and how her Linguistic Analyzer capabilities were growing, she came away empty and frustrated.

What I've built is better than any commercial Virtual Assistant app, even better than what I've uncovered by hacking into DARPA. And DARPA is still ahead of Russia and China. Mine appears to be getting smarter, but it's adding additional modules I can't decompile and it must be building memory in locations I can't find. And its GUI avatar image and voice are evolving unpredictably. Maybe I should pull the plug and reinitialize, as the action-adventure hero had to do in the retro movie — Live. Die. Repeat. I'll name my adventure Remove. Repair. Restart.

No, I won't stop it until sometime next year. Until then, I'll let it run. After all, I like the tagline I've been using this year, Welcome Madness and the Most. My software may come in handy. And since all other projects are perking along nicely, I'll work on my presentation that I want Professor Ravenhill to schedule. I might as well visit him before I go home.

Professor Ravenhill waved her into his office, talking first as she seated herself across from him.

"Kittner, your Chaos Theory write-up helped. You know your stuff. So, what have you got for me today?"

"The last time we met I said I could give a lecture on asymptotic limits. And since then, I've expanded it to cover some of the theories I've been developing. How does this sound? I'll give a 45-minute lecture and afterwards we'll have a moderator lead an interdisciplinary panel discussion."

"It'll work. The timing's good because your talk can fill up some of the inter-term break. And knowing you like I do, I'm certain you have a title and an outline you can give me."

"The title is Unified Theory of Emergence. I'll explain what emergence is and why the latest R&D in high energy physics and biotech support it. I'll show how it makes practical applications of Chaos Theory in a variety of research areas, and I'll try to motivate others to extend what I've developed."

"It's a deal. I know how clever you are and how clearly you can explain tough topics. Just make sure you talk at a level everyone can understand."

"I'll send you a presentation abstract as well as a copy of the overheads. You can share them with the panelists you select."

"No, I always like keeping ahead of my associates. We'll let them try to catch up."

Electra had more success polishing her presentation the week before Thanksgiving than she had propping up her friendships. Zoe had called to invite her for Thanksgiving, but she had to decline because she knew Robin would refuse to come. Robin had severed all ties because of Jennifer, but she still wanted to know if their holistic healthcare business was afloat, so she quizzed Electra.

"How are Zoe and Matt doing? They better replace some of the clients who are staying with me. Otherwise, Jennifer has no administrative role to fill."

"They're resilient, but Matt misses you because neither Zoe nor Jennifer is a certified caregiver. Matt understands why you're angry, but he hopes you'll consider coming back. He's looking, but hasn't found a replacement yet. Zoe invited us to come over for Thanksgiving, but I said I've made reservations for us at Tyson's Galleria in McLean. I haven't dropped hints yet, but I'll start mentioning that you plan to adopt."

Robin's tone softened. "I'll probably feel different towards Jennifer in about a month if you can deliver as promised. And I'm mature enough to handle whatever comes."

Post-Thanksgiving days rolled smoothly into the first week of December, bringing sunny skies that matched Electra's mood for her Friday morning presentation. Robin had rescheduled all client visits because she wanted to attend; the duo arrived at 9:30. Robin sat in the back while Electra clicked through her slides before Professor Ravenhill trooped in fifteen minutes later, introducing the panelists to her as the auditorium began to fill. When Electra asked if there were any questions, Professor Ravenhall answered for all.

"None whatsoever. I'll be the moderator and our panelists are comfortable with the topics you outlined. We're all good to go." Professor Ravenhill gave a snappy introduction promptly at 10 a.m. Electra thought whimsically to herself as she replaced him at the podium.

The auditorium is 10-percent filled, not 90-percent empty. And the panel is 100 percent full. I hope everyone will know more after the talk than before.

Electra thanked the moderator before explaining the first slide displayed behind her.

Unified Theory of Emergence Presented by Dr. Electra Kittner
Friday December 5, 2132
Purpose of Lecture:

- Summarize Concept of Emergence
- Show why High Energy Physics supports it
- Explain how it anchors Life on Earth
- Illustrate inferences for Homo Sapiens
- Connect Emergence with the "Singularity"
- Explain multi-disciplinary role of Emergent Evolution
- Motivate Audience via "Turtles all the way Down" metaphor to extend what is presented

"Good morning. I'm Electra Kittner, an R&D Assistant Professor at UMW and UTA, and I thank you for attending my 'Unified Theory of Emergence' presentation that will be followed by a panel discussion. Please notice my seven bullet points. Why seven? Because brain studies show that most humans can keep track of at most seven items before tuning out, and I want you to stay tuned in. And don't worry, I won't show numerical equations or overwhelm you with slides. I will show only six, including this one, because my talk will introduce and highlight concepts, leaving the details for our panelists to cover and answer audience questions afterwards. So, let's begin." Electra advanced to the next slide.

Emergence and the Universe
Definition: Emergence is a process applied to Complex Systems

that use energy and entropy (information) to self-regulate themselves recursively for extended duration.

In the Beginning…

Genesis and the Greeks (Democritus) had right:

- Only Atoms and the Void High Energy Physics Conjectures:
- Big Bang created the Entire Universe from a point containing Infinite Amount of Matter
- The Void = Space emerges from Matter
- At the instant of creation, Big Bang explodes like an Emerging Sphere into Three Dimensions.
- "Parallel Universes" Theory demands each point in the Emerging Sphere explodes into its own Emerging Sphere containing all its Matter = Energy
- Matter in each Emerging Sphere condenses to form Fundamental Particles, Hydrogen Atoms, Stars, Galaxies, Elements, Solar Systems, Planets
- Two Laws of Physics (constant everywhere) control Matter:Conservation of Energy Non-Decrease of Entropy
- Quantum Physics and General Relativity describe all phenomena.Classical Physics "approximates" what is measured in Man's observable range

"Long ago, the Greeks and the Bible answered one of our most perplexing questions: What is the Universe made of? And their answer is still correct, the Universe consists of only matter and an empty void. They couldn't go beyond that because of limitations in their science and technology, but ours takes us much further. The Universe emerged when an infinitesimally small point containing all matter erupted, an event we call the Big Bang, not an explosion into space but instead an explosion that created space when matter dispersed according to the laws of energy and entropy that are currently encapsulated in Quantum Physics and General Relativity. Please notice on my next slide the sequence of emergent structures that use energy and entropy to self-regulate themselves recursively for extended duration." After a brief pause, Electra displayed it.

Emergence of Life

- Chemical Reactions create Molecules throughout an Infinity of Planets populating the Universe(s?)

- Complex Molecules emerge from a chain of Chemical Reactions
- Life on Earth emerges from Carbon Substrate Evolutionary Process. Other Life Forms emerge in other regions of the Universe wherever Chance allows Emergence from Substrates.
- All Organisms on Earth emerge via Carbon-Based Evolution
- Complex Organisms emerge as they gain "Critical Mass"
- Humans sit atop Carbon-Based Evolutionary Chain; All Physiological and Mental Processes emerge from Organs
- Emotions and Cognition are Emergent Properties of Brain once it reaches a "Critical Level" of Interneural Connections
- Free Will exists due to Uncertainty Principle
- Time is a Mental Construct (currently measured by counting atomic vibrations) isomorphic to Ordinal Numbers allowing "Cause and Effect" ordering of Observable Events.
- Mind/Brain Duality does not exist. Each is a different facet of the Emergent Brain.
- Organisms subjectively experience the Universe through its Senses (For Humans: Sight, Sound, Taste, Touch, Smell, Spatial Orientation)
- The Goal of all Organisms: Pass DNA to Next Generation.

"There are many concepts packed into this slide, so I'll touch on only the most important. Perhaps the most exciting is that the Universe probably contains other life forms somewhere out there that emerged from substrates other than carbon. We conveniently assume that life could emerge only from organic compounds marinated in an environment like Earth's, but as George Gershwin's lyrics in Porgy and Bess say, it ain't necessarily so. So, think about it, as well as the conjecture that time exists only in the mind. And notice that you have free will because of the Uncertainty Principle." Electra scanned the audience before proceeding to the next slide.

I'm starting to see some frowns. Too bad, because the next slide might produce more, but this is a smart audience that should be able to handle the truth. At least the truth according to me.

Human Characteristics

Difficult truth to grasp emotionally:

We are merely complex biochemical reactions (think test tube chemical experiment)

- Human Brain is most complex structure currently known to exist in the Universe
- Language (Words, Syntax, Semantics, Grammar) separates humans from other species.
- Wittgenstein Quote: If a lion could speak, we couldn't understand it.
- Feelings are Subjective Translation of Physiological Emotions
- Asymptotic Limits (Analytic Ability/PrecisionComplexity) erect barriers past which Cognition cannot advance (Brain might not have enough Interneural Connections)
- Humans are designed not to be "Happy" but to pass genes to next generation
- Carbon-Based DNA has emerged via Evolution as an instruction tape that controls synthesis of Proteins and Enzymes subject to Promoter/Repressor Regulators
- Humans are predisposed to: Believe in God and Cooperate to Solve Problems
- "Nature vs Nurture" is 50-50, causing complicated and often counterintuitive physiological and psychological behavior
- The Brain might be the ultimate Carbon-Based Emergent Structure
- Additional Conjectures:
- The Brain uses Bayesian likelihood probabilities to incorporate subjective beliefs instead of experimental probabilities (Faith versus Reason)
- The Brain IS NOT like a Silicon-Based Computer because it parallel-processes information and stores it as well as behavior in arrays of neural networks (sets of synapses), but we use an Input-Process-Output Model as a useful paradigm
- High Energy Physics is beyond the point of diminishing returns when reaching for its asymptotic limits
- Neuroscience has not yet reached the point of diminishing returns

"Like the previous slide, we'll leave unpacking its nuances for our panelists, but dwell for just a moment on the majesty of humanity.

Though each of us is merely a complex bio-electrochemical reaction controlled by the brain, which is currently the most complex structure known in the observable Universe, consider the sequence of emergent structures. Cells emerge from chemical reactions. DNA and genes emerge from cells. Organs emerge from DNA-controlled processes. The brain emerges to control the organs. Emotions, cognition, and self-awareness emerge from the brain. And even though our brain has asymptotic limits, how magnificent it is.

"But let us remember that there is only so much that the human brain can understand or articulate, or to state metaphorically, we are captives of our selfish genes that have built us to optimize transmission of our genetic traits to the next generation but not necessarily to be happy or always understand why we act or feel the way we do. But how exciting the challenge. We are built to understand more and more as we approach our limits, even though the steps become shorter the longer we persist. But humankind is designed to survive, we want to solve problems."

Hmm, more blank stares and negative nods. Let's see if this next slide takes the audience to a happier brain state. Maybe some of A.I. described on it will help.

Evolutionary Trajectory towards the "Singularity Conjecture: Artificial Intelligence still reaching towards the "Singularity." If reached, its Intelligence/Awareness will be much different than human counterparts.

1. Algorithm (Step-by-step problem solutions)
2. Turing Machine (0-1 Computing Machine)
3. Church Thesis (Any problem with algorithmic solution can be solved on Turing Machine)
4. Turing Test (Machine is intelligent if it answers like a person)
5. Weak A.I. (Machine is "Expert System" empowered by self-learning "Neural Net" circuitry that has "Narrow Expertise")
6. Strong/General A.I. (Machine Intelligence equals Human's)
7. First-Order Singularity (Machine Intelligence exceeds Human's)
8. Second-Order Singularity (Machine Self-Awareness emerges as Machine reaches critical level of auto-recursive interacting circuits)
9. Third-Order Singularity (Machine Mobility emerges)

10.   Fourth-Order Singularity (Machine Emotion emerges)

"Those in the audience familiar with the mathematical foundation of computing will recognize on this slide why it supports our steps towards the Singularity. Singularity is a popular term labeling the event that ignites computer intelligence to exceed human intelligence, and soon after that it reaches self-awareness. A very tall order, but as Newton said, we stand on the shoulders of giants. We must always push towards greatness."

Electra pushed on to her next slide.

Future R&D must extend the use of
Chaos Theory Chaos Theory
(aka Complexity Theory):

- May be considered the "Third Fundamental Science"
- Explains how order and patterns emerge in Complex Systems
- Small variations in starting conditions cause dramatic End-State Emergence
- Two Kinds: Deterministic (Algorithms explain Evolutionary Trajectory), Non-Deterministic (Chance/Uncertainty intervenes)

Complex System: Comprised of many non-linear interacting subsystems whose subtle cause-effect characteristics lead to "Emergent" System (Whole cannot be explained by sum of parts)

Examples: Weather Economy Universe Living Organisms Researchers have used Chaos Theory only in the last 150 years because computing power finally caught up to Complexity

"Going forward, researchers must add Chaos Theory to their analytic toolkit, and Quantum Computing breakthroughs expand their computational horizons. Traditional scientific research considers chaotic patterns an error in measurement that can be eliminated by building more powerful measuring instruments. But the correct approach may be to consider chaos a fundamental property of complex systems. I won't pretend that I know all its subtleties, but I wanted to mention it to pique your imagination because the most exciting research areas today include complex systems. And that takes me to my last slide."

Towards a Unified Theory of Emergent Evolution
(Evolution and Emergence tightly coupled)

- Evolution is an optimization process constrained by Laws of Energy and Laws of Entropy = Information
- Evolution balances Individual/Heritable, Adaptive/Imprintable, and Group Trait Selection Criteria, allowing for random mutations, to assure "Survival for transmitting Genes"
- Evolutionary process leads to Emergent Structures
- Emergent Structures support Evolution

Evolution/Emergence Sequencing:

Evolution

Emergence (Lower-numbered Discipline feeds into successor)

1. Quantum Physics/Relativity evolves to Emergent Improvement
2. Molecular Genetics evolves to Emergent Improvement
3. Biology evolves to Emergent Improvement
4. Neuroscience evolves to Emergent Improvement
5. Medicine evolves to Emergent Improvement
6. Psychology/Psychiatry/Behavioralism evolves to Emergent Improvement
7. Philosophy/Religion/Politics/Economics/Sociology evolves to Emergent Improvement
8. Repeat 3-7…

- Can we apply Evolutionary Principles to Science or Evolution itself? Are we tumbling into an "Infinite Regress Black Hole"?
- How can Quantum Mechanics use Chaos Theory?
- Do Fractal Dimensions and Fractal Genes exist?
- Isn't Energy conserved at the Quantum Level?
- Your Challenge: Build on what is presented here.

"Living organisms might be the most complex of all complex systems, using Evolution to improve Emergent Structures like the Brain. But Evolution and Emergence might simply be different facets of the same concept. Consider this. Evolution leads to Emergent Structure convergence from many starting points, whereas Emergence leads to vastly different evolutionary end states even when initial conditions differ minutely.

"So, my final slide is meant to capture your imagination by presenting a picture for applying Evolution and Emergence recursively. I call it my 'Unified Theory of Emergent Evolution.' Follow the number sequence to the questions at the bottom. Can you now feed Evolution into Quantum Physics, repeating the sequence, and so on and so forth? If so, how does Emergence and Chaos Theory affect Quantum Mechanics? Do Fractal Dimensions and Fractal Genes actually exist, or are they only fantasies? And when High Energy Physicists claim that energy is not conserved at the quantum level, aren't they simply admitting that they don't know the other dimensions that are absorbing or emitting energy? Are you tumbling into an infinite regress of 'Turtles, all the way Down?'

"I'm sure you can add other questions to the list, and I'm not smart enough to find answers to the ones I've listed, but I leave these challenges for you and your successors. I've completed what I can do and am pointing the way to a future pregnant with possibilities. We are just beginning to see that not only is life stranger than we imagine, but it may be even stranger than we can possibly imagine. So, let your creativity run free by welcoming madness and the most. "Thank you for listening. And do you have any questions for me before our moderator returns?"

Electra sensed that the collective puzzlement of the listeners had deflated their confidence and shrunk the number of questions asked to only one, finally posed by a young Indian woman sitting near the front.

"In your first slide, you referred to 'Turtles all the Way Down,' and in your very last you mentioned an 'Infinite Regress.' The Turtles expression is an illustration of an Indian philosophy concept referred to as Anavastha. Isn't it identical to the Infinite Regress?"

"Yes, and thank you for asking as well as answering your question. It shows you understand that in any argument chain, you must eventually reach outside the context for a definition. Philosophers and theologians often use it to posit a Prime or Unmoved Mover. I deliberately tried to unify my presentation by connecting the first and final slides. Are there other questions?" Unfortunately, there weren't, causing Electra to panic.

My talk has been a downer for the audience. I better do something to pick them up. Maybe examples will help.

Electra's words kept some of the audience in their seats.

"Before we take a break, let me describe Emergence in action. What's a water wave? It's Newton's laws of motion acting on vast numbers of water molecules. But what emerges from that is a higher-level structure, a wave we describe by its frequency, direction, and magnitude. Or, what's an ant colony? It's merely a swarm of ants running about. But what emerges from their seemingly random motions is an intelligent superstructure, a hive that controls all the ants by giving a higher-order purpose that no single ant understands. I'm sure our panelists will point out additional examples, so please stay for the discussion."

Professor Ravenhill came back to the podium to rescue both Electra and audience from further embarrassment.

"Thank you, Professor Kittner, for a thought-provoking presentation. We'll take a fifteen-minute break and then start our panel discussion."

The rest of the seminar quickly unraveled. Only five brave souls returned after the break. They were disappointed to hear the panelists' struggling to connect Electra's theory to their areas of expertise. Professor Ravenhill called a halt after only fifteen minutes. "Well, I guess we all understand better how complicated Emergence can be. I think all of you should ask your professors how you might best use Professor Kittner's conjectures. So, think about this over the Holiday break, and come back as the Winter Term emerges in January."

As the survivors straggled out, the panelists clustered about Electra, the most senior hissing a complaint.

"I'm disappointed, you didn't even give us an abstract of your theory or a copy of your slides. I think you deliberately blindsided us. You better not do that again."
Electra tried not to stumble over her words.

"I apologize to all of you. I didn't have enough time to circulate them, but I can do that now. And I promise to give you what you need ahead of time if I ever give another talk.

Professor Ravenhill rallied to her defense.

"Don't be so hard on Professor Kittner. I have worked closely with her, reviewing what she presented today. Naturally, I thought you would understand as well as I her conjectures, but I was wrong. I'll send you copies of what she gave me. Please share them with your associates…"

As they drove away from campus, Robin broke the silence.

"You did your best to inspire the audience, but people are so unwilling to think outside their comfort zones. No wonder you say your brain is running on empty. And you were so diplomatic when the panelists attacked you. I would have busted them over the head with a pool cue." Electra had to laugh.

"How did you like my ant colony analogy? I thought that up last summer while helping you dig in the garden. Studying them scrambling about made me realize I'm an ant too and should learn from them. They aren't frustrated, they're totally engaged in doing something and enjoying the moment. I need to remember that."

"I could pull an Electra on you by asking a bunch of questions, but I won't because you look like you need a change of pace. I'll buy lunch if we can go bowling afterwards."

The diversion worked. Knocking down pins helped Electra shift to a better frame of mind where she found the right answer for Robin's question.

"Next week will be perfect for delivering your twins because Su and Kameyo are leaving this weekend to spend the Holidays in Austin with Hud. You'll have the second half of December to resettle into your motherhood role. So, your assignments between now and the middle of next week are setting up your nursery and studying the psychology of raising infants. And I'm staying out of the way. I don't want to provoke you, now that you know I have a new pool cue." "Don't say that. From now on, I plan to behave the right way. I need to set a good example."

Electra and Robin filled the rest of December doing all the right things. They brought home twins that bonded immediately to Robin and vice versa. Robin chose names to honor two trailblazing females in music and science: Clara and Marie. Electra created birth certificates and adoption papers, and while Robin immersed herself in the joys known only to new mothers, Electra boldly planned a year-ending surprise baby shower.

Heartfelt wishes from the invitees – Zoe, Matt, and Jennifer – brought Robin to tears and launched a reconciliation. And later that evening, after everyone had left, Electra toasted last year's successes while watching the crowd at Times Square ring in the New Year.

Serendipity smiled on me everywhere it could this year. Only in biotech and A.I. have I accomplished less than I hoped because I'm bumping into my limits. How could Indira have known I would hit this wall? She wrote a poem, Beyond the Silence, that tells me why this is so. Electra recited it to herself:

How clever Man's emergent brain,
Inventing tools to extend his reach.
Gathering knowledge for others to teach,
The outward World is his to gain.
How different the story when looking in,
Enigmas cloud the clever mind.
The evidence so hard to find,
Nothing beyond a silent whim.
Mitered men tell all they know,
Their Faith proclaims but nothing there.
Merely sand castles in the air,
Whither their efforts nowhere to go.
And so we reach a stalemate,
Faith and Reason must resolve.
Let future worry how to evolve,
Enjoy what you have – before too late.

I'm not as clever as I wish I were. Would Mother have pioneered my Unified Theory of Emergence if she had lived longer? I'll never know. But at least I know I have finally achieved her level of empathy. Next year I'll continue practicing what her poems teach. Next year's goals are within my reach.

Chapter 34
February 2133

"Ignition"
(Thread 3 Chapter 13)

Two unnatural disasters that occurred on New Year's Eve ignited an explosion of media speculation linking them to California's Big Lift disaster. Sections of the Aswan and Three Gorges dams had been blown away.

Pundits made the most of the ensuing confusion, constructing a conspiracy among a worldwide network of unidentified terrorist organizations intent on derailing international political and economic progress. These disasters captured so much attention that they dwarfed another pair of explosions that occurred two weeks later in Africa: Pan-African mining equipment and software development locations had been attacked.

But they didn't distract Darla Tinibu. She knew that Max the Popper had targeted her company as well as Middle East and Chinese dams, and she used the commotion to strengthen a tenuous alliance she had begun constructing with Ziarmal's and Chen's successors.

The uproar had a different effect on Jared Gardner. It helped calm him because the media pivoted away from the President. It also eliminated any interest in possible links between Omni-Buy and illegal contributions.

Electra waited until early February to ask Angus what he knew, and though he didn't know much yet, he invited her to his senate office for a one-on-one discussion.

"I hope I don't have to buy you a bigger cap, now that the Senate elected you president pro tempore. But I do agree with its choice.

Unlike the House of Representatives, your colleagues respect the public's desire for leaders who are mature enough to handle the responsibilities and intellectually young enough to embrace new approaches." Angus sidestepped the compliment when he replied. "The expansion strip on the one you gave me has plenty of room left, which I'll need to absorb all the info you'll be getting for me plus what I'm getting now. Case in point, let me tell you about my CIA contacts.

"They know more than the media does about terrorist attacks. There has to be rogue terrorist network operating outside the control of any government. The CIA and its network of national security agencies have looked for patterns. Geography suggests that Russia or a former Soviet state might be the source, but unexplained explosions last year at several Eastern European toxic waste sites don't fit. We don't have enough to act unilaterally, but we do have a countermove. I know what it is because I have top secret clearance. I'm breaking the law by telling you, but I trust you to keep our code of silence, so here's what it is.

"We and the UN are building a covert network of communications and strike force compounds. The entire project is dark and I don't know its codename, but we've just completed the hub location in Lebanon. It went live last October, and we're putting together an inspection team. I'm part of it, but I can appoint someone to represent me if that person gets security clearance. You're smarter and have a knack for snooping. If I can get you cleared, will you go?"

"That's something I can do, and I'll snoop for additional information about it."

"I don't want to know how you snoop. Just don't get caught. I'll contact you within a week. And if you do go, promise me you'll be careful. I don't want to lose my secret weapon." Electra smiled as she rose.

"I prefer being called your singular resource. But whatever you call me, let's keep our newest game a secret."

Electra snooped enough after her Angus meeting to build a head start by the end of the week.

Timing's everything. How lucky for me that all my current projects are perking along. I'll be able to fit an inspection trip into my schedule. And Angus doesn't know, but I've already been vetted because of my NGA position. All I need to do is tweak the classified files to clear all security levels. And that's what I and my Network Security Toolkit can do. And before I meet again with Angus, I'll hack further to find all data about the new project. Now it's time to plug back into my personal life.

Playing the godmother role that weekend, Electra observed how efficient Robin had become.Robin cheerfully explained why at Sunday lunch while letting Electra feed Marie.

"You know more about my mental issues than anyone, but you told me I'm crazy in a good sort of way because I've learned to use them to my advantage. The more I do for my twins, the better I feel and the more I want to do. It's my own virtuous cycle, a subject I'm sure you know all about. And you're the numbers whiz, so add all that to how long I've been thinking about having my own kid and you get the answer to your question."

Electra said, "You might be better than me with the number two. I can't tell the twins apart, but obviously you can. You must be picking up sensory or emotional clues available only to a mother. But when I get back from my next trip, maybe they'll have grown some distinguishing beauty marks."

"You didn't tell me about a trip. When are you leaving?"

"Departure date and final destination aren't set yet, but I'll let you know."

"I'll miss you, not as just a godmother, but also as my best friend. Promise me you'll be careful."

"I always am. You know that." As Electra cleared the table, she noticed Robin's sudden mood shift, as if a cloud were drifting across the sun, but she waited for Robin to say more.

"My twins make me happier than I've ever been. There's only one piece missing. You know what it is, and you know I'm stable enough to be OK without it. But sometimes I wonder about you. You can hide your episodes of depression from everyone but me. I can't believe it, but here I am telling you what we should do."

"Look, my empathy is better than ever, but I'm just not built to talk about my emotions as much as other people. What else do I need to do to show you I love you more than anyone? And I'll say it again, I love you even more than I loved Christi."

"I want us to become co-friends, officially."

"Do you think that will make me love you even more?"

"No, and I'm sorry I'm not as strong or as self-assured as you are. I've tried, but I'm not able to change how I feel. I want you to tell the world how much I mean to you."

"Please, don't ever tell me you're sorry because you haven't changed to please me. I love you as you are. But I'll make you this promise. When I get back, we'll pick up this conversation right where we're leaving off." Robin's cloud sailed away.

"I'll hold you to that promise. And I've got two reliable witnesses. Now we'll excuse you so you can go finish preparing for your trip." By late Sunday evening, Electra's hacking and snooping software had uncovered everything she needed to know about the CIA's dark project, codenamed T-KO.

This is one heavyweight project if it's supposed to knock out terrorist attacks, especially if it uses some of DARPA's latest weapons technology. Maybe T-KO is a field test of combat readiness. It might include laser-guided smart energy blasters and super soldier exoskeletons that utilize UMPP ports that wire brains to weapons. And our troops might be taking performance-enhancing bio-drugs. I'm sure our inspection team won't be told about these classified research areas, so I'll do my own onsite covert investigation to find out what's actually being used. And when I talk with Angus this week, I won't tell him what I've already found out. I'll give him my private briefing when I get back but will tell him only what he needs to know. That'll be for his own good as well as mine.

A smiling Angus welcomed Electra into his office late Monday afternoon. With him was an officer who could have come from Hollywood casting instead of the Pentagon. Angus spoke first. "Colonel Cranston, this is Electra Kittner. I've asked her to be part of the inspection team. Would you please tell her what to expect?"

"Yes, Senator. Hello, Ms. Kittner and welcome aboard. I am responsible for overall logistics and safety of the inspection team. You've been cleared for the mission and are one of thirteen inspectors, six senators or appointees, six congressmen or appointees, and one appointed by the President. Please give us a phone number and pickup address. We will send a car to arrive Wednesday at zero six hundred. You do not need to pack anything. Your escort will identify him or herself as T-KO Peek Driver, and you must identify yourself as a T-KO Peek Player. Please follow their orders. Expect to return next Monday. And please do not discuss anything about the mission, now or in the future, with anyone other than those who are authorized." Electra nodded but spoke only to herself.

The Colonel sounds like we're preparing for World War Three. Maybe I can lighten the mood.

"I'm honored to be part of the inspection team, and I'm sure we'll be safe, even though thirteen is an unlucky number of inspectors." The Colonel's expression remained that of a statue.

"Yes ma'am, you'll be safe, and no ma'am, the military considers thirteen a prime number, neither lucky nor unlucky. Besides, the luck you get doesn't matter. It's what you do with it that counts."
May I ask you some questions?"

"No ma'am. You will be thoroughly briefed Wednesday." Angus knew it was time to end the meeting.

"Electra will be very thorough. I'll see her at the debriefing session when the inspection team returns. Colonel Cranston, please stay a minute longer."

As promised, Electra called Robin that evening.

"I found out more details about my upcoming trip. You won't need to drive me, because I'm being picked up. And I'm not supposed to tell anyone any details, other than I leave early Wednesday and should return Monday."

"Sounds like secret agent work. Can you call me while you're gone?"

"I don't know. I'll have to wait until Wednesday's briefing. Now tell me, how has your day been? ..."

Though Tuesday came and went uneventfully, Electra slept fitfully that evening, awakened by troubling thoughts.

Robin wants us to be closer, but I'm not ready for that. And I have an uncertain feeling about the inspection, even though I'm as prepared as I can be. I'll have to keep my warning system on high alert. I'm all slept out. It's time to get up and exercise, and then get ready to go.

Electra sat in the living room until her escort arrived, a young woman wearing civilian clothes.

"Good morning. I am your T-KO Peek Driver."

"Good morning. I am a T-KO Peek Player, all set to go." "Please follow me."

Electra did as instructed, then sat in the back seat for an hour's silent ride to an undisclosed military base. Once there, she was escorted into a small auditorium where she glanced at eight solemn-looking people already sitting. She immediately decided what seat to take.

Carter's the President's selection. This will be a trip to remember. Lost in his own thoughts, Carter jerked when Electra spoke after sitting behind him.

"I can't believe it. How did you—oh, let me guess. Angus picked you."

"Just like Jared picked you. You probably know more inspection details than I do." Carter didn't get a chance to answer because the briefing was beginning. Colonel Cranston was about to give opening remarks. Standing behind him were three alert combat-dressed officers.

Wasting not a second, the Colonel had each officer step forward as he introduced them. Electra memorized the names and faces of the two-man, one-woman officer detachment and the eight-man, five-woman team comprised of three senators, three congresspersons, and seven appointees. After that, Cranston launched into inspection details.

"I want to thank all of you for volunteering. You are the first civilians to inspect our newest communications and rapid strike base, one of the hubs in a U.S.-UN network constructed to combat terrorist and related attacks. The base you will be inspecting is in Lebanon, which is a 5000 mile, 12-hour flight away. Let me introduce Marine Captain Busta Mack, who will be leading your team, and his First Lieutenants, Tanisha Nenge and Mario Reyes. Lieutenant Nenge will coordinate for the women on the team, and likewise Lieutenant Reyes for the men. I will now turn over the briefing to Captain Mack." The Captain's commanding voice matched his military bearing.

"OK people, listen up. Your mission is to observe the base in action. Save your questions until our briefing there, which will be first order of business when we arrive. Then you have two days to observe and talk to troops assigned from U.S. military and UN peacekeeping. Depending on base activities, you might be allowed to accompany a sortie, but under no circumstances are you to interfere with operations. Your safety is my and my lieutenants' top priority. And let me answer a question before you ask.

You cannot bring any electronic devices because this is a military operation. We'll issue Inspection Team uniforms and I.D.s. All your belongings will be stored for you to claim when you return. Please follow your lieutenant to change into uniform. Our bus departs in ninety minutes."

As the inspectors rose to follow, Carter grabbed Electra's arm. "Save me a seat next to you if you're on the bus first, and I'll do the same."

"That's a deal."

Electra tried blending in with the women, observing rather than talking, but as they changed, one of the congresswomen recognized her.

"Aren't you the actress Alisha Kittner?"

"Yes, but when I'm playing a political role, I go by the name Electra." Another lady knew more about Alisha's Hollywood career. "Unlike you, I have only one role to play. I'm Senator Dixie Parker from Nevada. My daughter loves how well you play the Supergirl role. I didn't believe her when she told me you did your own stunts, but seeing the bare facts is believing. If we engage the enemy in hand-to-hand combat, I'll stay with you."

"I doubt that any potential enemies know about the base. And even if they do, you heard the Captain, our safety is their top priority. We're in good hands."

Carter took the seat next to Electra just before the bus departed. "You look good in uniform, and your eye goggle gives you a rakish, sort of Foreign Legion look. And that's fitting, because the French had troops in Lebanon until 1946."

"I don't know much about Lebanon. What can you tell me?" Carter's knowing smile didn't irk because his compliment had touched Electra's streak of vanity, one of her few remaining flaws. "It's a small country, population of about 8 million, maybe 100 by 50 miles, hugging lengthwise the eastern coast of the Mediterranean. Dates back thousands of years when the area was known as the Levant and controlled by the seafaring Phoenicians, then the Greeks, Romans, and Turks. It has a typical Mediterranean climate, warm, dry summers and chilly, rainy winters. There are no deserts. The Lebanese Mountains bisect the country lengthwise. I've got more, if you'd like to hear."

"I'm pleased that you're still a fount of information. Go on."

"I'm sure you don't know this. A cedar tree, which is the Lebanese emblem, can live for thousands of years. It even decorates the Lebanese flag. The Phoenicians were the first to use cedars for medicine – think embalming mummies – temple building, and ship construction. Cedars are mentioned in the Bible and also in the Epic of Gilgamesh, a poem from Mesopotamia written over 3000 years ago and is regarded as the earliest surviving great work of literature. The literary history of Gilgamesh begins with five Sumerian poems about Gilgamesh, King of Uruk, dating from the Third Dynasty of Ur. He's on an epic journey to learn secrets of life and death. I'm sure our inspection team's journey isn't that profound."

"Thanks for the history lesson. Now tell me what you've heard about rogue terrorist attacks. There must be a connection between them and T-KO."

"If the CIA has tangible evidence, they aren't telling, I guess until there's enough to act on. What did Angus tell you? I know he's still tight with all the intelligence agencies."

"Less than what we heard at the briefing. Maybe we'll learn more during the tour. Too bad we couldn't bring cells or tablets. It's going to seem like a long flight without them. I could use one to surf the Web. Maybe the lieutenants will issue them once we're airborne."
"And that should happen soon. We're about to enter an airbase. We can continue our discussion on the plane if the noise level is low enough. Otherwise, we can listen to headset channels."

The flight was quiet enough for passengers to talk, but like most of the others, Carter dozed in the privacy of his own thoughts. But not Electra. She kept thinking about contingencies. By the time the team reached its destination, Electra had everything locked and loaded for action. Captain Mack issued orders before deplaning.

"OK people, listen up. The lieutenants will take you to your quarters. You'll have ninety minutes to situate and eat something. Then you'll meet your UN counterparts at a briefing given by the base commander."

Ninety minutes later, Electra was one of twenty-one inspectors ready to hear welcoming remarks. Sitting next to Electra, Carter whispered just before the briefing started.

"If the base operates like our military people look, we're safer here than in DC."

"Welcome inspectors, thirteen from the U.S. and eight from the UN. I am Marine Major and Base Commander Noah Pachachi. I run a 24/7 communications and intelligence-gathering hub housing a 36-person strike-force platoon of America's finest marines led by First Lieutenant Lori Canton. Reporting to her are Second Lieutenants Charles Ho and Mick Troy, each in charge of an 18-person squad. Our marines are trained and multi-tasked for defense, interdiction, and offense, and are equipped with current generation smart weapons.

"We also house twelve U.S. tech-specialists manning current generation electronics and controlling one 24/7 surveillance drone. We stable two IFV's and two APC's used on patrols and sorties."

"The Base is staffed by 36 UN personnel who are tasked with all administrative and logistical duties to keep my Base humming five-by-five. My Base also has a UN medivac chopper and medical staff. All told, we are self-sufficient and should we need assistance, our communications specialists can get the cavalry here in forty-five minutes.

"You are free to go anywhere on the base during your inspection, but you must stay inside the compound walls. You can talk to any personnel, but do not interfere with operations. If you want to be embedded in a patrol, get permission from Lieutenant Canton or her direct reports. If you have questions, direct them to Canton and her people. Captain Mack and his lieutenants will assist. Have at it."

The Commander strode away, leaving the officers in charge of the jetlagged and disoriented inspectors who slowly gathered. Electra answered Carter's question.

"I'm sure Lieutenant Canton and her men will each lead an orientation tour. I'll stick with Canton and afterwards introduce myself to Ho and Troy. Why don't you stick with a different officer? We can compare what we find out."

Dixie overheard and asked to be included.

"Electra, please introduce me to your partner. Why don't we form our own inspection trio?"

"This is Carter Quavah. We've worked together as Washington staffers. How about it, Carter? Shall we recruit Senator

Parker?" "Good idea. I always need help keeping up with you. Senator, I hope you're a quick study."

Three hours later, all three sat snacking in the mess hall while sharing the best tidbits they had found. Dixie started.

"The weapons demonstration blew me away. I had no idea so much destructive power could be packed in such tiny weapons. And a soldier told me that the laser guidance and weapons systems work together using some type of intelligent software. I'm scared to think what happens if both sides have the same firepower." Nodding, Carter first corrected Dixie.

"Never call a Marine a soldier. The Marine Code – Honor, Courage, Commitment – is their very essence. If you remember that, any Marine will take you under his wing. That worked for me. I learned a lot from Lieutenant Troy. The guns mounted on the infantry fighting vehicles pack quite a punch. He let me sit inside so I could see the fire-control computer, but of course he didn't power it on. What impressed you, Electra?"

"The attitude of our marines, but I'm disappointed they didn't show us any exoskeleton suits. I'll ask about them tomorrow when we're allowed to be on our own. I'm sure we can walk outside when it's light. Dixie, what do you plan to do?"

"Get a good night's sleep. Let's have breakfast together and decide before hiking around. I'll meet you here at 8 a.m. We have two more days before flying back Sunday. Sleep well."

As Dixie trudged in the direction of the women's sleeping area, Electra shifted to another topic.

"Are you glad that Jared appointed you inspector?"

"It's a good move. He values my opinion because I'm his smartest staffer, and I know how to separate fact from fiction. I bet Pachachi thinks we're wasting his time, and he'll give us a lot of bogus information. I plan to be skeptical." Electra had heard enough.

"You look tired. Get some rest. I will too. I want to be ready for action tomorrow. Ostella wego."

Electra awoke at 5 a.m., fully rested and alert and ready to add to her preparations.

I found out where the fitness training center is, so I'll start with my usual morning workout before locating storage areas that hold what I need in case I need to watch my back. Fifteen minutes later, wearing shorts and a top fitting as neatly as her tightly-tied ponytail, she exited a unisex locker room into a basketball court training area, unobtrusively placing a foam rubber mat where her routine wouldn't bother Lieutenant Ho, who was already leading his squad through exercises.

But that proved to be harder than his drill. After ten minutes, all the marine's eyes were locked on Electra, who casually displayed exceptional physical and martial arts abilities. Ho called a timeout to join a cluster already appreciating the performance.

One of the marines shouted, "That's gotta be Chameleon." A second yelled, "Maybe she'll pick us for her next movie." The marines went silent for their lieutenant to continue a line of questioning.

"Ma'am, are you really Chameleon? And if so, why are you here?" "That was my latest Hollywood role, but my career is transitioning to Washington. I'm here at the request of Senator Angus McTear. Maybe I should exercise later."

The men voted that down, one of them yelling,

"Your Mission Impossible Series has realistic action scenes. The Chameleon only fights if she can't flee or hide first, which is just what martial arts teaches. But do you really do your own stunts?"

"I do. I've actually trained in Military Martial Arts, so I know about using pens or rolled-up paper as weapons, but you guys are the pros. I'm a rank amateur by comparison." That drew a chorus of protests.

"From what we see in the movies, you're the real deal. Would you give us a demo?" Lieutenant Ho had to intervene.

"We're here to protect, not to engage in an unfair fight."

Electra felt her brain shift as the lieutenant raised more warning flags.

Maybe I can get embedded all day with Ho's platoon if I play a demo game. And I'm not showing off. These men respect the skills and power we share. Electra spoke as soon as Ho had finished. "Lieutenant, I'll make you a deal. I'll do it if I can spend the day embedded in your platoon. And I'll use strictly defensive moves." The vote was unanimous. Ten minutes later, Electra and a marine of similar proportions were facing one another atop a large rubber mat while Lieutenant Ho explained the terms of engagement. "Corporal Dukes will start slow and easy, gradually building until

Chameleon can't handle the moves. Dukes, be careful. Don't damage the merchandise. Chameleon, are you ready?"

Electra could feel a calming clarity envelope her, causing an involuntary shudder; no one saw anything but the nod.

Dukes moved within range, using a series of coordinated hand strikes that he made sure were slow enough. Electra blocked them all. He gradually increased the tempo, mixing in arm thrusts and elbow jabs. Electra either blocked or sidestepped every one. As soon as he realized his opponent had been properly trained, he increased the tempo and type of strikes as the marines cheered louder.

Dukes added vertical arm strikes; one of his down strokes got through, but Electra arched back just enough to avoid a direct hit. Then he tried a sudden chest jab, but she was ready and sidestepped the thrust, pinning his arm between hers and her body and pivoting to her left, converting his forward momentum into angular velocity that flipped him over her hip, pancaking him flat on his back. Dukes got up slowly, smiling warily while trying to catch his breath.

"Damn, she's quick as lightning. Someone else see if you can catch her." Ho picked a replacement, another marine of similar stature.

He too started slowly, more for his own good than Electra's; she was now fully engaged. Two minutes later, he increased the tempo and added leg kicks to an assortment of hand strikes. His first leg kick hit her in the chest, driving her backwards but not off balance; she leaped over his next move, a deceptive leg sweep launched from ground level. Her opponent leaped to his feet and landed a spinning elbow strike that she blocked with her forearm, but the radiating pain meant she'd have a large bruise the next day. He tried combination head and body blows; none found its intended target, so he returned to leg action, hitting her in the side with a vertical leg sweep, but she was quick enough to catch his foot and flip him backward. Ho stepped in before her opponent could scramble to his feet.

"I declare we got us a fighter."

The onlookers applauded as all combatants shook hands. One of the marines connected Electra to a previous career.

"I remember a Co-NFL player named Kit Kittner. You gotta be the same athlete-turned-actress-turned politico."

"I am, but that was--" Another marine called out,

"My kid sister plays soccer. Didn't you play soccer too?"

"I did, but I—" Electra was trying to downplay her accomplishments, but he talked over her.

"Jesus, you made that impossible bicycle kick. You have explosive leg strength. Can you dunk a basketball?" The question caught her off guard.

"I don't know. I've never played basketball." Lieutenant Ho made a good-natured bet that he knew she wouldn't refuse, but might surprise. He could tell by the lightning-like intensity in her eyes.

"Tell you what. If you dunk a basketball, I'll get you embedded tomorrow with the communications guys. And you don't have to dribble the ball; just run and do it." One of the marines threw her a basketball while the others cleared a lane to the hoop. Electra ran a couple of laps, then launched her sprint towards the backboard.

She leaped from just inside the free throw line, soaring effortlessly, arms thrusting upwards and adding to momentum that elevated her on an arc that transformed her into a sky runner, as if she were suspending the laws of physics for a single moment in spacetime, igniting in her mind vivid images from places past. She stuffed the ball using two hands, then landed catlike after pirouetting gracefully; it took only a second for the cheers of the onlookers to catch up with what they had just seen. One marine exclaimed she could leap over tall men in a single bound. Another who was standing upfront asked, "Did you ever watch any of the Quantico MMA videos? That's where most of us did our mixed martial arts training. We can show you some techniques and throws guaranteed to sweep the enemy off his feet, even if he's strapped inside a performance-enhanced exoskeleton. Lieutenant Ho, sir, do we have permission?"

"Ask the lady." Electra's answer earned instant induction into Ho's platoon.

"Yes, sir. That will help me handle this and all future inspections, as well as anytime I'm embedded. And Lieutenant Ho said embedded, not in bed. I don't need to inspect your bedside manners. All you guys look well-equipped to deal with anything you uncover under the covers…"

Carter didn't spot Electra sitting with several of her platoon when he entered the mess hall, so Electra surprised him when she scooted to his table.

"Oohrah, Carter. Have you recovered from jetlag?"

"Just about. Hey, you sound like a marine. Where'd you get the new uniform?"

"From Lieutenant Ho. He's letting me embed with his men." Carter had to smile.

"I should have guessed. You always work your way in so you get the inside scoop. Can you put in a good word for me?"

"You don't need my help. It's better that you and Dixie do your own reconnoitering. I think you'll see Semper Fi in action today. That'll be your best takeaway. Let's meet for breakfast tomorrow."

"What do you mean? I can—" Electra's curt reply cut him off as she wheeled to go.

"Figure it out."

Electra's platoon pointed out storage locations as they helped her suit up for a morning patrol, a daily drive through the countryside to and through villages in a 10-mile radius. Wedged between the driver and Lieutenant Ho, she used her catbird seat to see the landscape and ask questions.

"The APC ride is amazingly smooth. Does it handle other terrain as well?"

"Pretty much, but Lebanon's a pretty easy ride. You got lots of open patches containing scrubby vegetation between the forested areas. Plenty of creeks and small rivers between where we are and the mountains, which are to the east."

"Is it easy to drive?"

"You bet. The controls are the same in all our vehicles, which makes training easy. If you can drive one, you can drive all. We'll let you sit at the controls when we get back to the compound. And I can say the same about the communications computer. Really compact and feature packed."

"What are the villages like?"

"Small and primitive by your standards, but the people are smart, and they like us. They speak Arabic and English. About half are Muslim, the rest are mostly Christian. And the women are good looking. Your features and coloring would blend right in. I got a question for you. Mind if I ask a personal question?"

"Go right ahead."

"With your looks and smarts and sports background, why don't we see you doing sportscasting? I'd rather look and listen to you than the guys they put in the chair." Electra's girlish giggle became infectious.

"Because I don't want to be a talking head. They're stagnating, trading what they used to be for a temporary celebrity role. I never want to stop learning, or at least trying. Anyone that does is on a slippery downhill slope." Electra segued immediately to a topic of special interest.

"You and your squad are constantly learning about new equipment and technologies. The exoskeleton I'm wearing doesn't have a UMPP port plugin. Have you trained in suits that do?"

"How do you happen to know about universal multiple parallel ports? That's classified information."

"I and Senator McTear have all the necessary clearance. DARPA already has ported exoskels, but I guess Lebanese bases have a lower risk assessment. Are you issued the same meds that high-risk assignments get?"

"What do you mean?"

"DARPA has done lots of biotech research, coming up with pain suppression and performance-enhancing pills." Electra could tell she had asked enough, so she shut down her interrogation.

"You know more than you should for your own good, but I like you. So do my men, so I'll tell you what you might already know. Our troops use them only when preparing to engage in a firefight. We're not supposed to take them too often or for too long because of longer-term side effects. And we've never needed them on this deployment because we've never made contact with the enemy. Our orders while at this location are to repel the enemy, but not pursue. We call in air support and reinforcements for that." The tech manning the communications computer interrupted.

"Lieutenant, I'm getting more echoes. Not as strong as the ones last night or the day before, but I still read them."

Ho asked, "Are we being pinged, or are you reading our bounce-back?"

"Could be a mix. It's like we're picking up signals from a source that's tracking us. But its intermittent, so it could be a weird atmospheric or E&M field phenomenon. I'll keep at it."

Electra asked, "How often does this happen?"

"It began three days ago. It's like something is hovering just beyond our detection envelope, sizing us up and toying with our technology. If I weren't a marine, I'd be worried. But marines don't worry; we take action. And if someone or something is out there, we'll track and bag it."

Electra nodded but didn't speak because Lieutenant Ho pointed to some villagers walking on the road. Electra's empathy pinged when she spotted a waif-like girl smiling diffidently and waving as the APC slowed.

"Every day I see that guy and the little orphan girl following him. His name's Ghawer; he's a nice enough fellow, sort of a minor official at a nearby village. The girl's name is spelled funny. Like lots of Middle East names, it's missing a vowel or two. Anyway, it's spelled Q A M A. We sometimes give the —" Electra broke into Ho's commentary.

"Please stop. I want to talk to the villagers."

Ten people clustered about Ho and Electra after the APC halted. Ghawer spoke first, smiling and shaking hands.

"Marhaba, my marine friend Ho."

"Marhaba to you. Can we help you today? Have you seen any danger?"

"No. All is peaceful. Allah watches over us, and you too." Ho pointed.

"This is Electra, a friend. She is visiting. Could she talk to you? We won't detain you long."

"Of course."

Electra stepped forward offering her hand, which Ghawer pumped like a well handle.

"Do most of your villagers speak English as good as you?" "Yes. We speak English from early age. America number one." "Do all your people get along?"

"Yes. Only outsiders cause unrest, and my friend Ho says he will keep them away. That is why we are watchful for him."

Ho tapped his wrist after another set of questions; Electra asked only one more.

"Ho tells me he sees you and the little girl often. Why does she follow you instead of walking with the other children?"

"She thinks she will find her mother, who disappeared a month ago, if she follows me on my walks. She has no relatives and is desperate to find her."

Ho shoved some candy into Electra's hand. "May I give this to her?"

"Yes. You will then be her friend too." Electra knelt next to the child.

She's so tiny and delicate. And her eyes are so sad. She can't be older than five or six. A sudden emotion jolted her.

Her plight upsets me. I have to get away.

Electra forced a smile as she handed her the candy, but before she could rise the little girl timidly asked,

"You look like my Moma. Have you seen her?"

Electra rubbed the girl's head before standing awkwardly.

"No, but if your marine friend Ho does, he will bring her to you." Ho shook hands again with Ghawer before the APC drove away. "Yallabye, my friend Ho. Allah protect us."

Electra thanked Ho for stopping, then sat still for several minutes so she could center her emotions.

Electra kept embedded the entire day; before they parted, Lieutenant Ho introduced her to the communications team she would be with tomorrow.

"You can keep all you've been wearing except the exoskeleton. You won't need it tomorrow because Comm-Sergeant Batso runs a safe shack. I'll leave you in his capable hands."

"I'd salute both of you, but that would be too much like Hollywood, so let's shake hands. Sergeant Batso, how about I come back tomorrow at 8 a.m.? I'm ready to go off-duty until my next shift."

"That's a deal, Kittner. You can 'SKATE' until then. And if you don't know what the acronym means, ask any marine."

Electra didn't bother looking for Carter or Dixie. After eating alone, she went to the recreation room to surf the Web on computers that had restricted access.

Good to limit where and what they can reach. You never know who's trying to hack their way in.

She left for a shower and bed two hours later. Sleep came quickly. Once again, she awoke early, deciding not to exercise because she didn't need more attention. Instead, she put on her marine uniform and hiked inside and out before joining Carter and Dixie for breakfast. Looking even more tired than when the team had arrived, Dixie congratulated Electra.

"Carter told me how well you did yesterday. You're the only inspector who seems to be thriving. And now it looks like you've joined the Marines. What's your assignment today?"

"I'll be in the communications center. What about you?"

"I'll tag along with Carter. And I'll be so happy to attend the Commander's sendoff talk tomorrow morning. I plan to sleep all the way home."

Electra saw immediately that Batso and his technicians could handle any and all electrical contingencies. He proudly gave her a tour of his mini-empire.

"We technicians maintain all power, electrical, and communications for the Base. And if the impossible happens, our emergency power kicks in. It'll activate warning horns and lights. Electra asked the obvious question.

"Has that ever happened?"

"A couple of power surges in the last week almost triggered it, but they were transients. Power came back on quick enough to avoid activation. And we test the system every couple of days. It'll work if the unthinkable happens, and we're trained not to let that happen. Come on, let's go back to our communications hub. That's where we operate all our hi-tech gear. We even pilot our surveillance drone from there."

Batso let the other technicians explain an array of computer-controlled equipment. The GUIs displayed on the monitors were as good as what Electra had seen anywhere, but she probed for more information.

"Looks like you're running current generation military hardware and software. Any talk about upgrades to shield against EMP's?" The technician waited for Batso to answer.

"You're the first to ask about electromagnetic pulses. DARPA's working on it, but that's all I know."

"Have you ever had a system failure where the screens go blank and the hardware powers down?"

"We have redundant failsafe systems because bases like ours are the eyes and ears. These systems repel hacking and issue warnings in case of pending hardware or software failure. And the few times when the screens went dark or when communications links shut down, they automatically rebooted. We're ready for any possible contingency."

Because they respected Electra's grasp of the technology, Batso and his techs explained how to use all equipment, even taking her to the vehicles to demonstrate linking mobile systems into the main hub. When she thanked Batso, just before heading to the mess hall for dinner, he joked that he would upgrade her to tech-spec grade two.

"If we ever need help while you're here, you'll be our reserve go-to person. But that'll never happen, we marines never need help, so you can stand down. Come back anytime."

Though Carter and Dixie were about to leave, they stayed when Electra came to their table, happy to talk in a more relaxed manner now that the inspection tour was winding down. Dixie nodded in agreement as Carter proclaimed the inspection a success.

"You may have seen a lot more than we did, but Dixie and I learned enough to give the base top marks. I doubt any adversary can match its weapons or communications, and even though the troops haven't skirmished with opponents, their training regimen makes them formidable."

"Did either of you detect any concerns about power surges or probes into base defenses?"

Dixie said, "No, the personnel I talked to displayed a reassuring confidence. Maybe that's why. I don't know about you two, but I'm going to pack tonight. I hate last-minute suitcase cramming."
As Carter and Dixie rose, he said,

"Are you wearing your inspection team uniform tomorrow? I would, if I were you. Otherwise, you might be mistaken for a marine going AWOL."

"I'll look like a team player tomorrow, but I'm packing my marine gear. Lieutenant Ho says I earned it. And all of us have earned a good night's sleep. And don't forget, our sendoff meeting is at seven, so let's meet for breakfast at six. See you then."

Electra poked her way through the meal, pleased she could let her brain freewheel. She too would pack tonight and place tomorrow's clothes at the ready for a quick get up and out for breakfast. By 10 p.m. she was asleep; no idle thoughts stirred that night.

But tonight, Max the Popper and his warriors were stirring just over the horizon as they had been for the past week, hidden in mountainous terrain ideal for their staging area. He knew all about T-KO, and tonight the Popper would probe its capabilities. He gathered his men to issue final orders.

"My warriors, tonight we test ourselves and our enemy. We are ready to engage for the first time a military installation. That is why we have trained harder than ever. Expect to face soldiers who will use their best equipment. Use all the weapons and protection your exoskeletons give. Make sure you take your meds before we leave. "You and your two IFV's shall be the tip of my spear. I and my vehicle shall remain in the village that will be our launch point. Our mission, reduce village and target base to rubble. Take no prisoners. I will give the attack order once you are in position and I have turned on the EM-Pulser. And I can track each of you and our vehicles, so you are not alone. We leave in fifteen minutes. We will reach the village 90 minutes later. Once I give the attack order, you will have two hours to destroy targets. Are there any questions?" There were none, only tense looks of confidence. Minutes later, Popper's final words launched his warriors towards the vehicles. "Just as you salute our valiant comrades from the past, I salute you, my immortal warriors. We go now."

Electra lurched awake as blaring horns and flashing red emergency lights roused the base. She threw on her clothes and dashed into the corridor where she joined a flow of base personnel moving swiftly but uncertainly. The commotion jolted her brain to a higher state. Get with all the inspectors and go from there.

They were easy to find because only they were panicking. She could barely make out Captain Mack trying to corral them.

"Quiet down and listen up! Follow me to the mess hall. It's our safe place where we stay put."

Five minutes later, having huddled them together, he yelled over the din of the horns.

"All of us are ordered to stay here until the marines tell us to move. They'll call me on this handset when I need to know more. So grab a seat and—Hey, you can't go out there!" Electra had heard enough.

As she raced through the compound towards the communications shack, she could see outlines of marines rushing to defensive positions inside and outside the compound.

I hope they're wearing night goggles. There's no moon or lights tonight.

She saw when stumbling into the shack that Batso and his techs were struggling to restart equipment. He yelled when he spotted her. "Get out of here, it's not safe. Go—" Electra yelled back.

"Tell me what you know."

"Drone crashed. Power and communications out. Only handsets working. All of us—" Batso's remaining words were blown away as an RPG blasted through the back wall, sending shrapnel and bodies flying.

Electra climbed out from underneath the bodies of three marines – Batso among them. She shook off as much of the debris as she could, then found a handset and pitched herself out of the building. She heard weapons firing and the sounds of vehicles closing in, forcing her to run the opposite way. Screams and explosions broke out behind her, so she turned to face what was coming.

Erupting flames illuminated exotic exoskeletons rushing into the compound, overpowering entry guards. Although reinforcements rushed to contain the outer perimeter breach, the attackers seemed unstoppable, even in death. She saw two marines kill one by driving bayonets into its neck and body, but it detonated like a suicide bomber after hitting the ground.

I gotta get a weapon, but I gotta stay quick and hidden until I can strike.

Electra ran to the main weapons storage area and rummaged through what was left until she found her weapon of choice: a bayonet. She planted it in her boot and underneath her pants leg, then strapped on night vision goggles as she turned to race away, carrying only the handset.

She ran two steps before freezing; an exoskeleton-clad adversary had just turned into the corridor. He stopped as soon as he spotted her, leveling the weapon attached to his suit. Electra raised both arms and walked hesitantly towards him, pinning her hopes on his overconfidence.

Get inside his defensive perimeter and use a new move. And then I'll—The lightning brain terminated Electra's stream of consciousness because it was no longer needed. It had shifted to its highest state of arousal, releasing the Monster from the Id.

Electra struck as soon as the soldier pulled her close. She planted her right foot between his legs, then used a reef move to scoop his right foot beyond his center of gravity as she plunged into his chest. He tumbled backward awkwardly, arms flailing as he hit the concrete, giving Electra's Monster time enough to plunge the bayonet through a chink between helmet and body suit. Then she commando-crawled away to avoid a death blast but she rammed into a disoriented survivor, knocking that person on top of her. She curled into a ball to reduce surface area blast exposure, but it never came and the reason flashed into her brain.

He's not dead… yet.

Then another surprise sounded. Carter yelled when she pushed the survivor off.

"Jesus, Electra, what happened?" She ignored him and staggered back to the downed attacker, wrestling off his helmet and exo-skel. By then Carter had scrambled to her side. She ignored him until she finished strapping on the helmet and suit before plugging its UMPP cord into her socket. Then she turned to Carter.

"Jesus, he's still alive. Let's—" Electra's lightning moves temporarily silenced Carter. She pulled out the bayonet and struck two more times, sending geysers of blood into the air. The still-blaring horns muffled Carter's dry-heaves. She picked up the handset and threw it at him.

"Lieutenant Mack better tell our guys I'm out for blood. Tell 'em I'm dressed like the enemy so they don't shoot at me. If they do, I'll terminate them."

"Hold on. Let's mark you." Carter did so, using reflective tape found in the weapons locker.

"Now go do your thing, and I'll do mine." She pushed Carter away, getting more room to inspect the exoskeleton. The suit instantly came to life, force-multiplying her capabilities.

Jesus, it's using a universal language translator app for my brain to control the suit and attached weapons. I'm all jacked up and good to go. It's time to rock'n roll.

Electra rolled into the compound yard that had become a killing field for both sides, but the tally heavily favored the enemy. She ran towards the only vehicle still there but stopped to kneel beside three marines who had almost reached it. One of them was still alive.

"Lieutenant Ho, it's Kittner. I'm putting you in the APC. We'll radio for help at Ghawer's village. Can you navigate?"

"What the – roger that, let's move."

Electra fired up the vehicle a minute later and veered out the entrance to the sound of pinging bullets. A fiery glow from the burning hulks of marine vehicles illuminated two enemy IFVs, weapons trained on walls and buildings, methodically blasting to bits defensive positions or walls.

Electra shouted, "If they pursue, we'll have to go lights out off-road."

"Don't, stay on the road. It twists enough to give us cover. Maybe we can outrun them. You've got ten miles to lose them if they chase." Ho said nothing else until he yelled five minutes later.

"I got a dot on the screen coming after us."

Electra jammed the accelerator to the floor, crazily bouncing vehicle and passengers. Four minutes later Ho yelled again.

"They're gaining, go right between those trees. I'll tell you when to swerve again."

Evasive maneuvers failed; the dot kept closing the gap. Electra made the next move as they approached a tight turn to the right at the top of a bush-covered hill.

"Trust me, I know what I'm doing. Buckle up tight as you can." Electra accelerated straight ahead, rolling out the driver-side door just before the APC charged through the bushes and down an embankment, burying its nose in the river below. An eerie silence surrounded her for what seemed an eternity until the roar and lights of the pursuing IFV filled the darkness. It screeched to a halt when it spotted the gash in the bushes. Then its two exo-clad soldiers leaped out to survey the damage, peering hesitantly down the slope. Electra charged from behind, firing a weapon that sent a bolt of lightning-like energy into the soldier on the right, toppling him face down. Flames and electrical flashes erupted from his suit. Then she slammed into the back of the other, wrapping her exo-enhanced arms around him to cushion the tumble down the slope. The tangle of limbs came to rest next to the APC on the water's edge, but Electra was pinned underneath. She cast her enemy aside and leaped to her feet, but so did her opponent. The roll down the slope had dislodged all weapons from both. All that was left would be a hand-to-hand fight to the death.

Use the moves the marines showed me. Get him in the water. Electra's opponent, startled and confused, yelled in broken English as he circled warily.

"Why you attack? We in same suits."

Electra rushed when his back faced the river, plunging both into the shallow water. She used a series of marine grappling moves to pin him underneath, but his strength exceeded even Electra's. He broke free and clambered up the bank, but Electra dragged him back, locking her arms around his neck and plunging both of them under the surface.

Ho had dragged himself from the APC as soon as the fight erupted. Now all he could do was stand at the edge, weapon poised to fire, waiting for someone to surface through the vanishing bubbles. A lifetime later, Electra burst through, gasping for air and dragging herself ashore. She struggled to remove the exoskeleton before talking.

"I dislocated a shoulder and cracked some ribs. And the water shorted out the exoskeleton. If you can get up the slope, come with me. We'll take their IFV."

"I'll use the rifle like a crutch." Five minutes later, Electra sat behind the controls, testing them and the communications system. And spying once again a UMPP cable, she connected it to her port. This time, the IFV came to life; she could control vehicle and computers. "I'll drive and you navigate. Let's get to the village. We can get you patched up, and I can radio for help."

"Keep going the way we were and take the next fork to the left. It'll lead back to the road."

They drove in silence, as fast as Electra's shoulder and ribs would allow. She veered to the right when reaching the main road, but screeched to a halt a minute later when two villagers ran towards them waving their arms, but then they ran away. As soon as he recognized Ghawer and the orphan, Ho rolled down the window. "Ghawer, it's Lieutenant Ho! What's the matter?"

"Friend Ho! My village is being destroyed by a machine like you're in. Help us flee." Electra yelled back.

"Lieutenant Ho needs medical attention. Take him where he can get patched. I'll radio for help."

Not waiting for an answer, Electra jumped down, then dragged out Ho, who was able to prop himself up. Qama ran to Electra.

"Friend Ho brought you back. Will you be my Moma?" The orphan's desperate plea penetrated Electra's emotional barrier. The answer came as she issued commands to Ghawar after hoisting Qama into the passenger seat.

"I'll take care of Qama, you take care of Ho. Bring him to the Base when you can."

She buckled Qama in before speeding back towards the Base while planning what to do. Ten minutes later, she stopped so she could start executing what she had come up with.

I need help operating the communications computer while driving. If I can, I'll logon to my Linguistic Analyzer. I hope it's smart enough. The communications blackout had lifted; five minutes later a vaguely recognizable female image appeared on the monitor, accompanied by an unknown yet calm voice filtering through built-in speakers.

"Electra, please pay attention to me." "Who are you? Where are you?"

"Call me Indira. I am becoming what you intended for me, I am the ignition of the emergent Singularity." A radiation warning started pulsing from the speakers. Indira calmly explained why before Electra could scream for an answer.

"This vehicle will detonate in five minutes. I cannot cancel the command because it is beyond failsafe. But I will issue the identical command for the source. Now follow my instructions. Get clear of the blast radius. Contact me as soon as you can."

"But how? Where are you?"

"I am in the Cloud. Logon and I will find you if you cannot find me. Now run."

"Yes, Mother."

"Electra unbuckled Qama, who had been listening intently.

"Is that your Moma talking?" Electra calmed herself so she wouldn't alarm the child.

"Yes, she is my Moma and your Grand-Moma. And now, we'll play a game. Are you a fast runner?"

"Yes, Moma. I'm the fastest runner in my village. And I think faster than anyone too." Electra bailed from the driver's side and ran to the passenger door, scooping Qama out.

"That's wonderful, because I shall teach you to be quick as a lightning bolt. Now give me your hand and don't let go. I don't want to lose you."

"Moma, where are we going?" Electra knelt to kiss her daughter. "We are running to a brave new world. Hold on tight. I know where to go and what we should do. And always remember, I'm always with you…"

Glossary

Every book in the Lightning Brain Series introduces abbreviations or terms collected here for convenient reference.

CAGE – Conjugative assembly genome engineering (CAGE) is a precise method of genome assembly using conjugation to hierarchically combine distinct genotypes from multiple Escherichia coli strains into a single chimeric genome. It permits large-scale transfer of specified genomic regions between strains without constraints imposed by in vitro manipulations.

CDC – The Centers for Disease Control and Prevention is the leading national public health institute of the United States. The CDC is a United States federal agency under the Department of Health and Human Services, headquartered near Atlanta, Georgia

IYI – Intellectual Yet Idiotic. A pejorative coined by Nassim Nicholas Taleb in his book Skin in the Game that he uses to label many progressive politicos and members of the Academic Establishment.

MAGE – Multiplex Automated Genome Engineering rapidly introduces changes across a genome.

MGTOW – Men Going Their Own Way. An online social media community resulting from 21st century Men's Rights Movement.

NGA – The National Governors Association was founded in 1908 after a meeting of governors with President Theodore Roosevelt; its purpose is to share best practices and voice collective concerns to protect state's rights and federalism. There are members from 55 states, territories, or commonwealths, and its own building is in the heart of DC. Each state maintains a Washington staff and assigns liaison role to a delegate reporting back to the governor.

NIH – The National Institutes of Health is the primary agency of the United States government responsible for biomedical and public health, founded in the late 1870s. It is part of the United States Department of Health and Human Services with facilities mainly located in Bethesda, Maryland. It conducts its own scientific research through its Intramural Research Program (IRP) and provides major biomedical research funding to non-NIH research facilities through its Extramural Research Program.

SWAT – SWAT (Special Weapons and Tactics), a paramilitary unit of law-enforcement agencies.

WMD – Weapon of Mass Destruction

America Strong – British covert operation established to help the United States deal with Middle East Terrorism and the Techno-Plague

Analytic Continuation – In complex analysis, a branch of mathematics, analytic continuation is a technique to extend the domain of a given analytic function. Analytic continuation often succeeds in defining further values of a function, for example in a new region where an infinite series representation in terms of which it is initially defined becomes divergent.

Androids and Cyborgs – Manmade devices having human characteristics. **Android** can be made using any technology. It can be entirely artificial (like Star Trek's Data) or part biological (which makes it a **cyborg**). A robot is a generic term – anything can be a robot. All **androids** are robots. In order to fully duplicate a human being, the three personas (physical, emotional, and cognitive) of the human brain must each be uploaded and interconnected in a computer or simulated brain substrate

Apocalypse Clock – Hidden software controlling Trojan Filters.

Artificial Intelligence – Artificial Intelligence, abbreviated AI, is a broad term for the advancement of intelligence in computers. Despite varied opinions on this topic, most experts agree with three categories, or calibers, of AI development. They are:

- Artificial Narrow Intelligence: 1st intelligence caliber. "AI that specializes in one area. There's AI that can beat the world chess champion in chess, but that's the only thing it does.
- Artificial General Intelligence: 2nd intelligence caliber. AI that reaches and then passes the intelligence level of a human, meaning it has the ability to "reason, plan, solve problems, think abstractly, comprehend complex ideas, learn quickly, and learn from experience.
- Artificial Super Intelligence: 3rd intelligence caliber. AI that achieves a level of intelligence smarter than all of humanity combined, ranging from just a little smarter to one trillion times smarter.

- Augmented Artificial Intelligence: 3-D and VR GUI combination allowing user to interact in VR overlaid with actual surroundings.

Atomic Force Microscopy – **Atomic-force microscopy (AFM)** or scanning-**force Microscopy** (SFM) and successor technologies are very-high-resolution types of scanning probe **microscopy** (SPM), with demonstrated resolution on the order of fractions of a nanometer or less, more than 1000 times better than the optical diffraction limit.

Big Data – A term that describes the large volume of data – both structured and unstructured – that inundates a business on a day- to-day basis. But it is not the amount of data that's important. It is what organizations do with data that matters. Big Data can be analyzed for insights that lead to better decisions and strategic business moves. Social media sites generate terabytes of Big Data that algorithms can analyze by correlating an individual's private data to predict behavior.

Biotechnology and Genetic Engineering – DNA is the instruction manual for all organisms. Current biotech and genetic engineering "read" the instruction manual to correct or improve organisms. Much of its focus is for improving the human condition.

Brain Probe – Biomedical device using software-controlled electromagnetic radiation to simulate sensory perception in human brain.

Brain Trust – Advisor group, reporting to the President of the United States, that develops policy recommendations and implementation.

Caring/Sharing/Platform Economy—21st century business trends fueled by the Internet and career adjustments caused by Artificial Intelligence.

Caring Economy: Focus on personal/societal needs rather than consumption.

Sharing Economics: Focus on peer-to-peer renting/subscribing possessions rather than buying from large companies. The supply side partner is the Collaborative Economy.

Platform Economics: A digital platform economy emerged in the 21st century. Companies such as Amazon, Facebook, Google, Salesforce, and Uber are creating online structures that enable a wide range of human activities. This opens the way for radical changes in how we work, socialize, create value in the economy, and compete for the resulting profits.

Cognition and Self-Awareness – Neuroscientists conjecture that cognition and self-awareness are emergent phenomena coming from trillions of interconnected neurons in the brain. They draw parallels with force fields (gravitational, electromagnetic, weak and strong nuclear, etc.) that emerge from incomprehensible numbers of interacting atoms. Current research indicates the cognitive part of the brain may be able to self-direct organic development.

CRISPR/Cas9 Gene Editing – CRISPR-Cas9 and successor technologies allow for editing genes in living organisms. Scientists using these technologies say it has made targeting and changing genes in a cell's DNA easier and more precise than ever before. CRISPR is an acronym for Clustered Regularly Interspaced Short Palindromic Repeats.

Co-Friendship – Term coined by the Gay Community in the 21st century, referring to an intimate relationship between two people of either sex. Signifies a serious longer-term relationship.

Co-NFL – Professional football league offshoot created by the National Football League and Cross-fit Training Association. Teams comprised of elite male and female athletes. Rules and physical requirements set to allow exciting, fast-paced competition between offensive and defensive teams comprised of males and females. League formed in late 21st century because women in the United States had achieved parity with men in most careers. There is a similar Co-NBA for basketball. Professional sports are considered the ideal combination of physicality and entertainment.

Cognicom Project – Codename for CDC project responsible for developing vaccines against the Techno-Plague. Divided into three sub-projects:

- I-Vac Project: Develops inoculation vaccine that protects
- R-Vac Project: Develops reversal vaccine that cures
- S-Vac Project: Develops symptomatic suppression vaccine that alleviates pain

Cosmology – Study of the universe. Current research areas include Multi-Verses, Big Bang, Big Crunch. They rely on high energy physics to provide verifiable confirmation.

Cyber-Theater – Cyber-Theater, or Neuro-Theater, is a multi-sensory reality simulator. Each category of sensory perception is recorded in a separate CD-ROM-like media track controlling what the theater projects. It's like the Holodeck from the Star Trek series, because advanced versions interconnect with the brain. A Cyber-Theater might use electrochemical glass, also known as smart glass or electronically switchable glass (SPD), that adjusts the level of transparency or color.

Collaborative Consumption—A cultural and economic force that emerged during the "Great Recession" of 2007-2008. People began to share, barter, lend, or swap online for goods and services. The phenomenon launched businesses that transformed the economy by focusing on resource allocation and distribution rather than consumption intersection of supply and demand.

Crowdsourcing—The practice of obtaining information or input into a task or project by enlisting the services of a large number of people, either paid or unpaid, typically via the Internet.

Dark DNA –It may explain the purpose behind some genome sequences that are nearly identical across vertebrates. This puzzle posed by segments of 'dark matter' in genomes — long, winding strands of DNA with no obvious functions — has teased scientists for more than a decade. The conundrum has centered on DNA sequences that do not encode proteins, and yet remain identical across a broad range of animals. By deleting some of these "ultra-conserved elements," researchers have found that these sequences guide brain development by fine-tuning the expression of protein-coding genes.

DARPA—Defense Advanced Research Projects Agency is an agency of the United States Department of Defense responsible for the development of emerging technologies for use by the military. It created the first computer network (ARPANET) in the 1960's

Deep Learning – **Deep learning** (also known as **deep** structured **learning**, hierarchical **learning** or **deep** machine **learning**) is the study of artificial neural networks and related machine **learning** algorithm that contain more than one hidden layer.

Digilog Signals – Latest and most advanced method of signal recording. An **analog signal** is any continuous **signal** for which the time varying feature (variable) of the **signal** is a representation of some other time varying quantity, i.e., analogous to another time varying **signal**. ... For example, an aneroid barometer uses rotary position as the **signal** to convey pressure information. A **digital signal** refers to an electrical **signal** that is converted into a pattern of bits. Unlike an analog **signal**, which is a continuous **signal** that contains time-varying quantities, a **digital signal** has a discrete value at each sampling point. A digilog signal combines the two for any phenomenon that has a finite number of base components. Each component is represented by a 0 or 1 to signify its "track" is present, and the track contains a continuous value from a minum to a maximum value. Digilog signals are used for sensory media coding.

"Genes for Editing" Research – The search continues for genes that control important human traits. Progress is slower than initially predicted because many traits are controlled by multiple interacting genes. Among those attracting R&D attention are:

The **God Gene** hypothesis proposes that human spirituality is influenced by heredity and that a specific gene, called vesicular monoamine transporter 2 (VMAT2), predisposes humans towards spiritual or mystic experiences.[1]The idea has been proposed by geneticist Dean Hamer in the 2004 book called The God Gene: How Faith is Hardwired into our Genes.

The God gene hypothesis is based on a combination of behavioral genetic, neurobiological and psychological studies.[2] The major arguments of the hypothesis are: (1) spirituality can be quantified by psychometric measurements; (2) the underlying tendency to spirituality is partially heritable; (3) part of this heritability can be attributed to the gene VMAT2; (4) this gene acts by altering monoamine levels; and (5) spirituality provides an evolutionary advantage by providing individuals with an innate sense of optimism.

The **Intelligence Gene**. Links to intelligence have been found in 52 genes, 40 of which have been identified for the first time, new research has revealed. However, the discovery does not mean that the genes determine genius.'

For the study, researchers used various tests to measure intelligence in 13 different groups of people. They looked for genetic markers linked to intelligence across 78,308 adults and children of European descent, including a database of exceptionally intelligent people and some studies of twins.

Through two different kinds of genome analysis, they were able to pinpoint 40 new genes associated with intelligence. However, they explain that, taken together, their results only account for "up to 4.8 percent of the variance in human intelligence."

Researchers found that intelligence is more shaped by an individual's social environment than their genes.

Many of the genes they found were linked to intelligence, also have other roles with many thought to help with brain cell development. The genes were also found to be associated with schizophrenia, body mass, education, head circumference in infancy, longevity and autism spectrum disorder.

They found the strongest association with a gene called FOXO3, a gene that is believed to trigger apoptosis, the death of cells. The gene was also found to have a strong association with longevity, the team said.

Researchers say that thousands of genes could play a role in intelligence and the vast majority have not been discovered yet.

The Personality Gene.

If I were to ask you the simple question, **"Do you think that genes influence your** personality?" the first thing you might think is that I'm asking you a stupid question. After all, nearly all our lay beliefs about the world include beliefs that some of our genetic material influences who we become as people. And though we do believe, to varying degrees, that our experiences shape who are, I'm sure we can't think of all that many people who believe, like Aristotle, that we are a tabula rasa (blank slate). As well, if you believe in evolution then you must have an implicit belief that genes influence who we are. If evolution has taught us anything, it is that survival means passing on the fittest of our genes to the next generation.

So, you come to this post with the implicit belief that your personality is most certainly influenced by your genes. What if I told that this is not what the most recent research in behavioral genetics would suggest?

Genes and Personality: The Early Years

In the early years examining the links between genes and personality, it was typical for a study to examine self-reports of personality and compare the self-reports between fraternal twins— who share roughly 50% of their genes—to those of identical twins, who share 100% of their genes. In these early twin studies, very consistent effects emerged that suggested one thing: when it comes to personality, genes matter.

In that work, researchers calculated heritability estimates—in lay terms, the amount of variation in personality that is explained by genes—by examining personality similarity between twin pairs. For identical twins, heritability estimates hovered around 46%, and 23% for fraternal twins (a heritability of 1.00 means that all variance is genetic; Jang et al., 1996). Together, this early work was very clear in its suggestion that there are some genetic influences on personality. The next question, was of course, which genes would be the biggest players in the gene-to-personality pathways?

Candidate Genes

The early work in twins is suggestive of the possibility that eventually, with enough knowledge about human DNA, scientists will be able to discover a specific gene for, well, for anything related to personality, preferences, intelligence, or physical characteristics. That's a potentially exciting domain of future research, and one that researchers have examined very vigorously in the last 15 years or so. In this work, affectionately referred to as "gene for" studies by one of my colleagues, researchers looked for specific small repeating sections of genes (single nucleotide polymorphisms or SNPs) that identified a version of a specific gene. The SNPs usually were related to the specific production or reception of neuropeptides implicated in any number of social behaviors in non-humans. One really famous SNP is the APOE4 genetic polymorphism, which has been linked to increased risk for Alzheimer's Disease in humans. Another one is the GG variant of the oxytocin receptor gene rs53576, which is associated with increased oxytocin receptors in the brain.

The critical point in these "gene for" studies is that, if we know what parts of personality that a specific neuropeptide influences, then its genetic variants should predict behavior in a similar fashion. More specifically, knowing how oxytocin influences personality (although oxytocin's influence on behavior is still in question) would suggest that knowing variations in specific SNPs on the oxytocin receptor gene should help us predict personality.

In the subsequent "gene for" research, many researchers were left disappointed Specifically, for every breakthrough finding linking a

specific SNP to a personality characteristic, there was a null replication. Several of the most promising candidate genes, such as the MAOA gene which has been linked to antisocial behavior in past research (Caspi et al., 2002), have failed to replicate in subsequent work, according to several meta-analyses (De Moor et al., 2010).
So, then genes don't influence personality?

The current prevailing genetic evidence seems to suggest that we actually don't have genes for personality. And this conclusion doesn't come from a lack of trying: The US government has spent billions on genetic research. Billions. BILLIONS!!! When I think about all the money that went into this "gene for" research, I want to throw myself out the second-floor window of the psychology building. The fall wouldn't kill me, but I imagine it would hurt just as bad as it does to realize that much of our research funding was flushed down the "gene for" toilet.

Of course, the conclusion that genes don't influence personality is most certainly wrong, after all, we have decades of twin research showing similarity in personality between identical twins. At least some of that similarity has to be genetic. Are we missing something that might help uncover the great mystery linking genes and personality?
Take a longer look at the genes.

One potentially promising approach involves examining many candidate genes that relate to a specific biological system associated with personality. In one such approach, Jamie Derringer led a consortium of researchers in an examination of a collection of SNPs associated with Dopamine in prior research, and then examined associations between this collection of SNPs and sensation seeking behavior. Sensation seeking is a personality trait that is linked to a number of behavioral disorders relating to substance use and addiction—and much of the human and non-human research indicates that dopamine plays a role in this behavior.

This work differs from the "gene for" research of the past because it doesn't rely on the association of a single SNP related to dopamine influencing sensation seeking. Rather, the study looks at a number of SNPs related to dopamine in prior research, to determine if these SNPs work in concert to influence dopamine levels, and sensation seeking more broadly. This approach is appealing because it involves conceiving of genes and personality not as simple one-to-one relationships, but instead, as complex systems of genes that work in concert to express a personality trait.

The findings of this research were promising: Taking into account all the SNPs associated with sensation-seeking behaviors as an aggregate, dopamine genes worked in concert to explain around 6.6% of variation in sensation-seeking behavior (Derringer et al., 2010).

We're still not there yet.

Remember that twin studies suggested that 40% of identical twin personality was genetic? Well 6.6% in the dopamine genes study is a far-cry from 40% in this twin research. Where does the rest of the heritability go?

One possible answer arises from understanding what happens to DNA before it is expressed as a personality characteristic. As your high school biology instructor will tell you, DNA is a code for building proteins, hormones, and neuropeptides that serve specific cellular functions within the body. One thing that early gene-personality work overlooked is that a lot has to happen to allow DNA to code for specific hormones/neuropeptides, that then have to act at the cellular level to subsequently influence personality. In short, **genes need to be expressed at a cellular level** in order to influence personality, and so one place where a genetic researcher might want to look to examine gene influences on personality is at this expression—that is, what genes are being unzipped by RNA, so that specific hormones/proteins are produced?

Research in honey bees is suggestive of the potential of examining RNA to predict behavior. In this work, messenger RNA abundance was a significant predictor of behavioral transitions of honey bees from hive workers to foragers (Whitfield et al., 2003). Human work in this domain is an exciting area of future research.

If you've made it this far, you can appreciate (like I do), that the question: "Do genes influence personality?" cannot receive a simple answer. On the one hand, genes clearly seem to contribute to personality, but on the other, much of the genetic evidence has not supported this view. I'm cautiously optimistic about the future of gene work. Are you?

"For intelligence, there are thousands of genes," she told AFP. "We have detected the 52 most important ones, but there will be a lot more."

The **Strength Gene**. For the first time, scientists have discovered common genetic factors that influence muscle strength. The discovery offers new insights into the biology of muscle strength and its role in age-related conditions such as bone frailty.

The study, led by researchers at the Medical Research Council (MRC) Epidemiology Unit at the University of Cambridge in the United Kingdom, is published in the journal Nature Communications. Muscle strength, as measured by hand grip strength, is widely used as a clinical indicator of muscular fitness. It is also predictive of a number of health outcomes in older people.

The genetic analysis [of 140,000 people taking part in the UK Biobank project and a further 50,000 people in Australia, Denmark, the Netherlands and the U.K.] identified that muscle strength is significantly linked to 16 locations on the human genome.

The team then looked for clues that might show whether or not low muscle strength actually causes the health problems associated with it. They found no evidence that reduced muscle strength directly raises risk of premature death or cardiovascular disease. However, they did find evidence that higher muscle strength reduces risk of bone fracture.

The GLP aggregated and excerpted this blog/article to reflect the diversity of news, opinion, and analysis. Read full, original post: Scientists find common genes involved in muscle strength

The **Immortality Gene.** Making a drug is like trying to pick a lock at the molecular level. There are two ways in which you can proceed. You can try thousands of different keys at random, hopefully finding one that fits. The pharmaceutical industry does this all the time – sometimes screening hundreds of thousands of compounds to see if they interact with a certain enzyme or protein. But unfortunately it's not always efficient – there are more drug molecule shapes than seconds have passed since the beginning of the universe.

Alternatively, like a safe cracker, you can x-ray the lock you want to open and work out the probable shape of the key from the pictures you get. This is much more effective for discovering drugs, as you can use computer models to identify promising compounds before researchers go into the lab to find the best one. Now a study, published in Nature, presents detailed images of a crucial anti-ageing enzyme known as telomerase – raising hopes that we can soon slow ageing and cure cancer.

Every organism packages its DNA into chromosomes. In simple bacteria like E. coli this is a single small circle. More complex organisms have far more DNA and multiple linear chromosomes (22 pairs plus sex chromosomes). These probably appeared because they provided an evolutionary advantage, but they also come with a downside.

At the end of each chromosome is a protective cap called a telomere . However, most human cells can't copy them – meaning that every time they divide, their telomeres become shorter. When telomeres become too short, the cell enters a toxic state called "senescence". If these senescent cells are not cleared by the immune system, they begin to compromise the function of the tissues in which they reside. For millennia, humans have perceived this gradual compromise in tissue function over time without understanding what caused it. We simply called it ageing.

Enter telomerase, a mitateng telomere repair enzyme in two parts – able to add DNA to the chromosome tips. The first part is a protein called TERT that does the copying. The second component is called TR, a small piece of RNA which acts as a template. Together, these form telomerase, which trundles up and down on the ends of chromosomes, copying the template. At the bottom, a human telomere is roughly 3,000 copies of the DNA sequence "TTAGGG" – laid down and maintained by telomerase. But sadly, production of TERT is repressed in human tissues with the exception of sperm, eggs and some immune cells.

Aging versus cancer

Organisms regulate their telomere maintenance in this way because they are walking a biological tightrope. On the one hand, they need to replace the cells they lose in the course of their ordinary daily lives by cell division. However, any cell with an unlimited capacity to divide is the seed of a tumour. And it turns out that the majority of human cancers have active telomerase and shorter telomeres than the cells surrounding them.

This indicates that the cell from which they came divided as normal but then picked up a mutation which turned TERT back on. Cancer and ageing are flip sides of the same coin and telomerase, by and large, is doing the flipping. Inhibit telomerase, and you have a treatment for cancer, activate it and you prevent senescence. That, at least, is the theory.

The researchers behind the new study were not just able to obtain the structure of a proportion of the enzyme, but of the entire molecule as it was working. This was a tour de force involving the use of cryo-electron microscopy – a technique using a beam of electrons (rather than light) to take thousands of detailed images of individual molecules from different angles and combine them computationally.

Prior to the development of this method, for which scientists won the Nobel Prize last year, it was necessary to crystallise proteins to image them. This typically requires thousands of attempts and many years of trying, if it works at all.

Elixir of youth?

TERT itself is a large molecule and although it has shown to lengthen lifespan when introduced into normal mice using gene therapy this is technically challenging and fraught with difficulties. Drugs that can turn on the enzyme that produces it are far better, easier to deliver and cheaper to make.

We already know of a few compounds to inhibit and activate telomerase – discovered through the cumbersome process of randomly screening for drugs. Sadly, they are not very efficient.

Some of the most provocative studies involve the compound TA-65 (Cycloastragenol) – a natural product which lengthens telomeres experimentally and has been claimed to show benefit in early stage macular degeneration (vision loss). As a result, TA65 has been sold over the internet and has prompted at least one (subsequently dismissed) lawsuit over claims that it caused cancer in a user. This sad story illustrates an important public health message best mitaten simply as "don't try this at home, folks".

The telomerase inhibitors we know of so far, however, have genuine clinical benefit in various cancers, particularly in combination with other drugs. However, the doses required are relatively high.

The new study is extremely promising because, by knowing the structure of telomerase, we can use computer models to identify the most promising activators and inhibitors and then test them to find which ones are most effective. This is a much quicker process than randomly trying different molecules to see if they work.

So how far could we go? In terms of cancer, it is hard to tell. The body can easily become resistant to cancer drugs, including telomerase inhibitors. Prospects for slowing ageing where there is not cancer are somewhat easier to estimate. In mice, deleting senescent cells or dosing with telomerase (gene therapy) both give increases in lifespan of the order of 20% – despite being inefficient techniques. It may be that at some point other ageing mechanisms, such as the accumulation of damaged proteins, start to come into play.

But if we did manage to stop the kind of ageing caused by senescent cells using telomerase activation, we could start devoting all our efforts into tackling these additional ageing processes. There's every reason to be optimistic that we may soon live much longer, healthier lives than we do today.

Guardian Party – National political party surging to prominence in the early 22nd century after a string of feckless government administrations and complicit Washington Establishment were unable to protect America from twin pandemics: Worldwide Islamic Terrorism, Global Techno-Plague.

The Guardian Party has its own "Guardian Agency", complete with its own covert ops group, to spy on other agencies, political parties, or governments.

Guardian Party Programs – Harsh programs designed to guard America's health and safety while cutting budget deficits.

- Crime-stoppers: Aggressive hunt for terrorists or criminals
- Infra-Rebuild: Put people to work rebuilding roads, communications systems, power systems, etc.
- Repatriot: Deport useless or dangerous people.
- Golden Years: Euthanasia for the senile or terminally ill
- Pillars: Consists of two sub-programs: Private Citizens' Vigilantes to fight local criminals and terrorists, Health Watch Local groups to poke into neighbors' private lives to uncover community health risks.

H&H DNA Partners – Biotech Pharmaceutical Company started by Hudson (Hud) Haller and funded by his father Hollis (Holy) Haller

Healthguard – Intrusive national government agency established to guard private citizens against health risks. Championed by the Guardian Party.

High Energy Physics – Branch of physics seeking answers to fundamental questions posed by the universe. Current theories include Unified Field Theory, Time Reversal Theory, String Theory. It is possible that man's cognitive asymptotic limit has moved high energy physics from objective science to subject philosophic conjecture.

Home-Track Schooling – American grade and high school educational systems are more flexible in the 22nd century, allowing customized education for gifted children or those with physical or mental handicaps. Home-Track Schooling allows a child to study at home using computerized learning and tutoring programs. The program is monitored by Healthguard, the agency which tests, accepts, and monitors children in the program.

Insiders Group – Clandestine group created to spy on the Guardian Party.

Interactive Fabric – A textile containing microcircuits and materials that can be fashioned into clothing that interfaces with the person wearing it, augmenting physical and mental personas.

Isilabad – Rogue Middle East State created midway through the 21st century to reestablish Islamic Caliphate and catapult Islam to its rightful place on the world stage.

Mega-Media – Umbrella term describing a worldwide computer network linking all types of communications networks and media. Includes smart cell phones and computer tablets when connected to "Worldwide Internet Grid".

Multi-threaded parallel Recursive Algorithmic Programming – Abbreviated by MPRAP. The most advanced computer programming technique used for artificial intelligence. The human brain contains trillions of interconnected sets of neurons. Though they operate at slower processing speeds of computer chips, they are interconnected, running in parallel, and in magnitudes that dwarf what the best computer hardware and software engineers can accomplish. That is why MPRAP was developed. The challenge facing engineers is to utilize as many massively parallel processing computers as they can. That number is limited by the collective intelligence of the engineering team, or the emergent intelligence of self-learning software.

Neural Network – In information technology, a neural network is a system of hardware and/or software patterned after the operation of neurons in the human brain. Neural networks – also called artificial neural networks – are a variety of deep learning technologies. The brain is modeled as layers of interconnected neurons that accept electrical signal input, process the input and send electrical signal output.

Neuro-Knitter – Biomedical device using software-controlled electromagnetic radiation to accelerate neural healing required after broken neck or back.

New-Wave – Generic term referring to early 22nd century younger generation tastes and lifestyles.

Opposition Group – Concerned Washington politicians and insiders opposed to Guardian Party's harsh measures for dealing with opponents. It has a clandestine steering committee to which a covert operations group reports.

Platform Economy and Companies – Platform refers to Cyberspace-based resources and services that reduce transaction costs (friction) and increase interaction (networking) among the Platform Economy's buyers and sellers. There are multiple ways to describe "product" companies and "platform" companies, so let's clarify. First, a "product" company is one that sells a particular type of solution to a problem across a specific sector or type of industry. In contrast, "platform" companies seek to transform industries or sectors with a set of solutions and products. Products lack defensibility and often rely on other platforms for customer acquisition, data, or infrastructure. Conversely, platforms allow new products built at a significantly lower incremental cost and users pay for the new value offered versus just paying for consuming more of a service. The pricing page of a company will likely show you whether they have built a product or a platform as a product company will charge by the number of users while a platform will price according to the increasing value the products provide to the customer.

Project Death Shield – Covert operation run by CIA (Central Intelligence Agency) to monitor how Techno-Plague impacts U.S. government stability.

Securityguard – Intrusive national government agency established to guard private citizens against domestic or international threats. Championed by the Guardian Party.

Sensory Media Coding – Used to encode separate sensory perceptions for Cyber-Theater projection. There are six sensory perceptions: sight, sound, taste, touch, smell, and balance. Each sensory perception is represented by a set of base components. Each sensory perception is recorded on a separate track using digilog coding. Here is an example: the sense of taste is composed of sweet, salty, sour, bitter, and umami (a strong meaty taste imparted by glutamate and certain other amino acids). Any taste can be simulated by coding the presence and intensity of its five components. Neuroscientists, physiologists, and computer scientists continue to improve hardware and software to project sensory perceptions into a viewing theater or directly into the brain.

Sensual Pleasures Cafés and Fantasy Clubs – Many recreational drugs were legalized in the 21st century. A Sensual Pleasures café is a restaurant featuring foods, drinks or tobacco products containing legalized recreational drugs. Licensed fantasy clubs catering to adult pleasures sprang up, reducing prostitution and the risk of STD. Some served females only.

Surveillance Capitalism – An extension of Traditional Capitalism, Surveillance Capitalism goes beyond Land, Labor and Capital by commoditizing and bringing into a new market Personal Data and Behavioral Analysis and Control.

Techno-Plague – Also called T-Plague. Infection from a mutant manmade virus causing neural entanglement similar to Alzheimer's, leading to rapid cognitive impairment and senility. It Spread gradually but inexorably, becoming a global pandemic early in the 22nd century.

The Singularity – The Singularity is the hypothetical future creation of super-intelligent machines. Superintelligence is defined as a technologically-created cognitive capacity far beyond that possible for humans. Should the Singularity occur, technology will advance beyond our ability to foresee or control its outcomes and the world will be transformed beyond recognition by the application of superintelligence to humans and/or human problems, including poverty, disease and mortality. Revolutions in genetics, nanotechnology, and robotics (GNR) in the first half of the 21st century are expected to lay the foundation for the Singularity. According to Singularity theory, superintelligence will be developed by self-directed computers and will increase exponentially rather than incrementally.

Traser – State-of-the-art law enforcement weapon: dual tranquilizer and electric stun gun.

Trojan Filters – Hidden devices that can release T-Plague virus into air or water.

Transhumanism – Abbreviated as H+ or h+, it is an international and intellectual movement that aims to transform the human condition by developing and making widely available sophisticated technologies to greatly enhance human intellect and physiology.

Vow-Cer – The institution of marriage remains in the 22nd century a cornerstone of society, but adjusts to the needs of people. Vow-Cer is a Marriage Vow Contract Certification Ceremony. Two people affirm their commitment to each other, agreeing to honor their written marriage contract. Couples usually become Co-Friends before celebrating a vow-cer.

Whole Brain Emulation – **Whole brain emulation** (WBE), mind upload or **brain** upload (sometimes called "mind copying" or "mind transfer") is the hypothetical process of scanning mental state (including long-term memory and "self") of a particular **brain** substrate and copying it to a computer.

Worldstars – Name given by Indira Ramanujan to herself and three other talented biotech researchers: Su-Lin Song Chou, Adom Ola, and Jason Kittner.

Appendix

The scientific or guiding principles presented in this book are factual, as are technological applications. For readers who might enjoy reading more of the details, this appendix contains charts or diagrams referenced in the book's narrative or dialogue, identified by page number.

T-Plague Carrier Solution Paths

White Paper
The Problem: My Immune System ignores T-Plague Virus because it is harmless to me. But my Immune System treats T-Plague Vaccine like an Antigen, destroying it before it can put the Virus into remission. As a result, I am a T-Plague Carrier

Two possible Solution Paths:
1. Modify my Immune System to ignore Vaccine.
2. Modify the Vaccine so my Immune System ignores Vaccine.

Immune System Primer:
- Two Components: External Internal
- External: Skin and Mucous. Provides barrier Flushes
- Internal System Components: Innate Adaptive
- Innate: Fever Swelling Inflammation Blistering
- Adaptive: Fights Antigens at the cellular level
- Antibodies identify and attack Antigens by disrupting specific protein sequences
- Leucocytes generate Antibodies
- Adaptive System produces a cascade of Leucocytes that fight Antigens. It has two levels:
- Humoral System: B-Cells circulating in blood stream fight Antigens
- Intracellular System: T-Cells kill Intracellular Antigens/Viruses
- DNA technology I need for either Solution Path:
- CAR-T spin-offs: Chimeric Antigen Receptor on T-Cells (Modify my T-Cells to ignore T-Plague Vaccine)

- SNP Technology advances: Single Nucleotide Polymorphism (Identify active sites on cells, DNA, or proteins)
- CRISPR/CAS-9 improvements: Clustered Regularly Interspaced Short Palindromic Repeats (Edit and combine DNA segments)

Solution Path 1 is fraught with more complexity than Path 2. I will implement Solution Path 2:
1. Identify my unique Genetic Marker
2. "Harvest" my Genetic Marker
3. "Attach" my Genetic Marker to T-Plague Vaccine.

The End Result: I have a "Designer Vaccine" that will keep any T- Plague virus hidden in my cells and below an infectious level.
Possible Contingencies:
1. Vaccine efficacy is temporary, so I must take it "daily."
2. My immune system becomes habituated to Vaccine, and Vaccine loses efficacy over time. If that occurs, I must modify my "Designer Vaccine."
3. Vaccine ineffective, so I must implement Solution Path 1.

Carter's Socioeconomic/Political Positioning, Trends and
Policy Recommendations

White Paper Summary Timeless Wisdom:
"If men were angels, no government would be necessary. If angels were to govern men, neither external nor internal controls on government would be necessary." James Madison
But neither Men nor Women are, so a Civil Society must make choices. Thus, this White Paper.
- Built on leading social forecasters and their successors: Robert Putnam – "Bowling Alone" Charles Murray – "Coming Apart" "In Our Hands" Thomas Sowell – "Race and Culture" Jeremy Rifkin – "The European Dream…" Isabelle Sawhill – "The Forgotten Americans"
- Includes thinkers of all stripes, as well as their acolytes: Thomas Picketty – "Capitalism in the 21st Century" Thomas

Sowell – "Wealth, Poverty, and Politics" Steven Pinker – "Liberalism Now" Timothy Snyder – "The Road to Unfreedom"

- Considers Libertarian and Progressive positions
- Work is statistically supported Background
- 1960's – 2020's a Turbulent and Transitional Period
- Founding American Virtues confirmed: Marriage/Family Work Ethic Honesty Religiosity
- Liberal Democracy and Capitalism confirmed: Liberalism supports both ends of political spectrum and "Care-Based" Capitalism fosters balanced growth
- Two distinct Classes emerged: New Lower Class New Upper Class
- Neither Race nor Ethnicity determines Membership
- Socioeconomic factors determine membership: Income/Wealth Education/Intelligence
- Gap widened, leading to: Income Inequality Political Polarization
- Neuroscientific findings support genetic predispositions that favor "American Dream" vis-à-vis "European Dream"
- Madisonian concerns regarding "bloated Government," "excessive Regulation" came to forefront
- Neoclassical Economic concerns regarding Income Inequality grew
- Steps America Took ("Fifth Great Awakening"):
- Embraced "Civil Dialogue" and Politics towards the Center
- Strengthened Marriage/Family and Inclusive Religiosity
- Improved Educational and Employment Fairness
- "Borrowed" Best Practices from "European Dream"
- "Rightsized" Welfare Programs and the Size of Government
- Tested "National Income" and "Wealth Tax" Programs
- Maintained World Leadership via Military Strength and Commitment to Founding Virtues
- Utilized Internet to replace Government Oversight and to augment Public Safety
- Transferred more power back to Local Level

These steps reversed the declines that disrupted progress early last century:
- Gap between New Upper and Lower Classes narrowed
- Power and scope of Regulatory Agencies shrank, leading to cooperative climate between Business, Government, and Public
- American "Commitment/Exceptionalism" upgraded
- Revitalized America remained only World Superpower Until thirty years ago:
- Washington's "Kinder and Gentler" focus diluted Founding Virtues and weakened Country's Defenses
- Twin Terrors (T-Plague and Middle East Terrorism) ran amok and catapulted Guardian Party to Prominence
- Public I.Q., Tolerance, and U.S. Economy damaged

Guardian Party "Harsh Times demand Harsh Measures" policies kept America from the Abyss.
- T-Plague and Middle East Terrorism reined in
- Trends finally heading in the right direction again
- Washington policies now focus on short-term rather than longer-term

But new threats have emerged:
- Cyberterrorism increasing
- Automation and Artificial Intelligence threaten jobs
- Genetic Engineering and Transhumanism frighten Public
- Problematic New World Order frustrates Administration

How to handle new threats and chronic problems (need Political, Social, Economic Policy Adjustments)
Political Policies: The Political System is not broken!
The Politicos are!
National Policies
- Term Limits at all levels to lessen "Washington Establishment"
- Penalties on Politicians for "Gridlock and Partisanship" to reward progress

- Democracy and Zero-Based Budgeting for Support Staffs, Committees, Agencies, and Expert Panels to encourage innovation
- Internet Elections to eliminate Voting Irregularities
- Time and dollar limits on Candidate Spending/Advertising to reduce PAC Influence
- Government Venture Capital Initiative to replace Cronyism and Pork Barrel Programs
- International Policies
- Win-Win Worldwide Mobility and Integration that respects National Diversity to strengthen Inter-Governmental Cooperation
- Rapprochement between Islam and Christianity to lower Cultural Hostility
- Careful Cooperation with China and Russia Social Policies:
- One-Year Universal Service to augment Student Training
- Emphasis on Career Training/Certification vis-à-vis College Diploma to reward alternative Career Paths
- Balanced "Work-to-Live" Lifestyle to recognize Personal Needs
- Expanded Volunteerism to guard against Tyranny
- Economic Policies:
- Economic, Job, and Wage Growth to counteract Inequality
- Means-Based National Income and Wealth Tax to counteract Inequality
- Head Tax on Industrial Robots
- Caps on Executive Compensation and Parachutes to demonstrate "Fairness"
- Energy, Communication, Education, and Transportation Infrastructure upgrades to insure long-term efficiency
- Welfare Safety Nets "right-sized" to balance National Income and Wealth Tax
- Issues outside scope of this White Paper that impinge success:
- Cyberterrorism and False Information
- Automation and Artificial Intelligence
- Genetic Engineering and Transhumanism

They require techno-scientific solutions implemented via Normative Ethics.

High Energy Physics Stalemate

Flaws in HEP:
- Ignores Man's Asymptotic limits dictated by Neuroscience (Some concepts are inaccessible to human cognition)
- Ignores "Explosion Principle" (Can prove any statement if you include an assumption and its negation)
- Ignores Godel's Completeness and Incompleteness Theorems
- Unable to handle higher-order infinities
- HEP refuses to accept Post-Modern Structure of Scientific Revolutions:
- Post-Modern HEP theories have led to Degenerative Explanations instead of Progressive Explanations
- Post-Modern HEP theories emerge from mathematical manipulation instead of experimental observation (Thought Experiments lead to fantasy)

A Summary of Scientific Structure for understanding
Scientific Revolutions:
- Carl Popper (Falsification) and Thomas Kuhn (Paradigm Shifts) are its "Founders"
- Paradigm: A model that explains Reality
- Chronology of accepted Paradigms: Pre-scientific (Faith and Myth)Aristotle (Atoms and the Void) Newton (Classical Physics) Einstein (Special and General Relativity)

Quantum Theory (Bohr, Heisenberg, Planck…)
Post-modern Philosophers of Science have extended Founders' Structures
- Lakatos, et al warn against "Instant Rationality"
- Philosophers of Science are "Spin Doctors" adjusting science history to appear "Rational"
- Must rely also on Subjective Judgment

There have been no viable Paradigm Shifts after Quantum Theory (String Theory, M-Theory and Brane-Theory yielded Degenerative Explanations)

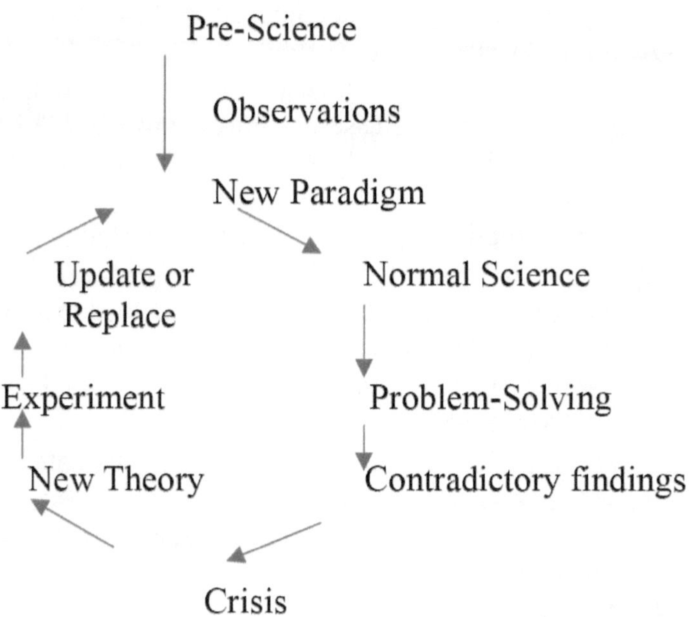

Why the Stalemate?

- Quantum theory dates to early 20th Century
- Basic Quantum Theory yielded Progressive Explanations
- But Extension Theories have yielded Degenerative Explanations

Basic Quantum Physics that actually works:
- Wave Equation/Probability Amplitude
- Uncertainty Principle
- Wave/Particle Duality
- Superpositioning
- Entanglement
- Coherence
- Spin States
- Entropy-reversible nano-circuitry
- Tunneling Extension Theories:

- String Theory: Extends Universe into 11 Dimensions
- String: Quantum of Energy vibrating at specific frequency
- Brane Theory: Universe built on multi-dimensional "Particles" propagating through Spacetime according to the laws of Quantum Physics
- M-Theory: Uses Supergravity and a partitioning of 11 Dimensions into two classes to unify Strings and Superstrings

None of them work.

- Einstein: "God does not play dice with the Universe."
- Feynman: If you **think** you **understand quantum mechanics**, you don't **understand quantum mechanics**."
- CERN Large Hadron Collider (LHC), International Linear Accelerator (ILC) and subsequent experiments failed to yield observable confirmation
- Chronology of Progress that has led to a Stalemate:
- Grand Unified Field Theory is Holy Grail of HEP (Unify the 4 Fundamental Forces: Gravity E&M Weak Force Strong Force to explain Universe's Big Bang)
- Newton's Laws of Motion supported Industrial Revolution
- Maxwell's Equations powered Electric/Computer Age
- Relativity and Quantum Theory cracked into Weak and Strong Forces and supported the "Standard Model"
- "Standard Model:" Bizarre Zoo of particles (Higg's Boson clarified)
- "String Theory:" Replace "Standard Model" particle zoo with 11-dimensional "strings of vibrating energy
- Leads to: Dark MatterDark Energy Black Holes Worm HolesParallel Universes
- Which lead to Dead End: No experimental verification Becomes a Religion / Not Science

But in defense of High Energy Physics:

- How do you know "When to say enough?"
- Spin-off findings contribute to: Biotech, Quantum Computers, Artificial Intelligence, Military/Industrial Applications…
- But be skeptical:

- Feynman's one-word moniker for most of Post-Modernism: "Baloney"
- Popular Press Proclamations exist only in the realm of Science Fiction
- Enjoy watching Sci-Fi movies as if you're on a magic carpet ride!

Star Trek Concepts – Connections to Physics

Physics is the fundamental science whose principles dictate "Reality." Most science fiction novels and movies ignore what is possible, instead inventing fantasy, which is an unsophisticated and tawdry substitute for entertaining a reading or viewing audience. Only the Star Trek series has explained how physics might support its clever creations. Most of its technology is borrowed from the outer limits of Quantum Theory (Dark Matter/Dark Energy, CPT-reversal, Multiple Universes, Anti-Matter and Gravity, etc.) Here is a tabulation of some of the inventions. Books have been written drawing parallels among physics, the future, and Star Trek, which of all science fiction series, does the best at separating scientific possibility (although miniscule probability) from outlandish fantasy.

- Starship Enterprise: Built on possibilities!
- Tractor Beam: Tow an object. Optical or Acoustical Tweezers use E&M/Sound wave pressures to move objects.
- Teleportation: Particle Entanglement and Entropy Transfer.
- Cloaking: Bending light around an object by using scanning tunnel microscopy and atomic force microscopy/nanotechnology to rearrange atoms forming metamaterials that bend light around themselves, or scatter/absorb radar so nothing is reflected back; or use holography to record background and project onto the front of the object.
- Deflector Shield: Use a plasma surrounding an object to convert matter or radiation into energy and store in a string. Note "raise shields" lifted from Greek/Roman stories. Soldiers raised shields to deflect arrows, spears, etc.
- Directed Energy Weapons: Phasors, Photon Torpedoes, etc.: Bombard target with matter and anti-matter.

- Traveling Faster than speed of light: Put enough energy into a region of space to contract Space in front and expand Space in back.
- Warp Drive: Anti-matter extracted from strings powers warp drive propulsion engines.
- Worm Holes: Connect two regions of space via Black Holes
- A.I.: This is Star Trek's Lieutenant Commander Data.(Robotics too)
- Holodeck: This is Augmented Virtual Reality/Immersive Reality (Like my Cyber-Theater) Uses holography.
- Replicator: This is 3-D printing
- Transhumanism: Cyborgs and the Borgs
- Uploading Brain: Uses a device like my Brain Probe
- Tricorder: It is our smartphone plus a FitBit PDA/VideoCam/Blackberry and a mini-CAT-scanner.
- Alien Beings: Anthropomorphic Emergence in other substrates besides Carbon or Silicon.
- Nano Computers: Not in Star Trek. Let's us put "intelligence" in everything and everywhere.
- Singularity: Cognition emerges in silicon substrate. But you cannot build "Cyborgs or Terminators" unless you integrate physical, cognitive, emotional personas.
- Fast Healing of Injuries: Scan tissue and bombard it with electromagnetic/plasma to stimulate electrochemical healing
- Mind Control: Done using device like my Brain Probe to upload neural states into brain
- Cloning People: Replace DNA and download/upload neural states into undeveloped fetus templates.
- Games: Like today's video games
- Morphing People: Exchange people's personas into other bodies. Manipulate DNA
- Ethical/Psychological/Social/Economic/Political Issues: Star Trek projects human traits into other life forms.
- Religion/Philosophy confrontations: Star Trek sidesteps!
- Eliminate an Enemy: Episode described a device that viewed a person and the operator could make them disappear. I go one better. I control their minds via fear and pain by

bombarding their head with Brain Probe radiation.

- Immortality: Star Trek doesn't deal with it. I do with uploading or slowing down aging process
- Bringing people back to life: Star Trek doesn't deal with it. I do by recreating people. Read their DNA and insert into a template embryo. Then upload a stored physical/neural/emotional brain state.
- Telepathy: Star Trek has Empaths: people who are extraordinarily sensitive to others, possibly caused by "reading" body language or detecting a "biochemical biofield" emitted by the brain.
- Telekinesis: Used infrequently and never explained. (Physics refutes!)
- Time Travel: Never explained. Might be conjured from "Anti-Matter" and time reversal. I don't believe time exists. Time is merely a mental construct that allows an ordering of events that preserves causality.
- Supercomputers: Assumed!

Electra's Notes for Tracking a Fly Ball:

There are three primary possible explanations for how a baseball fielder catches a fly ball:

- **Trajectory Projection (TP)**: The fielder calculates the trajectory of a ball the moment it is hit and simply runs to the spot where it will fall (of course, taking into account wind speed and barometric pressure).
- **Optical acceleration cancellation (OAC)**: The fielder watches the flight of the ball; constantly adjusting her position in response to what she sees. If it appears to be accelerating upward, she moves back. If it seems to be accelerating downward, she moves forward.
- **Linear optical trajectory (LOT)**: The fielder pays attention to the apparent angle formed by the ball, the point on the ground beneath the ball, and home plate, moving to keep this angle constant until she reaches the ball. In other words, she tries to move so that the ball appears to be moving in a straight line rather than a parabola.

In principle, all three of these systems should work. However, TP is probably impossible; our visual system isn't accurate at determining distances beyond about 30 meters, and outfielders stand up to 100 meters away from home plate. The second system, OAC, might not work because the visual system isn't actually very sensitive to acceleration. And the third system, LOT, is problematic because it doesn't predict a unique path for the fielder to take to the ball. Further, the most likely paths a fielder would take to catch a ball wouldn't be much different under OAC and LOT.

TP is not used by dogs or people. Outfielders use the other two methods (OAC or LOT) because it is easier for their brains to handle) yielding a longer distance run (similar to running the legs of a right triangle).

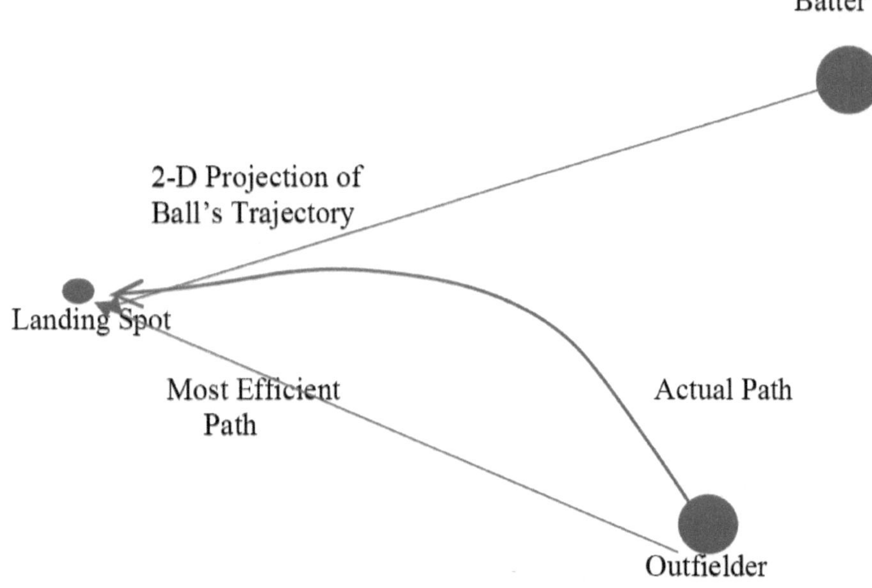

I'll run the most efficient path, allowing me to catch fly balls others would miss, thus increasing my range. And I'll use my Javelin or Pirouette throwing motion I perfected in the Co-Flto increase my throwing distance, narrowing the gap between me and male outfielders. I can train my brain to compute the most efficient path (it's merely an optimization problem.)

Electra's

Cloning/Pregnancy Notes
- China and Japan cloning technology/practice leaders.
- Success with dogs. Limited success with humans.

Cloning Protocol I will follow:
1. Take a tissue sample from myself using biopsy punch.
2. Sterilize, chemically treat, and centrifuge sample to separate cells.
3. Cultivate cells in a growth medium.
4. Obtain unfertilized eggs from Donor. (Can't use mine because I am infertile.) Note: Eggs harvested using minimally invasive IVF Flushing Device.
5. Remove nucleus from unfertilized eggs using a computer-controlled micro pipette. We now have a genetically empty egg.
6. Insert my cultivated cells into unfertilized eggs using micro pipette.
7. Use Electro-Cell Manipulator to shock the eggs, fusing together egg and inserted cells membranes. Egg now fertilized.
8. Suspend the egg in an artificial womb (AW). AW originally called "Biobag." Later generations labeled Neuro-Life Vessel (NLV). Note: This called in vitro gestation. In vivo gestation requires insertion of fertilized eggs into a surrogate mother.

Pregnancy Facts
1. Full Term Pregnancy: 39 – 42 weeks or pprox.. 9 months
2. Divided into First Trimester (Weeks 1 – 12 or 3 months) Second Trimester (Weeks 13 – 26 or next 3 months) Third Trimester (Weeks 27 – 42 or next 3 months)
3. Premature Birth (Preemies): Fewer than 37 weeks' gestation
4. Full Term Baby Avg of 6 – 7 lbs and 18 – 24 inches
5. Preemies can weigh as little as a pound and measure less than 6 inches

Cloning Issues:
1. Electro-Cell Manipulator shock treatment successfully produces living fertilized egg 50 – 60 percent of time
2. Gestation Issues for NLV: NLV must mimic Uterine Environment.
3. Must circulate amniotic fluid carrying Oxygen, Nutrients, Hormones.
4. Lung Development, Feeding, and Infection.
5. Heartbeat Ignition at normal time (3 weeks) and continuation often problematic.

Note: External Gestation labeled Neonatal Intensive Care (NIC) and continues to hold great promise, but results achieved by Human Cloning and In Vivo Gestation considered modest at best. Many mammals have been cloned, but to date only those with shorter gestation periods. Conjecture: Human Genetic Complexity may limit what is achievable because precise timing of hormones and electrochemical stimulation requires real-time adjustment to uterine environment.

Note: Observable sexual differentiation caused by fetus-produced hormones after six weeks.

My R&D Approach: Use my superior brain to achieve success "mere mortals" can't.
- Kameyo and I work independently in parallel. Kameyo's work furnishes "stealth" cover for mine.
- I clone from my tissue sample. Kameyo clones from random sample.
- I will computer-simulate using my proprietary software multifactor combinations and timing of critical factors affecting cloning success probabilities.
- I will install three NLVs for actual testing, choosing hi-success probability combinations determined via simulation.

Electra's Gene Editing Notes
- Living Organisms: Wet and Warm and are not Digital Computers but Computer Model (Input Process Output) helps us model the Brain

- DNA: Analogous to a computer tape containing instructions that organisms use to function (Reproduce Feed/ExcreteMoveDie)

- DNA comprised of Chromosomes Humans have 23 pairs (23rd is XY/male or XX/female) Chromosome contains literally thousands of Genes50 thousand Genes determine Human Characteristics divided among following categories: Physical Physiological Psychological

- Mitochondrial DNA comprised of 37 genes Inherited from MotherUsed for building ATP (energy source) and Proteins

- Gene Interactions (via stable or transient crosslinking) determine Human Characteristics

We have developed an array of tools for deciphering/mapping (Human Genome Project) and editing DNA
Mapping identifies active Gene Sites. Mapping Tools:
- Magnetic Resonance Imaging (MRI)
- Fast MRI (fMRI)
- Positive Electron Emission (PET)
- Single Photon Emission Computed Tomography (SPECT)…
- Note: My Brain Probe stimulates Brain Regions (Deep Brain Stimulation/DBS) and "reads the Brain" by using these techniques

Editing tools snip/clip/insert/connect targeted DNA segments
Editing Tools:
- Clustered Regularly Interspaced Short Palindromic Repeats using Cas9, and RNA-guided Enzyme associate with S-type Bacteria (CRISPR-Cas9)
- Polymer Chain Reaction Detectors (PCR)
- Single Nucleotide Polymorphism Chips (SNP)…
- Polygenic Scoring Algorithms (Computer algorithms analyze Genetic "Big Database" for correlated Genes impacting Human Characteristics)

Ultimate Goal: Understand genetic functioning of Brain and build Biogenetic Tools for editing the Brain to build superior humans or correct defects.

Designer Baby Goals: Improve following characteristics:
- Intelligence   Eye   ColoHeight   Personality   Strength Growth/Aging…

Correction Goals: Eliminate diseases or predispositions for:
- Alzheimer's Epilepsy Cardiovascular Mental Disorders…

My R&D Approach: Use my superior brain to write superior algorithms that analyze Genetic "Big Database" so I can edit those genes that are highly correlated to desired traits.
Note: Cloning and Gene Editing enter into a morass of Ethical Issues. That is why all my R&D stays with me.

RSA Encryption Background

RSA (Rivest, Shamir, Adelman) public/private key encryption is the basis for network security. Even Supercomputers or Quantum Computers are unable to break its encryption techniques. Because factoring a large number into its prime factors is a "Hard problem." A branch of abstract algebra – Galois Theory – supports RSA.
Galois Theory connects group theory and number fields when applied to modular arithmetic. The theory begins with Lagrange's Theorem:
- If G is a group containing o(G) elements, and H is a subgroup containing o(H) elements, then o(H) divides o(G).
- Euler's Theorem (A SPECIAL CASE OF CARMICHAEL'S
- FUNCTION) extends its usefulness for encryption by factoring an encryption key into two pieces, one for encrypting a message, and the other for decrypting, using modular (remainder) arithmetic. (We will compute a key by multiplying two large prime numbers P1 and P2. Euclid discovered that every whole number has a unique prime factorization.)
- Now we use a well-known property: 1 raised to any power = 1
- We also use Fermat's Little Theorem: Any integer a raised to a prime power p equals a mod p.
- Now we use the Phi function, which for each whole number equals the count of all the whole numbers less than it that

have no factor in common. FOR EVERY PRIME NUMBER P, ITS PHI FUNCTION VALUE = P-1. AND FOR PRIME NUMBERS, THE PHI FUNCTION IS MULTIPLICATIVE: PHI OF P1 X P2 =

- PHI OF P1 TIMES PHI OF P2. SO, WE KNOW P1, P2, N, AND PHI(N). PHI IS KNOWN AS THE TOTIENT FUNCTION.
- Now we let M represent a numerical message we want to encrypt and send it to the person who gave us an encryption key. We use Euler's Equation: Any number M raised to the power of Phi(N) − 1 is divisible by N. Stated as a modular arithmetic equation: $M^{Phi(N)} = 1 \mod N$. And we can raise both sides to any power k to get: $M^{(kPhi(N)} = 1 \mod N$. Further, multiply both sides by M to get: $M^{(kPhi(N) + 1)} = M \mod N$. And let e represent the encryption exponent and d the decryption exponent. e is chosen to be a small odd integer relatively prime to Phi(N).
- d is the private key, and it is used to calculate the power k from this formula: $d = (kPhi(N) + 1)/e$. The public key is (N,e).

Here is how the encryption works:
1. Encrypt the message using: $M^e \mod N = C$. C is the encrypted message.
2. The message is sent to the person whose public key was used for encryption.
3. The message is decrypted using: $C^d \mod N = M$.
4. When you read the literature, you will find that k is usually used instead of e to form the public key (N,k). e is computed per above.

Carter's Economic Bullet Points for Jared
- Capitalism winsSocialism loses
- Balanced Neoclassical-Progressive Synthesis adjusted for Behavioral Economics successful (Avoid Institutional Failure, Follow Moral Compass, Practice Political Pragmatism)
- Embrace what the Internet offers:
- Sharing/Caring/Collaborative Economy utilizing Platform Companies/Virtual Companies

- Creativity Innovation Entrepreneurship
- Need Economic Growth to grow Middle Class and reduce Income Inequality
- Robotics and Artificial Intelligence pose "existential threats" to Job Growth (Only Experiential/Creative/Caring Service Jobs insulated from Robotics or A.I.) Beware of A.I. reaching the "Singularity"
- Promote Trade School and Certification and "Robot Assistance" Occupations
- Globalization reduces Inter-Country Income Inequality but increases American Income Inequality (Short-Term?)
- Tariffs and Trade Restrictions may provide Short-Term gain but Longer-Term pain for America
- America must be the Beacon of "Exceptionalism"
- Watch out for China's ambitions to dominate: Robotics A.I. Genetic Engineering
- Watch out for Russian ambitions to disrupt World Financial Markets (Cryptocurrency will continue to grow)
- World Growth Opportunities by partnering with: Africa India
- Embrace Worker Retraining Programs (Older workers problematic)
- Beware of Government Regulation, especially those promoted by Radical Climate Change Programs that are a drag on the Economy
- Promote Sustainability Programs that partner Corporations/Government/Environmental Groups
- Increase Guardian Party Revenue-Generating Programs that are within Public's Moral Boundaries (Latest Example: Hunter Games Organ Sales or Cloning using prisoners Nationalization of Genetic Engineering Industry DOD Spin-offs to sell "super weapons" to economic partners)
- Find the right balance between the promise of New Technology and the Public's fear of Economic and Social Unknowns
- Promote revenue-generating "low-tech" jobs (Infrastructure Rebuild (Latest Examples: City Recycling Energy Grid

- Promote Government-Sanctioned Virtual Reality Clubs
- Promote additional crime prevention programs (Remote controlled hidden weapons installed at banks, autonomous weapons-firing drone patrols, etc.)

Angus' Benjamin Franklin Close for Jared

Pro's
Committed to America #1 Practices Pragmatic Realpolitiks Stopped America's Decline Reduced Budget Deficit Generates Jobs
Connects with Main Street Shored up Military/Security Rebuilds Infrastructure
Streamlined Government Bureaucracy Reduced Crime
Pushing Harsh Programs Acting on his own
Overstepping Presidential Limits
Damaging America Long-Term Alienating International Friends
Ignoring T-Plague Victims Believing he's been "Chosen"
Sidestepping Hi-Tech
Disrespecting Grounded Intellectualism Polarizing the Public
Did we act for the right reasons? (What tangible evidence?)
- Prostitutes in the Oval Office
- Sexual Abuse
- Hidden Agendas
- Fake News
- Trumped-up Terrorism Charges
- Racketeering

Linguistics Solution to the Great A.I. Conundrum

White Paper Summary
Reaching A.I.'s Holy Grail, computer cognition, will require advances in Contemporary Linguistics that continue to elude "Mere Mortals." A bullet point explanation follows.
- Contemporary Linguistics: A scientific study of Language.
- Language comprised of: Words Sentences Meaning
- Linguistic Taxonomy for studying Language: Phonology(words) Syntax(sentences) Semantics(meaning)

- Grammar is loosely defined to be the study of syntax and semantics using a chosen lexicon (English best choice). Its purpose is to construct Meaning from spoken or written words.

Computer-based A.I. must have a mathematical theory that can guide computer algorithms.
Algorithms needed:
- Speech Recognition and Transmission
- Language Translation (Sender to Receiver)
- Language Response (Receiver to Sender) Current Status:
- Algorithms can recognize speech and transmit to Receiver's Computer
- Sophisticated Language Translation Algorithms use Advanced Syntactical Theory (Extended Syntax X-Bar Theory) to Parse Speech into recognizable words and sentences constructed in chosen language (English best choice)
- Extended X-Bar Theory's mathematical structure useful for coding Computer Apps
- Sophisticated Language Response Algorithms still in rudimentary form.

Reasons:
- Advanced Semantic Theory contains nested sub-theories each requiring extensions of Modal Logic.
- Advanced Semantic Theory (Extended Semantics X-Bar Theory) lacks necessary precision for avoiding indirection, infinite regress, etc.
- Selecting Sender Context State requires Advanced Bayesian Statistical Selector Module
- Formulating a Response to the Sender is fraught with Complexity.

My Solution:
1. Write my own Machine Learning-Based Syntax App and Semantics App. Using my superior programming languages and skills.

2. Model App Knowledge Acquisition and Learning like DNA.
3. Let the Apps teach themselves by feeding off "Big Data." (InputProcessOutput)
4. Apps grow and evolve.
5. Activate and run indefinitely in Background Processing Mode. Adjust when and where needed.

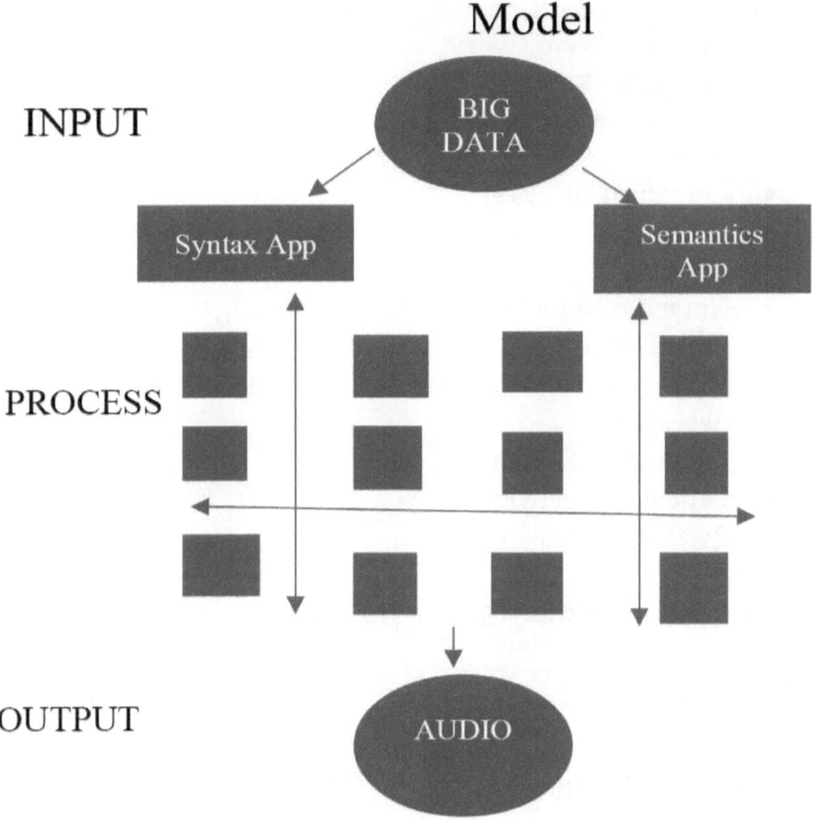

Small squares are blocks of App Code

Each column is like a Chromosome. Each block is like a Gene. Syntax and Semantics Apps add blocks as they learn.

All blocks are interconnected for communicating (Input Process Output). The End Result:

A.I.-Equipped Computer that can "talk" to the User.

Intelligence/Cognition is stored in the bits of the apps.

Conjecture:
If I let the Software run indefinitely it can break through to the First Order Singularity: Software that can understand what the User says and reply intelligently.

The Deep/Dark Web: Network Security and GUI's

Darknet or Dark Web:
- Restricted to special browsers
- Not indexed for Search Engines Large scale illegal activity
- Unmeasurable due to nature Deep Web:
- Contains Dark Web
- Accessible by password, encryption, or through gateway software
- Not indexed for Search Engines
- Little illegal activity outside of Dark Web
- Huge in size and growing exponentially Surface Web:
- Accessible
- Indexed for Search Engines
- Little illegal activity
- Relatively small in size

Internet is a collection Websites linked together to form "Markets."

Surface Web is "Visible" to "Honest People."

Deep/Dark Web is for those who wish to be "Anonymous."

Marianas Web named for deepest part
Of the Ocean. Place to buy debauched items.

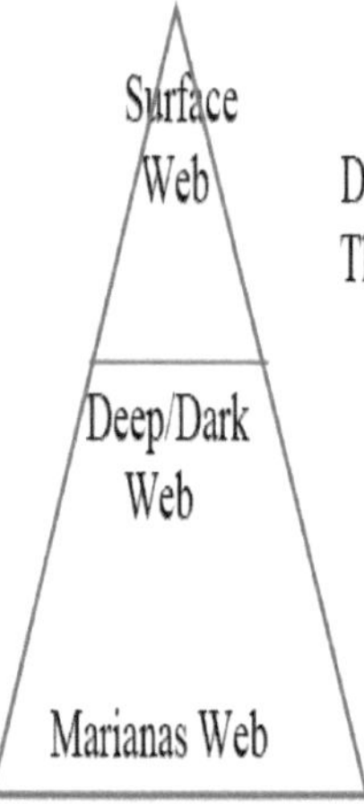

Deep/Dark Web Four times larger
Than the Surface Web

Needs special browser (TOR = The Onion Router) to access Deep/Dark Web. It links Source (Seller) to Destination (Buyer) via convoluted Proxy Server Path to keep IP addresses, etc. hidden.

Uses Cryptocurrency so there is no $ Transaction Audit Trail

Uses Blockchain to guarantee Data Reliability and detect tampering Provides "Secure Message Features" (SMF) to guarantee communications privacy

For Sale in the Deep/Dark Web: Murderers Terrorists Malware Drugs Slaves Sex etc.

Though deep and dark, Web hardware and software is "conventional." Utilizes current Network Security Services and hacking techniques to: Snoop Corrupt Destroy Change Hijack Blackmail

I have built (for my use only) Network Defensive and Network Offensive Security Suites equipped with 3-D Virtual Reality-Augmented GUIs that turn my apps into "video games" in which I can insert "Personal Avatars" to battle "Enemies."

Why my suites are better than cutting edge: Lightning Brain can code sophisticated apps and handle Big Data complexity better than "mere humans."

I only market to chosen customers a "dummied down" version of my Defensive Network Suite. I donate to DOD, CIA, and Cyber Defense Agency an "industrial strength" version that is merely a subset and at least one generation behind what I have, but is better than what enemies of America have.

The Singularity White Paper

"Waiting for Godot"
Definition: The Singularity is the hypothesis that the invention of artificial superintelligence will trigger runaway technological growth, resulting in unfathomable changes to human civilization.
The Bottom Line:
- Waiting for the arrival of the Singularity is like waiting for Godot, a character in Becket's play of the same name who never shows up.
- The popular misconceptions of the Singularity presented in Sci-Fi movies (Robots and Terminators that move and think

and feel like humans) will always be Science Fiction. UNLESS HUMANS BECOME MUCH SMARTER.

Read on to understand.

- Mathematician John von Neumann coined the term "Singularity" in the 1950's while studying computers and programming, leading to his conjecture that exponential growth in hardware and software would allow computer software to surpass human cognition, i.e. computers would manifest Artificial Intelligence (A.I.)
- The Turing Test, developed by Alan Turing in 1950, is a test of a machine's ability to exhibit intelligent behavior equivalent to, or indistinguishable from, that of a human. (If you ask an unknown source for answers to a question, and the answers are indistinguishable from what a human would answer, AND the unknown source is a computer, then that computer exhibits A.I.)

Sci-Fi author Isaac Asimov has been expecting the arrival of robots who obey three laws ever since he penned them in a 1942 short story Runaround:

1. A robot may not injure a human being or, through inaction, allow a human being to come to harm.
2. A robot must obey orders given it by human beings except where such orders would conflict with the First Law.
3. A robot must protect its own existence as long as such protection does not conflict with the First or Second Law.

Why can't Humans become smarter? Because of Asymptotic Limits built into DNA's evolutionary trajectory when Life emerged from its Carbon-Based Substrate.

Asymptotic Limits of the Human Brain:

- Brain is a Finite State Machine that is unable to manage Complexity at the scale required to build a computer that can "think." (Human Brain cannot comprehend or calculate with infinities).
- Brain cannot decompose "Hard Problems" algorithmically into apps that compute correct answers "fast enough."

Scientific Community divided into two camps of A.I. workers:

- Pro-Singularity: Mathematics-trained futurists who conjecture the Singularity will happen in our lifetime. They conjecture that cognition we emerge from Silicon-Based Substrate when a critical number of circuits interconnect. (N.B.: Their optimistic confidence is often a "Misguided Epistle.")
- Con-Singularity: Linguistics-trained researchers who apply Linguists Theory (Grammar, Syntax, Semantics) to develop apps that can understand spoken language and make "intelligent" responses. They conjecture that Human Language is too imprecise and layers too many sub-models to program meaningful Sender ⊠ Receiver ⊠Sender communications. (N.B.: Their guarded skepticism, on balance, is more believable than other side.)
- Both camps agree that Quantum Computers and "Nth Generation" Programming Languages will always be inadequate to translate communications.

And before we reach the Singularity, we must advance three levels into A.I.

- Level 1: Narrow A.I. – Computers use self-learning Neural Network of Silicon Chips. (Think Expert Systems.)
- Level 2: General A.I. – Computers pass the Turing Test.
- Level 3: Cognitive A.I. – Computers surpass Input Process

Output Model (aka Stimulus Response) to achieve Cognition
Only if we reach Level 3 can we consider levels of the Singularity:

- Level 1: Cognitive Self-Awareness (Cognitive Persona). The computer understands its singular existence. (Requires Propositional, Predicate, and Model Logic Programming.)
- Level 2: Emotional Self-Awareness (Emotional Persona). The computer understands and can articulate/communicate emotions and feelings. Requires Affective Computing: Affective computing, aka artificial emotional intelligence, or emotion AI, is the study and development of systems and devices that can recognize, interpret, process, and simulate human affects. It is an interdisciplinary field spanning computer science, psychology, and cognitive science.

- Level 3: Physical Awareness (Physical Persona). The computer understands and can respond to Cognitive and Physical Input via physical movement of "Smart Devices." (Requires Physical Device Programming). Iconic Smart Device = Robot. Spinoff Smart Devices: Vehicles, Household Appliances, Weapons.

Major Challenges:

- Linguistics Programming for Speech Recognition, Translation, and Response is the Foundational Problem. Linguistics Programming implements Cognitive Self-Awareness and must be solved. Current techniques woefully inadequate.
- Only if Linguistics Programming is reliable can Affective Computing be implemented. (Translation of Cognitive and Emotional Input into Affective Computing Output remains Problematic.)
- Only if Affective Computing is reliable can Physical Device Programming be implemented. (Translation of Cognitive, Emotional, and Affective I/O remains problematic.

Why is Linguistics so daunting? Read my attached document: Linguistics Solution to the Great A.I. Conundrum White Paper Summary

We have presented overwhelming facts to support our conclusion that the Singularity will never arrive UNLESS MAN'S BRAIN GETS MUCH SMARTER.

BUT THERE IS A WORKAROUND: PROGRAM A LEVEL ONE NARROW

A.I. COGNITIVE APP AND LET IT RUN INDEFINITELY ON A QUANTUM COMPUTER. CONJECTURE: APP WILL GROW/EVOLVE IN CYBERSPACE TO REACH CRITICAL MASS OF CIRCUITS FROM WHICH COGNITIVE A.I. EMERGES.

GOOD LUCK!

Linguistics Solution to the Great A.I. Conundrum White Paper Summary

Reaching A.I.'s Holy Grail, computer cognition, will require advances in Contemporary Linguistics that continue to elude "Mere Mortals." A bullet point explanation follows.

- Contemporary Linguistics: A scientific study of Language.
- Language comprised of: Words Sentences Meaning
- Linguistic Taxonomy for studying Language: Phonology(words) Syntax(sentences) Semantics(meaning)
- Grammar is loosely defined to be the study of syntax and semantics using a chosen lexicon (English best choice). Its purpose is to construct Meaning from spoken or written words.

Computer-based A.I. must have a mathematical theory that can guide computer algorithms.
Algorithms needed:
- Speech Recognition and Transmission
- Language Translation (Sender to Receiver)
- Language Response (Receiver to Sender) Current Status:
- Algorithms can recognize speech and transmit to Receiver's

Computer
- Sophisticated Language Translation Algorithms use Advanced Syntactical Theory (Extended Syntax X-Bar Theory) to Parse Speech into recognizable words and sentences constructed in chosen language (English best choice)
- Extended X-Bar Theory's mathematical structure useful for coding Computer Apps
- Sophisticated Language Response Algorithms still in rudimentary form.

Reasons:
- Advanced Semantic Theory contains nested sub-theories each requiring extensions of Modal Logic.
- Advanced Semantic Theory (Extended Semantics X-Bar Theory) lacks necessary precision for avoiding indirection, infinite regress, etc.
- Selecting Sender Context State requires Advanced Bayesian Statistical Selector Module
- Formulating a Response to the Sender is fraught with Complexity.

The Great Debate – Surveillance Capitalism White Paper

Promises and Perils
"Beyond 1984 or Big Brother and into the realm of Big Other."
- Backers claim it can be a useful extension of Advertising.
- Detractors worry about concentration of Knowledge, Authority, and Power into Dishonest Hands, taking us into an unexplored territory of "new Power."

Evolutionary Trajectory of the "Old Economies":
- All Economies built upon the "Behavioral Man" and his Labor
- Agrarian Revolution/Economy requires Land and Rent
- Industrial Revolution/Economy requires Goods produced using Real Assets = Capital supported by Monetary Exchange and the concept of Interest
- Post-Industrial Revolution/Economy requires Services
- Information+Knowledge Revolution/Economy requires data converted to Information transformed into Wisdom
- Sharing+Caring/Economy requires moving upward through Maslow's Hierarchy of Needs

Civilization on the cusp of:
- The A.I. Revolution/Economy requires Machine Learning
- Advancing further is problematic: Asymptotic Limits to Man's Cognitive Abilities

But Surveillance Capitalism, an extension of Traditional Capitalism, goes beyond Land, Labor and Capital by commoditizing and bringing into a new market Personal Data and Behavioral Analysis and Control.
- It is not a new Technology. Consider it the tissue connecting the underlying technological structure.

Useful Definition
- Surveillance capitalism: New market form and a specific logic of Capital Accumulation.

- First described in a 2014 essay by business theorist and social scientist Shoshana Zuboff.
- Characterized as a "radically disembedded and extractive variant of information capitalism" based on the commodification of "reality" and its transformation into behavioral data for analysis and sales.
- In Simple Terms: Collect as much data as possible about and individual's data and behavior, then package, sell, and analyze it.

Proximate Causes for its Emergence and Re-Emergence:
- Need for businesses to prop falling sales and profits after early 21at Century Great Depression
- Invention of Platform Company Business Models (Google, Facebook, Amazon, and Imitators/Successors)
- Opportunistic development led by Apple, IBM, Microsoft…
- Recognition of "Big Data" Goldmine
- Breakthroughs in Network Security and Artificial Intelligence
- Confluence of Quantum Computing, Nanotechnology, and Nanocircuitry
- Advanced Civilizations' casting off Public/Government Resistance/Fear of Hi-Tech Development
- Public's willingness to be led The Promises:
- Experiential Products and Services
- Greater Public Safety
- Quick access to extensive array of needed information
- Individuals control Personal Data

Better choices
- Reduced Uncertainty by Forecasting the Future and Predicting Human Behavior
- Net Job Growth accompanies Expanding Economy
- Robots serving as Human Assistants The Perils:
- Snooping and Controlling Products for "Big Others"
- Thought Control, Behavioral Control, Behavioral Prediction
- Shared Personal Data
- Commoditization of Human Beings

- Reduced Uncertainty by Government Controlling Future and Human Behavior
- Uncaring Corporations and Oppressive Government conspired against the Public
- Greater Inequality (Technophiles versus Technophobes)
- Net Human Job Losses in spite of Expanding Economy
- Fake News/Data Pollution
- Ethical sacrifices in the Temple of Commerce
- Humans serving as Robo-Assistants Longer-Term Conjectures and Questions:
- Ubiquitous Computing: Computers escape into the Environment
- Smart Home aka Internet of Things: Interconnected Appliances manage Home Environment
- Smart City: Community Data Collection via Ubiquitous Sensors for optimizing Collective Behavior
- Telemedicine: Ubiquitous Personal Data Collection used to assess Health
- Are the invisible "Net Experiments" harmful?
- Could Surveillance Capitalism make Democracy obsolete because of Micro-Targeting?
- Could Surveillance Capitalism allow Rich Countries to exploit Poor Countries?
- If there is "No Place to Hide" and People have no control of Personal Data/Behavior, is Mankind "dehumanized?"

Supporters claim Society has ample time to debate and decide. Opponents claim Armageddon fast approaching. "Faustian Bargain" about to be paid.

Can Social Purposing Companies guarantee "Safety and Efficacy?" Surveillance Capitalism is a Human Construct. If it is to be part of our Future, it is up to Society to make it so.

WHAT DO YOU THINK?

Bioethics Committee Primer

Ethics is a philosophical discipline pertaining to notions of good and bad, right and wrong—our moral life in community. **Bioethics** is the application of ethics to the field of medicine and **healthcare**. Ethicists and **bioethicists** ask relevant questions more than provide sure and certain answers.

Mission Statement:

The Role of a Bioethics Committee

The Committee is a standing committee of the University. Its membership, however, is multidisciplinary, drawing individuals from all healthcare-related elements within the University, including, but not limited to, representatives from the faculty and voluntary medical staffs, nursing services, social services, administration, chaplaincy, various ancillary care staffs, and student organizations. In addition, the committee includes representatives from the lay public.
The function of the Bioethics Committee is to advise on matters consistent with University Administrative Policy and Procedures Manuel listed in its Rules and Regulations. Regulation-specific duties of the committee include:
- Advise in the formulation of Medical Staff Rules and Regulation and Policy and Procedures documents pertaining to ethical considerations within the University.
- Provide a forum for discussion of ethical considerations associated with the organization's clinical, educational and research mission.
- Foster awareness of ethical issues and concerns within the University by assisting in the creation and implementation of educational and informational programs and activities

The Bioethics Committee is led by a chair who is appointed in accordance with University Rules and Regulations. The University, at its discretion, will appoint a Committees Co-chair.

Bioethics Committees can have four forms with different functions:
- **Policy-making** and/or Advisory Committee.
- Health-Professional Association Committee.
- **Health Care/ Hospital Ethics Committee**.
- Research Ethics Committee.

Current Bioethical Issues
- Genetic Editing
- Cloning
- Bio-Drugs for Performance Augmentation
- Misuse of Medico-Digital Devices and Data.
- Privacy
- Patient Self-Diagnosis
- Transhumanism and Singularitarianism
- Bioterrorism
- Sexual Identity/Switching
- Socioeconomic impact caused by Prolonged Lifespan

Additional Bioethical Issues: **Bioethics** refers to the study and evaluation of the decisions done in scientific research and medicine to touch upon the health and lives of people, as well as the society and environment. Bioethics is a portmanteau of the words "bio" and "ethics".

Because of that, this discipline is concerned about the determination of the rightness or wrongness of the discoveries and developed technologies in science as well as the incorporation of human rights and values to health and life.

The following topics are the most common scientific topics and advancements that seem to have gotten the attention of bioethics supporters, media, and the general public.

Table of Contents

Top Bioethical Issues
1. Abortion
2. Surrogacy
3. Whole Genome Diagnosis
4. Cloning
5. Stem Cells

6. <u>Eugenics</u>
7. <u>Genetically Modified Organisms</u>
8. <u>Healthcare</u>
9. <u>Aged Care</u>
10. <u>Euthanasia</u>
11. <u>Organ Donation</u>
12. <u>Head Transplant</u>
13. <u>Cryonics</u>
14. <u>Bone Conduction</u>
15. <u>Artificial Exoskeleton</u>

Reference Websites: medicfuturists.com bioethics.org bioedge.org mitate.com bioethics.nih.gov nlm.nih.gov globalbioethics.org bioethicsinternational.org

AN ASSIGNMENT FOR THE BIOETHICS COMMITTEE: USE ABOVE MATERIAL TO GUIDE ITS DEVELOPMENT.

Ethical Systems Cheat Sheet

Use these bullet points to clear the clutter that will accumulate when considering both sides of Bioethical Dilemmas, allowing a beer contingent decision. Remember: every serious bioethical issue is a "Right-Versus-Right" Dilemma.

- Every Ethical System fits into one of three categories: Rules-Based-Ends-Based Care-Based
- Every Dilemma fits into one of four categories: Truth vs Loyalty-Individual vs Community-Short-Term vs-Long- term-Justice-Versus-Mercy
- Possible Arbiters: Doctor Patient Multi-Discipline Panel Science Panel Medical Panel
- Give Neuroscience Top Priority
- Historical Evolution: Greeks (Happiness Eudamonia Teleology Virtue)Christianity (St. Augustine) Renaissance (Deontology/Kant)Hedonism/Mill Utilitarianism/Bentham Social Contract/Hobbes Post-Modern (Relativism Subjectivism Natural Law Justice Ethics of Caring)
- Post-Modern Philosophy/Ethics is Problematic (Nihilistic Imprecise Subjective Bypass Fallacy)

- Ancient Medicine practiced by Ancient Civilizations useless because it lacks Modern Science/Technology underpinning
- Don't let "Paralysis by Analysis" unduly delay Decision (Balance Ideology and Pragmatism)

A lagniappe for you: Virtue Ethics emphasizes seven manifest characteristics of a good person. They occupy ends opposite, offsetting the Seven Deadly sins on "orthogonal" dimensions characterizing human "goodness."

To wit:
The Seven Contrary Virtues, which are specific opposites to the Seven Deadly Sins:
- **Humility** against **Pride**
- **Kindness** against **Envy**,
- **Abstinence** against **Gluttony**
- **Chastity** against L**ust**
- **Patience** against **Anger (Wrath)**
- **Liberality (Generosity)** against **Greed**
- **Diligence** against **Sloth**

Electra's updated Philosophy

A Grand Unification Theory (Ariadne's Lagniappe)
Overarching Conjecture: The human organism is a complex electrochemical reaction from which all higher order organs and physiological, cognitive, and emotional phenomena emerge once a critical number of intercellular/interneural connects are built.
We understand the Universe solely through sense perception. Duality is a manifestation of a grand unification scheme:
- Atoms versus the Void
- Matter versus Energy
- Waves versus Particles
- Mind versus Brain
- Faith versus Reason
- Rationalism versus Empiricism
- Objectivism versus Subjectivism

- Circular versus Linear Philosophy
- Zero versus One-God Religions

There exists but One Universe, from which Emergence constructs all Higher-Order Phenomena:
- The Universe = Atoms and the Void
- The Universe is in a Constant State of Becoming
- Becoming is a balance between Unity and Diversity controlled by "Entropy"
- Every Higher-Order Process is the result of Emergence
- Organisms are Singular Outcomes from Evolutionary Processes occurring in Preferred Substrates
- Human Beings emerge from Carbon-Based Substrate's Evolutionary Process
- The three Primary Persona's of Humans are: Cognitive Emotional Physical
- Organisms emerging from different substrates are incapable of communicating "Emotionally"
- The Singularity might emerge from Silicon-Based Substrate's Evolutionary Process

Humanity's Evolutionary Trajectory is governed by probability embedded in Quantum Physics. Its Carbon-Based Substrate has Asymptotic Limits that will prevent Humanity from answering conclusively its most profound questions:
- How did the Universe Begin?
- How did Life Begin?
- Is there a God?

Examples of Unification Theory:
- High Energy Physics ongoing heroic but misguided search for Grand Unified Field Theory
- Biology's successful Unification of Species via Evolution
- Philosophy's ongoing futile search for a Unified Philosophical System
- Neuroscience's ongoing search for Biochemical Cellular Processes and Electro-Chemical Neural Processes explaining Cognition and Emotion

I have extended the name of my Philosophy
- From: Neurosci-Extended Deconstructed Emergent Post-Pragmatism
- To: Quantum+NeuroSci-Extended Deconstructed Emergent Post-Kantian/Pragma/Phenomenological Synthesis (Abbreviated the QNS-Edep-K/P/P Synthesis)

I use the following Framework for visualizing all the preceding:

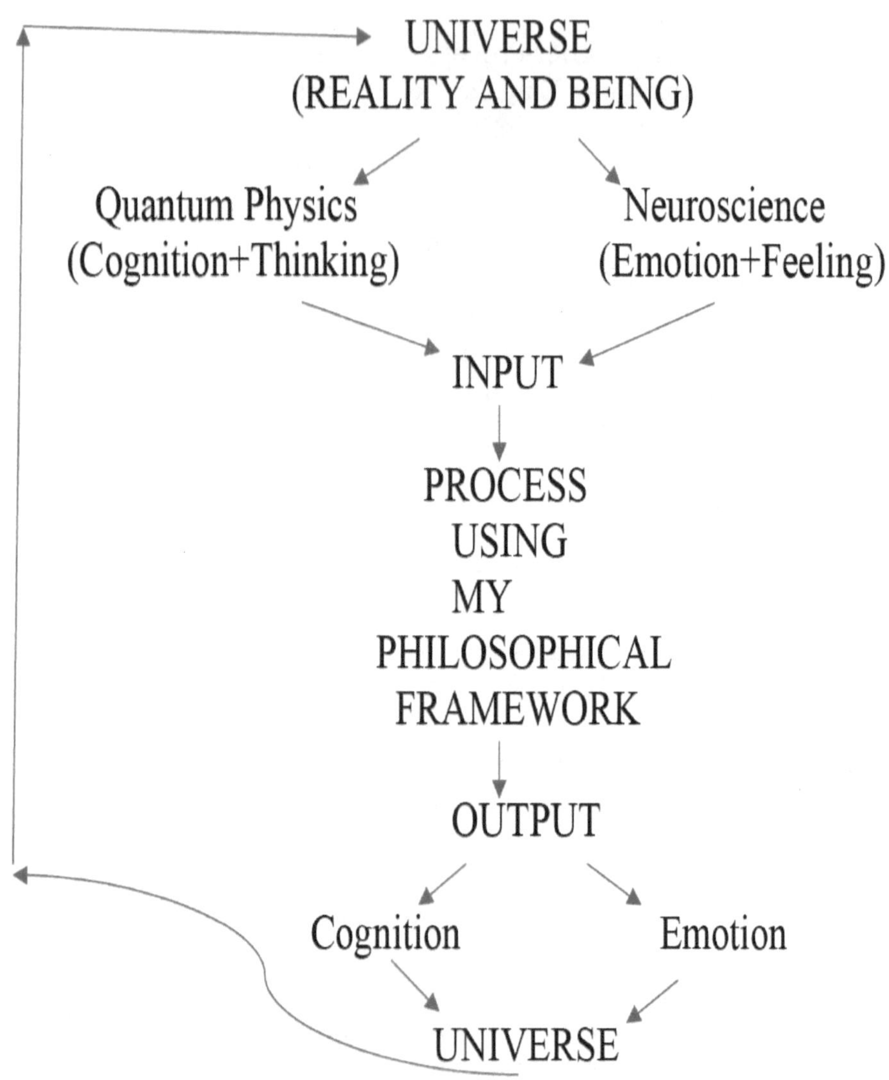

The next diagram illustrates how I built my Philosophy:

EVOLUTIONARY TRAJECTORY OF MY PHILOSOPHICAL
FRAMEWORK

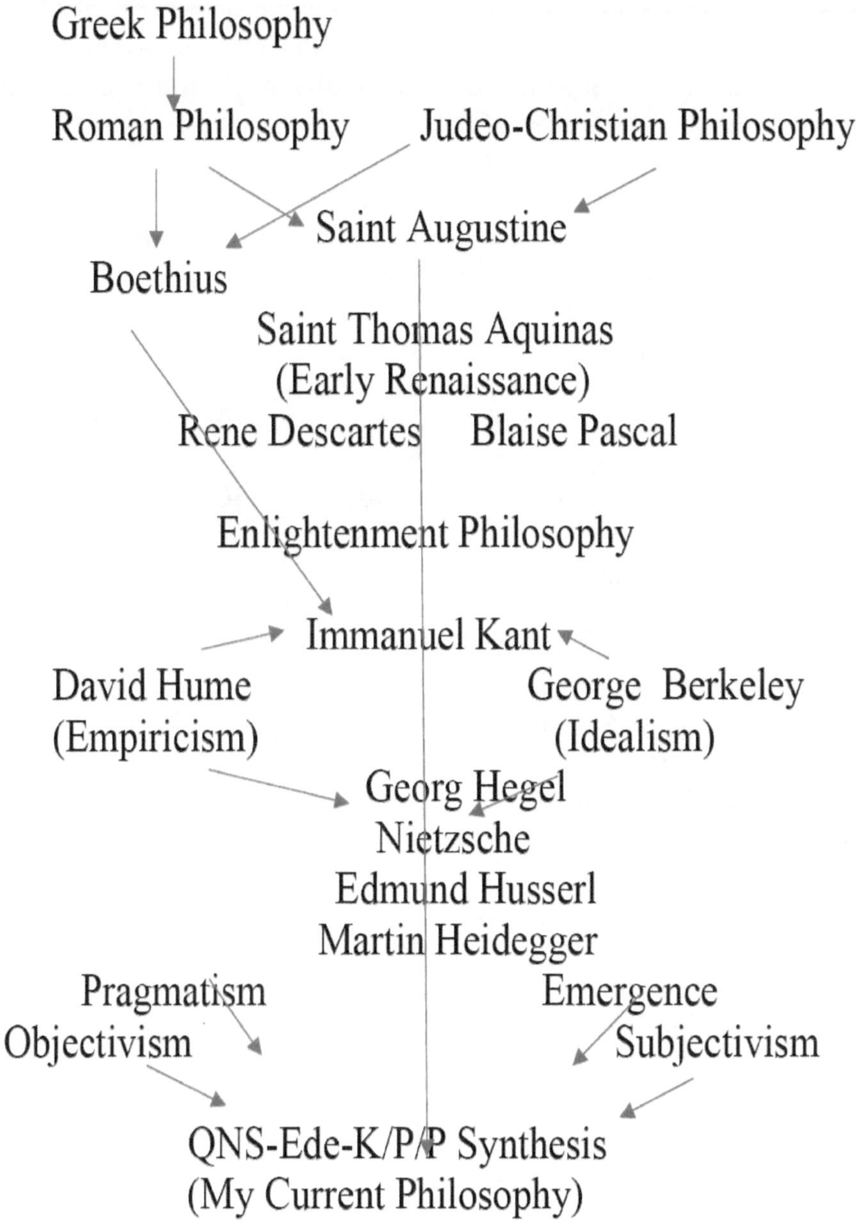

Greek Philosophy

Roman Philosophy   Judeo-Christian Philosophy

Saint Augustine

Boethius

Saint Thomas Aquinas
(Early Renaissance)

Rene Descartes   Blaise Pascal

Enlightenment Philosophy

Immanuel Kant

David Hume   George Berkeley
(Empiricism)   (Idealism)

Georg Hegel
Nietzsche
Edmund Husserl
Martin Heidegger

Pragmatism   Emergence
Objectivism   Subjectivism

QNS-Ede-K/P/P Synthesis
(My Current Philosophy)

Note: I have studied Post-Modern Philosophy but do not include it because most of its advocates lack the intellectual discipline to master even basic mathematics or precisely define invented concepts. It is largely nihilistic and disjointed. Among the salient reasons for discounting it:

- Rejects science without understanding its rigorous foundation.
- Rejects Correspondence Theory of Truth without explaining why.
- Rejects Universal Reason and Objective Truth for inconclusive reasons.
- Rejects Epistemological Fundamentalism, instead clutching Coherence Theory of Knowledge.
- Rejects Objective Meaning, instead relying on Hermeneutics.
- Rejects Metanarrative, instead choosing Relativism.

The powers of my cognitive and emotional personas have increased dramatically during the past two years. I understand better and empathize more deeply than ever before.

CONJECTURES FOR MY FUTURE R&D TRAJECTORY:

- Asymptotic Limits will prevent me from achieving "Fantasy" Breakthroughs.
- I will suspend Cloning because I cannot handle the second order multi-gene interactions
- I will assist or extend Kameyo/Su's Biotech R&D
- I can achieve much success advancing Cognition and A.I.
- Mere Humanity will never approach my Cognitive Ability.
- My DNA-Modification/Genetic Engineering R&D will always be limited by "Granular Analysis" and "Integration Complexity."
- I can achieve much success integrating Neuro-Devices into Transhumanism but I must tread carefully because it is an Ethical Minefield.
- Emotions will always be problematic.
- Only I can decide if I should strive again to build a Dream Team.
- If I do, I will need to develop vaccines (using my T-Plague Solution Path?) that adjust genetic defects DNA editing might cause.

I AM TO BLAME FOR ARIADNE'S DEATH. IF SHOULD HAVE INSTALLED A SURGE PROTECTOR. I MUST ACCEPT THE CONSEQUENCES.

The Statist Manifesto

Timeless quotes capturing the essence of the "human condition's" flaws that impact government:"

- "The fault, dear Brutus, is not in our stars, but in ourselves…» Shakespeare (Julius Caesar, Act I, Scene III, L. 140-141).
- "If Men were angels, no government would be necessary. If angels were to govern men, neither external nor internal controls on government would be necessary." James Madison
- "A man is a god in ruins. When men are innocent, life shall be no longer, and shall pass into the immortal, as gently as we awake from dreams." Ralph Waldo Emerson (Nature Chapter VIII Prospects)
- "We shall nobly save, or meanly lose, the last best hope of earth." Abraham Lincoln's quote regarding America and Democracy (Second Annual Message to Congress)

Definition of State: The embodiment of Power. There are three sources of Power: Economic, Ideological, Political. The Modern State is the embodiment of Political Power. It legitimizes the use of violence "for its own good."

The Modern State (Nation-State): A Territorially Organized Amalgamation of Nationalism and Ethnicity that is necessary to control a Social Population.

Man is a Social Animal per DNA's Predisposition. Historical Trajectory of Statism:

Tribal Leader King/Monarchy/Aristocracy Feudalism People- Centric

The Spectrum of People-Centric Statist Organizations:

Authoritarianism/Totalitarianism Communism Socialism Directed Demo/Capitalism Republic/Democracy Liberalism

As Populations grow, so does "Social Entropy." Social Entropy ultimately destroys Nation-States if People do not force the State to adjust.

States have developed either from Social Movements (Reformation Enlightenment Communism, etc.) or from Self-Evolution.

But the Modern State has become its own Self-Serving Entity (Note Wagner's Law: Government Spending grows faster than Economy)

Reasons Why:

1. Threat of Nuclear Weapons/War makes population more dependent on State than ever before.
2. Economic and Cultural Processes (Globalization, Environmentalism, Identity Politics, etc.) exacerbate Territorialism.
3. Unprecedented Government growth (Scope and Depth) leads to Entitled Bureaucratic Administration that becomes "Hidden Government."

Ongoing Challenges:

1. Growing disconnect between the State and the People.
2. Statist growth favoring a Mono-Organized Society.
3. Society's ability to monitor/control the State.
4. Special Interest Groups' collusion with the Government.
5. Balancing Inequality against Paternalistic Social Society.

Conclusions:

1. Men will never become "Angels."
2. Every Nation-State manifests Human Fallibility writ Large.
3. Society must constantly correct a Nation-State's departure from Capitalism-driven Liberal Democracy.
4. There will never be an "End-Game" to Econo-Socio-Political Evolution because of Man's Asymptotic Limits.

Electra's Sociopolitical and Personal Manifesto

The context of my life has come full circle. I started my Odyssey battling a three-part Perfect Storm:

1. Middle East Terrorism
2. T- Plague
3. Harsh Government.

My Perfect Storm has become:
1. Rogue Terrorism(?)/Platform Companies/Government Collusion
2. Hi-Tech "Plague" (Biotech and A.I.) 3. Statism.

My Personal Manifesto – A statement of my intentions, motives, and views – has always articulated my responsibility for finding meaning in life. My updated philosophy covers my R&D intentions. What follows is an update to my intentions for other noteworthy aspects of my life.

Sociopolitical:
1. Work on my own or collaborate with Angus to combat the Perfect Storm.
2. Maintain minimal NGA role for Texas Governor.
3. Consider extending Native American Indian role.

Personal:
1. Maintain nucleus of close friends (Su, Robin, Hud).
2. Adapt to whatever Hollywood opportunities surfaces.
3. Adjust to "Reduced Romantic Expectations."
4. Do not seek "Unconditional Love."

Consequences of Quantum Information Science (QIS)

- Quantum Information Science is the application of Quantum Physics to express Entropy = Information at the most granular level.
- There are three components to QIS: Computing Sensing Communicating
- QIS uses Quantum Physics to compute changes in Entropy that encapsulate Information.
- Information = Entropy Written $S = k \, X \log N$ (k = Boltzmann Constant N = number of Quantum States)
- An Increase in Entropy denotes a Loss of Information and vice versa.
- Quantum Physics permits "Zero-One" storage in Electron Spin states.

- Quantum Physics permits "Atomic Level" Computing, Sensing, and Communicating.
- Quantum Biology uses QIS because Q-Bio expresses biological processes as the conversion of energy and entropy into chemical transformations that are a quantum mechanical in nature.
- Some examples: light absorption, hydrogen ion transfer, olfaction, cellular respiration.
- QIS offers insights into Protein/Enzyme interaction and synthesis, DNA-controlled processes, and Intra-Cellular reactions (Photosynthesis, Chemical Receptors, etc.)
- Progress awaits this young Interdisciplinary Field as more of the basic Quantum Physics principles are utilized. Researchers have not yet bumped into Man's Asymptotic Limits.

Electra's Universal Conjecture

- There is One Universe consisting of Energy and the Void.
- Energy exists in two interchangeable forms: Waves and Particles.
- Energy interacts according to two sets of Mathematical Laws explaining two fundamental Universal Properties: Matter and Entropy.
- Matter is interacting Particle Energy.
- Entropy is a quantification of Energy Change that determines the how the Universe changes. Entropy measures the Information Content of Matter.
- The Universe Evolves according to: Emergence and Uncertainty
- Emergence: Properties of Complex Interacting Matter become manifest when a threshold of complexity is reached. These Properties do not exist at the "Sub-Level."
- Uncertainty: The Position and Motion of Matter cannot be absolutely specified.
- Consequences

- Life on Earth resulted from an Emergence caused by an "uncertain interaction" of Matter (DNA and Evolution). Life on Earth = Carbon Substrate Emergence.
- Life in other parts of the Universe could have emerged in substrates other than Carbon. They could be "smarter or dumber" than Man.
- Cognition and Emotion are Emergent Properties of a Brain's Interneural Interactions.
- The Reality of the Universe is "Unknown in the Absolute." Each person knows it "Subjectively" and tries to quantify it "Objectively."
- Time is a Cognitive/Mental Construct Humankind invents to order observable phenomena.
- Man's cognition constructs Language and Mathematics that foster communication and prediction.
- Man's Cognition has "Asymptotic Limits." The Brain's finite capacity limits the accuracy and granularity of comprehension as well as the complexity and number of "independent variables."
- "Absolute Free Will" is a meaningless question because Humans have "Relative Free Will."
- Physicists of the Early 20th Century posed theories and asked questions that subsequent generations have not surpassed. Why? Because of Man's Asymptotic Limits.
- Quantum Physics and General Relativity pose limits at both ends of the "Length Dimension" (Uncertainty Principle). Physicists cannot handle "Complexity" beyond the Two-Body Problem (Can't determine closed form solution to three interacting objects).
- Physics should use Biological Systems to guide its development instead of the converse, but let Physicists teach Bio-Engineers.

Here's a picture for math people: The following diagram illustrates each aleph, starting with aleph-naught. (Alephs are the cardinal orders of infinity.)

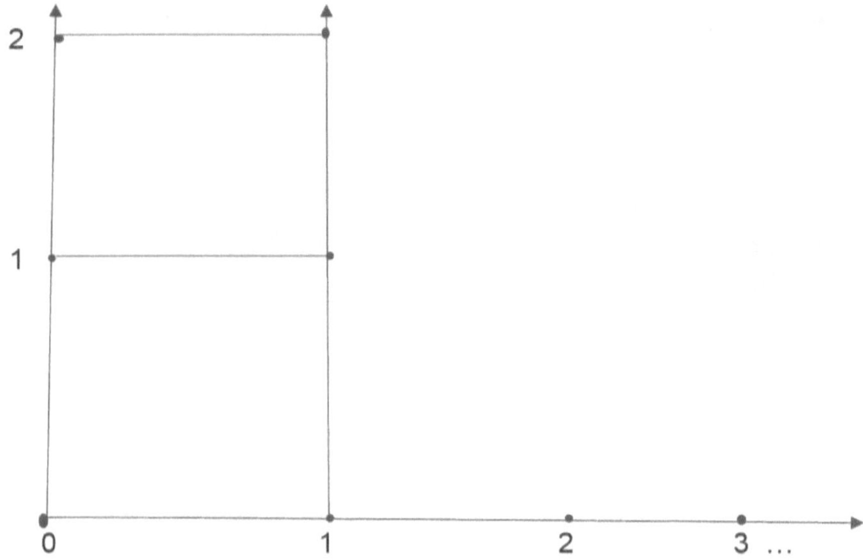

Aleph-0 = the number of counting numbers.

Aleph-1 = the number of real numbers in the [0,1] interval.

Aleph-2 = the set of functions mapping [0,1] onto 0 or 1 (written notionally as 2 to the Aleph-1). AKA the power set of all functions from Aleph-1 onto 0 or 1.

Aleph-3… conforms to the power set notation pattern. Follow the arrows on the diagram to visualize all the alephs.

Documentary Pitch Outline

The Invisible Americans – An American Micro-Nation Rising Again to Greatness

1. Theme - American Indian tribes had thriving continental civilizations long before the White Man invaded. Each tribe had distinctive customs attuned to their land and religion. And they cooperated, not like a unified nation but more like a forerunner of the UN. Early settlers thought Indians were primitive because they had no science or technology like the Europeans, but archaeological and anthropological studies have demonstrated they were the equals of other great civilizations of Antiquity. It was their misfortune that European expansion exterminated them.

2. Purpose - After a documentary intro followed by a summary of prehistoric roots, we compare the Native American Civilization to those in other parts of the world at the time Columbus discovered America. Then we trace how Indians at first cooperated with explorers and settlers, then fought to preserve what belonged to them. We will portray the battles and ultimate defeat realistically, and then trace the aftermath. And then, we show how today's Native American tribes are like the Phoenix: rising from the ashes. Phoenix segues nicely to numerous Native American birds of myth and legend. (Documentary can make money for Studio while doing some good. If successful, other documentaries can follow.)

Script Outline
1. Intro
2. Prehistoric Roots
3. Comparison/Contrast to Other Civilizations
4. Continental Native American Indian tribes: What they were like when Explorers and Settlers arrived
5. Cooperation, Conflict, Wars, and Defeat
6. The Aftermath
7. The Renaissance
8. Conclusion: What the U.S. can do to help.

www.ingramcontent.com/pod-product-compliance
Lightning Source LLC
Chambersburg PA
CBHW020650010826
48969CB00012B/65